Lightning on a Quiet Night

A Novel

By Donn Taylor

Lighthouse Publishing
of the Carolinas

PRAISE FOR *LIGHTNING ON A QUIET NIGHT*

From the hiss and pop of the gas heaters to the description of the soda fountain, Taylor paints a colorful picture of small town life in a bygone era. His characterization is so accurate you recognize yourself and your friends among the townspeople. A most enjoyable book.

~**Sadie and Sophie Cuffe**
Authors of *Arrow That Flies* and *The Heart Knows*

A unique and intriguing story expertly told with compelling characters and an ending that left me sighing with satisfaction.

~**Roger Bruner**
Award-winning author of *Found in Translation* and *Lost in Dreams*

Those of us from small towns like to believe in their residents' virtue, in their local legends, as the folks in Beneficient do, but when a girl is found murdered, suspicions creep in along with dark, sinister threads of revelation. Donn Taylor's ability to set us up without our seeing it coming is masterful. His historic detail is amazing as he threads us in and out of the eye of the needle until we have no idea where we're headed. Skillfully written.

~**Linda S. Glaz**
Author of *The Preacher's New Family*

LIGHTNING ON A QUIET NIGHT BY DONN TAYLOR
Published by Lighthouse Publishing of the Carolinas
2333 Barton Oaks Dr., Raleigh, NC, 27614

ISBN: 9781941103319
Copyright © 2014 by Donn Taylor
Cover design by writelydesigned.com
Interior design by Karthick Srinivasan

Available in print from your local bookstore, online, or from the publisher at:
www.lighthousepublishingofthecarolinas.com

For more information on this book and the author visit: www.donntaylor.com

Brought to you by the creative team at LighthousePublishingoftheCarolinas.com:
Courtenay Dudek, Barbara King, Michele Creech, Rowena Kuo, and Eddie Jones.

Library of Congress Cataloging-in-Publication Data
Taylor, Donn.
Lightning on a Quiet Night / Donn Taylor 1st ed.

Printed in the United States of America

Dedication

*To Mildred, the Northeast Mississippi girl
who taught me the meaning of love, and
who honored me in marriage more than
six blessed decades ago . . .*

*"She speaks in trust that only grace allows,
Modestly unaware her softness, strong—
Stronger than stone or steel—holds up this house
In love, to let the house hold up the sky."*

Acknowledgements

This is a work of fiction. Coosa County and the town of Beneficent are fictitious, as are all other places where action occurs in the novel. Weather in the novel is not literal, but is a selection of typical weather phenomena from the winters of 1947 – 1951. Prices mentioned are those current in 1948, and Jack's $6000 debt in that year is equal to about $58,200 to $58,800 in 2013 dollars (www.bls.gov.data/inflation_ calculator.htm and www.dollartimes.com/calculators/inflation.htm).

All individual characters in the novel are fictitious, but they are modeled on the everyday citizens of Mississippi whom the twentieth-century naturalistic novelists largely ignored.

Social terms used in the novel are those customarily used by citizens of good will in 1948. In all cases I have avoided the anachronism and intellectual poison of twenty-first century political correctness.

Biblical quotations from Brother Smallwood's funeral sermon in Chapter 6 are taken from, in order, Psalm 89:48, Genesis 3:19, Revelation 21:4, Isaiah 25:8, Romans 12:12, and 2 Corinthians 6:10. Those from his church service in Chapter 38 are 2 Chronicles 7:14 and Colossians 1:19–20. The quotation Jack remembers in Chapter 32 is Jeremiah 17:5.

Quotations of Robert Browning's poetry are taken from first editions held in the Armstrong Browning Library, Baylor University, Waco, Texas.

For historical research, I am indebted to the Lee County Library, Tupelo, MS, to Ms. Lynne Mueller of the Mississippi State University library, and to the Mississippi Department of Archives and History. Professor Rick Johnson of East Texas Baptist University provided translations from biblical Hebrew. Bernell Smith provided details of Mississippi basketball history.

For many helpful comments on the manuscript, I am indebted to my critique group: Jan Tichner, the late Don Dilmore, Robert Wilson, and Cathy Messecar. Cathy and her husband David also advised on details of agriculture, as did Charles Stubblefield. I am indebted to Wanda Dionne for chapter-by-chapter comments and innumerable helpful suggestions.

Special thanks to my agent, Terry Burns, for leading me to Lighthouse Publishing, and further thanks to my editor, Courtenay Dudek, whose editorial skills greatly improved the novel. Thanks also to Elizabeth Easter for helpful suggestions and to beta readers Roger Bruner, Ginger Aster, Nancy Kimball, Courtenay Dudek, Regina Smelzer, Barbara Warren, and Diana Austin.

I would also like to express appreciation for Ivory Doakes, housekeeper extraordinaire, whose many kindnesses have seen Mildred and me through difficult times.

Lastly, I am deeply indebted to Mildred Taylor, my wife, for assistance on historical research and for her consistent encouragement, understanding, and fruitful suggestions throughout the writing. I am even more indebted to her for her sound literary judgment, on which I rely when mine falters.

*The righteousness of the righteous shall not
deliver him in the day of his transgression . . . .*
—*Ezekiel 33:12 (KJV)*

*'Tis mad idolatry
To make the service greater than the god. . . .*
—*Shakespeare, Troilus 2.2.56–57*

Chapter 1

The northeast Mississippi town of Beneficent, "A Town As Good As Its Name," had never known a murder until Friday, January 9, 1948. Nor, in the oldest memory of its 479 citizens, had the town known a single felony.

Until the fatal moment, that January day progressed as hundreds had before. The winter dawn came late, struggling through clouds and fog to shed a dull gray light more kin to night than day. Cold rain fell to drench the thrush-brown land, and stolid hardwoods thrust black skeletal limbs upward against an iron-gray sky. Farmers revised work plans in deference to the rain, and storekeepers pondered its effect on weekend sales. But more than rain would be required that night to keep them from the Coosa County basketball tournament, an event as fundamental to their lives as seedtime and harvest. From all corners of the county they came in mud-spattered pickups, the less affluent in mule-drawn wagons, to converge on Beneficent. All brought good spirits to share an experience that came but once a year.

Yet among that cheerful crowd one stranger would come unwilling . . .

In her bedroom in the darkening evening, Lisa Kemper stared at the rain that drummed against her window. She did not want to be there at all.

How shall we sing the Lord's song in a strange land? The psalmist's words leaped unbidden into her mind, but she shut them out. She was *not* here in captivity, the puddles in her yard were *not* the waters of Babylon, and she would *not* sit down by them and weep.

Still, she hadn't bargained for this. After her mother's death last August, she'd postponed graduate school for a year to help her father adjust to life as a widower. Then she would get on with her studies— that is, if she could ever decide what to study. But when she made that decision in August, she never dreamed Stephen Kemper would leave his position with an Indiana corporation to manage the small chemical plant the company was building in Beneficent.

From first sight, she detested this backward town. She abhorred the unkempt fields and unpainted barns nearby, so different from the well-tended farms of Indiana. Most of all, she abhorred the boastful motto "A Town As Good As Its Name" and the complacency of the townspeople who thought they made it that way.

But she would get through this year, somehow. She had promised.

A car's headlights flashed across her window. That would be Hollis Wilson, the newly elected state senator who would escort her and her father to the basketball tournament. People expected them to attend, he said.

"Are you ready, Lisa?" Stephen Kemper's voice carried from the living room.

"I'm coming, Father."

A critical glance in the mirror confirmed that her new gray suit brought out the blue of her eyes and emphasized her trim figure. But not too much. And if the locals thought she was overdressed, that was their problem. With a final pat at her dark brown hair, she scooped up her raincoat and headed for the living room.

Miraculously, the rain suddenly stopped, though low clouds scudded by overhead. Maybe Senator Wilson had fixed the rain as he had so many things to help them fit into the community. Lisa wondered how an insignificant mud hill like Beneficent could produce someone like Wilson. He was handsome as a movie star—a war veteran, she'd heard, and people bragged that at age twenty-five, he was the youngest senator in the state's history. She didn't doubt that he was, but she did doubt that anyone had bothered to research it.

"You'll enjoy the tournament," Wilson said. "It's one of the great events of the year."

Lisa answered with a smile and followed him out the door, her father close behind. For her father's sake, she'd make sure people thought she enjoyed the tournament.

At the wood-frame gymnasium beside the town school, mud-spattered pickups crowded the gravel parking lot and spilled out into the street. Wilson parked a block away, and they walked back through laughing, faceless crowds that drifted through the darkness.

The din heightened as they entered the gym. Before Stephen Kemper could protest, Wilson paid the sixty-cents admission for the three of them. He and Lisa proceeded into the stands while Kemper dropped off to talk about his plant's security with a red-faced man who wore a badge. Lisa caught the words "... no real crime here, just kids' pranks." She found that hard to believe.

"Sheriff Rainwater isn't kidding," Wilson said. "In my lifetime I can't remember a single crime being committed here. Not one. But that doesn't tell the whole story. It's a town of good Christian people trying to live good lives. That's what makes it different."

Lisa threw him a skeptical glance.

He laughed. "I know it's hard to believe. Just give it a chance and you'll see."

When they found seats, a man in overalls came to belabor the senator about a tax problem. Lisa tried to interest herself in the game. Typical girls' basketball, she thought—the Beneficent Pantherettes' three forwards matched with Shady Creek's three guards on one half of the court, the opposite situation at the other end. Whoever wrote the rules didn't think girls could run full court.

One Beneficent forward, a short girl with chunky-muscled legs and a straw-colored ponytail, consistently got the best of her guards. The other players showed little skill.

Soon bored with the game, Lisa surveyed the crowd, composed mostly of men in overalls and tired-looking women who held small children. Mostly disreputable, she judged, or at best . . . just *ordinary*.

Like the sandy-haired man who stood watching the game from the corner of the end line. In his mid-twenties, she guessed. Moderate height, moderate build. He wore brogans, khaki work clothes and a dark waterproof jacket. Neat enough, but still thoroughly ordinary.

Then Miss Ponytail took her eyes off the game to wave at that man. He grimaced and pointed at the guards moving the ball toward her from the far court. Ponytail wasn't ready and dropped their pass before recovering. Lucky not to lose it.

Her gaze followed the sandy-haired man to the refreshment stand. A darkly handsome, statuesque woman of perhaps thirty intercepted him there. Even at this distance she seemed to radiate an aura of sadness. The woman tried to hold the man in conversation, but he broke off and joined a male group that included Lisa's father.

Strange little mini-dramas . . . That ordinary man no sooner walked into the gym than two women tried to attract his attention. A redneck version of Frank Sinatra? But the woman at the refreshment stand was too old to swoon like a bobby-soxer. Or was she a case of arrested development? Such odd people! Lisa thought she would never understand them. But she had to try. Her father's success here might depend upon it. She had to try, though the placid tempo of their lives dragged against the lively beating of her heart. It felt like running in mud.

"Panther!"

The sudden word and a slap on Wilson's back shook Lisa out of her thoughts. She found the senator locked in an odd handshake, with each man grasping the forearm of the other. The newcomer was a tall man wearing an olive-drab field jacket that sported the well-known brass eagle pin that signified honorable discharge from military service.

"Lisa," Wilson said, "this is Jimmy Fletcher, the big gun from our 1942 team."

He was certainly big enough—at least several inches above six feet. She wanted to ask about the handshake, but the bleariness in Jimmy's eyes stopped her.

"Big gun, big goon," Jimmy said, his speech slurred. "This young senator and two, three others helped—only Beneficent team t' play in the state tournament."

Lisa nodded her response without comment. She'd already heard boasts about that team, always in the same words: *We'll never forget the team of 'forty-two*. She'd bet that team was as dinky as everything else in town, and whoever heard of a team called Beneficent Panthers? Nevertheless, she filed the state tournament fact as something she and her father should remember.

But Jimmy Fletcher was speaking to her again. "Most folks said it was a good team." He met Lisa's eyes for a second, then dropped his gaze and shuffled away, slightly off balance.

Mississippi is a dry state. So how did he manage to get tipsy? And what kind of a handshake was that?

"Sometime I'll have to tell you about our team," Wilson said. "Hey! There's Jack Davis." He pointed to the corner of the end line, where the same ordinary man had returned to watch the game. "He was a member of our team."

Jack Davis, Lisa thought. *The ordinary man has an ordinary name*. While she'd been distracted, the girls' game had ended and the boys' game begun. Beneficent had quickly gained the lead and someone had called time out. Then she saw that Miss Ponytail had lined up as a cheerleader. For some reason she felt drawn to the girl.

"Who is that cheerleader?" she asked. "The one with the ponytail."

Wilson grinned. "That's Callie Rakestraw. Her brother—"

Lisa lost the rest of his statement, for another mini-drama occurred. As the cheerleaders leaped and cheered, Callie Rakestraw twirled her pleated white skirt, displaying chunky legs and showing that she wore her basketball uniform beneath the skirt.

Lisa saw Jack Davis scowling at her from the end line. When he beckoned, Callie beamed and ran to him. His scowl deepened. They gestured and seemed to quarrel. Callie stalked away, hands on hips. She twirled her skirt again and threw Jack a glance that should have turned him into stone. The town might be filled with good people trying to live good lives, but that didn't mean they were immune to anger. She filed the incident for future reference.

She watched in boredom until the game ended, then looked to see if more sparks would fly between Callie and Jack Davis. But he had disappeared. Callie appeared to make a point of seeking out a young player who wore the number four, and they walked away holding hands.

A second triangle. The first was Callie, Jack, and that older woman. The new one was Callie, Jack, and Number Four. Both could be catalysts for crimes of passion, and it looked like Beneficent might not be as virtuous as Senator Wilson claimed. She would have to wait and see.

On the ride home, she congratulated herself on learning things that might help her father with the locals. They liked talking about their team of 'forty-two, so she would draw them out about that. And they were always ready to sing the virtues of Beneficent. But if the state was dry and Beneficent so virtuous, how had Jimmy Fletcher found the liquor that made him unsteady? She wouldn't ask that question. And she wouldn't ask about the two Jack Davis triangles she'd observed. She'd just watch to see what came of them. Feeling a bit smug, she decided that a stiff upper lip would get her through the rest of this year. Then back to civilization and graduate school—that is, if she could ever decide what to study.

***

When the game ended, Jack Davis drove his 1938 Chevy pickup to his farm four miles west of town. Rain threatened but none fell, and the clouds had lifted to a high overcast. Far to the southeast, lightning flickered, too distant to bring the sound of thunder.

Despite the cold, Jack lingered on his front porch to savor the quiet night, so different from the turbulent nights he'd known overseas during the war. Beneficent was a good town with good people, and he relived with pleasure each meeting he'd had with its citizens that night. Presently, he considered the striking brunette Hollis Wilson escorted to the tournament. Hollis would need a showcase wife when he ran for governor a few years from now. That woman would meet the requirement.

Jack himself had no time for the two women who'd complicated his life lately. Callie Rakestraw would outgrow her schoolgirl crush. But Vesta Childress, the school librarian who'd intercepted him at the refreshment stand, was another story.

Even if he'd felt inclined, though, he had no time. The mortgage on his new acres of choice bottom land hung above him like an anvil suspended by a thread. Farm work would never pay it off, so he labored extra hours at any construction job he could find. That left him scarcely time to sleep. But in three more years, if he could hold this pace, he'd have clear title.

Lightning flickered again in the southeast, followed by a faint rumble of thunder.

Somewhere out there the evils of this world still strike like lightning. But here in this blessed place all things are quiet, the air washed cold and pure.

***

Later that evening in town, Sheriff Claiborne Rainwater parked beside his home. The tournament had brought no trouble except two genial visitors who'd drunk too much, and he'd found sober drivers to take them home. He thanked the Lord again for letting him be sheriff of a county where nothing ever happened. He could already taste the cup of coffee his wife would have waiting for him. It kept some people awake, but for him it acted like a sedative. He could use the sleep. He'd been on his feet since breakfast, and he wasn't getting any younger.

Across town, Stephen Kemper brooded on his problems with building the new plant. All his life he'd worked with chemicals that behaved in predictable ways, and he felt out of his element dealing with unpredictable people. Like that difficult contractor out of Memphis, often absent from the job and full of excuses why work wasn't done. If things didn't get better quickly, Kemper's company would send someone else to finish the project. He mustn't worry Lisa about it though. Better to keep his troubles to himself.

And in Vesta Childress's home that evening, blue flames burned low in the butane heaters. Their steady hiss was punctuated now and then by a faint popping sound from impurities in the gas, and the flame flickered yellow before subsiding into blue.

Vesta shivered as she entered the house, for the night had turned cold. She'd made a fool of herself again trying to attract Jack Davis's attention. She should have remembered his love of basketball, remembered it from that magic year when the late William Bradley, the man she'd consented to marry, had coached the team of 'forty-two and she'd marveled at each tactical adjustment he made.

She moved through the few rooms she still occupied and turned the heaters to full high. They would hold back the cold darkness that seemed to press against the house from all sides.

The house itself stood isolated among trees, its rear entrance huddled against a wooded hill. A long, curved driveway formed its only connection to the main road in front. Vesta's father had valued privacy to the point of obsession. The ivy he'd planted long ago now entwined on the trellised front porch as if to make sure the house could not run away. Even now, the furniture stood where it had when Vesta was a child.

Idly, she moved to the oak secretary in one corner of the living room. A half-wall topped by dowels separated that room from the dining room. Shadows from the dowels formed a pattern of bars on the wall above her. On the secretary rested a photograph of Vesta and William Bradley, taken the day they announced their engagement in November 1941. He smiled forth from the picture, handsome and self-assured as he had been in life. She, too, smiled with the happiness she'd known in the radiance of newfound love. The photographer had caught her with one hand shyly fondling a wisp of her long brown hair.

For a long time she studied the photograph, then touched the tightly braided bun behind her head, tugged briefly at the collar of her blouse that lately felt a bit choking, and opened a well-marked book to Amy Lowell's poem "Patterns." Vesta knew it by heart, but she still traced its lines with her finger.

Her eyes moistened as she read about a lady in the distant past whose tragedy so resembled Vesta's own. The stiffness of the lady's clothing and the constraints of society denied fulfillment of her ripe woman's body. Yet she dreamed of bathing in a wooded bower, unconstrained, each touch of the water intimate as a lover's caress.

So like Vesta's own dreams of fulfillment in marriage to William Bradley.

The gas heaters murmured and burned with a blue flame. Air in the room remained hot and dry. Out of Vesta's mouth came an involuntary sound from beyond spoken language. Her vision now too blurred to read, she formed the remembered words with her lips. For in the poem, the lady's dreams were shattered like her own, condemning her to a life unfulfilled, hedged in by societal constraints and the lady's stiff, corseted clothing.

The gas heaters popped and flickered yellow, and the deep-lined shadows of dowels grew darker on the wall. Vesta's fingers tugged again at her collar as her lips pronounced the poem's climactic words:

For the man who should have loosed me is dead.

As she had done so many quiet nights before, Vesta Childress sank forward upon the book, rested her head upon her arms and wept.

Chapter 2

Jack Davis went to sleep in peace but woke in terror. Clawing his way up into the cold darkness of his house, he knew what had happened. He had dreamed The Dream again, the familiar details all in place.

He'd dreamed that he walked through woods like those of the Vosges Mountains in France, where he'd known savage fighting. But unlike the Vosges, these dream-woods exuded calm so deep it seemed tranquility itself had come alive.

Then in an instant, the woods that had murmured safe assurance shrieked mortal danger. For some unknown enemy had set an ambush. The man's faceless form remained half-hidden among the leaves, but one dread shape showed stark and clear. From among fern fronds, the enemy's pistol pointed directly at Jack's heart.

In that eyeblink of time, Jack realized he could not bring his own weapon to bear before his enemy blasted the life out of him. There the dream always ended, in the certainty of imminent death.

Now fully awake, Jack didn't remember seeing ferns in the Vosges. But in those harried days he'd been too busy to notice things like that. He pushed the question aside, for it seemed there was something he had to do. Something urgent.

There was. The phone was ringing. From the intervals between rings, he knew it had been ringing for some time. Dressed only in the undershorts and T-shirt he slept in, he felt his way through darkness into the hallway where his old-fashioned box phone hung on the wall. The wooden floors felt cold beneath his feet. Rain was falling again, drumming steadily on the roof.

Jack lifted the phone's receiver to his ear and spoke into the mouthpiece. "Hello?"

"Jack?" Worry throbbed in the woman's voice. "This is . . . Cornelia Rakestraw." She paused as if reluctant to say more. But her next words came in a rush. "Is Callie with you?"

Jack's temper flared. What kind of man did she think he was? Then he realized how frantic she must be to ask that question.

"No, ma'am," he said simply, then added, "Is anything wrong?"

It was a dumb question, but he had to say something. What time was it? Feeling along the wall, he twisted the knob of the ancient rotary light switch, one of the first installed in Coosa County. Through the kitchen door he could see a clock.

Two-fifteen. No wonder Mrs. Rakestraw was frantic.

"Callie hasn't come home. We don't know where she is." Her words tumbled out half-spoken, half-sobbed.

"Maybe she spent the night with another cheerleader and forgot to call in." Jack didn't think it likely.

"She didn't. We've phoned all of them." Another sob. "Hiram is out looking for her, but I had to stay here with little Clem. Jack, you don't know how hard it was for me to make this call. But I was desperate. Callie has such a crush on you, she'd do anything you ask. I almost wish you did have her there because I know you'd do the right thing."

Jack's temper rose again. How could this woman think he'd seduce a child, much less the sister of his teammate Clyde Rakestraw, killed in action on a distant island? But Mrs. Rakestraw was worried sick, as any mother would be. He forced his anger down and controlled his voice. "Mrs. Rakestraw, there's never been anything between Callie and me. Is there any way I can help?"

A long pause.

"I don't know. The only place Hiram knew to look was the all-night truck stop on Highway 78. That's twenty-five miles away. Can you think of any place else? If you could . . . I know it's a terrible night out . . . but . . . but *could* you?"

Rain spattered on the roof and made trickling sounds in the gutters. The last thing Jack wanted was to go out in this weather. But Clyde Rakestraw, if he were still alive, would be out there looking for Callie.

Jack felt the weight of responsibility descend upon him like a leaden overcoat, as it had so often in the past. He heard his voice saying, without volition, "I don't know any place, Mrs. Rakestraw. But I'll go out and try."

Her effusive thanks still echoed in his ears as he re-donned his work clothes and a heavy outer jacket. He topped these off with an old hat and the olive-drab plastic raincoat he'd bought from Army surplus. Gloves, too. No use freezing his fingers.

Turning his Chevy pickup around, Jack glanced by habit toward the old Miller place a quarter mile to the west. The house was deserted now, and the land belonged to him, but his eyes still turned that way as they had when he was a child. Long ago, the lights of that house had reassured him of his playmate, Lucy Miller. Next day they'd play again midway between the houses. That world was now so distant . . .

Back to business, Jack told himself. He cranked down the driver's window and adjusted the truck's spotlight to supplement his headlights. The inside control for the spotlight was broken, and he chided himself for not having it fixed. His arm would get soaked, but he'd need the extra light where he was going.

He hadn't told Mrs. Rakestraw the whole truth. He knew of three places, just off the westward road, where teenagers often parked. If any still lingered there, the news would be bad. He thought of the ramshackle pre-war cars many people still drove. On a night like this they'd keep the engine running and the heater on. A rusty muffler and leaky floorboards were all it would take. Carbon monoxide would do the rest.

The gravel road from Beneficent to Cherry Grove, twenty miles west, wound through varied terrain. The fertile north-south valley where Beneficent nestled gave way, four miles west, to rolling hills. Jack's farm straddled the border of valley and hills. From that point westward, the hills grew steeper and higher while the farms grew scarcer and scrubbier. Eventually, the twisting road topped a ridgeline and dropped down to the swampland of Branch Creek, which marked the county line. Bootleggers there operated first in one county and then the other, depending on which sheriff was more aggressive at the time. Beyond the creek, the road climbed through similar terrain, arriving again at open fields near Cherry Grove.

Unhampered by traffic at this hour, Jack avoided the road's well-defined ruts and drove wherever the gravel lay thickest. No use in getting stuck. The Chevy's windshield wipers cleared the steady rain, but fogging windows kept him busy wiping with an old towel. Maybe someday someone would invent a defrosting system that worked.

He drove directly to the nearest of three places he suspected, a fifty-yard-square clearing on a hilltop crisscrossed with vehicle trails. He shifted into low gear to climb the narrow track up from the road and stopped on the first firm ground that let him view the entire site. Using his spotlight and getting his left arm wet in spite of glove and raincoat, he confirmed that no cars remained.

He followed the same procedure at the other two places, each more rugged than the one before it. He found no cars. Rain came harder, spattering fiercely on the metal roof of his cab, and lightning flashed. At Branch Creek, Jack turned around and headed back toward home. This time he crept along in low gear with his window down. Ignoring his drenched and aching left arm, he played the spotlight first on one ditch and then the other.

At the driveway to each farm, he searched for recent car tracks in the mud where gravel was thin. He found plenty. And why not? The county tournament had given most of the residents good reason to come home late. The Rakestraw's driveway, three miles west of his own, showed one set of fresh tracks—apparently Hiram Rakestraw's as he began his search.

Haunting memories from that farm crowded in on Jack: the basketball goal nailed up above the barn door, the dirt court worn smooth before it. On many an off-season afternoon, he and Jimmy

Fletcher and Clyde Rakestraw had practiced together while ten-year-old Callie looked on. Jimmy and Clyde, both six-feet-three, played one-on-one against each other. Jack's five-eleven couldn't compete. So he passed the ball to each in turn, learning in the process how to give his receiver an advantage over the defender.

That supporting role often left him standing idle, so he taught little Callie basic skills of the game. He hadn't thought about it then, but now he understood why she had a crush on him. No one else paid her any attention.

His spotlight still on the Rakestraw driveway, he wondered if he should stop and tell Mrs. Rakestraw he'd found nothing. If he did, he'd have to stay until someone brought definite news. Maybe all night.

No, he'd phone her from home. Then he could get a hot shower. He thought longingly of the shower. With that and an hour or two of sleep, he'd be ready for a full day's work.

He released the clutch and continued his search, shining the spotlight on each ditch in turn. Lightning flashed more frequently now, with thunder crashing close behind. Strange about lightning: It wrought destruction wherever it struck, but it also showed things one wouldn't ordinarily see in the world's prevailing darkness.

At length, between lightning flashes, he played his spotlight on the driveway to the old Miller place. He saw no tracks, for here the gravel lay deep and heavy as it did in the entry to his own place. Eight years ago, Mr. Miller had gotten stuck in his own driveway and swore it wouldn't happen again. The lot of large, high-quality gravel he brought in was more than he could afford, so he and Jack's father bought it together. Their extravagance paid off, for both driveways remained in top shape despite heavy use by farm equipment.

Should he search the hundred yards of twisting driveway up to the Miller house? Teens never came there to park. From his house just over the rise, he would have seen reflections of their car lights.

The wet cold chilled him badly now, and that hot shower looked better and better, but he couldn't tell Mrs. Rakestraw he'd searched everywhere unless he actually had. Gritting his teeth to prevent chattering, he turned into the Miller driveway. As before, he directed the spotlight first left, then right, working toward the circular turnaround before the house.

Nothing.

He played his spot on the house. No sign of tampering. Still locked as tight as when he'd checked it a few days before.

Jack eased his truck into the second half of the turnaround, shining the spot along the deeper ditch where water collected. Still nothing. He eased into the final quarter of the circle back toward the main drive.

Lightning flashed again.

There. In the ditch.

In the darkness, he played his spotlight on the ditch, and something red reflected. He backed his truck up and pulled forward again as close to the ditch as he dared, shining the spot directly on the bright color.

"Oh Lord, no."

The words sprang out involuntarily. He wept.

She lay on her back in the ditch, arms spread in either direction. Muddy water swirled over and about her from the abdomen down. Her red-and-white warm-up jacket lay open, revealing her cheerleader costume. Her ponytail, bound with the red ribbon that reflected in Jack's spotlight, flowed out behind her head like the tail of some sodden comet. Her mouth had dropped open, and her dark eyes stared sightlessly into infinite space. But most horrible of all was the unnatural ninety-degree bend in her neck.

Jack had seen violent death before, knew it too intimately from a score of battlefields. But there it was expected. Here in Beneficent it was alien, an intruder from some brutal foreign land.

Ignoring the pelting rain, Jack leaped from the truck. He knelt and made the futile but necessary check for signs of life. The body had already stiffened in the winter cold.

Mechanically, Jack climbed into his truck and drove home.

Shivering, dripping water and tracking mud on the hardwood

floor, he groped his way to the phone and dialed Sheriff Claibourne Rainwater's number.

After the sixth ring, a sleepy male voice answered. "Yeah?"

Jack took a deep breath, knowing his words would brand the mark of evil forever on his beloved Beneficent.

"Sheriff, this is Jack Davis. I just found Callie Rakestraw's body at the old Miller place. She's been murdered."

Chapter 3

Saturday, January 10

At mid-morning, Lisa Kemper and her neighbor Rose McKenzie lingered over coffee at Rose's kitchen table.

"Is something wrong, Lisa? You're not your usual self." Rose gave her guest a questioning glance.

Without either woman's planning it, their mid-morning coffee break had become a ritual. Lisa began her day by feeding Stephen Kemper his breakfast and getting him off to work. Then she had little to do until he came for lunch at noon. Rose followed a similar routine in launching her husband, Ralph, to their farm north of town. Recently retired from teaching math at Beneficent High, Rose was a bulky, energetic woman in her sixties who needed no help with her housework. She'd usually finished the essentials by nine o'clock and found herself looking for ways to fill out the morning. When the Kempers moved in next door, she wasted no time before inviting Lisa over for coffee. Despite their age difference and Lisa's distaste for all things in Beneficent, friendship developed quickly. It provided Lisa her only island of compatibility in Beneficent's vast sea of estrangement.

Rose brushed a strand of gray hair from her forehead and asked, "Has this rain got you down? Or is there something more?"

Lisa looked away. Could her malaise be that obvious? But Rose's probing eyes showed more sympathy than curiosity. With a sigh, Lisa decided to take the older woman into her confidence—partly, at any rate. Her moods and emotions would be fair game, but she wouldn't say what she thought of Beneficent.

"It's not the rain or the cold," she said. "It's just that most of the time I feel so useless." That much was true even without mentioning her estrangement. Helping her father make a good impression in town wasn't an all-day job. In fact, most of the time she had no job at all. After good-mornings, she and her father held little conversation. She knew that problems in building the new plant occupied his mind, but she missed their former closeness. Even in the evenings he seemed withdrawn, worrying over how he'd get one thing or another done.

"I'm no help to Dad in dealing with that troublesome contractor. I'm not doing anyone any good, and I'm wasting a year I could spend in graduate school."

Rose arched an eyebrow. "What will you study there?"

Lisa looked away again. "I'm not sure. Business or library science, I guess. Maybe sociology. That's what my friend Alex is studying."

And what do I really feel about Alex? Her uncertainty seemed to encompass everything.

"Business, library science, and sociology?" Rose asked. "They're very different. Which one really interests you?" In spite of the blunt questions, Rose's face showed genuine interest.

"I don't know. I did okay in all three."

Rose sniffed. "I have a better idea. Take a clerical course, get a job at a hospital and marry a doctor."

Lisa felt herself blushing. "You're so sure of things, and I feel so . . . so *uncertain*." There! She'd confessed it. She was so different from Alex, who was always so definite.

Rose's eyebrow arched again. "*You* uncertain, Lisa? You look like confidence itself."

I must be putting up a good front.

"And me?" Rose gave a laugh as deep and burbling as a man's. "Child, at my age I'd *better* be certain!" She continued more soberly. "When the right thing comes along—man or profession—you'll have no trouble at all making up your mind. In the meantime, you need something useful to occupy your time."

Rose paused in thought. "Library science? I've heard Miss Childress say she needs help in the school library. Would that interest you?"

"It certainly would. I used to read shelves." It would also give her useful contacts in the community.

"I'll talk to her, then," Rose said. "She could use some friendship, too. It's kind of a sad story—"

A banging on the front door interrupted her, and a woman's voice shouted, "Miz McKenzie! Miz McKenzie! Have you heard the news?"

"Come in," Rose called, then whispered to Lisa, "Watch what you say. That's Effie Dean Telebit, the worst gossip in town."

The door opened and closed. Heavy steps sounded from the hall, and a breathless middle-aged woman with half-combed hair rushed through the kitchen doorway. "I don't have time to sit down," she said, apparently oblivious to the fact that Rose had not asked her to. "Have you heard about Callie Rakestraw?"

A chill gripped Lisa. She'd never heard of Callie until last night, yet this felt like hearing bad news about a friend.

"What about Callie?" Rose asked.

"She's been murdered." Mrs. Telebit glowed with excitement.

"Oh, no." Rose looked stricken. "Murder? Are you sure?"

"Sure as God made little green apples." Mrs. Telebit warmed to her subject. "They found her laying in a ditch with her clothes all wet and her neck broke. She might've did the clothes by herself, but for sure she didn't break her own neck. The little flirt has been asking for it, people say."

"I don't have to ask which people." Rose's voice carried a distinct bite, then softened. "Poor Mrs. Rakestraw. She lost a son in the war, and now she's lost Callie. What happened?"

"Most folks say one of the Gypsies got her."

"Gypsies?" The question sprang from Lisa's lips before she thought. She hadn't heard about them.

Rose explained. "Folks call them that, but they're really people of Italian and Greek descent. About thirty families live in a trailer park south of town. The banker, Harry Pendleton, brought them in three years ago to work in his new shirt factory."

Lisa remembered a sprinkling of swarthy complexions among the crowd at the ball game last night, and she'd seen the man named Jack Davis laughing and talking with several dark-faced men.

"They say Callie ran around with some Gypsies at school," Mrs. Telebit said. "Boys, most prob'ly, knowing Callie." She paused and surveyed her audience. "But I got my own ideas."

"Just tell what you *know*." Rose emphasized the last word.

"It was Jack Davis what found her. About three-thirty this morning, he says, in a ditch on the old Miller place. I got my own ideas about that, too. At any rate, Jack called Sheriff Rainwater."

Lisa caught her breath. Only last night the sheriff had told her father Beneficent had no real crime.

Mrs. Telebit's giggle brought Lisa's mind back to the conversation. "Hey, now. Sheriff *Rainwater* sure has the right name." She paused for effect. "'Cause he had to go out in the *rain* and get soaked while he looked at the body." No one laughed, and her voice grew conspiratorial. "I bet I know what kind of looking he did—"

"Had Callie been . . . molested?" Rose brought the discussion back to facts.

"Hasn't nobody said, but I bet it wouldn't be the first—"

"So we don't really *know*. Why was Jack Davis out there at that time of night?"

"He says Miz Rakestraw asked him to hunt for Callie, but that sounds fishy to me. Personally, I don't think no Gypsy done it. Mighty convenient that Jack owns the Miller place now, with the old house empty. I bet him and Callie'd been carrying on, and then he found out he'd got to cover his tracks—"

"Nonsense. You know better than that." Rose's tone of voice closed the subject.

Mrs. Telebit seemed to realize it, for her eyes left Rose and focused on Lisa. "Oh. You're the one Hollis Wilson's been squiring around."

Lisa felt herself flush. "He has been very helpful to my father, but—"

"I have to go now," Mrs. Telebit broke in. "I got to give Mrs. Pendleton the news." She hurried toward the door.

"I'm sure you will," Rose said, making no effort to see Mrs. Telebit out. She waited silently until the door closed, then put her hands to her cheeks. "Poor Mrs. Rakestraw."

During Mrs. Telebit's prattling, Lisa had felt a weight growing heavy in her stomach. It became sickening as the gossip's information blended with her own memory of Callie's quarrel with Jack Davis at the tournament. She wanted to be alone to think about it, but she shouldn't leave until Rose came to grips with the news.

"I saw Callie Rakestraw last night," Lisa said, hoping to offer a bit of comfort. She couldn't mention the quarrel she'd seen. Not now. "Callie played a good game and did well as a cheerleader. Such a pretty girl, and so much alive—Oh!" Lisa stopped, shocked as she realized what she had said.

Rose, smiling through tears, reached across the table and patted her hand. "It will take time for us to learn how to talk about it." She sighed. "Pay no attention to Mrs. Telebit. She never gets things straight. By the way, do you know Jack Davis?"

"I haven't met him. Senator Wilson pointed him out last night."

"Jack has known enough of death before this. Lucy Miller—the neighbor girl he grew up with and everyone assumed he'd marry—well, she died of leukemia while Jack was overseas. Then his parents were killed in a car accident, and he couldn't get home for the funeral. For some reason, the Army didn't find him till it was too late."

"Mrs. Telebit said Jack owns the Miller place?"

"Lucy was the child of her parents' old age. Mrs. Miller died when Lucy was eight, and Mr. Miller had his hands full scraping a living out of that little farm. Lucy spent as much time at the Davis house as she did at her own. Like I said, everyone thought Lucy and Jack would marry, and I guess Mr. Miller already thought of him as a son. When Jack came back from the war, Mr. Miller was in a nursing home. When he died, it turned out he had no heirs and had willed the farm to Jack."

She sighed again. "That's four deaths of people close to Jack, and I suppose you'd have to add Clyde Rakestraw. They both played on the team of 'forty-two, and teammates were close as brothers that year. Now we have to add Callie . . ." She stared into space, seemingly lost in memories.

"Senator Wilson told me a little bit about that team." Lisa shared the older woman's sadness, but the sick feeling in her stomach kept growing. She needed to be alone. "If you'll be all right, I think I'd better go."

"I'll be fine. You have to understand that everyone we've talked about is either one of my students or the parent of one." She stood and flashed Lisa a smile. "Now, about finding something for you to do: We have to go on living in spite of bad news. I'll ask Miss Childress about your helping her."

"I'll appreciate anything you can do." Lisa left quickly, the churning in her stomach still growing. In her mind's eye she saw again the angry exchange between Jack and Callie—apparently something about Callie's displaying her legs—and then Callie's departure hand in hand with the boy who wore number four. Lisa couldn't miss that triangle's potential for jealousy. Perhaps for jealous rage. Perhaps for murder.

Rose McKenzie obviously rejected Mrs. Telebit's suspicions.

But Lisa couldn't help wondering.

Chapter 4

Sunday, January 11

"I thought you'd want to know what was going on in town." Hollis Wilson lowered himself onto the Kempers' sofa.

"We certainly do." Stephen Kemper answered for himself and Lisa. "We heard they cancelled the tournament because of that girl's death. We stayed home from church—thought people would want to deal with it without having to worry about outsiders."

"Church was pretty grim." Wilson made a visible but unsuccessful attempt to relax. "Everyone looked kind of stunned. Shocked, I guess, that something like that could happen in Beneficent. The Rakestraw family wasn't there. When Otis Hahn and I visited them yesterday they said they wanted to grieve in private for a while."

"Otis Hahn?" Stephen Kemper asked. "I haven't met him."

"Owns a small farm south of town," Wilson said. "Family friend, teammate of Callie's older brother. As I said, the Rakestraws didn't come to church, but Jack Davis came in spite of everything."

"In spite of . . . ?" Lisa stopped abruptly. No use mentioning Jack's quarrel with Callie.

"Jack's had a rough two days," Wilson said. "He and the sheriff took the bad news to the Rakestraws. Mrs. Rakestraw was pretty broken up about it, and her husband had all he could do to keep her calm. So Jack took little Clem out and did the farm chores for them. Then he went home and did his own. All that time he was soaked through from looking for Callie. It's a wonder he didn't catch pneumonia."

Lisa's curiosity got the better of her. "You said you and Otis Hahn visited. Was he part of the team of 'forty-two?"

Wilson showed a grave smile. "Yes, and Jimmy Fletcher came by before we left. That made it complete."

"More team of 'forty-two stuff?" Kemper asked. "I keep hearing about it."

"I don't wonder," Wilson said. "I hope you won't think I'm boasting when I say it's become a local legend."

"We'd like to hear about it," Lisa said. Another chance to learn what made the locals tick. "Does that odd handshake have something to do with it?"

"It sure does." Wilson's laugh showed his dark good looks to advantage—blue eyes sparkling under jet-black hair. "It's supposed to be a handshake the ancient Romans used: each man grabs the other man's forearm. We saw it in a movie and adopted it for our team. Silly, I guess. But that time was special: Pearl Harbor came and the war started … All five of us were draft bait, and that brought us close together— made us more than just a team. We knew that year would be our last fling, so we made it count."

Wilson's eyes looked beyond the house walls, back to that golden time. "This might be hard to understand, but basketball has always been important here. Our schools are too small for other sports. Last night's county tournament was fun, but the ones that really count come in February. It takes four of them to find the state champion. All those things came together for us: Pearl Harbor, basketball, the coach, the team, the tournaments …"

He paused and gazed into space.

Lisa prompted, "You made it to State in 'forty-two?"

Wilson startled, but recovered quickly. "Yes. We won the first two tournaments outright and won enough in the third to get into State. We lost there by three points."

"Do your teammates still live around here?" Stephen Kemper asked.

Wilson frowned. "All but one. Clyde Rakestraw—Callie's older brother—he was killed on Okinawa." A smile replaced the frown. "You may have seen Otis Hahn at the tournament—kind of a fat man with two small boys, a wife and a baby. From the size of his family you can tell he was 4-F. The only thing a Mississippi farmer can plant in January is babies. Otis is living proof."

Lisa and her father smiled in response. Her father prompted again, "The war made a special bond among you?"

Wilson nodded. "It made us close. Very close. We knew we'd have to go. The only question was when. Our coach, William Bradley, joined the Marines the day after Pearl Harbor. The team wanted to join up, too, but he made us promise to wait till graduation. We did it for him."

"Who coached you then?" Stephen Kemper asked.

"The principal sat the bench with us, but he didn't know the game. Mostly we argued it out among ourselves."

"And after graduation?"

"We all went to join up the next day, but Otis flunked the physical. Flat feet. Clyde Rakestraw and Jimmy Fletcher chose the Marines. Jack and I went with the Army. All but Clyde came back. And Coach Bradley. We lost him on Tarawa."

Stephen Kemper smiled. "And all four of you—the survivors— paid your respects to the Rakestraw family yesterday. That's real loyalty."

Wilson looked embarrassed. "I guess you could say that. The war cast a shadow over us that year, but we had fun times, too. The night we won Regional—that's the second of the four tournaments—we got back to town around midnight. We all lined up abreast on the highway and joined arms like that crazy handshake."

He laughed. "There we were after midnight with our arms locked together, marching up and down the highway and making the traffic pull over . . . lucky there was gas rationing and not many cars. But around two o'clock Sheriff Rainwater told us to go home or we'd sit out the next tournament in jail. We had some really good times."

He laughed again and stood. "That's enough history for today. I have to go meet some people. I just wanted to check in and bring you up to date, but I guess you got more than you bargained for."

As Lisa and her father protested, he added, "I don't think the Callie business will affect building your plant."

After Wilson left, Kemper said to Lisa. "I don't seem to be affecting it very much myself." He turned into his bedroom and shut the door.

Left alone, Lisa's enjoyment of Wilson's story lapsed into deeper estrangement. A wave of uncertainty swept over her. She couldn't help her father with his troublesome contractor, she was a stranger surrounded by an alien culture, and she carried the guilty knowledge of Callie's quarrel with Jack Davis.

Should she take that knowledge to the sheriff? And if she did, would the sheriff believe her?

***

Monday, January 12

Lisa's mid-morning coffee with Rose McKenzie held her estrangement and uncertainty at bay, but they attacked in full strength the moment she returned to the silence of her house. Work seemed the best solution, so she went shopping for the week's groceries.

Though no rain fell, wet and cold weather remained. It chilled her through her raincoat as she walked the quarter mile to Beneficent's lone grocery store. Inside, an elderly man wearing an apron introduced himself as Willie Grant. In a drawling voice he told her the day's specials. From these she selected pork chops and looked for vegetables to go with them. The choice was limited.

As she brought her purchases to the counter to pay, the man she recognized as Jack Davis came in. Dressed in khaki pants and a dark jacket, he looked as ordinary as he had at the tournament. *Ordinary of ordinaries*, Lisa silently paraphrased. *All is ordinary.* Then apprehension crept in as she remembered the man's quarrel with Callie. She turned away from him and gave full attention to her groceries.

"Pardon me, Miss Kemper." The male voice came from behind her.

She turned and found Jack Davis standing only three feet away. Her apprehension ratcheted up into fear. It kept her tense in spite of his easy smile and unexpected softness in his gray eyes. She managed an uncertain word.

"Yes?"

"I'm Jack Davis, Ma'am. I talked with your father at the tournament Friday night, and I wanted to welcome you into town. We think it's a good place to live, and we like to have other folks come enjoy it with us." He made a half-wave gesture with one hand, a strong hand that reminded Lisa of Callie's broken neck.

Still fighting tension, she said, "Thank you. We're looking forward to it." *Meaning my graduate school afterwards.*

"Moving to a new place isn't easy," Jack said. "Everything here must seem awfully foreign to you."

Foreign isn't the half of it.

But she muted her answer. "I do feel like a foreigner. You expect the big things to be different, but the little ones take you by surprise. Like broccoli. I can't find it in the grocery store."

Jack laughed, and his eyes grew softer. "That's a lost cause. Local taste runs to green beans and lettuce."

"I guess I have a lot to learn." That seemed a safe reply.

He grew earnest. "Everyone does in a strange place. They laughed at me in the Army when I asked about turnip greens and black-eyed peas."

What a stupid conversation. Doesn't he think of anything but vegetables?

To change the subject, she asked, "The Army? What did you do there?" She had to be nice to these people.

The softness left his eyes. "I was in Europe."

He said nothing more. The silence grew tense.

"But what did you *do* in Europe?" Lisa would not be put off.

He showed a bland smile. "I was in Italy, France, Germany. What I did most was remember Beneficent, Mississippi. I saw a lot of rotten things over there—the war, the societies themselves, what I could see of them. Plenty of rotten Americans, too. It's so different here." He grew earnest again. "I think that's because people here are basically good."

"You've revoked original sin?" Lisa's voice carried more edge than she intended. He looked taken aback, and she remembered she needed to make a good impression. "I . . . uh . . . I'll try to keep an open mind."

His smile widened. "We'll fill it with good things."

She made no reply.

When the silence grew awkward, he pointed toward her sack of groceries. "That's kind of heavy. Can I give you a ride home? My truck is right outside."

She scooped up the groceries and hugged them to her body. "No thank you. After all these rainy days I need the walk." She wasn't about to ride in a truck with a strange man she thought might be a murderer. Not if the temperature were twenty below zero instead of today's thirty-five above.

"I'm glad to have met you," he said. "Give my regards to your father. We appreciate his bringing in a new industry." He turned and headed into the produce section.

On the walk home, Lisa tried to make sense of the encounter. The man had shown her none of the anger she'd witnessed in his quarrel with Callie. In fact, he'd been the very picture of solicitude. But he'd given her one of the dumbest conversations she'd ever had. Broccoli, green beans and lettuce, indeed!

Then realization struck. Jack Davis was the first person in Beneficent to see her situation from her point of view. Maybe that conversation wasn't so limited after all.

But what was he hiding by ducking her questions about Army service? Was he one of those 'rear-area commandos' she'd heard about—people who'd sought out low-risk, menial jobs? Or had he done something too dishonorable to admit? That would fit with the anger he'd shown Friday night.

So which was the real Jack Davis? The one with the soft smile who'd empathized with her plight as a stranger? Or the strong-handed angry one who might be a murderer?

The man was an enigma. She'd be wise to steer clear of him.

Chapter 5

Monday afternoon, January 12

"We don't have much to go on, Mr. Patterson." Sheriff Claiborne Rainwater leaned back in his swivel chair, folded his hands across his paunch and cautiously surveyed his visitor. He'd had the worst weekend he'd known in twenty years as sheriff, and today had begun no better. The tournament's cancellation on Saturday crushed his hope of finding witnesses there. When no leads opened up, he knew he was in over his head. He called the state police for help.

Surprisingly, it arrived quickly—a huge, red-faced detective named Ben Patterson and a cigar-chewing grouch reputed to be the state's best forensic pathologist. Now the grouch was busy with the autopsy. Patterson appeared to be in his mid-thirties and wore a blue-checked suit that made him look big enough to out-wrestle a grizzly bear. He paced back and forth in the sheriff's office as if it were a public restroom and he was afraid to touch anything.

Rainwater knew why. He and the visitor would circle each other like dogs meeting in unknown territory. He had to learn if Patterson was a grandstander who'd try to push him out of the investigation. Patterson had to find out if Rainwater was anything more than an incompetent hick sheriff.

"Suppose you tell me what you've got." Patterson's voice sounded like a frog talking through a tuba.

Rainwater looked longingly at the half-smoked cigar in his ash tray. "After the game Friday night, the girl asked a kid named Ronnie Parker to drive her home."

"*She* asked *him*?" Patterson stopped pacing in mid-stride.

"Why don't you sit down?" The sheriff's irritation must have showed, for his visitor complied. The chair groaned under the big man's weight—at least two hundred fifty pounds. "Yes, *she* asked *him*," Rainwater continued. "She had a kid's crush on an older man named Jack Davis, and she'd just had a argument with him."

"What kind of argument?"

"Callie was a cheerleader. Jack says he told her she was making a spectacle of herself by flipping her skirt around. She didn't take kindly to criticism."

"What business was it of his?"

"None, I guess, but it makes sense to people around here. Jack and Callie's older brother was teammates back in 'forty-two. Great team—played in the state tournament. But Clyde Rakestraw got killed in the war, and Jack says he thought he ought to tell Callie what Clyde would've if he'd been here."

"What did she do?"

"According to Jack, she says, 'Dancers do it in the movies. Why shouldn't I?' Then she twirls her skirt at him and gives him a hard look. He figures after that it was up to her parents. He don't know what happened later. Says he went straight home and slept till Miz Rakestraw phoned him to go look for Callie."

"And Callie?"

"She asked this kid Ronnie Parker from the boys' team to drive her home. He'd been trying to date her, but she'd froze him out. Now he thinks she's ready for whatever. So after a while, he pulls his truck over and makes a play for her."

"Did she give?"

"He says what she give him was a elbow in the ribs. But that don't discourage him for long. He drives on, but he tries again about a mile west of the driveway where her body was found. He puts his arm around her, and she takes his hand like she's going to kiss it. Instead, she bites his finger, yanks the door open, and says leave her alone or she'll walk home."

"And he let her?"

"He's pretty mad, checking to see if his finger was bleeding, so he says she can walk to Hawaii for all he cares. She slams the door and walks west along the road. The rain had let up for a while, and home was only a couple of miles away."

"What did Ronnie do?"

"After he sulks a while, he sees he can't let Callie walk home. Not if he ever wants to get another date in this town. So he drives after her and asks her to get back in the truck. But now she won't talk to him. To get away, she walks east, back toward town. He turns his truck around and asks her again—begs her, as he tells it. But she does another turnaround and heads west toward home. By this time he's really mad. The truck is pointed toward town, so he drives home and goes to bed. He says that's the last he hears till I find him about nine o'clock the next morning."

Patterson rubbed his red face with a huge paw. "Did he see any other traffic?"

"Says he saw two cars or pickups headed west, but it was night and he can't give no description. Wouldn't have done no good, anyway, since all the trucks and most cars are black." He wrinkled his nose. "Identifying trucks'll be easier when they begin making 'em in different colors. But that don't help us now. Anyway, we're on radio in four counties, asking those drivers to come forward."

Patterson made no response.

Rainwater ran a hand through his hair. "I think Ronnie's telling the truth. I didn't say why I was asking questions and he was defiant as could be. Finally, he lost his temper and blurted out the whole story. Said he hoped she wore her feet off up to the ankles. But when I told him she was dead, he went all to pieces. Kept saying it wouldn't've happened if he'd done what was right."

Patterson again listened in silence.

The sheriff quirked one corner of his mouth. "Ronnie's folks are no help. His dad kept talking about disgrace to the family. I told him it *would* be a disgrace if he didn't stick by his son. He didn't like that, either. The boy finally quieted down so we could finish up. He'd got teeth marks on his finger, like he said. They don't match up with his own teeth, either."

Patterson threw him a questioning look.

"Yeah," Rainwater growled, "I did get photographs of the bite marks. But not of Ronnie's teeth. They aren't going nowhere."

Patterson's expression made it clear he didn't appreciate the humor. "No other cars were reported?"

"None. If we find the drivers of the two westbound cars, they may have seen some. Eastbound, prob'ly, 'cause the body was found a mile east of where Ronnie let her out."

"Anything special about the body?"

"Not a mark on it except the broken neck. No signs of violation. She still had her basketball uniform on under her skirt."

Patterson gave the sheriff a probing glance. "Any chance some of your colored folks had a hand in this? We have enough trouble without a lynching or a race riot."

"I doubt Callie'd get in a car with 'em, 'specially that time of night. If someone forced her, she'd put up a fight. But like I say, there wasn't a mark on her except the broke neck." Rainwater shook his head. "Still, I got deputies talking to everyone who lives along that road, white or black. I'm also checking that bunch of Gypsies in the trailer park south of town. No reason to think they're involved, but gossip don't need a reason. People are already saying a Gypsy must have done it."

Patterson gave the sheriff another straight look. "What about this fellow Davis?"

"Grew up here, never in trouble. Steady. Never flashy, just always did his part. Since he came back from the war he's worked himself near to death paying off the note on his farm."

"Vet'ran, huh? Sometimes those guys go off the deep end. What did he do in the war?"

"Served in the Army. Doing what, I don't know." At Patterson's raised eyebrows, he added, "Won't hurt to find out."

The detective nodded with more satisfaction than Rainwater liked. "You say Mrs. Rakestraw asked him to go out in the rain and look for Callie? That was asking a lot."

"The woman was desperate. She called Jack because Callie was sweet on him an' she thought maybe they'd got together at his place. She could ask Jack to go looking because he and her dead son was friends. That team of 'forty-two stuck together close as two thin layers of glue. They still do. When any two of 'em meet, you'd think it was a family reunion."

Patterson looked skeptical. "How'd he know to look in that particular spot?"

Rainwater shrugged. "If he did what he says he did, he'd looked ever' place else."

The door opened and admitted Wilt Sorrel, the coroner, who had worked with Rainwater for years. Wilt granted Patterson a nod, then spoke to the sheriff. "The pathologist says we can release the body for the funeral."

Rainwater nodded. "Thanks, Wilt."

Sorrel headed for the door, but turned back for a parting shot. "First pathologist I ever saw with less sense of humor than the corpse."

Patterson grinned. "That's the guy I brought up here. He didn't like getting called away from his Sunday fishing." He stood up. "One other thing. I have to find a place to stay."

"Two choices," Rainwater said. "You can bunk in my spare bedroom if you like. Mama will feed you breakfast and supper, but you're on your own for lunch. The other choice is Mrs. Telebit's Beth-aven Boarding House. You can take your meals with her or eat downtown. The drugstore/café ain't too bad." He surveyed Patterson's six-and-a-half-foot length. "Either way, you'll have to sleep catty-wompus on the bed 'cause we don't got one that'll fit you."

"Thanks. No reflection on Mama, but I'll try the boarding house."

Patterson paused in the doorway and rubbed his huge hands together. "Tomorrow I'll talk to Ronnie Parker and Jack Davis. No problem about your interrogation, you understand, but maybe I can jar something new out of them."

Rainwater sighed. It looked like a rough week ahead.

Chapter 6

Tuesday, January 13

Morning broke cold and clear beneath a steely sun that brought glare without warmth. That afternoon, Lisa watched Callie's funeral with a special sadness carried over from her mother's death short months before. As outsiders, she and her father had wondered if they should attend at all. But Rose McKenzie thought attendance and sympathetic interest would further their acceptance in the community. Lisa had made a move in that direction Monday afternoon by telling Sheriff Rainwater about Callie's quarrel with Jack Davis. The sheriff thanked her and said he'd look into it. But his deadpan facial expression and monotone voice hadn't changed, so Lisa couldn't tell if he believed her.

She and her father sat near the back of the church, still wearing their coats in the inadequately heated sanctuary. Stephen Kemper wore the worried frown that lately had become habitual. Lisa couldn't tell if he fretted about problems with the building contractor or about the day's yet-unsolved mystery. Earlier that morning she had found a fifth of Jim Beam whiskey beside the milk delivered to their front porch. At the tournament, her father had jokingly complained to a group that included Sheriff Rainwater about having to give up his before-dinner cocktail in this dry state. Now he suspected someone was setting him up for an arrest.

The church organ sounded, and Lisa watched the dark-clad congregation drift in with melancholy faces. The faces showed shock as well as sorrow, combined with lack of comprehension of the terrible thing that had happened among them. One part of Lisa's mind said it served them right. No town could be as virtuous as they claimed Beneficent was. But her better part tried to empathize with their sorrow.

She, like everyone, listened as the organist played traditional hymns, but somehow the hymns lacked their usual assurance. Consolation seemed to drain out of the music before it reached the congregation.

The most somber sight of all was the flower-bedecked casket at the front of the church. It remained conspicuously closed.

Everything at this funeral was being done as it should be, yet Lisa had an uneasy feeling that something was missing—some subtle element that made the difference between sorrow consoled and sorrow unassuaged. Puzzling about this, she reexamined the congregation.

Behind the mourners' bench, as pallbearers, sat Hollis Wilson, Jimmy Fletcher, Jack Davis and a fat man of about the same age, who Lisa thought must be Otis Hahn.

Even here the team of 'forty-two holds together! Her imagination might be running away with her, but it seemed almost as if the dead Clyde Rakestraw sat among them.

Lisa wondered again about Jack Davis. Rose said that everyone now knew the story of Friday night's events, and a few of the townspeople thought either Jack or Ronnie Parker had killed Callie. Jack had found the body, and Ronnie was the last person known to have seen her alive, but most people thought no one in Beneficent could have committed such a crime. They said it had to be an outsider, probably one of the Gypsies. Lisa's rational mind told her to remain neutral until real evidence surfaced. Then she remembered Jack's scowl as he watched Callie twirl. Even an ordinary man like Jack might kill in a jealous rage.

Still studying the congregation, she recognized Ronnie Parker as the Number Four she'd seen holding hands with Callie. He sat alone in a side row, his parents nowhere in sight. Everyone who entered looked his way and sat somewhere else. Lisa doubted that the boy could ever live down his horrible mistake. If this was the good Christian community everyone claimed, where were its compassion and forgiveness?

As the church filled and the seats near Ronnie remained empty, Jack Davis whispered something to the man Lisa took to be Otis Hahn. Jack left the other pallbearers, moved to Ronnie's pew, and placed his arm around the boy's shoulders. Ronnie put his head in his hands as Jack whispered to him.

So, rather than condemning Ronnie, Jack felt compassion for him. A person with that kind of empathy couldn't commit murder, could he? But that scowl at Callie …

A movement from Otis Hahn caught her eye. The big farmer lumbered over to sit by Ronnie's other side. Lisa wondered if Hollis Wilson would follow, but he and Jimmy Fletcher remained where they were.

The organ music swelled and the mourners entered: Cornelia Rakestraw with a handkerchief wiping tears that never stopped, her husband Hiram stoic and stony-faced beside her, and young Clem stiff-collared in his Sunday best, red-eyed but determined.

Then four men took places on the platform. One was the pastor, a short, plump man known as Brother Smallwood. The others were the triumvirate of deacons who, Rose said, "ran the church." Lisa had met the one with the perpetually worried expression—Harry Pendleton, president of Beneficent National Bank. She'd also seen the burly, bald-headed Jacob Weaver, a reformed bootlegger, at his filling station/garage on Main Street. The third, a tall, thin man whom Rose termed "skinny as a scarecrow on a diet," had to be Shiloh Simpson—town mayor, chairman of the deacon body, and owner of the town's laundry and dry cleaners.

At Simpson's nod, a strikingly beautiful young girl came forward from the choir. Lisa had noticed her at the tournament. How could anyone not notice her? Expensively dressed and elaborately coiffed, she looked like a model in a fashion magazine. Why had the girl bothered to go to the tournament? She never seemed to watch the game. Once in a while she took out a compact and mended her makeup. Otherwise, she simply looked bored.

As the organ played an introduction, Lisa marveled at the perfection of the girl's face—completely dry-eyed, every precise stroke of mascara untouched by tears.

Her song was Albert Hay Mallotte's familiar setting of "The Lord's Prayer." The girl's rich soprano filled the church without apparent effort. It was beautifully controlled: each note precisely on pitch, each entry flawless. Technically perfect, but completely devoid of feeling. As emotionally blank as the girl's expressionless face.

After the song, each deacon eulogized Callie's short life. Harry Pendleton, his worried frown more somber than ever, told of her baptism at the age of ten. Jacob Weaver spoke of her high spirits and athletic skill. Shiloh Simpson praised her devotion to her parents. The congregation remained attentive, but it seemed to Lisa that the deacons' words flowed past them without effect.

When the deacons finished, Brother Smallwood read familiar passages from the Bible. As at her mother's funeral, Lisa found herself moved by the grandeur of the words: "What man is he that liveth, and shall not see death?" ". . . for dust thou art, and unto dust shalt thou return . . ." Yet someday "there shall be no more death" because Christ "will swallow up death in victory." "Until that glorious day of His coming," the minister said, "we must hold ourselves rejoicing in hope, patient in tribulation . . ." though often "sorrowful, yet alway rejoicing . . ."

When he closed his Bible, Brother Smallwood spoke first of consolation for, as he said, Callie's faith meant her soul was already in heaven. "So our grief is for our loss of someone we loved, and for the sudden and brutal nature of that loss."

He added that he understood the shock everyone was feeling, for everyone believed no such crime could happen in Beneficent. "But maybe we've been complacent," he said. "Perhaps we've thought that being good people made our community proof against the evils we read about every day in the newspapers or hear on the radio.

"But now our complacency is challenged: an evil act has taken the life of an innocent girl." He paused before adding, "And let there be no doubt of that, for an autopsy has confirmed that she died in innocence."

So much for Mrs. Telebit's gossip. Lisa almost smiled at the thought.

The congregation, attentive at first, now grew restless.

"What we must understand," the pastor continued, "is the legacy of Eden. Since then, the tendency to evil is the heritage of all mankind—including Beneficent, Mississippi. No one is so virtuous, nor any community so good, that evil cannot enter. We pray that God will 'deliver us from evil,' but our final deliverance comes only in death. And on this day our beloved Callie Rakestraw has received that deliverance."

Brother Smallwood paused, and through that silence Lisa heard a few mutterings and an uneasy shifting of positions among the congregation.

The pastor cleared his throat. "We can hope this evil came from outside our community, but we must admit the possibility that it came from within. While we wait for the police to find the guilty party, let us be conscious of our own potential for evil, and let us be in prayer that our own hearts will be right."

He had all the words right, Lisa thought as Brother Smallwood closed with prayer, but she could see that his message had not been received. He might as well have said nothing.

The organ sounded again as Jack Davis and Otis Hahn rejoined the other pallbearers and removed the casket from the sanctuary. The congregation then wasted no time in leaving. Their set expressions showed their reluctance to accept what had happened.

In the departing crowd Lisa saw a huge, red-faced man wearing a blue-checked suit that seemed ludicrously out of place at a funeral. The detective from Jackson, she guessed. She'd been warned about him. His gaze bored into the passing faces as if he read guilt in every mind. That was one man she hoped she'd never meet!

Lisa expected people to linger and talk outside the church as she'd seen after other services. Instead, they moved quickly away, some muttering vague disclaimers:

". . . nobody from this town . . ."

"Bet one of them Gypsies . . ."

". . . pastor has his nerve . . ."

". . . got to be some outsider . . ."

Lisa listened in silent amazement. She saw now that many people, perhaps the entire community, shared the same hardcore belief in Beneficent's virtue. Callie's murderer might turn out to be someone from outside the community, but sooner or later these people were going to receive a terrible shock. Her distaste for the town told her they deserved that shock. Yet underneath the distaste, her heart ached for the pain they would suffer in their day of disillusionment.

Then she wondered: Why had it begun to matter to her, a stranger in their midst?

Chapter 7

Wednesday, January 14

Lisa attended the evening prayer meeting—not in hope of spiritual sustenance, but as part of her program to gain acceptance in the community. Stephen Kemper, morose from another day's lack of progress at the chemical plant, said he lacked energy enough to make the effort.

Lisa wore the gray suit she'd worn to the tournament and again found she was overdressed. Some thirty people attended, about half of them women, and all thirty stared as she entered. The only person she really knew was Rose McKenzie, though she'd been introduced to the pastor and two of his three main deacons. Among the others, she recognized only Jack Davis, who acknowledged her presence with a nod and a smile that sent a shiver down her back when she remembered his quarrel with Callie.

She sat in silence as the pre-meeting chatter moved around her. No one knew if the sheriff had made progress about Callie's murder. Surprisingly, people seemed concerned less about the crime itself and more about what it would mean to the town's reputation.

One man in overalls spoke angrily, "We've spent years telling people Beneficent is a town where good people spend their time doing good things, and now some outsider comes along and wipes it all out. We're still as good a town as ever, but people won't remember that. All they'll remember is that somebody got killed here."

At that point, the pastor, Brother Smallwood, called for attention and opened with a short prayer. Then he divided the congregation into four groups, taking one himself and assigning his three chief deacons to the others.

Lisa and Jack ended up in the group led by the skinny chairman of deacons, Shiloh Simpson. Simpson asked each member to read or recite one verse of scripture that held special meaning.

Jack Davis spoke without hesitation. "You all know how much people in Beneficent did for me while I was overseas. But you did something for me that you may not know about. There were a lot of bad things going on over there, and I saw a lot of guys surrender to them. Remembering Beneficent was what kept me straight. No matter how much evil existed out there in the world, I knew there was one place where goodness and love were the order of the day."

He paused and took a breath. "So my verse comes from Psalm 133: *Behold, how good and how pleasant it is for brethren to dwell together in unity!*"

The group murmured in assent, but Lisa's temper rose. *Unity, my foot! Callie's murder knocks that 'virtuous community' idea into a cocked hat.* She remembered her question from their grocery-store conversation. *Does he think somebody has revoked original sin?*

She knew the exact verse he and everybody else needed to hear! She searched her Bible frantically as other people read or recited. Where was it? There! Psalm 53!

When her turn came, Lisa looked directly at Jack and read in a voice that came out louder than she intended:

> *Corrupt are they, and have done abominable iniquity:*
> *there is none that doeth good.*
> *. . . Every one of them is gone back . . .*
> *there is none that doeth good, no, not one.*

The group grew dead silent. Everyone looked at Lisa as if she'd thrown a rattlesnake into their midst. Everyone but Jack. He looked at her, too, but a smile spread slowly across his face—whether accepting or rejecting her rebuke, she could not tell.

In the silence, Shiloh Simpson cleared his throat with a sound like a thunderclap. "Folks," he drawled, "I guess that's enough scripture. Brother Conroy, would you lead in prayer?"

At this request, an elderly man mumbled at considerable length. Lisa couldn't make out many of the words, but those she could asked divine help for a remarkable number of people with a greater catalog of ailments than she'd ever imagined. At least the bowed heads kept people from staring at her.

When Brother Conroy finally said "Amen," she left quickly. She didn't feel like explaining herself to anyone. She'd come there to help her father gain acceptance in the community, but her outburst had only pushed her—and him—further out of it. And it left her more uncertain than ever. She could finish out her year here. But would she have to do it as an apostate?

***

Driving back to his farm after prayer meeting, Jack chided himself for making a mess of things. He believed goodness actually *was* the norm in Beneficent, and it *had* been his spiritual anchor during the war. Callie's murder was the great exception to that goodness. All the more reason to reemphasize the town's virtues, especially with that newcomer in their midst. In the prayer meeting his good feeling toward the community had welled up inside him. And Lisa Kemper was there. He was much too conscious of her presence across from him in the prayer circle. She had a smooth olive complexion and deep blue eyes. Nice figure, too . . .

For reasons he didn't understand, he wanted her to see the town as he did. So when Shiloh Simpson asked for a scripture verse, Jack chose the one from Psalm 133.

Although he thought of Lisa as Hollis Wilson's girl, he admitted his fascination for her. Especially the quick intelligence in her eyes. But those eyes flashed anger at him as he recited the psalm. He knew trouble was coming as he watched her page furiously through her Bible. Sure enough, she attacked him with Psalm 53: *there is none that doeth good, no, not one.*

The words still stung as he remembered them. He knew they were true, but in practical terms wasn't it a matter of percentage? People here slipped once in a while in small ways. He himself did. But they spent most of their time doing things that were good and worthy. He couldn't imagine anyone in Beneficent doing anything really evil. There was Callie's murder, of course, but he still hoped it was done by an outsider. There were plenty of them around for the tournament.

Given what he'd heard of Lisa's background and education, Jack could understand her impatience with Beneficent. He wanted all the newcomers, including the Gypsies, to see the town as he did, and he might even confide that he knew it wasn't perfect yet. He'd wanted to explain all that to Lisa. But as the meeting broke up, someone distracted him with a question. When he looked, she had gone. Sometime soon he'd find a way to talk with her. She was Hollis Wilson's girl, but he didn't guess Hollis would mind a little Chamber-of-Commerce conversation.

***

Thursday morning, January 15
With time for the morning coffee break approaching, Deputy Woodrow Wilson Brown watched gloom descend on Sheriff Rainwater's face. It always did when Detective Ben Patterson entered the office. *No,* Brown corrected himself, *Patterson didn't enter a room. A man that big* invaded. The huge man's entry ended Brown's banter with the sheriff, but the signs of frustration on the detective's face gladdened his heart.

"How'd you make out questioning the suspects?" Sheriff Rainwater asked. His face assumed the customary deadpan expression Brown admired.

"Oh, the questioning went fine." Patterson carefully lowered his bulk onto a protesting chair. "The problem was getting answers. Those two would make a clam sound like a gossip columnist."

"Even the kid?"

"Ronnie Parker? He told me the same story he'd told you. But when I tried to cross him up he got quiet as a church mouse with laryngitis. Kept telling me to look it up in his previous statement."

"You didn't push him around none?"

"I leaned on him a little, but no rough stuff. He's just a kid. Besides, I think you're right that he didn't do it."

"And Jack Davis?"

"He's a different story. I went to his place yesterday and found him out in the boondocks chopping pine trees. Got a good pair of shoes all muddy while I was looking for him."

Rainwater grunted. "The shoeshine boy at the barber shop'll fix 'em up for you."

"So I found out. Gave him an extra dime for it, too. Your man Davis is a hard case."

"He's got a clean record." Rainwater looked into space beyond his visitor—a sure sign, Brown knew, that the sheriff was leading him on.

"Clean record?" Patterson's lips pressed tight. "Maybe so. But Jesse James was clean, too, till he robbed his first train."

The phone rang and Rainwater answered. "Yes, Mr. Kemper," he said. "Advice? No sir, all I can do is tell you what the law says." A pause. "You found a fifth of Jim Beam on your porch beside the milk bottles?" The sheriff winked at Brown, then turned back to the phone. "Was the seal broken?"

Another pause. Ben Patterson leaned forward, suddenly alert. Brown suppressed a chuckle.

The sheriff's face remained inscrutable. "If I was you, Mr. Kemper, I'd open it up an' enjoy it . . . No, sir. Possession is not agin' the law. It's the *sale* that's illegal . . . That's right. You can buy it in Memphis and bring it home as long as you don't sell it, but be careful about the seal. Sometimes they ring in some local stuff what can strike you blind . . . No, sir. I wouldn't have no idea who brung it, but lots of folks are grateful for your building the chemical plant . . . No trouble at all, Mr. Kemper. If ever'body was as law-abiding as you, we wouldn't never have to worry about no crime."

Ben Patterson looked incredulous. "Someone left a fifth of Jim Beam beside the milk?"

Rainwater's face remained blank. "That's what the man said. Wasn't no crime committed, so it wasn't none of my business. What was you saying about Jack Davis?"

Patterson looked disgusted. "Did you ever try to talk to a man who's chopping trees? I'd get out three words of a question, his axe would go 'whack,' and I'd have to start over. All he said was that if you brought him in for questioning, he'd answer anything I asked. Otherwise, nothing at all."

Rainwater's eyes flickered. "You're a lot bigger'n he is. What happened when you offered to get rough with him?"

"Not much. He was very polite when he reminded me who was carrying the axe." Patterson scratched his head. "Sheriff, maybe I better stick to the technical end of this case and let you handle the interrogations."

Rainwater gave a benign smile. "Okay, Ben. However you want to work it."

Deputy Brown clamped his jaw to suppress a laugh.

Two other deputies entered and one reported, "We've finished checking on the Gypsies, Sheriff. There must be a hundred in that trailer park, and you never heard such a racket. I don't see how Mr. Pendleton stands 'em at the shirt factory."

Rainwater grinned. "The noise won't bother him as long as the factory makes money. Was the Gypsies clean?"

"All but one was clean as a new-bought whistle."

"What about him?"

"His name is Guido Bramante. A bunch of people saw him at the girls' ball game Friday night. He'd been drinking and was making remarks about the players, including Callie Rakestraw. But nobody sees him after the boys' game starts, and the next anyone knows is when he comes in drunk and cussing at three in the morning. Woke several families up. Somebody hollers that his noise will wake up the dead, and he yells back that when he lays someone out for dead they don't never wake up."

Rainwater gave a curt nod. "Bring him in for questioning. He sounds like a bad actor, so don't forget to fingerprint him."

The deputies left. Ben Patterson shook his head. "This is *some kind* of dry county you have, Sheriff. A Gypsy comes in three sheets to the wind, and somebody runs around delivering whiskey with the morning milk. Don't tell me you have cows that give whiskey."

"Not yet," Rainwater said, "but I'll pass that idea on to the agricultural experiment folks down at State College. How are you and Mrs. Telebit getting along?"

"Oh, fine." Patterson stretched. "She keeps asking who the murder suspects are, and I keep naming your deputies."

"That's very considerate of you. Is the bed okay?"

"I have to sleep catty-wompus, like you said, but that has advantages. I sink in so deep the other two mattress corners fold back over and keep me warm. A man could make a fortune selling mattresses like that."

After Patterson left, Deputy Brown asked the sheriff, "Will we ever let on that you had me put the whiskey on Mr. Kemper's porch?"

"Not till Gabriel takes over from Louie Armstrong."

"That wasn't no easy job," Brown complained. "I like never've convinced the bootlegger it wasn't a raid, and then he tried to bribe me with a whole case. How come you sent me on a fool's errand like that?"

Rainwater squinted. "Call it a housewarming gift. I never could stand to see a good man go thirsty. But now he's had his welcome. From here out, he's on his own."

Chapter 8

That afternoon found Lisa looking forward to more interesting work in Beneficent. Rose McKenzie had kept her promise to ask Vesta Childress if Lisa could help as a volunteer in the school library. Vesta and Lisa agreed to meet in the drugstore/café to see what they could work out.

A sudden false spring that morning pushed back the winter weather, so Lisa chose a spring-spirited yellow dress for the occasion. She walked the quarter-mile of Beneficent's potholed streets to downtown, stepped carefully across the railroad that divided the town in half, and crossed Main Street to the one-block business district on its far side. A few muddy pickups were parked at the curb, with the inevitable mule-drawn wagon nearby.

Five unshaven elderly men in overalls occupied a bench in front of the drugstore. They concentrated on a checkerboard resting on a nail keg before the bench. Otherwise, the street was empty. As Lisa approached, the men looked up and stared until she thought they'd never seen a yellow dress before. She wished she'd worn something more subdued.

She wondered if she should speak to them, but at the crucial moment Jimmy Fletcher's tall form emerged from the drugstore, and all eyes turned toward him. When he saw Lisa, he planted himself in her path.

"Hello, Miss Kemper." Jimmy hovered over her with the boyish grin she remembered from Friday night's ball game. Looking up at his height made her neck hurt.

She felt herself flushing. "I . . . uh . . . it's Mr. Fletcher, isn't it? I think Senator Wilson introduced us at the tournament."

That ought to keep the record straight for this audience.

"Welcome to Beneficent, Miss Kemper." Jimmy took a step toward the street, effectively pinning Lisa between him and the men on the bench. "Can I give you a tour of the town? I got a special truck for jobs like that. I call it 'Mayflower.'"

Lisa put an edge in her voice. "That's very kind of you, Mr. Fletcher, but I have an appointment."

Jimmy moved closer and his grin widened. "Do you know why I call my truck 'Mayflower'?"

"I know exactly," Lisa snapped. "That was a bad joke the first time I heard it, and I have no intention of hearing it again."

She ducked between Jimmy and the bystanders to escape, but collided with the checkerboard. Checkers rolled on the pavement behind her, the fallen nail keg bounced with a hollow sound and someone muttered, "Dag-nab it!" Then she was safe inside the drugstore.

Safe, but furious that she'd made a spectacle of herself. Gratefully, she found metal racks of paperback books on both sides of the entry. They shielded her from observation while she recovered her poise. That done, she moved past the books and surveyed the store.

A long marble soda fountain counter ran the length of the left-hand wall. At a window in the rear, the pharmacist talked with a blonde female customer. Across from the fountain stood six of the round, marble-top tables common to drugstores nationwide. The customary wooden straight chairs were arranged around each table. These tables gave way, where the right interior wall had evidently been removed, to square cafe-style tables covered with red-and-white checkered oil cloth. Clattering kitchen sounds came from the rear of that section.

An attractive middle-aged woman behind the fountain asked, "May I help you?" The quality of her clothing proclaimed her proprietress rather than employee.

"Thank you," Lisa said, "but I'll order when Miss Childress comes."

The woman introduced herself as Mrs. Harding, then checked her wristwatch. "School's out. Miss Childress should be here any minute. I'll come back then."

Lisa chose a marble-top table where she could watch the door. She hoped she and Vesta would prove compatible. Rose McKenzie had filled her in on Vesta's past, the "sad story" interrupted by Mrs. Telebit's revelations.

A local girl and new college graduate, Vesta had taken a job at Beneficent High in August, 1941. She'd had better offers but gave priority to caring for her invalid mother. With flowing brown hair and a quiet beauty blossoming into full womanhood, Vesta was much sought after by eligible males. The competition ended at Thanksgiving, though, with the announcement of her engagement to William Bradley, the well-respected history teacher and basketball coach. They were perfect for each other, everyone said.

But in December the Japanese attacked Pearl Harbor, and Mr. Bradley joined the Marine Corps the next day. His death on Tarawa ended Vesta's romance and brought the sadness that now hovered around her like an aroma of morbid perfume. Her mother's death a year later freed her to pursue better opportunities, but for reasons never stated she remained in Beneficent, living in the same house and working at the same routine year after year. A very sad story, Lisa agreed.

The door of the drugstore opened. Instead of the librarian, though, it admitted Jack Davis. Lisa sighed in relief when he disappeared among the bookracks without looking her way. She remembered their encounter at prayer meeting, and she still wondered about his quarrel with Callie Rakestraw. She didn't care to meet him again just yet.

The pharmacy customer turned out to be the young singer from Callie's funeral. Privately, Lisa thought of her as "Miss Beauty Queen." Made up to perfection again today, the girl gave Lisa a monotoned "Hello." Her facial expression remained completely blank. But before reaching the door, she flashed an animated smile at someone Lisa could not see among the bookracks.

In a clear voice, the young beauty exclaimed, "Hello, Jack."

The masculine reply sounded pleased. "Hi, Precious. How are you and your folks?"

Lisa almost blushed. *How can a grown man be so familiar with that … that child?*

The girl's smile twinkled again at the unseen man. "Daddy and I are fine, but Mama caught cold at the funeral." She showed him her package from the pharmacy.

"Tell her I hope she gets well soon," Jack said. "And remember me to your father."

"Okay." As the girl left, her expression subsided again into boredom.

Lisa was certainly seeing the community today. Understanding it was something else. Then things got worse.

Mrs. Telebit bustled in, her lips drawn tight beneath angry eyes. Mrs. Harding's face instantly reddened. Deliberately, she turned her back on her customer and stalked into the kitchen. Just as deliberately, Mrs. Telebit looked in the opposite direction. Soon afterward, a Negro woman came from the kitchen and waited on Mrs. Telebit, who departed as angrily as she had come. When the door closed behind her, Mrs. Harding returned to the soda fountain and showed Lisa the sweetest of smiles.

Lisa didn't know what to make of their animosity. It certainly didn't accord with the town's claims of virtue.

She had no time to think about it, for the door admitted a tall, statuesque woman who moved directly to Lisa's table. "I'm Vesta Childress," she said. "Are you Lisa Kemper?"

The woman's navy blouse and skirt were skewed an inch or more in different directions, largely negating the attractiveness of her ample figure. She wore her hair swept back and disciplined into a bun, though one unruly wisp fluttered loosely on her forehead. From time to time, absently, she pushed it back toward its place. Her face revealed a settled sadness, and her manner radiated the message that life was to be endured rather than enjoyed.

At the tournament, Lisa had seen this woman trying to hold Jack Davis's attention at the refreshment stand. She fumed silently. Mr. Davis apparently kept a harem of all shapes and sizes. But she pushed her irritation aside and said, "I hope I'll be able to help you in the library, Miss Childress."

"Call me Vesta." Instead of sitting across the table from Lisa, the older woman sat beside her. She spoke to Lisa, but kept looking hopefully toward the door. "The work is simple, but few people would find it interesting. Can you afford two mornings a week?"

"Even three. Or afternoons. I can start tomorrow."

Vesta frowned. "Mornings are better. Afternoons are hectic, and Fridays are completely impossible."

She brightened as the door opened, but squinted in disappointment when it admitted Hollis Wilson. The handsome senator threw Lisa a casual salute, then said to someone hidden among the bookracks, "Sorry I'm late." Vague sounds of masculine conversation followed, and presently Wilson and Jack Davis emerged together.

Suddenly energized, Vesta beckoned them to the table. Lisa felt embarrassed for both of them. She could understand that teenage beauty's interest in a man in his mid-twenties, but Vesta had to be on the high side of thirty. In her irritation, Lisa made a point of speaking mainly to Senator Wilson. She'd come for a business meeting, but this was turning into a social.

Mrs. Harding came and entered into brief badinage with the two men. As they talked, Lisa noticed Jack Davis's hands clasped on the table, his sleeves rolled up almost to the elbow. Strong hands, quite capable of overcoming a small girl like Callie Rakestraw. Strong forearms, too, but appearing smooth under their light rug of sandy hair.

Enough of that. She'd come here to talk business.

Wilson asked the two women, "What will you have?"

Vesta ordered a lemon Coke from the fountain. Lisa, chilled from her walk, ordered hot chocolate.

"With or without marshmallow?" Mrs. Harding asked.

Lisa looked up in surprise. "With, please. The marshmallow is the best part."

"I thought I'd better ask," Mrs. Harding said. "Jack takes his without."

Jack laughed. "I'll still take it without. But you can give mine to her. Two ought to be better than one."

Lisa protested and thought the matter closed until her chocolate arrived, graced by two marshmallows. Mrs. Harding gave Lisa a knowing look that seemed to imply a shared secret. Lisa thanked Jack, but her irritation returned, more insistent this time. Could the middle-aged Mrs. Harding be another member of The Jack Davis Harem?

And what about Callie? Lisa looked again at Jack's hands.

". . . construction job finished," Hollis Wilson was saying. "So what comes next, Jack?"

Jack shrugged. "I get on the telephone and find something else. I have to stay ahead of the interest on that bank note."

"He does more than stay ahead of it," Wilson said to Lisa, then asked, "Does your father still have problems with his contractor?"

"Dad can't pin him down about specifications, and the man is gone so often . . ."

Wilson frowned. "Cinder-block walls on a concrete slab can't be that complicated. If your father's company hadn't insisted on a contractor out of Memphis, plenty of local men could do the job. They'd be more responsive, too."

Wilson broke off as four men in work clothes gathered at the soda fountain. He laid a quarter and a nickel on the table to pay for the drinks and, with a murmured "Excuse me," joined the group at the fountain. A round of laughter followed. In their conversation, Lisa caught only scattered phrases: ". . . rural electrification . . . 'forty-seven . . . record-breaking year . . ."

Her mind drifted back to Jack's hands and Callie Rakestraw, his too-familiar greeting to Miss Beauty Queen—*"Precious"* indeed! But Jack had comforted the ostracized Ronnie Parker at the funeral, and he understood Lisa's frustration about broccoli. Jack's hands and Callie and marshmallows. How did they all fit together?

Vesta leaned forward on the table. "Well, Jack, what *are* your plans now?"

Jack turned with obvious reluctance from watching Senator Wilson and his constituents. "I'll take any job I can find till spring plowing."

He glanced at Wilson again, then said to Lisa. "Hollis sure knows how to politick. He'll go a long way."

Vesta also addressed Lisa. "Hollis always knows what he wants and he knows how to get it. In the Army he got himself assigned to a headquarters in Atlanta and took college courses at night. That let him finish his law degree within a year after discharge. He always comes out on top."

Half-listening, Lisa saw that Jack still watched the Senator work the small crowd. The original group dispersed and was replaced by a succession of others, including several couples. Wilson had them all smiling as they left.

Jack turned back to Lisa. "With that talent, he'll be elected governor someday."

Vesta gave a hollow-sounding laugh. "If he's going to be governor, he'd better find a good wife." She spoke directly to Lisa. "With his good looks that shouldn't be hard to do."

Lisa put a certain coolness into her reply. "He has been very helpful to my father." She changed to a safer subject, making a point of talking to Vesta rather than Jack. "Do you often have weather this nice in January?"

"Two or three warm spells every winter," Vesta answered. "They don't last long. In a day or two we'll be back to cold and wet."

"But our cold and wet isn't as bad as they have in Europe," Jack put in. "They're having their worst winter in years over there. Not enough coal for heating, and food is still scarce. On top of that, Russia keeps making trouble. Mostly around Berlin, but in other countries, too. Like Czechoslovakia, and the Communist guerrillas in Greece."

How did a farmer like Jack know about things like that? Lisa concealed her surprise and murmured, "I hope something can be done."

"Only relief work, for the present," Jack explained. "For the long haul, Congress is looking at foreign aid plans by Secretary of State

Marshall and Representative Herter. It looks like Congress will side with Marshall."

He looked again at Senator Wilson, who was now listening on the telephone. "On second thought," Jack said, "Hollis won't ever be governor if he lets people work him to death."

Lisa pretended she hadn't heard and turned to Vesta. When she looked back, Wilson had rejoined the group. "Let's go, Jack," he said. "I've found you a job. Will you excuse us, ladies?"

Lisa was glad to, but Vesta asked, "Magazines tomorrow, Jack?"

"You can count on it." His voice sounded flat, formal. Then he said softly to Lisa, "Give my regards to your father."

Lisa thanked him but felt relieved as he and Wilson left. She'd had enough embarrassment for one day, and she was beginning to have doubts about Vesta. If Jack and "magazines tomorrow" were that important to her, then Fridays couldn't be as impossible as she'd claimed. Another member of The Jack Davis Harem, perhaps? But if Jack was such a Casanova, why hadn't he made a play for her?

Angrily, Lisa dismissed the thought and asked again about the library. Vesta agreed for her to work Tuesday and Thursday mornings. That settled, Lisa asked for advice about her encounter with Jimmy Fletcher and the checker players.

"Don't worry about Jimmy." Vesta rolled her eyes. "He's a textbook case of overgrown boy."

"That may be," Lisa countered, "but I didn't appreciate his trying to pull the Mayflower joke on me."

Vesta looked confused. "Mayflower joke? What's that?"

"An old one. The boy says, 'I've named my car Mayflower.' When the girl asks why, the boy says, 'Because so many Puritans have come across in it.'"

Vesta looked blank for a moment and then said, "Oh." She swallowed hard. "I see why you didn't appreciate it."

When they left the drugstore, Vesta stood by while Lisa apologized to the checker players. They accepted graciously, and one conceded that Jimmy "wuz standin' a mite close."

As Lisa walked home through the growing chill and pondered the afternoon's events, she noticed a young boy standing in the road ahead, watching her. She had seen him at the tournament and again after the funeral. On both occasions he'd stood near a group but not in it. A born outsider, she'd decided. But why was he staring at her?

"Hello," she said as she stopped in front of him. He was several inches shorter than she, and she guessed his age at about twelve. His uncouth appearance was part of what she detested about Beneficent, yet for some reason her heart went out to him.

"Can I help you?" she asked.

He gulped once and blurted, "Your yard is full of water. I'll dig a ditch and drain it."

"Why do you want to do that?" Something seemed out of kilter.

"Because good people do good things." He gulped again. "I want to be a good person."

The Beneficent self-image again. This time it made an ignorant boy feel guilty.

"That's very commendable," she said, "but I'll have to ask my father. What's your name?"

"Buddy." His body fidgeted, but his gaze held hers.

"I'll call you Buddy if you like, but what's your real name?"

He looked at the ground. "Albert Eugene Robinson. It's awful."

Lisa struggled to keep from laughing while her heart moved her toward consolation. But how? "That's a beautiful name," she said. "The problem is that you haven't grown into it yet. It's like wearing a suit of men's clothing and having it hang all loose around you. But in a few years you'll fill out the suit nicely. You have to grow into names, too. Yours will fit when you're grown, and you'll be proud of it."

"That's what Mama tells me, except for the part about the suit. Maybe you're right, but right now the name stinks."

"I tell you what, Buddy. I'll talk to my father about draining our yard, and you talk to your mother. Give me your phone number and we'll work something out."

Lisa continued toward home, still trying to make sense of things. Her determination to find out what made Beneficent tick kept getting tangled up with understanding her own reactions to it. She should be happy to find useful work in the library, but mostly she felt confused. The most dramatic event in town was Callie's murder, yet everyone in the drugstore talked around it as if it had never happened. Was everyone in denial? And what should she make of the hostility between Mrs. Harding and Mrs. Telebit? Her encounter with Jimmy Fletcher still rankled. She resented Vesta's and Jack's attempts to match her with Hollis Wilson. And she found Jack's over-familiarity with Miss Beauty Queen offensive.

In a montage of images, she saw marshmallows, Callie Rakestraw, Jack's hands, and broccoli. She didn't know what to think. Fortunately, she told herself, she didn't have to think of Jack Davis at all.

She came in sight of home just in time to see her father, Hollis Wilson, and Jack Davis drive away in a pickup truck.

The false spring suddenly felt cold as deep winter. Her father had enough trouble just getting the chemical plant built. This new involvement might mean that both he and she were not finished with the enigma named Jack Davis.

Chapter 9

As Jack and Hollis Wilson drove from the drugstore to the Kemper residence, Wilson explained his phone conversation with Stephen Kemper. That morning, Kemper had decided to settle his differences with the troublesome Memphis contractor once and for all. He found no one in charge at the work site, where eight slow-moving workmen shifted materials from one stack to another. He watched the desultory effort for an hour, then left to phone Sheriff Rainwater about a different problem.

"What kind of problem?" Jack asked.

"He didn't say." Wilson waved the question aside and continued. The contractor was present in early afternoon when Kemper returned, but work crept along at the same lazy pace. Kemper confronted the man about evasiveness and lack of progress. The contractor cursed, walked out, and said he wouldn't be back. Wilson thought the man was trying to make Kemper choose between a relatively small cost overrun and the greater expense and delay of starting over with another contractor.

Stephen Kemper awaited them in his driveway with a briefcase in his hand and a glum expression on his face.

"Take the contractor at his word," Wilson advised. "He told you to get somebody else, and you're legally entitled to believe him. He's broken the contract, but he probably thinks you'll beg him to come back. He's betting you can't find anyone to meet your deadline."

"He's right," Kemper said, "I've called every contractor in four counties. The postwar boom has them all overcommitted."

Wilson shook his head. "You can finish the job sooner and with less expense if you work directly with subcontractors."

Kemper frowned. "I don't know any. And if I did, I wouldn't know what to tell them. I'm a chemist, not a construction engineer."

"Jack knows most of them, and he's done a lot of construction work. Hire him as your coordinator or whatever you want to call it, and you'll finish on time." When Kemper still looked doubtful, Wilson added, "You have something else going for you. The locals want to prove they can do the job better than outsiders, and their talk will keep that Memphis character from getting another contract in this part of the state."

Kemper's eyes flashed. "We'll give it a try." He turned to Jack. "What kind of salary will you want?"

Jack grimaced. "First, let's be sure I can do the job. I'd like to look at the plans and see what's been done."

Kemper pointed to his briefcase, and all three climbed into Jack's pickup. At the construction site they found that forms had been laid for the building's concrete floor. Materials lay piled about haphazardly, and eight men lounged among the stacks. They watched the newcomers with curiosity but without ambition.

Jack studied the plans, then paced off the approximate dimensions for the concrete floor. The forms, already enclosed, came up short by several feet.

He approached the loafing workmen. "Do you men work here?"

"Yep." The spokesman was an unshaven middle-aged man who chewed a toothpick. "Leastwise, we do when there's somebody to work for." He shifted the toothpick. "Who's gonna pay us for today?"

Jack met his gaze. "I'll see that you get paid. If you're here at eight tomorrow morning you can keep working at the same wage. We'll extend those forms to the length the plans call for. I'll need an accurate count of these materials, too."

Light flickered in the man's eyes. "There's more forms hid behind that pile of girders. I figgered we might need 'em if somebody reputable come along."

Jack grinned. "Good. We'll see you tomorrow, then."

As the men left in a battered pickup, Jack made a more thorough check of preparations to lay the slab. By the time he finished, he was certain he could do the job.

Kemper and Wilson agreed that the contractor's cheating on measurements would prevent a suit for breach of contract.

"What will you tell your company about this?" Wilson asked.

Kemper snorted. "Nothing. If I report a problem, they'll solve it. But they'll blame me, take the credit for themselves, and never again give me room to breathe. In two weeks I'll have progress to report. Then they'll have no choice except to approve what I've done." He turned to Jack. "You see how much I'm depending on you. Have you made a decision about your pay?"

Jack shook his head. "I'd rather you figure what the job is worth and let me worry about getting it done."

Kemper raised an eyebrow. "That's good enough for now, but we'll talk again when I've put pencil on paper."

They shook hands on it. Jack dropped Kemper and Wilson off in town, then drove home. This job would take a good bite out of his note at the bank, but some parts of it lay beyond his knowledge. He'd worked for men who had that knowledge. He hoped he'd worked well enough for them to share it.

***

That evening in Vesta Childress's home, blue flames again burned low in the butane heaters, their hiss still punctuated by faint popping sounds from impurities in the gas. The flames flickered briefly yellow from the impurities. As always, Vesta kept the air hot and dry to hold back the cold outside.

Seated at the oak secretary, with dowels from the half-wall casting bar-like shadows above her, she bit her lip and reviewed the day's embarrassments. In the drugstore she'd made a fool of herself again with her play for Jack Davis. He was friendly enough, and he always thanked her for letting him read the magazines in her library. But he was just as friendly to everyone else, from children in the church up to the oldest crone.

Crone. The word struck fear into her heart. Someday she would be a crone. That wasn't what bothered her, though, for it was inevitable. What bothered her was the thought that she'd become a crone without enjoying the fullness of youth.

She tugged at her collar, which again seemed too tight, and gazed at the photograph of her and William Bradley. With him she'd known high romance and promise of fulfillment, but his death on Tarawa had ended that. So what was left for her now?

She listened to the low hiss of the butane heaters. In dozens of ways she'd let Jack Davis know she wanted more, but distant friendship was all he offered. He was six years younger than she, but who else was there in this tiny village?

As she had done so often in grief, she turned to poetry for consolation. Opening the book at random, she read:

> *With thee conversing I forget all time,*
> *All seasons and their change, all please alike.*

No consolation there, Eve speaking to Adam in the Garden. That was the relationship Vesta had hoped for with her Adam, William Bradley.

Tears formed in her eyes as she opened the book again at random and read:

> *I have no wit, no words, no tears;*
> *My heart within me like a stone*
> *Is numbed too much for hopes or fears.*
> *Look left, look right, I dwell alone . . .*

Ah! Count on Christina Rossetti to understand. Yes, Vesta did dwell alone, and it looked like she might live that way for the rest of her life. So what solution did Christina offer?

My life is like a frozen thing,
No bud or greenness can I see:
Yet rise it shall—the sap of spring;
Oh Jesus, rise in me.

Her heart fell. Yes, Jesus would greet her at the end of life, and her resurrection would bring glorious happiness. But what about the long, empty years of this life? Something within her rebelled and said Jesus was no help here. She faced a life frozen in winter without bud or greenness.

The faint hiss from the butane heaters grew louder and the flames burned darker blue. Shadows from the dowels grew darker on the wall. Vesta's fingers tugged once more at her collar. Then once again she rested her head upon her arms and wept.

Chapter 10

For Lisa, the next two weeks passed as rapidly as a montage in a movie. Working in the school library with Vesta filled the empty hours and lessened her haunting sense of uselessness. For her father's sake, she took care to make a good impression and learn all she could about the town. Students and teachers welcomed her with courtesy. Yet while some images in the montage suggested she was gaining acceptance, others reminded her she was still an outsider.

Like the dead squirrel she found on her porch the second morning after her drugstore visit. First there was that bottle of whiskey, and now a dead squirrel. If someone was sending her and her father a message, what on earth was it?

But she quickly forgot the incident among pleasant contacts at the school. Her acquaintance with the boy named Buddy grew into genuine friendship. His plan to ditch the Kemper's yard proved too ambitious, but to avoid letting him down, Lisa hired him to trim the hedges instead. Buddy's eyes sparkled at the idea, and he bubbled with suggestions. One day while they spoke about it in the library, "Miss Beauty Queen" walked by.

Buddy glanced up and said, "Hi, Precious."

"Aren't you being too familiar with that girl?" Lisa asked. She bridled at remembering Jack Davis using that term of endearment to the girl.

Buddy's mouth dropped open. "Gosh no, Miss Kemper. That's her *name*."

Lisa caught her breath. "What?"

"It's her *name*," the boy repeated. "That's Precious Pendleton, the banker's daughter." His voice took on a tone of awe. "Sweet names run in the family. Her mother's named Honey."

So when the girl met Jack Davis in the drugstore, he was only calling her by name. But hadn't Precious greeted Jack a bit too eagerly? Lisa decided to learn more about her.

When questioned, Vesta Childress arched her eyebrows. "Precious makes straight *As*. She spends most of her time waiting for everyone else to catch up. There's nothing in town to challenge her, so of course she's bored."

The girl herself confirmed Vesta's word. "Miss Kemper," she asked when Lisa helped her with a research project, "don't you find Beneficent awfully dull? I know I do. But Mama says things will be different when I go off to college. That's when life really begins."

Precious obviously needed more than she was getting at school to prepare her for college. Moving cautiously, Lisa suggested a few books that might give the girl a broader perspective.

Over coffee, Rose McKenzie told Lisa more about Precious and her family. "No better man in town than Harry Pendleton," she said. "He loves his family almost to death—dresses them like Paris models and sends Precious to Ole Miss every week for voice lessons."

Rose warmed to her subject. "Harry refused to be church treasurer because as bank president he reviews every check the treasurer writes. He said it wasn't good business to have the same man write them and review them, too."

"He owns the new shirt factory, doesn't he?" Lisa asked.

Rose laughed. "He almost lost his own shirt on that one. His partner—a Memphis man—backed out at the last minute and left Harry five thousand dollars short. Heaven knows how he found the money, but he did. Now he's sole owner, and the town is richer by the thirty families of Gypsies that came with it."

Curious about relationships, Lisa mentioned Jack Davis's name to Precious.

The girl's boredom dissolved into sudden animation. "Daddy says Jack will have the best and biggest farm in the county in five more years. Jack thinks a lot of Daddy, too. I guess that's why he treats me nice. You know—almost like I was grown up."

So much for the Jack Davis Harem, Lisa thought. And so much for making hasty judgments. Rumors connecting Jack and Ronnie Parker with Callie's murder had died down with news that Sheriff Rainwater had a suspect in custody. But the Jack Davis that people spoke so highly of was the same Jack Davis who'd quarreled with Callie Rakestraw. Lisa couldn't reconcile the two images. She shuddered when she remembered his scowl.

Nor could she escape hearing about Jack even at home. "He's got construction back on schedule," Stephen Kemper boasted. "The men like him because he listens but isn't easily fooled. He's never showy. He just quietly finds ways to get things done."

In the library, Lisa found herself wondering about Jack and Vesta Childress. Despite the librarian's statuesque beauty, she dressed severely and without ornament. Yet Buddy confided that "Miss Childress always wears perfume on Fridays." Lisa remembered Vesta's anxiety in asking Jack, "Magazines tomorrow?" Could that explain the mystery of Friday perfume?

The harem again? Her familiar uncertainty returned.

Then more images tumbled into her montage. Another dead squirrel on her front porch suggested a planned harassment campaign, so she and her father talked to Sheriff Rainwater about it.

"Ain't no telling who's doing it," the sheriff said. "Could be some local who don't want the chemical plant built, or it could be that rascally contractor you fired." He shifted his cigar to the other side of his mouth. "I wouldn't lose no sleep over it, though. The worst part is that if you don't know who brung the squirrels, you don't dare eat 'em."

The situation might not be dangerous, but it emphasized their status as aliens.

Lisa continued to hear talk about the Beneficent team of 'forty-two, so she researched the library's files of the county newspaper. Skipping the first two tournaments, she began with the team's two games in the North State tournament.

She'd heard that Jimmy Fletcher and Clyde Rakestraw had averaged eighteen points apiece all season long, but in the North State games, neither scored more than ten. Contrary to all she'd been told, Jack Davis scored nineteen and sixteen points in the two games while Hollis Wilson scored eight and twelve. The team's losing game in the state tournament showed similar figures.

She asked Hollis Wilson about it while they drove to the nearest movie theater, located fifteen miles south in the town of Shipley.

"Not many people know that story," he said. "Gasoline was rationed, so most of our fans couldn't get to the tournaments." He slipped into fond remembrance. "At North State, defenders were good enough to hold Clyde Rakestraw down. And they double- and triple-teamed Jimmy whenever he got the ball. Jimmy was born stubborn, so he kept forcing shots instead of passing off. We were twelve points down at the half. That's when Jack laid down the law: if Jimmy didn't pass to the open man, that would be the last game we'd ever play together."

He looked a question at Lisa as if to confirm her interest. "Jimmy hated taking orders, but he hated losing even more. So he did pass off, and Jack and I made enough shots to get us into the state tournament."

Wilson seemed to look beyond the road ahead of them. "That's the way it always was. Whenever we got in trouble, Jack found a way to get us out. We were always a team. Jimmy was a problem at times, but in the crunch he'd do what was best for the team."

By this time Hollis had taken Lisa to several movies. She liked riding in his Ford convertible, and he was a good conversationalist when they were alone, but the minute they stepped out of the car he spent time with his constituents. Sometimes hours of time, while Lisa fell silently into the role of attractive backdrop. She didn't doubt that he'd be elected governor someday, but she felt sorry for any woman he might marry. And that raised another complication.

"People have already linked your name with Hollis's," Rose warned. "If you don't date someone else, they'll have you married before the year is out."

"I have a friend in Indiana," Lisa said. "He's asked to come for a visit."

That night she answered Alex's letter and invited him. He'd almost proposed to her last year at school. She didn't know what her answer would have been if he had. For that matter, she didn't know now. That confounded indecisiveness again! She hoped his visit would clarify her feelings. She didn't know how his aggressiveness would play in Beneficent, but his coming would at least quash the gossip about her and Hollis Wilson.

Lisa's montage also included curiosity about the animosity she'd seen in the drugstore between Mrs. Harding and Mrs. Telebit. She'd asked Rose McKenzie so many things that she hated to bring this one up. It was too likely to hit a sore spot. Whenever Lisa thought of it, she postponed the question for another time.

Thursday morning of the second week brought another dead squirrel to Lisa's porch, and that brought back her feeling of alienation, stronger than ever. In her living room late that afternoon she brooded, looking for meaning in the scattered images of her montage. Stephen Kemper had gone to Memphis on business, so she was alone. As the evening darkened, Lisa's brooding sank into a lonely restlessness that bordered on depression.

The telephone rang. It was Hollis Wilson, asking her to another movie the following night.

Lisa remembered Rose's advice. "I'm sorry," she said, "we've already made other plans." She hoped Hollis wouldn't ask her to define *we*.

No answer came, and for a moment Lisa thought the line had gone dead. Then for the first time she heard Wilson sound unsure of himself. "Well . . . uh . . . another time perhaps." He paused, then added, "I hope your plans work out."

When Lisa hung up, the house seemed suddenly empty. Her loneliness and alienation deepened. What would it take, she wondered, to assuage this feeling of malaise?

The doorbell sounded. Her uncertainty grew, for darkness was closing in and visitors would not come this late. She thought again of the dead squirrels. Could her late visitor be the person who'd left them?

Nonsense, she told herself. Still, fear walked with her to the door. She forced herself to open it.

Outside, on the darkened front porch, stood Jack Davis.

Chapter 11

For Jack, the same two weeks were filled with endless details of building the chemical plant. In the evenings he telephoned construction men he'd worked with to get advice on various parts of the job. He and two friends installed the plumbing that weekend so the concrete floor could be poured when weather permitted.

Hollis Wilson found a subcontractor who could provide the concrete. Tuesday brought several temperate days—the capriciousness of Mississippi winter again—and by Friday noon the concrete had been poured. When the work crew finished all that could be done until the floor had set, Jack sent them home and went to read the week's magazines at the school library. On his tight budget he couldn't afford to subscribe to news magazines, so he'd asked Vesta Childress if he could read them after school on Fridays. The arrangement let him keep abreast of the world situation, but it also brought him a new problem with Vesta . . .

As he read, Jack frowned over the worsening situation in Berlin and Czechoslovakia. The thought of another war repelled him, but he felt driven to know what was going on, no matter how unpleasant.

His new problem made him pay a price for his reading. Vesta Childress hovered near the back of his chair, at times leaning on it to ask if he had everything he needed. Her closeness and her open-ended question stirred impulses he knew he must suppress. The sadness she radiated and the too-sweet fragrance of her perfume didn't help. He knew she would go out with him if he asked, but that wouldn't be the end of it. She'd want something permanent. From high-school days, his admiration for William Bradley had spilled over into affection for Vesta, but it was the affection one felt for an older aunt. Anything beyond was more than he could give.

He finished the magazines, politely foiled Vesta's attempts to keep him there, and drove home. This couldn't go on, he decided. He had to find a solution for Vesta's loneliness.

He got home just after dark, fatigued and ready for bed. But from his porch he saw a flickering light in an upstairs window of the old Miller house. Suspicion and anger rose in him. No one had any business there, and it was near the place he'd found Callie's body. Had the murderer come back to hide some incriminating bit of evidence?

Without lights, Jack felt his way through the hallway of his house into his parents' room. From a bureau drawer he took his father's old-fashioned Colt revolver. He hadn't looked at it in more than a year, so he made sure it was loaded with an empty chamber under the firing pin. In the hallway again, he discarded his thoughts of confronting the intruder alone. There might be more than one, and he might have to use the pistol in self-defense. He'd heard that a few people still linked him to Callie's murder. The fact of a suspect in custody would make no difference to them. If he shot someone, regardless of the justification, he would only confirm their suspicions.

On the front porch, he looked again for the light. It was still there—as dim as before, but definitely present. Jack eased back into the hall and phoned Sheriff Rainwater.

"I don't want to push the panic button, Sheriff, but someone's poking around inside the old Miller house. I thought I ought to call you before I check it out."

The sheriff's bellow blasted his ear. "Don't you go nowhere till I get there. Meet me down on the main road, and we'll go in together."

Jack tucked the revolver in his belt and headed toward the road, walking on soft ground beside the driveway to avoid making noise on the gravel. Sheriff Rainwater arrived ten minutes later. Jack climbed into the patrol car, and they drove openly up the Miller driveway and stopped in front of the house. Jack started to get out, but Rainwater stopped him.

"Leave that weapon in the car," he said. "If there's any shooting, I'll be the one what does it."

Jack complied without comment. The sheriff handed him a flashlight and kept one for himself. They circled the house and found that a rear window had been forced open. Jack let them in the back door, and they advanced to the stairway.

The sheriff focused his flashlight on the top of the stairs. "You up there," he called. "This is the sheriff. Come out with your hands up. If we have to come up, we'll come shooting."

From upstairs, a raspy voice whined, "Don't shoot. I'm coming." A bearded, dark-complexioned man of middle age and medium size appeared above. His work clothes were mud-stained and his hair looked like it hadn't been combed for a week.

Sheriff Rainwater held the light so the man could see the Colt automatic pointed at him. "Anyone else up there?"

"No, sir. Just me."

"If there is somebody, you'll be the first one to get shot. Now, what are you doing here?"

"I swear there ain't nobody else, Officer. I was just passing through, looking for a place to spend the night."

Rainwater directed the man downstairs, spread-eagled him against the wall and frisked him. At the sheriff's nod, Jack took his own flashlight upstairs and made a hasty check. The rooms were bare, for Mr. Miller had auctioned off his furniture when he went into the nursing home. Only one room was disturbed, and that held only a stub of candle, a pile of discarded food tins, a knapsack, and a moth-eaten Army blanket.

Jack carried the knapsack and blanket downstairs and reported his findings. "He's been here several days. Too many empty food tins for one day."

Rainwater had kept his man spread-eagled. Now he prodded him with the flashlight and growled a question. "What's your name?"

The intruder winced and muttered, "Uh . . . Abraham."

"Abraham what?" The sheriff prodded him again.

"Uh . . . Abraham Martin."

"Well, Mr. Martin, how many days have you been here?"

Martin tried to shrug his shoulders, but his off-balance position against the wall foiled the attempt. "Three, four days, I guess."

"And where was you before you was 'just passing through' our neighborhood?"

"Jackson."

"How long had you been in Jackson, and what was you doing?"

"Maybe a month. I was working on the roads."

Rainwater handcuffed the prisoner's hands behind him. "Well, Mr. Martin," he said. "I'm taking you in for illegal entry, and I wouldn't be surprised if you spent some time working on the roads for Coosa County. And while you're making that positive contribution to society, we'll find out where you really was this past month. I'm real curious about that."

He marched the prisoner out to the car.

Jack retrieved his revolver and asked, "Want me to ride in with you?"

Rainwater shook his head. "No need. Check the house again in daylight. Then come in and sign a complaint."

Jack agreed, then walked home across the ridgeline, ground so familiar that he needed no light. Obviously, the prisoner knew more than he'd admitted. Just as obviously, Sheriff Rainwater saw at least a chance the man was Callie's murderer. Jack doubted it, but he'd leave that to the sheriff.

In the rapidly chilling night, his thoughts returned to the chemical plant project. Plenty of work there to keep him busy, and Mr. Kemper had been generous about his pay. In the few days he'd known Kemper, Jack had grown to like him. He was a good and fair man, but miscast in building of a new factory. He'd do well enough when the plant was finished and he could concentrate on chemistry again.

Jack's thoughts turned to Kemper's daughter, as they had too often since that afternoon in the drugstore. She seemed so very sophisticated and sure of herself. She'd cut him short in the grocery store, stung him hard at that prayer meeting, and he'd missed his chance there to explain what he felt about Beneficent. Lisa obviously had no use for either him or the town, but he had to give her credit: in most cases she didn't let it show. And she *was* attractive. He saw again the dark hair, olive complexion and blue eyes . . . Nice lips, too. Grimacing, he pushed the thought out of his mind.

From his front porch he looked back at the Miller house, now only a dark silhouette against the night sky. He'd always assumed he would marry Lucy Miller. They'd played together as children, enjoyed hand-holding friendship in high school, even shared a few kisses. That history had its downside, though, because now he had no idea how to angle for a date, much less flirt with a girl. That was one reason he hadn't dated since the war. Mainly, though, he'd been too busy paying off the note on his farm.

Now he felt vague stirrings of a need for something more, and the image of Lisa Kemper kept appearing in his mind. But she was dating the handsome Senator Wilson, a man who had everything going for him. And someone said she had a boyfriend back in Indiana. If Jack asked her for a date, she'd turn him down flat. Besides, he didn't even know how to ask. He sighed, shrugged, and plodded into the house for sleep.

On Monday, the weather turned cold again, but the plant's floor had set long enough. For the next few days, Jack supervised laying the cinder blocks to form the building's walls. He double-checked the blocks' interlocking pattern and reinforcement with steel rods anchored in the floor.

Thursday found him completing that part of the job. By sundown, his crew had done all they could until more materials arrived on Monday. He dismissed them and drove into town to brief Stephen Kemper.

In the last stages of twilight, he walked onto the Kempers' darkened front porch. Mr. Kemper's new Frazer sedan was not in the driveway, but perhaps Lisa had driven it somewhere. Disappointment that he wouldn't see her took him by surprise.

He pushed the thought aside and rang the doorbell. After a long wait, soft footsteps approached the door. It opened a few inches, revealing Lisa instead of her father. Her hand rested on the wooden door, and she made no move to unlatch the screen that stood between them.

A rush of pleasure flowed through Jack. Confused, he stammered, "Uh . . . I need to talk to your father. Is he here?"

Concern, uneasiness—perhaps fear—showed in Lisa's eyes. Her gaze lowered from his and focused on the door latch. Her voice was hesitant. "He's not here at the moment."

Suddenly cautious, Jack took a step backward and saw her tension relax a bit. She couldn't be afraid of him, could she? He moistened his lips and said. "Perhaps I could leave a message." At her nod, he continued. "Please tell him the workers have done all they can until Monday. I've dismissed them till then."

She nodded again. "I will tell him."

In the silence that followed, she remained completely still, her hand on the door, making no move either to open it or close it. Her eyes seemed to look straight through him. He knew they conveyed some message. But what *was* that message?

"Thank you," he said. He half-turned and took another step away from the door. Looking back, he found her standing motionless, silently watching. Her eyes, deep blue, held the same expression he'd seen in Vesta's eyes. He turned to face her.

Strangely, he seemed to hear his own voice from a great distance. "Miss Kemper . . . There's a good movie showing down in Shipley tomorrow night. Ray Milland and Marlene Dietrich in *Golden Earrings*. Would you like to go see it with me?"

For a moment she remained motionless, solemn, her hand still holding the door. Then the blue eyes flickered and a faint smile graced the corner of her lips.

"My name is Lisa," she said. "And yes . . . I think I'd like to go."

Chapter 12

Friday, January 30

At eight-thirty a.m., Deputy Brown sauntered into Sheriff Rainwater's office just in time to see the lawman kick his desk and slap the back of his chair. Based on hard experience, Brown knew he had two choices. He could tiptoe around and wonder when the sheriff's legendary temper would explode in his direction, or he could take the problem head-on and hope to escape the fallout.

He chose the latter option. "Is something wrong, Sheriff?"

Rainwater's gray eyes glowered and he slapped the top of his desk. "Nothing's wrong, Deputy Brown. Not one cussed, cotton-picking, sheep-stealing, snake-bitten thing." He slapped the desk again. "You know we been holding that Gypsy, Guido Bramante, on suspicion of Callie's murder? It turns out he couldn't have done it."

Relieved to see the steam coming out of the sheriff's kettle before the lid blew off, Brown continued the treatment. "How come, Sheriff?"

Rainwater pounded the arm of his swivel chair. "'Cause while she was being killed, Bramante was sixty miles away, committing the stupidest burglary I ever heard of."

"How do we know that, Sheriff?"

Rainwater made a noise like spitting. "The fingerprints we took match the ones he left in a store in Holly Springs. So we got to send him up there to stand trial."

"At least we get credit for the arrest." Brown always looked on the brighter side of things.

"But you ain't heard the rest of it—" Rainwater broke off as Ben Patterson entered, wearing his blue-checked suit and a sardonic expression that suggested he already knew about Bramante.

"Here's more bad news," Patterson said. "The other fingerprint report came back from Jackson today. Jack Davis's truck had all kinds of prints, but none of them belonged to Callie Rakestraw."

Rainwater grunted. "How about Ronnie Parker's truck?"

Patterson showed a humorless grin. "Her prints were where they should have been if Ronnie was telling the truth. But there was nothing to help solve the case. I hear your Gypsy couldn't have done it, either."

The sheriff's florid face turned crimson. "That fool was so relieved when the fingerprints cleared him of murder, he was happy to confess to burglary. But that ain't all."

Patterson's face brightened. "What's his story?"

"He'd been drinking that night at the tournament, but he ran out of hooch. So he heads for Memphis to get more. Passing through Holly Springs, he realizes he don't have enough money. Then he sees the owner of a grocery closing up the store. That'd be about nine-thirty, by the owner's statement. With everything else in town shut down, Bramante decides to knock over the grocery."

Rainwater folded his hands over his paunch. "Getting into the store was no problem. He just kicks in the door. He busts the cash register open on the floor, and then he's the proud possessor of sixty-seven dollars and thirty-two cents. At least, that's what the owner says he lost. Talk about careless—Bramante leaves the door hanging half-open and fingerprints ever'where."

"When was the theft discovered?" Patterson asked.

"About eleven o'clock when the owner came back for something he forgot." Rainwater glared at Patterson. "Now comes the bad part. Instead of going to Memphis, Bramante drives back here to Coosa County to see if there really was bootleggers out there in Branch Bottom. That's like asking if a hound has ticks. And the bootlegger he finds not only sells likker, but runs a night club in his house." The sheriff's face showed outrage. "*Right here in Coosa County*, mind you, the man runs a cotton-picking *night club*."

Patterson raised his eyebrows. "I take it that's out of bounds?"

"Out of bounds?" Rainwater slapped the desk again. "It's off the face of the earth!" More calmly, he explained, "There's no way I can shut all them bootleggers down. Even the stupid state guv'ment knows that. The sale of likker may be illegal, but the state puts a sales tax on it anyway. You know as much as I do about the 'Black Market Tax,' and you know the state gets half its money that way. So I don't waste time chasing bootleggers that sell it like a package store."

Deputy Brown listened with as much interest as Patterson. He'd never heard the sheriff explain his philosophy.

"The way I see it," Rainwater continued, "it don't hurt if people take likker home with 'em. But when they drink it 'on premises,' they start picking fights and cut each other up. If that don't kill 'em, they drive home drunk and become a menace to ever'body on the road."

He looked up in satisfaction. "So that's where I draw the line, and it works real good. We haven't had enough DWI fines in this county to feed a redbug for a day."

Brown's curiosity got the better of him. "What we gonna do 'bout that night club, Sheriff?"

Rainwater ignored him and said to Patterson, "As I was saying, Bramante finds a guy named Shadrack Sullivan who's running a night club, and four witnesses agree he sat there drinking till two in the morning. Then he drives back to the Gypsy trailer park and raises the ruckus you already know about."

"What does Shadrack Sullivan say about it?" Patterson asked.

"He don't say nothing to me about it, 'cause I ain't talked to him." Rainwater rubbed his hands together. "And he won't know nothing, either. Not till around ten o'clock tonight when we go out there and shut him down."

Brown grew instantly alert. "We going to make a raid?"

Rainwater threw him a curt nod. "We'll shut Sullivan's place down tighter'n a mosquito hide stretched over a barrel head. Ain't *nobody* going to flout the law like that in my county. You go call them other deputies in here."

Brown moved to comply, but paused in the doorway.

Rainwater asked Patterson, "You come along with us, Ben?"

Patterson shook his head. "I'll pass on this one."

Brown's resentment of the big-city detective got the better of him. "'Fraid you might get shot, Mr. Patterson?"

The big man smiled. "I'm always afraid I might get shot, Deputy Brown. Someday I will. But when I do, it'll be by a real murderer. Not a two-bit bootlegger or some dumb deputy."

***

That Friday became a parade of frustrations for Jack. Before daylight, he woke to his familiar nightmare. In the dream he walked through woods with Eden-like tranquility. Then came the sudden plunge into horror as his faceless enemy pointed a pistol at his heart. As always, Jack woke in the split-second when he saw he had no escape from death.

He woke in the cold dark of his bedroom. For a few moments, from habits that had served him well during the war, he lay motionless and listened. He heard no sound except soft rain falling on the roof. Clad only in the T-shirt and undershorts he slept in, he rose and silently checked each room. The wintery air made goose bumps on his skin, and the wooden floors became dry ice beneath his feet.

Satisfied, he turned on the kitchen light and lit the gas stove. Five o'clock. No use going back to bed. As he waited for coffee to boil, he splashed water from the sink onto his face and wondered about the dream. A remnant from the war, probably. An alien thing that had no place in his peaceful Beneficent. A few hours of hard farm work should put it out of his mind.

After breakfast he threw himself into the work with a vengeance. Two weeks of long hours at the chemical plant had left much undone on his farm. The rain stopped before noon, though low clouds still threatened. Despite the cold, the work sent blood thrumming warm through his veins and, as he'd hoped, it banished the dream from his thoughts. But new frustrations arose, for the rain-soaked earth kept him from doing all he'd planned.

At mid-afternoon he showered, changed into clean work clothes, and drove his Chevy pickup into town. He'd planned to do several errands before his date with Lisa, but his schedule hit a roadblock in the floral concession at the drugstore. He'd wanted to put fresh flowers on the graves of his loved ones, but the delivery truck from the florist in Shipley had broken down.

"Come back in an hour or two," Mrs. Harding told him.

Jack made a quick calculation. If he read the magazines in the library now, he'd still have time for the cemetery visit before his date. He thanked Mrs. Harding and left.

On the sidewalk outside, he met Jimmy Fletcher and shared the team's ritual handshake.

"I'd been hoping to see you," Jack said. "I need another good worker out at the chemical plant."

"I can't handle it." Jimmy tossed his head and grinned. "I stay pretty busy these days."

Jack pressed his point. "Look, to become a real member of the community, you need a steady job. Right now you're just hanging around the fringes of everything. The money you saved during the war won't last forever."

Jimmy laughed. "It'll last a long while yet. Plenty of time later to get a job."

"We didn't make *that* much money in the service." Jack cocked an eyebrow. "You must have been lucky at poker."

"Try me sometime." Jimmy laughed again. "Try me anytime you've got money to spare." He gave a playful whack on Jack's shoulder and ambled away, still laughing.

Jack's frustration ratcheted up another notch. Jimmy had been born and raised among the bootleggers in Branch Bottom, and he'd never felt accepted in Beneficent, not even after stardom in athletics.

The only way he could join his teammates as fully accepted members of the community was to hold a steady job, but he'd always been too stubborn for that.

At the library, Vesta Childress had the magazines laid out. Jack was glad he'd arrived early. Late-studying students kept Vesta occupied, so Jack read for almost an hour without interruption. After skimming *Time* magazine, he studied the newly merged *US News and World Report* from cover to cover. Its editor, David Lawrence, usually saw into the heart of things. And there was good news. Congress seemed ready to approve Secretary Marshall's European Recovery Plan.

As Jack finished the county's weekly newspaper, the *Coosa Courier*, he felt someone leaning on the back of his chair. The cloying aroma of over-sweet perfume told him it was Vesta. Glancing up, Jack saw that the last student had gone. He felt a familiar uneasiness creep through him, the discomfort he always felt when Vesta stood that close. But he'd made up his mind what to do.

He stood, took a step away from her, and began his planned speech. "Vesta, you know how much I thought of Mr. Bradley."

"Yes, Jack. I know."

Her eyes held his expectantly, and he saw she'd drawn the wrong conclusion. "What I mean is . . ." He took another step back. "You and Mr. Bradley were like a second set of parents to me and the other team members."

"I suppose so." Her eyes grew watery, but no tears fell.

Awkward and self-conscious, Jack plunged on. "So I hope you won't hold it against me if I give you some advice."

"Of course not, Jack." Her voice half-choked.

"You're one of the most capable women I know. You have more talents than you can ever develop in Beneficent."

"Yes, Jack?"

"You need to move to a city like Memphis. You'll find opportunities there that Beneficent can never offer."

She said nothing, but pain reflected in her face.

Jack swallowed once and barged ahead. "Go there and take the first job you can get. Anything to keep you going while you find a job that fits your qualifications. Join one of the big churches. Meet new people. Find new friends. There must be a thousand possibilities there that you'll never find here."

Vesta's lips trembled. "I . . . I can't do it, Jack."

"Why not? You have what it takes."

"This . . ." Her voice faltered. "This is my home. I've always lived here in the house my father built. My memories are here. I can't bear to leave them and live in some strange place."

He took a step forward, determined to make his point. "Let the house go. You have to live your own life, not your father's or your mother's."

Vesta's voice filled with despair. "I can't do it. This is my *home*. Whatever happens, I will live here till I die." She covered her face with her hands.

Her misery drew Jack with an almost physical force, but he knew no way to comfort her. Words seemed inadequate. "I'm sorry, Vesta. I shouldn't have brought it up."

She said nothing, hands still covering her face.

Jack saw that further talk was futile. "I have to go now. Will you be all right?"

She half-turned from him and nodded, her face still covered. "Yes. Please go." She choked out the words.

"I'm sorry," he said again, and left. As he closed the door, he thought he heard a sob.

Outside, dark clouds still hovered low, but no rain fell. Jack chided himself for his failure. He'd tried to help someone he respected, even loved in a distant kind of way, but he'd only hurt her. Knowing that some problems have no solutions gave him no consolation.

Back at the drugstore, the delivery truck still had not come. He waited, but it arrived too late for him to make the cemetery visit before his date with Lisa. They'd have to stop there on the way to Shipley, he guessed. He was stuck with the flowers in any case. Some impression he'd make, he thought, taking a girl to a cemetery on their first date!

But Mrs. Harding proposed a solution Jack gladly accepted. It did not set him smiling as he loaded the mass of flowers into the cab of his truck, but it did lift some of his gloom. Thus far, everything he'd tried today had come out wrong. He could only hope for better luck on his date.

***

Vesta cried quietly for a while after Jack left, then removed the evidence from her face before walking home. When she stopped by her desk for her purse and carrying bag, someone knocked at the door.

"Come in," she called.

Jimmy Fletcher's tall form stepped through the door, the usual irreverent grin on his face. "Hello, Miss Childress. I thought you might tell me a book I could read."

"Why, Jimmy," Vesta said, "I didn't know you read for pleasure."

His grin widened. "I like to try out new things."

"There's a rule about lending books to non-students." Vesta brushed an unruly strand of hair from her forehead. "I have to be careful about breaking the rules. It could cost me my job."

"I'm always careful, Miss Childress." Their eyes met in silence for a moment. Then he asked, "What do you suggest?"

Vesta led him into the fiction shelves and looked under *B* for *Brontë*. Her fingers lingered over *Wuthering Heights*, but she took down *Jane Eyre*.

She remained facing the shelf. Jimmy stood behind her.

"You might like this one," she said. "It's about a girl, left alone in the world, who takes a job with a fine gentleman. He is much more experienced than she, and they face many difficulties before things finally turn out right for them."

"That sounds real interesting. I like your perfume, Miss Childress."

"Thank you, Jimmy." She held the book against her bosom and stood motionless.

His hands clasped her elbows and drew her back against him. She rested the back of her head against his chest. Neither of them spoke.

The book fell to the floor. Jimmy's hands held her close and turned her to face him. His grin unchanged, he whispered, "You're a lot of woman, Miss Childress."

She smiled at him through her sadness. "I hope so, Jimmy. I hope so."

Chapter 13

For most of Friday, Lisa fretted about her date with Jack. *That confounded uncertainty again!* In retrospect, accepting the date seemed almost involuntary. It certainly was against her better judgment. Thinking about it brought both a twinge of fear and a tingle of anticipation. The fear came from the lingering question of Jack's quarrel with Callie and its possible relationship to Callie's death. But where did the anticipation come from? These contradictory emotions puzzled her, so Lisa ordered her mind to take charge. To assure her safety, she would tell Jack—subtly, of course—that others knew about their date. If he became . . . *unpleasant* . . . she did not have to go out with him again.

She would also be careful, in dress and manner, to do nothing Jack could misinterpret. The mandarin collar of her teal-blue dress should send an unmistakable hands-off signal, but the movie's title, *Golden Earrings*, brought a special problem. The hit song from the film said that a woman's wearing gold earrings meant she belonged to the man she wore them for. To be perfectly clear on that point, Lisa chose a pair with small blue stones set in silver.

Steven Kemper welcomed Jack into the living room while Lisa put the final touches on her makeup. When she entered, she found the two men in easy conversation. They stood as she came in. Jack's gaze flicked from one of her earrings to the other, and a faint smile played across his lips. Lisa felt herself coloring, but Jack continued his greeting as if he hadn't noticed.

"I'm sorry about the weather," he said as he held her coat for her, "but maybe we can get through without more rain."

"It doesn't look too bad." She didn't like the low clouds, but she didn't want to sound timid.

"I have to apologize again," he said as they crossed the porch, "but can we make one stop along our way? A delivery truck was late, and I didn't get everything done."

"I don't mind." She assumed he meant to buy something from a store. When he opened the truck door for her, though, she found the middle of the bench seat crowded with a profusion of flowers.

She must have given him a questioning glance, for he explained, "I'd planned to go by the cemetery, but the flower delivery truck came too late. It won't take long."

Her heart sank. Cemeteries were isolated places, yet she'd agreed to be alone with him there. Most people thought Callie's murderer was an outsider, but she heard that a few still suspected Jack. As she climbed into the truck, she heard her voice saying, without enthusiasm, "It will be all right."

"I know it's inconvenient," Jack said as he started the engine. He fumbled with something on the seat, then handed her a corsage of two large gardenias. "Maybe these will make up for it. I hope this isn't too forward, but . . . Well, with all the other flowers on board, I couldn't *not* bring some for you."

"Thank you. They're lovely." This was the last thing she'd expected, and she hoped her surprise didn't show. She opened her coat and, perplexed, looked for a way to pin them on. Jack twisted the rearview mirror in her direction.

"Use this," he said. "I'll drive with the outside mirror."

She finished quickly and gave him back his mirror. "Rose McKenzie says this is supposed to be a good movie. If we like it, she and her husband may go tomorrow night." That should put Jack on notice that others knew where she was. And with whom.

He gave her a doubtful look but said nothing. Lisa felt a pang of conscience for implying distrust. Contradictions again. How could a man thoughtful enough to bring flowers turn out to be dangerous?

She need not have worried about someone's knowing whom she was with. It seemed half the people in town stopped what they were doing to watch them pass. Buddy Robinson waved to them from his front yard. Ronnie Parker hesitated on the sidewalk and stared. Mrs. Telebit stopped sweeping the porch of the Beth-aven Boarding House to get her eyes full. Ben Patterson, wearing his blue-checked suit, took time to glower at them.

Worst of all, Hollis Wilson and Jimmy Fletcher stood in conversation in front of the drugstore. Wilson favored them with a bemused wave, but a grinning Jimmy Fletcher thrust one fist into the air and shouted, "Go, Panther!"

Jack showed Lisa a pained expression. "Jimmy was always kind of enthusiastic."

"I can tell." She found herself smiling. Strangely, their mutual embarrassment lowered the invisible barrier between them. She relaxed and for the first time examined the truck. The green gasoline rationing sticker on the windshield caught her attention.

"A *B* sticker?" she asked. "I thought all farmers had *C* stickers."

"We did." Jack frowned. "But my parents' truck was destroyed in their wreck. When I came home, I had to buy another one. The *B* sticker told me it hadn't been driven much during the war. Somehow I never got around to taking it off."

At the entry to the cemetery, four miles south of town, two red brick columns supported a marble arch with the inscription *I AM THE RESURRECTION AND THE LIFE.* Jack turned in beneath the arch and followed a gravel trail circling among stately oaks that towered above the tombstones.

He stopped halfway around the circle and cut the engine. "You can wait in the truck if you like. I'll only be a minute."

Lisa hesitated, but her curiosity about the graves won out. Surely she'd be safe with so many people knowing who she was with. "I'd like to come along if you don't mind." She gestured toward the mass of flowers. "You'll need help to carry all of these."

She stepped outside into a silence so deep it seemed all sound had disappeared from the earth. The wind in the cemetery was still, though dark clouds raced silently by overhead. The afternoon light was fading. Full darkness would follow soon.

Jack led her to a small rectangular plot beneath a huge oak. On two tombstones Lisa read the inscriptions:

John Calvin Davis	*Sarah Boyd Davis*
Mar. 3, 1893 – Dec. 18, 1944	*Oct. 15, 1898 – Dec. 18, 1944*

Jack stood a moment in silence before the graves, then knelt to adorn each with flowers. Returning, he said to Lisa, "They argued for years about this place. Dad told everyone he bought a grave in the shade because he'd worked all his life under a hot sun. Mother reminded him his body wouldn't know if it was hot or cold, and his soul would be in heaven. She was afraid people would think he was a heretic. I think he did it to tease her."

"They sound like fun to live with."

"We had a lot of good times. I wish Dad had lived to enjoy the new land he bought. He'd waited a long time for those six hundred acres."

Jack led Lisa past the oak to a plot containing two more tombstones, one well-weathered and the other almost new. As before, she studied the inscriptions:

Robert Lee Miller	*Mary Wood Miller*
June 4, 1871 – Oct. 5, 1946	*May 14, 1888 – Apr. 8, 1933*

The Millers, the next-door neighbors who willed their farm to Jack. Her distaste for Beneficent faded for the moment as Lisa marveled at the two families' closeness. The Miller girl half-raised by Jack's mother after Mrs. Miller's death, Rose said. That was hard for Lisa to comprehend. She'd grown up in a fair-sized town where people made a point of keeping their distance.

Jack knelt and placed flowers on each grave, then walked past them to a smaller tombstone, similarly inscribed:

Lucy Sue Miller
July 8, 1925 – Aug. 23, 1944

Without pausing, Jack laid the last bouquet on that grave. "It's done," he said into the silence. Then, glancing at Lisa, he added, "I hope it didn't take too long."

"Not at all. I learned a lot while we were here." How could she have feared a man so devoted to this tender errand? His strong hands arranged the flowers so gently . . .

Leaving the cemetery, Jack pointed out Callie Rakestraw's grave, a raw earth mound as yet without a marker. Lisa wondered if Jack would someday put flowers there, but she said nothing. Any comment would raise the question of Callie's murder. She felt relieved when they turned onto the highway and the truck's steady engine-drone replaced the unearthly quiet of the cemetery. An uncomfortable silence hung between them.

She decided to break it and maybe learn something useful about Beneficent. "Tell me about your farm. They say you'll make it the biggest and best in the county."

Jack looked startled. "I don't care about biggest and best, but a prosperous farm does help the community." He turned on the headlights against gathering darkness. "It's hard to explain, but people here have done so much for me . . . It's like I owe it to them to build something good."

Lisa frowned. "I don't understand the logic in that." She didn't understand a lot of other things, like the odd thoughts he'd expressed at the prayer meeting.

Jack's hands tightened on the steering wheel. "It's hard to explain," he said again. His eyes looked far down the highway. "You know that my parents died in an accident while I was overseas?"

"Yes. I heard you weren't notified until weeks later."

"That's right. It happened in December of 1944, and the situation in Europe was confused. You've heard of the Battle of the Belgian Bulge?" At Lisa's nod, he continued. "I was out of pocket for a while, so folks here had to go ahead with the burial and catch me up on it when they could. That cost them money. Harry Pendleton, the banker, said he'd cover the expenses if I didn't get back. Dad still owed the bank six thousand dollars for our new land. Harry held the note open without payment as long as I was gone."

Jack gave her a quick glance before returning his gaze to the road. "That wasn't all Harry did. He had the farm sharecropped for me till I came home. He made a good job of it and wouldn't let me pay him a cent for his work."

"He's been very helpful to my father, too."

"He helps everybody. He brought in the shirt factory, you know. People try to pretend he's mercenary. They say things like, 'He'll sell you the shirt off his rack' but they're only kidding. He's as good a man as you can find, and others in town are almost as good. This may not make sense to anyone else, but I feel like I owe it to them to build the best farm I can."

"I think I understand." In spite of herself, Lisa felt drawn to a man who felt so deeply toward those who had helped him.

"About the farm," Jack said as Lisa mused on what she had heard. "I'd be happy to show it to you sometime."

"I'd like that," Lisa answered absently, her mind still intrigued by Harry Pendleton's generosity and Jack's response.

"How about tomorrow? Pick you up at ten?"

The questions jolted her alert. Dismayed, she realized she'd committed herself and couldn't get out of it without lying. "I guess so. Yes. Okay." She sounded as uncertain as she felt. Then caution asserted itself and she added, "I'll be having coffee with Rose McKenzie earlier, but ten would be fine."

Jack shot her a hard glance that she ignored by looking out the side window. Another awkward silence followed.

Thus far they had seen few cars, but now Lisa noticed a pair of headlights closing quickly from behind. Jack's speedometer showed fifty-five miles per hour. Lisa judged the other vehicle to be doing more than seventy, far too fast for this road. But instead of passing, the other driver locked in behind them—dangerously close behind, so close that the vehicles would collide if Jack slowed suddenly.

The trailing vehicle flicked its lights to bright, and the glare became blinding. Jack turned his rearview mirror up to protect his eyes and lifted an elbow to block the glare from the outside mirror. He kept his speed steady and his eyes on the road. The other driver blew his horn repeatedly.

"Don't look back," Jack said. "Maybe they'll go away if we don't respond."

Frightened and angry, Lisa complied. For once, she wasn't uncertain. She was determined those idiots would see only the back of her head. She refused to give them the satisfaction of seeing her fear.

Five minutes passed with the two vehicles locked in precarious relationship as Jack held a constant speed. Finally, the other car dropped back a bit and, with a roar from its poorly muffled engine, veered out to pass. As it came abreast, Jack hit the brakes so that the other vehicle shot by like a rocket.

In the light of Jack's headlights, Lisa identified it as a bright red pickup with hood vents painted so they seemed to emit orange flames. The overall paint job was sloppy—a do-it-yourself chore botched by amateurs. The truck's occupants were two men with ducktail haircuts, one of whom shouted something incomprehensible as he leaned out the passenger window and made insulting gestures.

Relieved, Lisa and Jack exchanged somber glances.

"I'm sorry," he said. "Those guys don't come from anywhere around here."

Beneficent's myth of The Virtuous Community again. Evil always invades from the outside; it never comes from within. She didn't share that view, so to change the subject she said, "You handled it perfectly. Let's not let them spoil our evening."

Jack's gratitude showed in his face. "We certainly won't."

Still, they drove in brooding silence until they parked near the theater on Shipley's main street. A number of people strolled along the sidewalk, and Lisa welcomed the relative safety they provided. She realized then how completely frightened she'd been. Jack must have been frightened, too. His eyes still blazed anger when he opened the truck door for her.

To lift their mood, Lisa showed a bright smile. "Don't look so grim. It's over, and we came here to enjoy the movie."

"So we did." He laughed, a bit self-consciously. "Afterwards, I'll ask you what you enjoyed most."

"I'll do the same," she said. "We'll make it a pleasant evening in spite of everything."

As they turned into the theater, though, she saw a familiar red pickup parked at the end of the block.

Chapter 14

In the theater, the first film of a double feature climaxed as Tarzan's elephants wreaked savage justice on a greedy ivory hunter. Next came a Porky Pig cartoon that set everyone laughing. By the time *Golden Earrings* began, Lisa had forgotten the red pickup. More than that, she'd forgotten her distaste for Beneficent.

The movie had her quickly entranced: the palpable calm after World War II, the mysterious golden earring delivered to the British brigadier (Ray Milland) at his London club, and the remembered story of his pre-war undercover mission to obtain a German chemist's secret formula. He completed the mission with the help of a clairvoyant Gypsy woman (Marlene Dietrich), but only after fighting the Gypsy king for the woman's love. As the movie ended with the lovers' postwar reunion, Lisa wished it could go on forever.

"A cup of chocolate?" Jack asked as they left the theater.

"I'd love it. But we made an agreement. What part of the movie did you like best?"

"Hard to say." Jack drove toward a section of town Lisa didn't know. "The ending, I guess. It makes you feel like things can come out right in real life, too. What about you?"

"I liked the ending, but Ray Milland's fight with the Gypsy king was good, too. Kind of comical."

Jack shook his head. "Strictly Hollywood. There's no way the fight could have lasted that long." At Lisa's quizzical look, he explained. "It looked more like a schoolyard tussle than a real fight. The brigadier was a professional soldier. He would have known how to disable his opponent quickly. Maybe that's why the scriptwriters played it for comedy."

"Call me naïve," Lisa conceded. "I never thought of it that way."

Jack parked the truck in front of a drab one-story brick building. "The bus station café doesn't look like much, but it's the only thing open after eight o'clock."

The café consisted of a long, narrow room with wooden booths on one wall and, on the other, a counter fronted by red upholstered stools. Two bearded men and a teenage boy occupied three of the stools. All three focused on conversation with an apron-clad fat man standing behind the counter. The elder of the bearded men looked about fifty, the younger about thirty. The counter man and the three customers stopped talking to watch as Jack and Lisa moved toward a booth.

Jack said something Lisa didn't catch to the man behind the counter. A few minutes later two mugs of chocolate arrived at their booth. Hers with two marshmallows, his with none.

At Jack's suggestion, they looked over the nickelodeon's offerings while the chocolate cooled. He put in a quarter and said, "You pick three, I'll pick two."

She chose two current hits, then exclaimed, "Oh! Here's an old one: 'I Had the Craziest Dream Last Night.' Do you know it?" She pushed the button and looked up to find Jack frowning.

"A bit too well," he said.

Had she stirred up a painful memory? "I'm sorry," she said. "Did I stumble onto an old flame?"

"Not exactly." He showed a rueful smile. "But for a moment I thought Marlene Dietrich wasn't the only clairvoyant in town. I'll tell you sometime. Maybe. But not tonight." He chose two records by Eddie Arnold, a name wholly new to Lisa. "When you hear the words to these," he said, "remember that present company is always excepted. They're just good songs."

"The same goes for my choices." Lisa sounded more defensive than she liked. Why were most popular songs about love?

They sipped their chocolate contentedly, and everyone in the café stopped to listen to the music. For a few moments, the golden tones of Harry James's trumpet and the full, plaintive voice of Helen Forrest transformed the drab café into a magic land where even the craziest dreams could come true. In the silence that followed, Lisa could hear the steady whir of the kitchen's exhaust fan.

"I heard that song when it first came out," Jack said, "I'd forgotten it, though."

Whatever the title meant to him, Lisa realized, it had nothing to do with an old love affair.

Next, the nickelodeon played the Eddie Arnold songs: "It's a Sin," followed by "I'll Hold You in My Heart (Till I Can Hold You in My Arms)." Now Lisa saw why Jack said they were just good songs. One part of her was grateful but, to her discomfort, another part felt something like regret. She wasn't supposed to have feelings like that until she was back in Indiana.

Time to think of something else. "I never liked country music," she said, "but that singer is good. His diction is perfect, and the electric guitar is played so cleanly."

"Steel guitar," Jack corrected. "That's Roy Wiggins. Nobody else can play it like that."

Lisa put on a mock-serious expression. "Why did he steal the guitar? Couldn't he just buy one like everybody else?"

Jack looked pained. "Stealing is more fun, I guess."

They burst into laughter. The men and boy at the counter eyed them curiously, then smiled. An aura of good feeling seemed to permeate the café, and Lisa realized she felt free and happy, happier than she'd felt since her mother's death. How could she feel like that in a place she disliked so heartily?

Her good feeling was short-lived. A poorly muffled truck engine sounded outside, then shuddered to a stop. Two men with ducktail haircuts slammed into the café. They stood heavily in the doorway and cast insolent stares at everyone inside. Both looked to be in their early twenties. One was the man who had leaned out of the red truck and made crude gestures. The other was powerfully built, about Jack's height but with a thick neck, barrel chest, and bulging upper arms that looked like hams.

With a shock, Lisa realized she'd seen men act that way before: in B-grade cowboy movies when the villain barged into the saloon looking for trouble. If these men were aping that behavior, they must have similar motives. She became uncomfortably conscious of her status as the only woman in the café.

The newcomers straddled the two stools nearest the door and ordered coffee, then held a muttered conversation punctuated by laughter and cunning glances toward Lisa and Jack. Presently, the larger one visited the restroom in the rear of the café. As he returned, he deliberately jostled their table. The impact rattled the cups. If they hadn't been almost empty, it would have spilled the chocolate.

The man faced Jack belligerently, but Jack smiled at him and said, "Pardon my table. I'll teach it better manners."

The other looked confused, but made no reply and rejoined his companion. Their laughter and glances toward Lisa grew more frequent, and their voices grew louder until Lisa heard a number of words she wished she hadn't. The counter man and the other three customers watched in silence.

At length, Jack turned to her and said, "Excuse me a minute." He was smiling, but his face had reddened, and his gray eyes were hard as he strode toward the troublemakers. Lisa watched his hands make palms-up gestures in what seemed to be a reasonable discussion. The heavier of the two men laughed and shook his head, after which Jack gestured toward the door. Both men rose and followed him outside.

In the silence, Lisa heard a hamburger patty sizzling on the grill. The smell of cooking meat replaced the café's odor of stale coffee. From the corner of her eye, Lisa saw the counter man step back from his grill and dial the telephone. The older bearded man whispered to the younger, who then led the teenager out the door where the others had exited.

Lisa's heart sank. She was a lone woman, helpless in a strange place with disreputable-looking people. In her misery, she closed her eyes and whispered a garbled, incoherent prayer—her first in a week or more, she realized with chagrin. "*Dear Lord . . . don't let them harm Jack . . . Keep him safe . . . Take care of us both . . .*"

The sizzling sound of the hamburger on the grill continued. The smell of burned meat filled the café.

"Missy?"

Lisa opened her eyes and looked into those of the older bearded man seated at the counter.

"Don't you worry none, Missy," he said. "I don't know what's happening out there, but me and my boy Josh'll make sure you get home all right."

"That's very kind of you." Her voice sounded hollow.

The counter man hung up the phone and squinted in disgust. "No help there. Sheriff's men are all out. Must be making a raid."

The bearded man spoke again to Lisa. "My name's Hudson. I'm from up near Tupelo. Your fella don't know me from Adam, but I know him. My middle son played basketball a-gin him before the war. That's the son we lost in It'ly. My older boy—the one sat beside me—he come back okay. Him and my youngest will see things don't get too far out of hand."

"Thank you," Lisa said. She felt she should say more, but she couldn't find words.

The door opened and Jack came back in. The knee of one khaki trouser leg was smudged with grime, and a few fresh red droplets bespeckled the other. He held a handkerchief to his left cheek. "I'll be another minute," he said. "The big guy wore a ring." He disappeared into the restroom.

Mr. Hudson's bearded son entered and said, "We was too late to do any good, Pa."

Hudson raised his eyebrows. "Then where's yore brother?"

"We got to pick him up at the hospital." A sly look in Lisa's direction suggested his words were meant for her.

"Hospital?" Hudson frowned. "What's he doing there?"

The son grinned. "A errand of mercy. Them scalawags didn't feel like driving. The big guy's busted nose was bleeding pretty bad."

Hudson nodded. "Guess he was asking for it."

"He was the lucky one." The son's grin broadened. "The other one had a knife."

Hudson scratched his head. "How come that was unlucky?"

"'Cause he's the one got his arm broke." He turned the grin toward Lisa. "Chile, you're travelin' in fast company."

Lisa nodded. Jack's return saved her from further reply. His cheek was cut but not bleeding and, as he paid the check, Lisa saw something like tooth marks gouged into the back of his right hand. They left quickly, though Lisa took time to thank Mr. Hudson again for his encouragement.

Outside, the rain had begun. They sat in the truck without speaking for several minutes while the heater half-defrosted the windshield. Jack finished clearing it with a rag, then put the truck in gear and pointed it north toward home. Beyond the city limits, night closed in around them. Emotionally drained, Lisa listened to the hum of the engine and watched the rain fall through their headlight beams onto the glistening blacktop highway.

"I'm sorry about what happened," Jack said presently.

"They were determined to make trouble. I'm just glad you weren't badly hurt."

Jack's voice grew earnest. "They're not locals. They come from forty miles south of here, a little town called Duck Bottom."

Lisa tried to suppress a laugh but did not succeed. "With a name like that, it's no wonder they left it."

That started them both laughing—deep, uncontrollable, satisfying laughter that swept away the evening's tension.

"You win the prize, Lisa," Jack said when they could breathe again. "I don't know another woman who could sit through all that mess and come out laughing."

"It was either laugh or cry," Lisa said, too much aware of the quiet tears now flowing freely. "For your sake, I'm glad those men didn't come from around here. I know how much you want your town to be perfect."

His head turned quickly toward her. "Thanks, but I'm not that foolish. Beneficent isn't perfect. We have things like that silly feud between Mrs. Telebit and Mrs. Harding."

"I know they don't speak, but no one has told me why."

Jack gave a sad laugh. "Years ago when Mrs. Telebit opened her boarding house, she made a big fuss about choosing a biblical name for it. For a joke, Mrs. Harding suggested the name Beth-aven. Mrs. Telebit snapped it up and, without telling anyone, had the name painted on her signs and printed in advertising. Things rocked along well enough for several months till someone told Mrs. Telebit what the name meant."

"What does it mean?"

Jack laughed again. "It's a biblical name all right, but it means 'Home of Nothing.' Mrs. Telebit didn't like being made a fool of, and she couldn't afford the cost of changing her advertisements. People say she called Mrs. Harding some unladylike names, and they haven't spoken to each other since."

"That's really sad. Mrs. Harding seems so sensible."

"She's a really sweet lady, and . . . Hey, what's that?"

Their headlights reflected from the windshield of an unlighted pickup parked facing south on the opposite shoulder. Jack pulled abreast of it and rolled down his window. The other driver became dimly visible in the darkness as he rolled his own window down.

Except for the two trucks, the road was deserted. They must be five miles out of Shipley and hadn't seen another car. Lisa's sense of isolation crept back, and she said another hasty prayer. She hoped Jack knew what he was doing.

"What's the problem?"

"We got a flat an' we got no spare." The reply came in a soft masculine drawl. Reflected headlights dimly revealed a gold tooth that contrasted with the speaker's chocolate-colored skin.

The crowded cab of the truck contained a Negro family of six persons, all dressed in their Sunday best. She guessed several had started out in the truck bed and were forced inside by the rain. The situation seemed to speak of some emergency.

This the other driver confirmed: a sister's funeral the next morning in a town twenty miles beyond Shipley. Stranded here for an hour, he planned to go on foot for help when the rain stopped.

"No help to find near here," Jack said, "but most Chevy trucks have the same five-lug wheels. My spare ought to fit."

Without waiting for an answer, he drove a hundred yards north, took two railroad flares from the glove compartment, ignited one, and dropped it onto the pavement. Maneuvering to keep his wheels on the blacktop, he turned around and ignited a second flare a hundred yards south of the parked truck. With both warnings in position, he again reversed course and stopped with the two trucks parallel and his own headlights illuminating the flat tire.

"No need for y'all to get wet," the other driver protested.

"I'm dressed for it," Jack said, "and I'm headed for home." He took a rain hat and Army surplus raincoat from behind the seat, struggled into them in the truck's cramped quarters, and stepped out into the rain.

While Jack worked in the glare of the headlights, Lisa talked with the family in the truck. They said they lived on a farm north of Beneficent. They had no telephone and heard of the sister's unexpected death almost too late to go to the funeral. They'd had one flat yesterday doing farm work and planned to get it fixed on their Saturday trip into town. With the press of time, though, they tried making the trip without a spare. It proved a bad decision.

Jack finished and threw the flat tire into the bed of his truck. "I'll leave it at Jacob Weaver's garage in Beneficent," he said. "You can drop mine off there when you pick yours up."

"We're much obliged to you," the other driver said. "I'll take good care of your tire." With a wave, he pulled back onto the road and headed south.

Jack struggled out of his rain gear and dropped it on the truck's floor. He took a handkerchief from his pocket and wiped his face and hands. Ahead of them, the railroad flare sputtered and died. The world outside grew black. Rain drummed softly on the truck's cab, emphasizing their isolation.

Still fighting back apprehension but determined not to show it, Lisa flicked the interior light on and surveyed Jack's condition. "You're all soaked."

"Not all." Jack's eyes, thoughtful and solemn, fixed on hers in the dim light but gave no certain message. "Only feet and hands, maybe a bit down the back. A hot shower will fix me up."

He put the truck in gear and drove, his eyes steady on the road. Lisa felt tension mounting but could find no reason. They'd seemed so much together until they found the truck with the flat. Why was Jack so taciturn now? Miserable again, she listened to the rhythmic thump of the windshield wipers.

As they drove into town, Jack sighed. "About that visit to the farm tomorrow, Lisa: I couldn't hold you to it after all that's happened tonight. It may be too wet anyway."

So that was the problem! Why hadn't he asked her about it instead of wasting all that time worrying? She didn't know if she wanted to visit the farm or not, but she certainly wouldn't let Jack make the decision for her.

She twisted around to face him. "You made a promise, Jack Davis, and you can't get out of it *that* easy. If it isn't raining cats and dogs, I'll expect you at ten tomorrow morning."

Jack chuckled. "You're a bear for punishment. After tonight, most girls would be calling up a migraine."

Lisa sat on the edge of her seat, her elbow on the dashboard, and looked him in the eye. "Did you enjoy the movie?"

"Yes."

"Was something wrong with the chocolate?"

"No."

"Are you ashamed of fixing that family's flat tire?"

"No."

"You shouldn't be. I've never seen a more generous act. That only leaves one thing. Do you think I blame you for what those troublemakers did? What kind of woman do you think I am?"

Jack's eyes glazed. "I think I'm beginning to find out."

"Then pick me up at ten o'clock tomorrow."

"Yes, ma'am." He threw her a left-handed salute, and the corners of his mouth quirked upward a fraction.

They parked in Lisa's driveway. "I can let myself out," she said. "You're wet enough already."

"Okay," he said. "I'm sorry about tonight."

Her hands flew to her hips. "Jack Davis, if you *dare* apologize again, I'll . . . I'll put marshmallows in your chocolate!" She slammed the truck door and ran for the porch.

Inside, her temper-inspired bravado deserted her. She'd enjoyed pleasant companionship with Jack in the café, but the night had put her on a roller coaster of emotions—fear, pleasure, despair, apprehension, near-hysteria in laughter and tears—and sudden, ill-understood anger at the thought of not making the farm visit.

She felt fatigued, too exhausted emotionally to think clearly about Jack Davis. The man was a continuing enigma: so kind to the family with car trouble, yet so savage with the men outside the café. The memory of Callie Rakestraw flitted through her mind. Jack was strong enough to have killed Callie, but Lisa's instincts now told her that was contrary to his character.

So why did she feel uneasy about the farm visit?

After the misfortunes of this ill-fated evening, surely nothing worse could happen?

Chapter 15

Saturday, January 31

Jack's first thought when the alarm clock jangled him awake was gratitude for dreamless sleep. His second, when he reached through darkness to silence the alarm, was that the clock had bitten his hand.

Then he remembered. He'd had a fight. The sequence flashed through his mind: his surprise backhand blow to the big man's nose and mouth as soon as they cleared the café door, his follow-up strike to the groin, then his grasping the man's head with both hands and yanking it down to meet an upward-thrusting knee. Strangely, he had little memory of the other man's attack: only the glint of a knife blade in semi-darkness, then the man on the ground with an arm broken at the elbow. He did not know when the big man's ring had cut his cheek.

As it had in the war, Jack's mind told him his actions were justified. But as always, he felt rotten about them. This morning, he felt even worse about bringing the sophisticated viciousness he'd learned in wartime into the innocence of his home territory.

Nothing could be done about it now, though, and he had a full day ahead. The bathroom mirror showed that his cut cheek was neither bruised nor swollen. The back of his right hand was both. He swabbed the teeth marks with iodine, as he'd done the night before, and hoped his Army tetanus shots were still effective. He taped a bandage over the wound, slipped on a pair of gloves, and went out to do the chores.

A cold, moist breeze chilled his face, but no rain fell. Mud slicks lay in isolated bare spots, but grass and pine straw made most of the ground walkable. That gave a green light for Lisa's visit. A rush of gladness surged through him at the prospect.

Easy, boy. You're poaching on Hollis Wilson's territory. And doesn't she have a boyfriend back in Indiana? You've got a farm to build. Don't get in over your head.

Still, he found much to admire in Lisa. Good sense of humor, quick mind, even playful. Almost too confident and spunky. Not a bit afraid to say what she thought, and unbelievably steady through last night's troubles. But those changeable moods! One moment she seemed at ease, and the next almost afraid of him.

He kept trying to solve this puzzle as he finished the chores and, later, as he drove toward Jacob Weaver's garage to deliver the stranger's flat tire. He found no solution.

Maybe it's not supposed to make sense. Maybe her moods will settle down today if nothing goes wrong.

***

Lisa woke with pleasant anticipation of her farm visit, but with something on her conscience. For the former, she dressed in dark blue wool slacks, a light blue sweater, and black moccasins. For the latter, nine o'clock found her knocking on Rose McKenzie's door in search of an answer and trying to forget the dead squirrel she'd just found on her porch.

"How was the movie?" Rose asked over their first coffee.

"You'll like it," Lisa answered. "There's something I need to ask, though." She recounted the previous night's events: the cemetery visit, the fight, and Jack's lending his spare tire to the Negro family.

"Lending the spare sounds like Jack," Rose mused, "but not the fighting. I don't think he ever had a fight at school. He's one of the few who didn't. What was your question?"

Lisa clasped her hands in front of her. "When Jack and the others went outside, I prayed about it. I guess I feel responsible for the two men's injuries. It didn't occur to me they'd be hospitalized."

"Did you pray they'd be injured?"

"No. I prayed for protection for Jack. Several times."

Rose cocked an eyebrow. "How about protection for yourself?"

"That, too. As soon as I thought of it."

Rose pursed her lips. "Your conscience has an overactive thyroid. We all feel bad when someone gets hurt. But if you only prayed for protection, you're not responsible for the way God chose to provide it."

"And I wonder about Jack. If he intended—"

"Menfolks have strange ways. We don't know what Jack was thinking. That's between him and the Lord."

"Do you know what Jack did in the war?"

"He served in the Army. In Europe, I think." Her eyes searched Lisa's. "Why all this interest?"

Why, indeed? Lisa looked down at her coffee cup. "No particular reason. He's showing me his farm this morning."

Rose smiled as if she'd heard a secret joke. "Have you made any more plans about graduate school?"

Glad to be back on safe ground, Lisa turned her palms upward in resignation. "It's the same old problem. I can't seem to make a definite commitment."

Rose laughed. "You don't want it badly enough. If you ever want something so much you think you can't live without it, you'll commit in half a second."

Lisa laughed with her. "I'm more likely to get hit by a streetcar in Venice. But I'd better go. It's almost time."

For the farm visit, she added a dark-colored heavy jacket and, at Jack's suggestion, galoshes to protect her shoes.

"I couldn't believe how trusting you were with that family last night," she said as they drove westward. "Do you think you'll get your tire back?"

"Probably." Jack's gaze never left the road. "If not, I'll have to make do with theirs." He pointed to the junction of two fence lines. "My land begins there."

Lisa noticed an immediate change in the quality of fencing. Jack's fences had sturdy, hardwood posts and diagonal reinforcing wires woven into the usual three strands of barbed wire.

Jack turned into a deeply graveled driveway and stopped. "You'll see a lot of things here that I'd like to change. I hope you'll look past them to the future . . . to what the place can be."

"You'll have to tell me what to look for."

Jack pointed along the driveway's upward slope to a one-story house at the top of the hill. "My house, for instance. Typical for this part of the country. Usually, people start with one room. Later, they add a kitchen behind it. As the family grows, they build another pair of rooms parallel to the first pair, with a kind of breezeway-porch in between. Then they enclose the breezeway to make a hall, and finally tack on a full-width front porch like the one you see up there. That was all done before my folks came."

"It looks solid enough."

"It is, but I'd want something better for my family. Maybe one of the new ranch-style houses with central heating."

Jack parked beside the house and led Lisa west about a hundred yards to the crest of a small ridge. Below, another hundred yards away, stood a two-story frame house that looked abandoned.

"The old Miller place," Jack explained.

Lisa's shoulders gave an involuntary shiver. *Somewhere over there Jack found Callie Rakestraw's body.*

As if on signal, raucous cawing sounded from the nearby woods. Jack turned keen eyes in that direction, then pointed. Seven crows were circling the top of a sweet gum tree, loudly protesting a raccoon that rested in the tree's highest crotch.

Jack laughed. "The crows think he's invaded their territory, and the coon doesn't know what to think. See how he keeps looking from one crow to another?"

Lisa laughed with him. "I sympathize with the coon. I know what it's like to be an outsider in a strange land." The image of dead squirrels on her porch flashed before her eyes.

Jack grew instantly serious. "I thought things were going well for you. Has anyone made you feel unwelcome?"

"Not really." She wasn't ready to talk about the squirrels. "It's just so different from what I was used to."

Jack's face showed relief. "My first months in the Army were like that. You have to keep telling yourself you'll get past it."

He pointed to a clay bank hedged over with Ligustrums. Their green leaves made vibrant contrast with their background of stark, skeletal hardwoods. "Last night's Tarzan movie reminded me. Lucy Miller and I used to swing on those hedges when we played Tarzan and Jane." He chuckled. "We never found anything to use for apes. We pretended Mr. Miller's cows were elephants till he found out and made us quit. He said running them spoiled the milk."

"That must have been fun," Lisa said, feeling more out of place than ever. "I'm sorry you lost Lucy."

Jack glanced away. "She was a sweet girl." His eyes darkened.

Visibly, he shook off the mood and pointed northward to the highest point of the ridgeline where an unpainted building towered above the surrounding trees. "Dad built the barn up there so Mother wouldn't have to look at it from her kitchen window. From the barn's hayloft you can see for miles in every direction. Not today," he added hastily. "It's too misty to see very much."

When they retraced their steps and circled to the rear of Jack's house, an open valley came into view. "That's what Mother saw from the kitchen window." As he looked out across the valley, his gray eyes seemed to look past what he actually saw and his deep love of the land showed in his face.

"There's a small creek down there," he said. "Water enough to feed a fair-sized lake. When I can, I'll build an earth dam yonder where the valley narrows. Then I'll stock the lake with fish."

He pointed eastward to a tiny orchard, no more than a dozen trees. "Half apple, half peach," he explained. "Plenty of blossoms in spring and fruit later on." He turned northwestward toward the distant barn. "More blossoms over there. That row of thirteen trees, all bare now, is dogwood. Dad planted them for Mother. You should see them around Easter. It becomes a wall of solid white, except that the middle one is pink. It's quite a sight."

"I'll bet it is." Lisa pictured it in her mind. Her gaze lowered to several weed-infested beds beneath the kitchen window. "Your mother must have loved flowers. And did that used to be a vegetable garden at the corner of the house?"

"Right on both counts." Jack warmed to his subject. "The flowers and blossoms because Mother and Dad liked beautiful things. The garden and orchard because they believed variety increased security."

His voice softened. "Our main crop every year was either cotton or corn, but Dad didn't stop with that. In the garden we grew enough for ourselves and sold the rest. The same with the apples and peaches. And milk. We kept three cows and a few beef cattle. On that bare spot over there we had a chicken coop—sixty or more laying hens—and across the ridge was a pig pen. The market for milk, eggs, and pork was always good. Dad believed in selling something every week of the year. That's how he financed the real money crops."

Lisa felt her interest growing. "It sounds like good sense. Will you follow the same plan?"

"Competition is tougher now." Jack started them walking across the valley toward the sparse woods on the next hill. "Small family farms will get squeezed out by the big commercial outfits. I'm setting up to compete with them."

"How will you do that?"

"My farm divides naturally into three parts. Each one has a different function."

When they reached the next hilltop, Lisa saw that the land dropped off into a long valley green with a winter cover crop. She caught her breath at its burgeoning fertility.

Jack pointed northward. "Up there where things get hazy, this field connects with the six hundred acres Dad bought five years ago. The new land extends east till it meets the highway north of town. This is good land for the main money crop."

They walked northward along the ridge, then turned west into wooded hills. "This middle section is too hilly for crops," Jack explained, "but it will make good pasture when the pine is cut out from the hardwood and the land is terraced to stop erosion. I keep twenty beef cattle now, but this section should support a hundred when the work is finished."

Never interested in farming, Lisa felt her heart reaching out toward the land. "It's beautiful," she said. "Now I understand what Precious Pendleton meant. She said someday you'll have the biggest and best farm in the county."

"She's never been out here to see it." His voice was abrupt. Too abrupt?

Lisa showed what she hoped was a reassuring smile. "She said she was quoting her father."

Jack looked relieved but made no comment. Farther west, they came to an area where cut pine logs lay among standing hardwood. Jack led her up a slope to the edge of a thick woodline.

"The good soil gives way to red clay here," he explained. "From here back to the Miller place it won't grow anything but pine. But that adds timber to my crops and pasture. I'll still have the variety Dad valued, but on a larger scale."

For whatever reason—the beauty of the land or the picture Jack had painted—Lisa felt her sense of estrangement subsiding. Maybe, just maybe, she was learning tolerance for Beneficent. "I can see why you love this place," she said. "And you've accomplished something you didn't set out to do." At his puzzled expression, she explained, "I no longer feel like that raccoon in the tree."

His smile came easily. "I'm glad you're here."

He took her arm, lightly, and led her along the woodline to a single pine that stood above a number of fallen logs. "Look south across that open area," he said, pointing. "Beyond the trees on the far side you can see the peak of my roof."

She turned from him to look. "I see the barn roof, but not your house."

"Here. Let me show you." He stepped close behind her, one hand on her arm, the other pointing over her shoulder.

As she looked, Lisa felt in harmony with her surroundings and free from the uncertainties that usually troubled her. She wondered idly if being with Jack had something to do with it.

And what . . . what was Jack doing? She felt his closeness and heard his soft voice asking, "Do you see it now?" Was she leaning against him? Were his lips brushing her hair?

She stepped away and turned to face him. "Jack . . . were you . . . ? Did you . . . ?"

Something slammed into the tree above them with a loud cracking sound. Before Lisa could react, Jack seized her shoulders and threw her down behind a fallen log. As she fell, she heard a far-away muffled thump like a gunshot. Only as her face plowed into the moist earth did she realize what was happening.

Someone is shooting at us.

"Stay down," Jack ordered.

As if she could stand up when he was holding her flat! She twisted her face up from the dirt to see what he was doing.

"Stupid hunter!" he muttered. Holding her down with one arm and keeping low himself, he took a white handkerchief from his pocket, waved it above the log and shouted, "Hey! Knock it off! There are people out here."

A few seconds of silence followed.

Then another bullet kicked bark off the log above their heads. Ricocheting, it whined its path away among the pines.

Before its echoes faded, Lisa heard the blunt thump of the rifle shot.

Chapter 16

For what seemed like eternity, Lisa and Jack lay behind the log, his arm across her shoulders holding her down. In horror, Lisa realized what had happened. *Someone shot at us. We might have been killed.* Her heart hammered at her ribs, and panic rose in her throat. She fought it down and breathed deeply, holding each breath as long as she could. Presently, her heart slowed, and she waited for a signal from Jack. He would know better than she how to handle this.

The woods were silent except for wind murmuring in nearby pines. Cold damp from the muddy earth seeped through Lisa's clothing, first at her knees and then her thighs.

Thank heavens I wore this waterproof jacket!

She tried to meet Jack's eyes, scant inches from her own, but his eyes scanned the terrain beyond the end of their log. His head tilted up in a listening attitude. In the quiet she could almost hear his mind working. A pleasant idea, she decided. But she had to let him know she wouldn't panic. His gaze returned to hers.

"Do you do this with all the girls?" she asked.

"Only the ones who look good with mud on their faces." The corners of his mouth smiled, but his face remained set. "I have to find out what's going on. You stay here. Don't raise your head till I come back. I'll call out before I come back. Understand?"

She gave a quick nod. "Be careful."

He took his arm from her shoulders and wriggled away with a strange, lizard-like motion. His elbows and knees, spread wide, seemed to carry his weight, yet his stomach remained flat on the ground. Beyond the log, he disappeared into a small depression.

Lisa checked her wristwatch. Eleven-forty. A restless breeze stirred leaves and branches above her. Cold damp from the ground climbed higher on her thighs. Desperately, she began to pray. First for Jack's safety, then her own.

Eleven-fifty. She shifted onto her left side, still pressing against the log. This place in the woods seemed isolated from other human life, yet she did not feel alone. Strange, since she'd felt such loneliness in her own home only two short nights ago.

Eleven fifty-five. What was Jack doing? Could this be some hideous joke played on her, like a snipe hunt?

Twelve noon. No. Jack might have wild ideas about Beneficent's virtues, but he was no practical joker. Her left side was soaked from ankle to hip, and she shivered from the cold.

Twelve-oh-five. Where was he?

"Hello-o-o-o-o, Lisa."

Jack's voice, she thought. Not nearby, but somewhere in the direction the shots had come from.

"Lisa, this is Jack." Closer now. "It's all right. It's safe to come out."

Was it really Jack? "Are you sure?" She bit her lip as she realized she'd given her position away. What if it wasn't Jack?

Footsteps, running toward her.

"Yes, I'm sure." The footsteps grew louder, and Jack appeared above the log. He took her hands and helped her to her feet. "Whoever it was has gone. Let's go get cleaned up and have some lunch."

"Lunch?" The everyday word sounded strange after their peril. Yet in spite of the tight grip of fear that bound every muscle, she felt ravenously hungry. "Yes, lunch," she said. "I'm ready to turn termite and eat this log."

As they walked south toward Jack's house, Lisa asked, "What did you see out there?"

"I found where he'd been. A scuffed place on the ground. Not much help."

They paused on Jack's back porch and assessed the damage to their clothing. Lisa's slacks were wet and muddy, and dark stains marred her jacket. Jack had caked mud on his trousers and jacket from his crawl, and dirty water oozed from the bandage on his hand. Lisa left her muddy galoshes on the porch. Jack pulled off his shoes and stood in sock feet.

Determined not to show her tension, Lisa threw Jack a mischievous look and gestured toward the mud on her clothing. "Can you spare this much topsoil?"

He visibly relaxed. "From that part of the farm, yes. If you'd taken it from the good crop land, I'd make you put it back."

Laughing together, they entered the house.

The door opened into a large kitchen with a blue linoleum floor. An open door in the opposite wall revealed a bedroom. To the right, another door opened into a hall. Nearby was a squat-legged refrigerator topped by external coils. The gas stove must have dated from the nineteen-twenties. In the middle of the floor stood an oblong metal-top table with four plain wooden chairs.

Lisa paused to take it all in. Jack had told her to see the future, not the present, she remembered. He'd had good reason. She moved to the porcelain sink. Above it, a window looked out across weed-ridden flower beds to the valley where Jack planned to build a lake. *It will be beautiful—* The thought was still incomplete when she saw its error. *No, it's beautiful right now. He will make it more so.*

Jack's voice interrupted her reverie. "Why don't you get cleaned up while I fix lunch? Bacon and eggs okay?"

"Fine. Where do I go?"

He pointed to the bedroom door. "Bath cloths and towels in the top right drawer of the chest. Bathroom is on your left."

She shut the bedroom door behind her. Across the hardwood floor, the gas heater was burning on high. So was the one in the bath. Jack must have lighted them while she gazed out the window.

Curious, she surveyed the room. One corner held a single bed with a white wrought-iron bedstead. The bed itself was covered with a crocheted spread and a patchwork quilt. No bedside table, only a small work table that held nothing but a wind-up alarm clock. An ancient floor lamp was sandwiched between table and bed. Everything was old and austere, but neat and clean.

The chest of drawers stood between two sheer-curtained windows that looked out onto the front porch. Which drawer held the bath cloths and towels? Top right or top left? She opened the top right and felt a flood of relief when she found them there. She took out one of each. Then she noticed that the bedroom's far wall was covered with bookcases, all filled with books.

She suppressed an impulse to browse their titles and entered the bathroom. An awkward monstrosity of a shower had been jury-rigged over the bathtub, but all else was plain and well-arranged. A soft-bristled shaving brush rested in a shaving mug on a glass shelf above the lavatory. Nearby lay a hairbrush and a half-used tube of toothpaste.

The water in the lavatory proved gloriously hot. Lisa scrubbed her hands and face with a vengeance and, guiltily, borrowed Jack's hairbrush to remove patches of sandy topsoil from her hair. Nothing could be done about her damp slacks, but she felt less chilled now that the house was warming up.

Back in the kitchen, she found Jack had been busy. Her galoshes, now clean, were drying by the back door. The bacon had been fried and the eggs were ready to cook. Coffee was perking on the stove, and the smell of toast rose from the oven.

Jack had changed shoes but still wore his wet clothes. "I hope you like scrambled eggs," he said. "That's the only way I know to cook them."

"I like them any way but raw," Lisa said. "Thank you for cleaning my galoshes. You didn't have to do that."

"No problem. The oven took time to heat and the hydrant is right by the porch."

Lisa's mind kept going back to the shooting, but she wasn't yet ready to talk about it. "You certainly keep a neat house," she said as Jack scrambled the eggs.

He laughed. "It's not always that way. The cleaning woman came yesterday." A worried look furrowed his brow. "I have to explain about that shower. We didn't have one until I came back from the war. I added it in too much of a hurry. But as soon as I have time I'll get someone to fix it right."

Lisa gave him a smile and a shrug. "I understand. My father says you like to see things done right."

As they ate, she asked about the proliferation of books.

"Most of them were Mother's," Jack explained. "She taught history at the high school till Dad talked her into changing careers."

"Have you read many of them?" Lisa remembered his knowledge of current events and his lingering among the paperbacks in the drugstore.

"Most of them. Mother taught me the reading habit early. She told me later it was the only way country people could keep up. She took me through a lot of history books and most of Shakespeare and Milton."

"Wasn't that awfully advanced for a teenager?"

Jack grinned. "I said she took me through it. I didn't say I understood. But I do like to read."

While they relaxed over a second cup of coffee, Lisa decided it was time for straight talk. "Being shot at was a new experience for me. Why would anyone do something like that?"

Jack hesitated before answering. "Some hunter, I guess. My land is posted against trespassing, but I haven't checked the signs lately. Some may have fallen or been removed."

Lisa pictured the dead squirrels on her porch. "But why would a hunter fire again after you called out and waved?"

Jack shrugged. "Some hunters would lose an IQ contest with a cricket. I've heard of deer hunters shooting cows by mistake." He swallowed the last of his coffee. "If you've finished, I'd better take you home before you catch a chill."

As they drove, a new constraint fell between them, one Lisa did not understand. She tried to reach across it. "Your farm is all that people say it is, Jack. I enjoyed the tour."

He gave a sardonic chuckle. "Everything except getting shot at. I'm getting to be a real jinx for you."

"Don't talk like that. You couldn't help what happened today. Or last night, either."

They found Hollis Wilson's Ford convertible parked in Lisa's driveway beside her father's Frazer sedan. Jack gave a low whistle. "This is going to be awkward."

"No, it isn't," Lisa said, fiercely independent. "I'll have as many friends as I like."

When they entered, their mud-stained clothing drew curious stares from Wilson and Stephen Kemper.

"It's all right," Lisa explained to her father. "We had a little accident, but no one was hurt."

"Someone with a rifle trespassed on my land," Jack said. "He fired close to us, and we had to dive for cover. That's where the mud came from."

Kemper said nothing, but Wilson asked, "Did you see who did it?"

Jack grimaced. "We never saw him, and he left no tracks. We don't even know which way he came or went."

"I drove the western road around noon today," Wilson said. "I didn't see any cars parked near your farm."

"Then he must have walked in from the other side," Jack mused. "Or maybe he cut across the old Miller place. There's another road half a mile beyond it." He turned to Lisa's father. "I'll talk to the sheriff about it, Mr. Kemper. I'm sorry to involve Lisa, but we can't let things like that go unreported."

Kemper frowned. "It can't be helped. I suppose we should be glad no one was hurt." He did not sound enthusiastic.

"If you men will excuse me," Lisa said, "I need to clean up. Thank you again, Jack, for a most interesting morning."

In her room, she thought again of the dead squirrels and wondered if today's rifle shots were intended for her. She would talk to her father about it, she decided, and pushed the question from her mind.

Through the walls came an unintelligible jumble of masculine voices, followed minutes later by the sound of a door shutting. Jack's truck engine started, then modulated pitch and timbre through several gear changes. The sound faded in the distance.

Without warning, a feeling of emptiness descended upon Lisa. In the familiar warmth of her own home, she felt suddenly alone.

***

Jack gave himself a lecture as he drove to the sheriff's office. Six kinds of fool he'd been, making a pass at Lisa! And an awkward one at that. He'd felt drawn to her ever since seeing her at the tournament, but in all honesty he'd only intended to show her an interesting view. Then there she was, so very close to him. He'd felt an overwhelming wave of tenderness. Then he'd startled her so much that she jumped away from him.

Getting shot at was a stroke of luck: it saved him the embarrassment of trying to explain something he himself didn't understand. Lucy Miller had never affected him that way. Lucy was placid, but Lisa was quick and lively. And now she'd never go out with him again because he'd been a fool.

Maybe that was a good thing. He had three years of hard work ahead before he could pay off the note on his farm. Until then, he had no business thinking about marriage. Especially with Lisa, who came from a different world and obviously didn't like Beneficent.

Marriage? How did that word pop up in his head? It wasn't part of his vocabulary.

He forced his mind back to the shooting. He'd simply reacted as he had in the war: throwing himself and Lisa flat behind the log, noting the time between the strike of the bullet and the sound of the shot. Before they hit the ground, he knew the rifleman was one hundred fifty yards due east of them, and in the same spot where they'd walked a few minutes before.

A careless hunter, he'd thought, until the second shot. Then he knew better, and knew he must leave his covered position to go after the shooter. An all-too-familiar terror from the war rose in him. Every time he'd forced himself to leave a covered position it became harder. Harder than ever, now, for this time he carried no weapon.

To compensate for that, he'd used all the woodcraft he knew. Yet in spite of all his skill and perseverance in the face of fear, his quarry had eluded him.

When Jack entered the sheriff's office with his mud-caked clothing, Sheriff Rainwater and Ben Patterson looked up in surprise.

"Jack," said the sheriff, "you got to give up this habit of rasslin' pigs in the mud." His gaze flicked to the cut on Jack's cheek. "Leastwise, you oughtn't mess with pigs what has tusks."

Jack grinned in spite of himself. "I wish that was the trouble. Somebody fired a rifle at Lisa Kemper and me on my place today. We never saw who it was."

Rainwater tented his hands. "You reckon somebody mistook y'all for deer?"

"Maybe on the first shot. After we dove behind a log, I waved a handkerchief and yelled. A few seconds later, another shot hit the log above our heads. That had to be deliberate."

The sheriff's eyes narrowed. "Could be, but some hunters can be remarkable dumb. Maybe he still thought you was a deer?"

"Most people don't hunt deer with these." Jack dropped two .30 caliber cartridge cases on the sheriff's desk. "They're for an Army M-1 rifle. I found them at the shooter's position. Can you do anything with them?"

At the sheriff's glance, Ben Patterson answered. "Probably not much till we can match them with something. But we'll try. I don't suppose you have an M-1 rifle around your place?"

Hot anger bubbled in Jack's stomach, but he fought it down. "No. I've kept Dad's .22 and Colt revolver, but no heavy rifles."

"We'll work on these cartridges," Rainwater said. "Meantime, can you think of anyone who'd want to shoot at you? Maybe only to scare you?"

Jack made a wry face. "Not from around here. This doesn't make much sense, but I did have trouble with two guys in Shipley last night." He summarized the events of the night before and ended by giving Rainwater the troublemakers' license plate number. "They might have gotten my license, too, but I don't see how they could have traced me this quickly."

"Neither do I." The sheriff pursed his lips. "So Miss Kemper was involved in both incidents?"

"She was a witness to both. I wouldn't say she was involved."

"My deputy in Shipley can check several things." Rainwater dialed the phone. "Caught up on your sleep yet, Jonesey? . . . Then whatcha been doing? . . . Naw, listen. Go check on a fracas outside the bus station café last night. Then hustle down to the hospital and find out what happened to two guys that got the worst of it. Who was they and where was they from? When did they leave the hospital and where did they go? Did they have a weapon in their truck? . . . Yeah, they might be mixed up in something else."

As the sheriff hung up, Ben Patterson stirred in the chair, which creaked under his bulk. "If you like, I can handle that license number. It's a weekend, but someone owes me a favor."

Rainwater nodded. "I'd 'preciate it." He turned to Jack. "An' I got one piece of good advice for you."

Jack met his gaze. "What's that?"

"Don't order no chicken-fried steaks." His face resumed its deadpan stare. "With the luck you're having, you'll catch lockjaw before they's cooked."

***

When Jack had gone, Rainwater reached toward the phone again. "Might as well find out what the Kemper gal's story is."

"Before you do," Patterson asked, "why didn't you tell Davis about the dead squirrels on her porch?"

Rainwater rubbed his hands together. "I wanted to find out if Jack knew about 'em. If he had, he wouldn't have been so positive them shots was meant for him. An' if I'd told him, he might've done some fool thing like staking out her place hisself. I've got deputies checking it when they can, and they'd have caught him doing the stake-out. We've got enough complications without making more."

"One other thing." Patterson leaned forward, the chair protesting beneath him. "I know we've got that Martin character in custody, but we don't have anything to connect him or anyone else to Callie Rakestraw's murder. Now, this Davis fellow can be real violent. He admits that he put two grown men in the hospital, and he's strong enough to break Callie Rakestraw's neck. Did you check his military record?"

Rainwater shifted uncomfortably. "I kind of forgot. But the way things is going, I don't guess I got much choice."

Chapter 17

Sunday, February 1

The sense of isolation that had plagued Lisa on Saturday afternoon stayed with her at church on the next day. Remembering the shooting incident was bad enough, but the dead squirrels on her porch told her Jack might be wrong in calling it an accident. Despite his words, he hadn't seemed too sure of it. Sheriff Rainwater's probing questions didn't help. Was he merely verifying Jack's version of the story, or did he suspect her of something?

To compound the problem, Alex had phoned last night. She'd enjoyed thinking of his proposed visit in the roseate haze of a distant future. At school last spring she'd enjoyed listening to his ideas—always fascinating, if unpredictable. And he'd seemed on the brink of proposing when they parted at semester's end.

But things looked different now, with his visit scheduled for the coming weekend. She had enough problems already: snipers, squirrels, trying to get herself and her father accepted in a town she didn't like—not to mention choosing a course of study for graduate school next year. To have Alex land in the midst of these would only add to her uncertainty. And what was this new feeling of incompleteness that troubled her lately? This longing for some vague something she didn't have and didn't even know the name of?

Now in church with her father, she tried to push these musings aside. Yet the unsettled feeling remained. Even the organ's sonorous prelude left her mood untouched as she watched the congregation assemble.

Little in the church had changed since Callie's funeral three weeks before. Buddy Robinson occupied one of the side pews, a hometown boy paradoxically as much an outsider as she. Ronnie Parker sat among empty seats as his quiet ostracism continued. He glanced up when Precious Pendleton passed on her way to the choir, but the bored beauty looked the other way. Precious was resplendent, as always, her makeup immaculately applied to perfect features.

Harry Pendleton, seated three rows from the front, carefully observed his daughter's passing. His obvious pride formed a strange combination with his perpetually worried expression. "Sometime late in the war he started carrying the world's troubles on his own shoulders," Rose said. "Now he's more worried-looking than ever. Most people blame the Russian situation."

Vesta Childress entered, her face unusually pale. The seams of her stockings were skewed in opposite directions. Lisa sympathized. She'd had enough trouble straightening her own.

Off to one side, Effie Dean Telebit sat on the edge of her pew and craned her neck for a better view of the congregation.

Always searching for gossip. I'll bet she can tell how many degrees out of true Vesta's stockings are. And she'll invent twenty reasons why Vesta looks pale.

Mrs. Harding sat on the opposite side of the church from Mrs. Telebit as their silent feud continued.

Wherever she looked, Lisa saw no spark of interest. Members of the congregation looked like what they were, Lisa thought: people satisfied with their own goodness who'd come there out of habit rather than genuine commitment.

But what about herself? Her only real commitment was to be seen in the right places so the community would accept her and her father. The thought brought a pang of conscience, but she pushed it aside and looked around again.

Jack Davis was nowhere in sight. Lisa felt a needle of disappointment and tried to explain her feelings. *I just want to be sure the rifleman didn't come back and finish the job.* For some reason, she hoped he would sit by Ronnie Parker as he had at the funeral.

As she watched, Otis Hahn brought his growing family to Ronnie's pew and folded the boy into the group. A few minutes later, Jack came in with young Clem Rakestraw, whose parents were absent. Lisa realized she hadn't seen them since the funeral, and the depth of their grief suddenly struck home to her.

She still felt strangely detached from the congregation as it labored through familiar hymns, and the choir worked through Sir John Stainer's setting of "God So Loved the World." Lost in her own thoughts, she only half-listened as Brother Smallwood began his sermon.

"Prayer is a mystery beyond human understanding," the minister said. "It's the mystery of communication between man and God."

That jerked Lisa fully alert. *How strange, his speaking on prayer when these last two days started me thinking about it.*

Her mind drifted off, though, as the minister retold biblical stories she'd known since childhood. Nor was she the only one drifting. Stephen Kemper's eyes were already blank. From the congregation came the sound of restless movement, punctuated now and then by stifled yawns. Lisa's gaze wandered to Ralph and Rose McKenzie, seated off to her left.

Rose sat primly straight and attentive, her burgundy suit enlivened by a bright paisley scarf. Ralph slumped beside her, almost dozing. He wore a dark blue pinstripe suit that must have dated from around 1940.

I'll bet he only wears it for Sundays, weddings, and funerals. At that rate, he'll never wear it out.

Ralph roused himself and, with one finger, appeared to draw diagrams on the back of Rose's hand. Rose's eyes remained focused on the minister, but she colored slightly, bit back a smile, and stopped Ralph's improvident artistry by covering his hand with her own.

Some signal understood only by the two of them, Lisa guessed. How wonderful after all these years to be still courting! With a twinge of envy, she hoped she'd be lucky enough to have a marriage like that. Someday, not anytime soon. Graduate school came first—

"Prayer is more than a grown-up letter to Santa Claus." Brother Smallwood's raised voice brought Lisa back to the sermon.

A letter to Santa? She remembered Brother Conroy's prayer the night she'd confronted Jack with Psalm 53. He'd launched directly into requests and piled them higher and higher right up to the "Amen." Now the pastor was saying that wasn't the way to do it.

"Prayer is two-way communication, but we have to begin by removing the obstacles. Confession, praise and thanksgiving come first." Brother Smallwood mopped sweat from his brow. "The example of the Pharisees shows us we can't come to God in pride. And we can't come to Him smug and self-satisfied, thinking we're a favored community."

Now he was stepping on the townspeople's toes. Or was that aimed specifically at Jack? Lisa looked for his reaction but found him gazing out at nothing, a brooding look on his face. Beyond him, a blue-checked suit drew her attention to Ben Patterson, whose eyes seemed fixed on one particular object. She followed his line of sight and, with a start, realized he was staring at Vesta Childress. Lisa looked away quickly, fearing her own gaze might draw the detective's attention. When she looked back, his gaze still focused on Vesta.

". . . And God is not a spare tire you keep locked in the trunk till one of your everyday tires goes flat."

If the pastor had been talking to Jack before, he was talking to her now. Yes, she'd fallen into depending on her own resources. That is, until that terrible moment in the café when she'd realized she had none. How desperately she'd prayed then! The next day, too, lying helpless in the mud on Jack's farm. Her prayers had been heard, she guessed. She and Jack were still here.

Then she remembered the driver stranded on a lonely highway with no spare tire. How abandoned he must have felt with nowhere to turn in time of need! She'd neglected her own privilege, but it was still available when she decided to use it. Maybe she should—

"The best athletes and musicians make a point of practicing regularly," Brother Smallwood said, "and the cumulative effect of their practice makes them excel. Prayer works the same way. When we practice it regularly and sincerely, something from God Himself flows into us and we become different people. We don't know how it happens, but all of those who experience it know that it *does* happen. And they know it changes lives."

Lisa's eyes focused on Precious, a beautiful bored manikin staring vacantly into space. The rest of the choir held similar poses. If Brother Smallwood was "preaching to the choir," he wasn't getting through.

Or to the congregation either. Jack was still brooding. Buddy Robinson seemed to be studying a stained-glass window. Hollis Wilson's handsome features showed only polite deference. Mrs. Telebit paid more attention to her neighbors than to the pastor, and Mrs. Harding looked everywhere except at Mrs. Telebit. Ben Patterson's gaze kept returning to Vesta Childress. And Otis Hahn absently scratched an ear with one hand while his other arm cradled a sleeping child.

In the entire congregation, only Ronnie Parker and Rose McKenzie seemed to listen. Ronnie's attentiveness had to come from his unhappy situation. He was shunned by his peers and, from all reports, received no support from his parents. He needed every word of encouragement he could find.

Ralph McKenzie's hand, imprisoned between Rose's two hands upon her lap, made some movement Lisa couldn't identify. Rose jumped, lightly slapped his hand, and stifled another smile. But her gaze never left the face of the minister.

" . . . Trouble with Job's three friends," Brother Smallwood was saying, "they based their advice on lessons learned second-hand. But Job had personal knowledge of God, developed from his own experience throughout a long lifetime. His prayers were acceptable."

Lisa winced. *He has me dead to rights. Okay, then. No more flat-tire prayers, and no more second-hand experience. I'll get to work and build my own. Who knows? I may even find the certainty I've been looking for—about Alex, about graduate school, about this isolation and loneliness I've been feeling.*

The congregation sang listlessly through the invitation hymn, and a brief benediction ended the service. Not a very successful one, from the looks of the congregation. Even Lisa's own mind had wandered. Yet, in spite of inattention, she'd been led to a commitment about prayer. A meager return, but it meant Brother Smallwood's efforts were not completely wasted.

Outside, Hollis Wilson stopped Lisa and her father to ask about progress on the chemical plant.

"Right on schedule," Stephen Kemper told him. "Say, a teacher named Oleta Brooks asked me to talk to her high school science classes about careers in chemistry. What should I know about her before I go?"

Wilson grinned. "She looks at you like you'd taken a litmus test and flunked, but her students learn a lot of science. She's a widow with one son, a chemistry major at Ole Miss."

As they talked, Lisa saw Jack emerge from the church with Clem Rakestraw. Ronnie Parker intercepted them and began talking to Jack. Young Clem gave Ronnie a hard look and moved away, sulking. Lisa couldn't blame him, given Ronnie's negligence toward Callie. Ronnie's agitated gestures showed the seriousness of the discussion. Jack answered deliberately, his hand on the boy's shoulder. Lisa wondered what they were talking about.

Off at one side of the crowd, Buddy Robinson stood alone, quietly watching, as always. Lisa made a note to call him about trimming her hedges when weather permitted. Farther to one side stood the huge bulk of Ben Patterson. His eyes flicked from one group to another, then followed Vesta's progress along the sidewalk. His staring made Lisa uncomfortable even when he directed it at someone else.

Other members of the congregation lingered in groups for conversation. She'd seen the numbness of shock on those faces at Callie's funeral, but now she saw the numbness of complacency. They seemed to have slipped back into the very thing Brother Smallwood was preaching against today. Or was their complacency a form of denial, a mask for underlying desperation that could not be assuaged until Callie's murder was solved?

Lisa felt a stab of regret. Then she wondered, as she had at the funeral, why the well-being of these people had come to matter to her, a temporary resident who would be gone to graduate school in the fall.

Chapter 18

All through the church service, Jack wondered why anyone would want to shoot at him. Except for the troublemakers on Friday night, he could think of no one. So he emerged from church doubly frustrated: He'd found no answer to his question, and his brooding distracted him from the service. He couldn't remember a thing Brother Smallwood had said. Worse yet, his dark thoughts had even kept him from looking at Lisa. He wanted to talk to her and see how she'd handled the dangers of the last two days.

But he had no opportunity. He and Clem Rakestraw found Ronnie Parker waiting just outside the church.

"I have to talk to you, Jack." Ronnie seemed ready to cry.

Clem made a point of walking away and turning his back.

"Jack, I've had it up to here with this town." Ronnie touched the top of his head. "Nobody speaks to me except you and Otis Hahn. And Brother Smallwood, of course. Even my parents don't say more'n they have to. I've had enough. I'm leaving this place."

Jack read the anguish in the boy's face. "What about the basketball team? People have started comparing you to the team of 'forty-two. You can't quit while you're winning."

"We're still winning, but it's not like it used to be." Ronnie looked downward. "The boys work with me on the court, but then they clam up. The locker room's like a tomb."

Jack searched for a solution. "I could talk to them, maybe bring Senator Wilson with me."

"No!" Ronnie pounded a fist into his palm. "If anything's done, I'll do it myself. The best thing is for me to leave."

"Where will you go?"

"I'll join the Army. That's why I wanted to talk to you. You've been there and you know what I should ask for."

Jack's first impulse was to voice opposition, but he suppressed it. "Why do you want to join the Army?"

"I've made a mess of things here. Got a lot to make up for." The boy spoke through clenched teeth. "The Army sounds like a good place to do it."

"I don't know, Ronnie." Jack searched for a way to put on the brakes. "The Russians are acting up around Berlin and trouble's coming to a boil in Czechoslovakia. You might be volunteering yourself into another war."

The boy's eyes blazed. "So much the better."

Jack wouldn't argue with that kind of emotion. "Well, if your mind's made up." He put his hand on Ronnie's shoulder. "I don't know what's going on with the Army now, but I know people who do. Give me a week, and I'll see what I can find out."

"That'd be swell, Jack."

"Promise me you won't do anything till we talk again. This is something you have to get right the first time."

"I promise." The youth gave a strained grin and walked away.

"Phew," Jack said to himself. He'd steered Ronnie away from precipitate action, but he couldn't stall indefinitely. The boy had a lot to live down. The Army might be the best place for him, but he'd fare better there if he finished high school. The problem was convincing him.

Jack filed the problem away and scanned the churchyard for Lisa. Disappointment struck when he couldn't find her. He scuffed a pine cone off the sidewalk and called to Clem Rakestraw, "Let's go home, Clem. This city life is getting me down."

***

That night after the evening church service, Buddy Robinson stood near a group of five boys and laughed until his legs refused to support him. Then he sat down in the street and laughed some more.

None of the group had planned this when they started walking home. It had just happened. Now they all stood or sat in the street and abandoned themselves to laughter as only the young know how to do.

The other boys were three to four years older than Buddy, but tonight they treated him as an equal. At times he even mingled with the group instead of standing outside and watching.

Maybe it happened because they put off going home and walked eastward to the city limits. At least that was where the dog barked at them. The dog remained hidden behind a board fence, but its deep, fierce bark meant it had to be huge. A German Shepherd, at least. Maybe even a Great Dane.

Presently, the dog quieted its fury. Then Jed Stoddard, who played center on the basketball team, barked back at it with a deep-throated sound almost as threatening. The dog began barking again and leaped viciously against the ramshackle fence. A second and a third dog joined in from neighboring yards, and soon the whole neighborhood erupted in a cacophony of baying, yipping, growling, howling, bawling, and bellowing that surpassed anything Buddy could remember.

All of the boys collapsed into laughter as unrestrained as the barking of the dogs.

The nearby dogs subsided in about five minutes, but the din from those in the town center and along the western outskirts continued long after.

When all was quiet again, Buddy decided to make his presence felt. In a contrived falsetto, he delivered a fit of soprano yips like a demented lapdog having a nervous breakdown. Jed Stoddard answered with his resounding bass. The original dog and his neighbors joined the chorus, and the entire performance was repeated throughout the town while the boys again surrendered to laughter, pounded each other's backs, and rolled in the street.

When the dogs finally ran out of breath and the boys' last laughter died away, Jed asked, "Wanna do it again?"

Buddy answered with another round of lapdog yapping, but before the canine chorus could respond, a gruff male voice shouted from a dark porch, "You boys git on home. You'll have ever' dog in town sick with sore throat."

"We wasn't doing nothing," Jed replied. He sounded almost innocent.

"Don't sass me, Jed Stoddard," the voice came back. "I know every one of you. If you don't git on home, I'll call your parents. An' if you come making noise again, I'll turn ol' Shep loose on you."

Jed gulped once. "Don't do that, Mr. Ricketts. We're going."

As they walked westward, he muttered under his breath, "You shouldn't 'a' threatened us, Mr. Ricketts. You just shouldn't."

A block later, Buddy left the group, the better to plead innocence if Mr. Ricketts did call his mother. He turned north to intersect the little-traveled road behind Vesta Childress's home. The small wooded hill between the road and the back of her house would shield him from her sight. Nor would anyone else see him, for no houses fronted on the seldom-used road.

He laughed again as he recalled his new friends' delicious mischief. They'd go on the loose again one of these nights, and Mr. Ricketts had better watch out!

Inwardly, Buddy savored his discovery of a principle that sooner or later warms the blood of every young man: adulthood is a crime that justifies whatever punishment youth can devise.

***

Wednesday, February 4

At ten o'clock in the evening, Jack sat reading at the metal-top table in his kitchen. At the chemical plant he'd worked too late to attend prayer meeting. Now, absorbed in one of his mother's old history books, he was only vaguely conscious of the kitchen sink off to his left or the dark window above it that opened onto the valley.

He'd read the book before, the great adventure of spanning the raw American continent with railroads to connect the Atlantic and Pacific coasts. He could use some of that pioneer grit now, though he was only building a farm.

This was a perfect setting for reading: a cloudy winter night with no wind stirring, the land so quiet he could hear the hiss of the gas heater in his bedroom. This was the kind of night he'd remembered, sometimes desperately, in steeling himself through the toughest moments of the war.

CRASH!

Something smashed into the wall opposite the window. Instinctively, Jack dove for the floor as shattered glass from the window fell around him. He was already crawling toward the hall when the sound of the rifle shot reached his ears.

He risked a quick look to see where the bullet had hit, high on the wall opposite the window, then crawled through the hall into his parents' former bedroom. His first reaction had been fear, but anger rose to overpower it. In that bedroom, he seized the old Colt revolver he'd carried the night he found the tramp in the Miller place. Next he found his father's .22 caliber rifle and slipped a box of cartridges into his pocket. Then he dropped from a hastily opened bedroom window to the ground outside and faded into the deepest shadows, listening.

His eyes searched out the darkness of the hill beyond the valley. The shot must have come from there, almost two hundred yards away. It was an impossible shot at night, except for the light from his kitchen window. As he watched, he loaded the rifle.

What should he do next? His .22 was no match for the high-powered rifle of his assailant. If he stayed where he was, would the other man grow tired and leave? Or would he guess that his quarry had left the house and pepper the area with bullets? Jack decided to change his position as soon as he could.

There! Across the valley, a muzzle flash lit up the night, and Jack heard the crack of another bullet into a wall somewhere near the kitchen. The flash would blind the rifleman for several seconds, so Jack sprinted fifty yards into the nearest woodline. His anger grew to white heat. The intruder was turning Jack's tranquil Beneficent into a war zone. Worse than that, someone was shooting at him on his own land. And, as it had on Saturday, the second shot proved that the first was no accident.

Jack paused in the woodline. He'd be foolish to let anger dictate his actions. Deliberately, he forced himself to plan.

The sniper had two possible routes of withdrawal. He could follow the fertile eastern portion of Jack's farm back to the highway north of town, or he could escape westward to the gravel road beyond the Miller place. If he chose the former, he had a two-hundred-yard head start. If Jack tried to close that gap, he could run head-on into an ambush. But if the trespasser headed west, the advantage passed to Jack. He was closer to that route than his adversary, and it was he who could set the ambush.

He jogged the first hundred yards down the well-known path, then slowed to a walk, his rifle held at ready. Every minute or so he stopped to listen, but heard nothing. Soon he came to his path's intersection with the best path heading west. That junction was the expected spot for an ambush, so he followed the westward trail for a hundred yards to a place where it crossed a clearing into impenetrable shadows.

Jack blended into those shadows and lay prone, his rifle covering the trail. He darkened his face and hands with dirt and pulled his sleeve down to cover the luminous dial of his watch. Then, motionless, he waited.

As adrenaline faded from his bloodstream, sobering thoughts replaced his anger. This was not a combat area where killing was expected. Though outgunned, he must try to capture his adversary rather than kill him. At worst, shoot to disable him temporarily. That increased his own risks, but it couldn't be helped.

He waited. The night grew colder. Jack wished he'd had time to throw a jacket on over his flannel shirt. His teeth wanted to chatter, but he clamped them tight and forced himself not to move. This was turning out to be the longest night he'd known since the war.

Certain that hours had passed, Jack shielded his watch with his hand and sneaked a look. Midnight. He'd only been there an hour and a half. Still, that should have been long enough if his man were coming that way. He decided to wait another half hour.

When that time passed, he gave up his vigil. With utmost caution, avoiding the main trail, he circled through the woods back to his house. He climbed in through the same window he'd exited and searched each room for an intruder. He found no trace. From the dark hall, he examined his kitchen wall. The bullet hole was where he remembered it, about fifteen inches below the ceiling. But now the wall contained a second hole within six inches of the first.

That raised a question. Was the unknown enemy an excellent marksman deliberately aiming high or an incompetent who'd made the same mistake twice?

Chapter 19

Thursday, February 5

Jack entered Sheriff Rainwater's office in mid-afternoon, fatigued from loss of sleep. He'd slept a couple of hours after the sniper incident, but rose early to call the sheriff's office. Perhaps he should have called before going to bed, but the stubborn independence of his rural heritage won out. He didn't want any deputies stomping around his place in the dark. In daylight, they could do the job in half the time.

The two who responded to his call grilled him thoroughly and dug the two slugs out of the wall. Accompanied by Jack, they found the sniper's position on the opposite hill. They collected two spent .30 caliber cartridges but no other evidence.

After they left, Jack supervised work at the chemical plant until time to sign his statement at the sheriff's office.

"I don't have no good news," the sheriff said. "Ben Patterson has took the first two cartridges to Jackson. Maybe we'll know something in a day or two. Meanwhile, we'll send last night's cartridges and slugs." He wiped his mouth on his sleeve. "Had any new thoughts about who might have it in for you?"

Jack shook his head. "Just those two guys in Shipley."

"The two from Shipley was otherwise occupied on Saturday." Rainwater leaned back in his chair. "Seems you busted that fella's elbow worse than the local bone-fixer could handle, so he shipped him up to some elbow-ologist in Memphis. They operated on him Saturday morning and didn't turn him loose till noon Sunday."

"I'm sorry," Jack said. "I didn't know what else to do when he pulled a knife."

Rainwater pursed his lips. "Don't you go getting conscience-struck. He done it at his own peril, and you periled him exactly like he deserved."

"I'm still sorry it happened. What about the big guy?"

"They fixed his broke nose at the hospital in Shipley. But the hospital folks in Memphis say he sat outside the operating room till about noon Saturday. That clears him." He fixed his eyes on Jack. "You can't think of nobody else?"

Jack turned his palms upward. "Not a soul."

They stared at each other across the desk.

The door opened and Deputy Brown entered, scratching his head. "Sheriff, we still can't find a place to put all that likker we cornfiscated."

"*Con*fiscated." Rainwater grunted. "The only *corn* is the stuff you can't find a place for. When the evi-dence room is full, pour the rest out. An' don't let me catch you drinking none."

Deputy Brown looked hurt. "Sheriff, you know I don't drink. I'm a Southern Baptist."

Rainwater showed his deadpan stare. "Just don't you get to be a backslid Baptist."

When Brown left, the sheriff turned to Jack again. "Okay, so you don't know anyone who has it in for you. But be careful. Pull your shades. Don't silhouette yourself against 'em."

Jack gritted his teeth. "I'll be careful."

Rainwater leaned forward so quickly he seemed ready to pounce. "And don't pull no more fool stunts like going after a man carrying a heavy rifle and you armed with a measly .22. He'd've blown you into the next county. But s'pose you'd shot him instead. Some grand jury'd have to decide what to do with you."

He gave Jack a sardonic look. "You don't know the new county prosecutor, do you? He's still mad 'cause he lost that special Senate election to Hollis Wilson. Now he's got to make a name the hard way by winning cases. He'd send you to jail as quick for stealing a three-cent postage stamp as he would for killing the postmaster." He sprawled in his chair. "Considering your fracas in Shipley, you don't need him to tell a grand jury you're a crazy war vet'ran what can't give up that habit of violence."

Wearily, Jack stood. "I get the idea."

Rainwater also stood. "I'll do what I can, but there ain't much to go on. Don't take no chances and keep your nose clean."

***

When Stephen Kemper and Oleta Brooks emerged from Beneficent High that afternoon, he felt more satisfaction than he'd felt in months. Each science class he'd spoken to showed genuine enthusiasm.

"I have to hand it to you," Mrs. Brooks said as they walked to their cars. "You had 'em on the edge of their seats."

She was a stocky, square-jawed woman with a sharp nose and dark hair streaked with gray. She had a habit of standing with one fist on her hip, cocking her head to one side and squinting at her audience. Kemper found it disconcerting, but Senator Wilson's description seemed a bit harsh. It wasn't really "like you'd taken a litmus test and flunked." It was more like you were an unknown chemical element and she wanted to find your atomic number.

"No, Mrs. Brooks," Kemper said, "*I* have to hand it to *you*. Those kids asked the right questions. I don't see how you've taught them so much with so little equipment. Nothing more complicated than a Bunsen burner. What did that student call it?"

Her laughter burbled. "Brother Smallwood's son. He called it a 'burn-sin' burner. I'll get him straightened out."

Kemper didn't doubt that she would.

Near the edge of the parking lot they paused. A few feet away on the street, a car drove slowly by.

"We're in for it now," Mrs. Brooks said. "That's Effie Dean Telebit. You've heard of her gossip?"

Kemper frowned. "I've heard. But what can she say?"

"What can't she?" Mrs. Brooks rolled her eyes. "Lord forgive me! But just between us chemists, I think of her as a member of the Halogen family."

"What?" Kemper stood perplexed, then broke into a grin. "Oh. I get it. Fluorine, chlorine, bromine, and Effie Dean."

Mrs. Brooks chortled. "That's the idea. Thanks again for coming." She moved toward her car with confident strides.

Kemper strode thoughtfully toward his. Basic equipment for a school lab couldn't cost very much. With a comparatively small investment, his company could provide these students a much better introduction to science. It wouldn't be bad for public relations, either.

***

When Lisa finished in the library that afternoon, she walked downtown with Precious Pendleton. The girl had responded to Lisa's interest, and a pleasing friendship developed. With her, at any rate, Lisa seemed to be accepted. Precious readily agreed to her suggestion of a soda in the drugstore.

First, though, they stopped by the bank so Precious could speak with her father. She walked past the bank's main entrance and led Lisa to an obscure side door. "Daddy's friends use this entrance," she confided. "They pretend to sneak in and out, and it makes people wonder if they got a loan or only talked about golf."

"That ought to drive Mrs. Telebit wild." The words slipped out before Lisa thought.

Precious giggled. "You learn pretty quick."

The door opened into Harry Pendleton's private office. Its colorful wallpaper differed sharply from the austere stone-and-metal decor of the front offices. The wall facing the door pictured an open meadow with a profusion of red and yellow flowers in the foreground, a scene repeated on the opposite wall. Those flamboyant colors contrasted with the cool green of trees pictured on the wall behind Pendleton's desk. Lisa studied them with pleasure while Precious spoke with her father.

"I've been admiring the scenery," Lisa said when the two had finished. "I haven't seen your office before."

Pendleton beamed. "The flowers make me feel warm in winter, and the trees keep me cool in summer." His worried expression returned. "I bought the wallpaper myself—wouldn't want to spend the bank's money for personal comfort, you know. By the way, Honey and I are looking forward to visiting with you and your father Saturday evening. It's nice of you to invite us."

"We're having a few people in to meet Alex Cavill, our friend from Indiana. Precious is most especially invited." That was part of Lisa's plan to expand the girl's horizons. Alex's ideas really sizzled when he got started.

In the drugstore, Lisa ordered a lemon Coke, and Precious chose a cherry soda. While they waited for their drinks, Precious took out a compact and mended her makeup. Lisa looked for a way to turn the conversation onto something constructive, but Precious saved her the trouble by mentioning a book Lisa had recommended.

"I'm more than halfway through *Pride and Prejudice*," she said. "Those people sure are different from us."

"How is that?" Lisa feigned ignorance to draw her out.

"Talk about arrogance! That Darcy thought he was better than everybody else." Precious showed more animation than Lisa had yet seen in her. "He may have been a nobleman, but *nobody* should make a proposal like *that*."

"He wasn't a nobleman," Lisa corrected, "but he was born into the gentry, and he did have more money than most."

"I don't care." Precious's eyes flashed righteous anger. "He still shouldn't have treated Elizabeth like she was *dirt*."

Images flickered through Lisa's mind: Precious snubbing Ronnie Harper in church, Precious ignoring the boys who hovered around her at the tournament. But here Lisa had to walk softly. "Perhaps . . ." She paused to moisten her lips. "Perhaps that's meant as a lesson for all of us on how to treat people. Did something else interest you?"

"Yes." Precious seemed puzzled. "Elizabeth and Darcy didn't only talk about clothes and crops and movies like people do around here. They knew a lot about all kinds of things."

Lisa let the bit about movies pass. "You'll be doing that, too, if you keep on reading. Two years from now at the university you'll find others who've done the same. You'll naturally draw together and share your ideas." She hoped Alex would set a good example on Saturday night.

"If I met somebody like Darcy," Precious said, "I'd do what Mama told me."

"What was that?"

"I'd eat raw onions and make him wish he was somewhere else."

Lisa laughed. "I'm sure that would work. But don't make final judgment on Darcy till you finish the book."

They turned to other topics, and soon Precious mentioned Alex. "I probably shouldn't ask, but is he your boyfriend?"

"No." Lisa felt herself coloring. "He's just a good friend from school."

Precious said nothing but showed an I-know-better-than-that expression.

Their drinks finished, Lisa paid Mrs. Harding a dime and a nickel, and they left. Turning toward the bank, they saw Jack Davis approaching. Lisa realized she was glad to see him. More than glad. She was delighted, and she wondered at her reaction. Did their getting shot at together produce that effect?

"Hello, ladies," Jack said. "How've you been?"

Before Lisa could speak, Precious answered, "Fine, Jack." She cleared her throat and threw Lisa a just-between-us-girls look. "I'm sorry I can't stay to talk, but Daddy's expecting me." She exited without waiting for a reply.

Jack cocked an eyebrow. "What's got into her?"

"I'm sure I don't know." Lisa hoped her face didn't show the blush she was feeling.

"I know you just came out of the drugstore," Jack said, "but could I interest you in a cup of chocolate?"

"I'm pretty agreeable." Lisa felt on safer ground.

Jack's eyes twinkled. "You're right on both counts."

"What?" Lisa groped for his meaning.

"You're both pretty and agreeable."

Now Lisa knew she was blushing. He'd used such a corny line, yet she found herself wishing he meant it. That made her angry, and her anger added to her blush. "Did you lie awake all night thinking that up?"

"I was up most of the night, but for another reason. That's what I want to talk to you about." He touched her arm and turned her toward the drugstore.

Inside, Mrs. Harding made a show of feigned surprise. "Welcome back, Lisa. I haven't seen you in so long I thought you'd left town."

"Two chocolates," Jack said as he guided Lisa to a table. He seemed to understand that she didn't want to be teased.

With a knowing air of diffidence, Mrs. Harding served the chocolates—Lisa's with two marshmallows, Jack's with none.

"You said you'd been awake most of the night?" Lisa hoped she was moving the conversation onto safe ground. For the first time, she noticed lines of fatigue on Jack's face.

His face grew grim. "Our rifleman came back last night. He put two bullets through my kitchen window."

"Jack, that's horrible!" Lisa felt as if she'd been struck. "Were you hurt?"

"Just inconvenienced. I spent part of the night trying to catch the sniper and the rest wondering if he'd come back."

"But what if he'd caught you instead? And if you'd caught him, would you—?" She couldn't bear thinking of Jack as either victim or—her mind shut down before she could finish the thought.

"You talk like Sheriff Rainwater." He gave a bitter laugh. "I meant to capture him, maybe wound him if I had to. Not a good idea, I guess. But his shooting at me again means you weren't his target on Saturday.

That's what I wanted to tell you."

"Thank you." Doubts still clogged Lisa's mind. "What will you do now?"

"There's not much I can do. Try not to get anyone else hurt . . . hope the guy goes away or the sheriff catches him."

She shook her head. "I'm sorry." The words were inadequate, but she could think of nothing better.

Jack shrugged. "At least we know he wasn't shooting at you. Now let's talk about pleasant things."

Reluctantly, she complied. "Are you free Saturday night? Dad and I are having a few people over for dessert. A friend of ours is coming to visit. We'd like you to meet him."

At the pronoun *him*, Jack's eyes narrowed. "You don't think I'm too dangerous to have around?"

"Of course not. I want . . . *we* want you to come. Around seven?"

He nodded. "I'll be there. Listen, I hate to run, but I have to get back to the plant."

"I always walk home. Thanks again for telling me."

After he left, Lisa sipped listlessly on the last of her chocolate. Jack might be right in thinking he was the rifleman's only target, but he didn't know about the dead squirrels on her porch. In her concern for his safety, she'd forgotten to tell him. The squirrels made another interpretation possible.

Jack and Lisa might both be targets for the sniper's malice.

Chapter 20

Saturday, February 7

Lisa grew more apprehensive as the evening approached.

"You've counted those dessert plates three times," Stephen Kemper complained. "The guests aren't due for fifteen minutes. Come relax."

Lisa stared at the kitchen table. "I want everything to be perfect. For your sake as well as Alex's. Tonight is the first time we've entertained in Beneficent."

Everything was perfect, her eyes told her. The damask tablecloth lay exactly in place. At the far end rested the pineapple upside-down cake she'd made last night with her mother's special recipe. At this end, the china dessert plates were neatly stacked, with silverware and napkins arranged beside them. Nearby were the coffee cups and saucers, along with glass cups for punch. The punch itself and whipped cream for the cake, she knew, sat cooling in the refrigerator.

She let her father lead her to a chair in the living room, but her tension remained. Alex's visit wasn't turning out the way she'd hoped.

He'd stepped off the train at six-thirty that morning, looking like the Alex she remembered: a solid six feet tall with rugged good looks, now a year older at twenty-seven. He had a straight, well-chiseled nose and flowing dark hair combed directly back from a wide forehead. His hazel eyes became almost hypnotic when he talked, and all his movements reflected a restless energy.

She'd found out quickly, however, that he'd changed. The decisiveness she'd admired last year now bordered on overbearing. In front of the small crowd that met the Saturday morning train, he swept her into a bear-hug embrace before she could resist. He'd have kissed her, too, if she hadn't managed to turn her head. He'd never taken that kind of liberty before.

After a few seconds she freed herself and said, "Alex, I'd like you to meet my father, Stephen Kemper."

"I'm glad to know you, sir." Alex gave Kemper's hand one vigorous shake before turning back to Lisa, leaving her father with mouth open to acknowledge the introduction.

"You're looking great," Alex told her. Before Lisa could answer, he asked, "What's on the program?"

Lisa grew acutely aware that a dozen or more people were watching, including the drugstore checker-players and Mrs. Telebit. "Uh . . . breakfast first," she stammered. "Then we'll get you settled. You're staying with the McKenzies, our next-door neighbors." That last was for Mrs. Telebit's benefit.

"Breakfast sounds good." Alex lifted his bag, gripped her arm with the other hand, and marched her toward the parked cars at the end of the platform. Her father followed, stony-faced.

Lisa didn't like her father's silence or the tightness of his lips as he drove them home. Alex filled the short journey with chatter about mutual friends at school. He kept it up through breakfast until Lisa said it was time to meet the McKenzies.

Rose greeted Alex graciously and guided him to her spare bedroom. While he freshened up, Lisa returned home to explain things to her father.

He wore a bemused expression. "You did say he had a strong personality."

"He wasn't that strong last spring, and he certainly wasn't that familiar. I'll have a talk with him."

One talk proved not enough. Three talks were required before Alex conceded that she did not welcome physical advances. He argued that society's old rules no longer applied because "times have changed."

"*I* haven't changed," Lisa replied. "We had a good friendship last spring. Let's keep it that way."

"I always held your hand then," Alex protested.

Lisa's chin tilted upward. "Only because you had sense enough to stop at the elbow."

Once Alex got the message, though, their old relationship seemed to return. Last spring, his twin enthusiasms had been anti-trust law and labor unions. This year he'd grown fascinated with socialism. He'd also read Ayn Rand's *The Fountainhead* which, as he explained it, argued that the world's few creative people should not be bound by law and custom, but should live however their superior intellects chose. Lisa listened, but with reservations.

When she showed Alex the town, his distaste seemed much like her own initial reaction, though much stronger. He kept asking why Lisa wanted to bury herself in Hicksville for seven more months.

Their stop in the drugstore went well enough despite the knowing grins of the checker-players. Lisa refused Alex's offer of chocolate and ordered a cherry Coke instead. She pretended not to notice Mrs. Harding's raised eyebrow.

These activities went satisfactorily, yet Alex clearly showed a harder edge than she remembered. He also had a new habit of drumming fingers. In spite of his good behavior, Lisa grew apprehensive about the impression he might make that evening. She worried, too, about how he would get along with the plain-spoken Ralph McKenzie. Rose had invited Alex for supper so Lisa would have free time to get ready for company.

Lisa had prayed for certainty about her feelings for Alex, but she felt more uncertain than ever as evening approached. That explained her tension as she checked and re-checked her preparations.

"How did things go with the McKenzies?" Lisa asked when Alex returned from supper.

"Okay." His fingers drummed the arm of his chair. "The food was all right, but the green beans were limp as spaghetti."

"They cook them longer down here. I'll serve you stiff ones tomorrow if I have to put starch in them."

The doorbell rang. Stephen Kemper ushered Vesta in and made introductions. "Alex, this is our librarian, Vesta Childress."

Alex's hazel eyes made a head-to-toe appraisal. "I'm glad to know you. You don't look like any librarian I ever saw."

Vesta's glance flicked to Lisa and back to Alex before she replied. "Thank you. I hope that's a compliment."

Rose and Ralph McKenzie arrived next, with Hollis Wilson and Jack close behind. Harry and Honey Pendleton, accompanied by Precious, completed the group. Soon all were comfortably seated in the living room.

Lisa surveyed her guests with pride. She felt certain they would modify Alex's unfavorable opinion of the town as they were modifying hers. Among the men, Harry Pendleton and Hollis Wilson wore conservative blue suits. Ralph McKenzie and Jack settled for clean work clothes and their Sunday-morning shoes, not too different in appearance from Alex's sport shirt and slacks.

Lisa had chosen the same teal-blue dress and silver earrings she'd worn to the movie with Jack. Vesta, her hair wound into the customary bun, wore her usual navy skirt and blouse—slightly askew, as always. Rose wore the gray suit she whimsically described as "experienced."

None of these could match Honey and Precious Pendleton. As always, they looked like models who'd just stepped out of a fashion magazine. Honey's dark hair and brown eyes made the perfect complement to Precious's blonde and blue. Alex seemed impressed with both of them. Too impressed with Precious, if Lisa read his eyes correctly.

After introductions, a silence fell. Honey Pendleton broke it with a well-placed question. "Where in Indiana do you come from, Alex?"

"From Gary. That's next to Chicago, you know. It's different because most of Indiana is farm country."

"And is this your first trip south?" Honey pursued the obvious question as everyone else visibly relaxed.

"Yes. I've never been south of the Ohio River before." Alex tapped his fingers on one knee. "It sure is different."

Stephen Kemper cleared his throat. "Your other travels have been eastward, haven't they? Military training in New Jersey and service in Europe?"

Lisa could have kissed him for moving the conversation into safe territory. To keep it there, she added, "Jack and Hollis served in the Army, too."

Alex asked Hollis, "Where were you?"

Hollis laughed. "I fought the Second Battle of Atlanta."

"The second *what*?"

"The paper wars," Hollis said easily. "I worked for a Judge Advocate section in Atlanta."

"Oh." Alex turned to Jack. "And what did you do?"

"I was in Europe."

"Where in Europe?"

Jack made an off-hand gesture. "Italy, France, Germany. Where did they send you, Alex?"

"To England." Alex rubbed his palms together. "I was a sergeant on General Eisenhower's operations staff. We spent over two years planning the Normandy invasion. Pretty stressful, that kind of thing—all of it Top Secret—having to get all the details exactly right . . ."

At school, Lisa had listened avidly as Alex told his story to groups of students, but what had seemed natural there seemed overblown among mature adults.

She moistened her lips and said, "If you'll excuse me, I'll serve the dessert. Precious, would you like to help?"

Lisa noticed that Alex's eyes followed every move Precious made. From the kitchen, faintly, she heard Jack saying, "From the result, Alex, I'd say you got most of the details right. What have you done since the Army?" Lisa couldn't make out the answer. A steady buzz of conversation continued, with Alex's voice dominating the others. Lisa's uneasiness grew.

When they were ready, Precious carried the first serving tray into the living room. Lisa picked up the second and turned to find her way blocked by Alex.

He reached across the tray and seized her shoulders. "I know you'll be glad to get back to Indiana. You'll die of boredom talking to these clods." His grip tightened. "Pah! Sad-eyed librarian, stupid teenager that doesn't say a word."

Lisa didn't know which displeased her more, his overly familiar touch or his insult to her other guests. "They're nice people and good friends," she said, "and if you make me drop this tray, I'll . . . I'll pour that punch all over you."

His angry hazel eyes glared. She glared back at him. "Alex?" Her voice made the question a command.

He grinned and dropped his hands from her shoulders. "Just teasing," he said, "but I liked it better with just the two of us." He preceded her into the living room.

Conversation slowed as the guests gave their attention to dessert. The pineapple upside-down cake drew raves, and several people complimented the punch. Reassured by these, Lisa relaxed. Her first entertainment in Beneficent would be a success.

Honey Pendleton, gracious as always, again focused on the visitor. "Alex, you still haven't told us your impressions of the South."

Instantly, Lisa's tension returned.

"It's really different," Alex said around a mouthful of cake, "like stepping back into the nineteenth century." He swallowed the cake and plunged on. "Everything is so rustic . . . the farms and all . . . *primitive*. I keep thinking any minute I'll stumble onto W.B. Yeats's 'small cabin . . . of clay and wattles made.'"

"Around here, the only thing that waddles is ducks." Ralph McKenzie looked around in satisfaction at his first pronouncement of the evening.

Alex seemed happy to explain. "Wattles are sticks woven together to make a wall or fence."

Ralph held his ground. "Down here we makes our fences out of barb' wire."

Stephen Kemper cleared his throat again. "Alex is taking a course in literature," he announced unnecessarily.

Precious suddenly came to life. "I'm reading *Pride and Prejudice.*"

Alex looked puzzled. "What's that?"

"It's a novel by Jane Austen," Vesta explained. "Have you read any Mississippi authors in your literature course?"

"Mississippi authors? I didn't know you had any."

Vesta continued smoothly. "When you get a chance, you'll want to read Eudora Welty and William Faulkner."

"Okay." Alex gave a quick nod. "Back to this Southern thing. Is everyone around here a farmer? I don't see any industry."

Concerned, Lisa looked to see how Alex's comments were being received. The Pendletons, McKenzies, and Vesta appeared cordial enough. Hollis Wilson and Jack sat easily in their chairs, though she could not read their expressions. She could still hope for the best.

"We're bringing in industry now," said Harry Pendleton. "That's what Mr. Kemper is doing here."

"Not so fast there." Ralph's face showed a mock-serious expression. "Mr. Kemper's a farmer, same as the rest of us. Farmers grow plants, and so does he. The only difference is, he grows *chemical* plants."

His laughter exploded. Everyone else smiled politely. Rose squeezed Ralph's arm and whispered something to him.

Alex forged ahead as if he hadn't been interrupted. "I'd heard the South was behind the rest of the country economically, but I hadn't seen it for myself—"

"Take a good look while you can," Harry Pendleton put in. "It's going to change now that the freight rates are equal." At Alex's blank look, he explained. "For decades, Southern industries couldn't compete because the freight rates gave the North an advantage. As much as thirty-nine percent. Qualitatively, Birmingham steel was as good as

Pittsburgh steel, but the freight rates made it cheaper for people in—say, New Orleans—to buy it from Pittsburgh."

He paused to let that sink in. "That went on for decades. Last spring, though, the Supreme Court ruled that the rates had to be equal. Now Southern industry can hold its own. With that and our competitive labor, the next twenty years belong to us."

Alex looked puzzled. "Competitive labor?"

Stephen Kemper intervened. "That means non-union. The lower cost lures Northern industries into relocating."

Alex turned back to Pendleton. "I suppose that means Negro labor. What will you do about the race problem?"

"Which one?" Rose entered the discussion. "There are so many problems here and elsewhere, and many of them do involve race."

Hollis Wilson's voice prevailed over several others. "In the Army I heard endless arguments about this. Let's put it this way. If we're lucky—both black and white—we'll get to evolve into our own solutions. If we're unlucky, outsiders will come in and try to do a generation's work in a week. Mrs. McKenzie is right, though. There are too many problems, and they're too complicated to solve over dessert and coffee."

Alex gave Wilson a look that could have been fired from a cannon. "Senator, Governor Thurmond of South Carolina wants the South to split with President Truman and the Democratic Party. Are you involved in that?"

"They haven't asked me." Wilson's manner remained genial. "When they do, I'll probably go the way the state party does."

"It doesn't sound very smart to me," Alex said. "If you split the Democratic Party, you'll ensure the election of any Republican that runs against Truman."

"Are you a Republican, Alex?" asked Harry Pendleton.

"No. I'm supporting Henry Wallace."

"Isn't he a—" Pendleton swallowed hard. "I mean . . . a *socialist* or something?"

"The closest thing I can find." Alex threw a challenging look around the room. "Capitalism is too inefficient to survive. The future belongs to socialism. With a few of the country's best minds managing things from the top, we can forecast market demand down to a gnat's eyebrow and fine-tune production to meet it. No waste, and everyone gets what he needs."

"It sounds good in theory," Stephen Kemper put in, "but it hasn't worked in Russia. They had people starving to death even before the war."

"You have to have good planners," Alex conceded, "and they have to have authority to move people from areas where jobs are scarce to places that need more labor. After the planners get the economy under control, they could apply the same principles to other problems. Religious tolerance, for instance."

Pendleton smiled benevolently. "That's a lot of control."

"Too much," Kemper said to Alex. "It sounds like the kind of control you and Jack and Senator Wilson just fought a war over."

Lisa had grown more and more uncomfortable as tension in the room mounted. She decided to intervene. "Would anyone care for coffee?" When several people responded, she added, "While I do that, Mr. Pendleton, would you tell us how you brought the shirt factory to town?"

Consternation showed momentarily on Pendleton's face, but he mastered it and, with good grace, retold the story everyone but Alex had already heard. He was still speaking when Lisa returned from the kitchen, but paused as she completed serving.

"Punch, anyone?" she asked. Several people raised their cups, and she acknowledged with a nod.

Precious sprang up and said, "Let me take care of it, Lisa. You sit down and listen." She headed for the kitchen.

Harry Pendleton resumed his story, and everyone listened courteously. Presently, Lisa saw Alex whisper something to her father and move out into the hall. Pendleton continued as if he hadn't noticed, and Lisa soon became fascinated. She'd heard most of it before, but certain details were new. Grateful that things were going smoothly again, she relaxed and began to enjoy the evening.

After a few minutes—quite a few, Lisa suddenly realized—Precious returned without the punch and whispered in her ear, "Alex needs your help in the kitchen."

Lisa gave her a searching glance but could read nothing in her manner. Precious crossed the room and whispered in her mother's ear as Lisa returned to the kitchen.

She found Alex there, red-faced and breathing hard, a handkerchief held to his left cheek. Fury flashed from his eyes as Lisa entered. "That little minx!" he muttered. The fast, hard breathing returned.

Lisa gasped. "Alex, what have you done?"

"What have *I* done?" he fumed. "That stupid teenager has ruined me!" He lifted the handkerchief from his cheek, revealing three deep scratches more than two inches long. Blood oozed from all of them and trickled down his cheek until he clamped the crimson-stained handkerchief back in place.

"Keep your voice down," Lisa ordered in a whisper as her anger rose to match his. "She didn't scratch you for nothing. Did you make a pass at her?"

In the silence, she heard people moving in the living room, their voices indistinct. A door opened and closed. Still whispering, she repeated her demand. "Did you?"

Alex looked away. "I wasn't hurting her."

Now Lisa was breathing hard. "You stay here," she ordered. "I'll talk to you later."

Alex stammered, "But . . . but what about my face?"

"There's iodine in the bathroom medicine cabinet. Right now, I don't care if you swab it or drink it." Lisa spun on her heel and moved to the living room door. There she stopped, forcing herself to breathe slowly and deeply. Her composure restored, she drew herself fully erect and stepped into the room.

The Pendletons and Jack had gone. "I'm sorry," Lisa said to those who remained. "Alex doesn't feel well. He asked me to make his apologies."

Rose looked concerned. "I'd better go home and make sure everything is ready for him. Stephen and Lisa, thank you both for a most stimulating evening." She and Ralph left quickly.

Hollis Wilson and Vesta Childress both spoke their thanks, and Vesta accepted Hollis's offer of a ride home.

In the newly emptied living room, Lisa felt an ache rise in her throat. Finally, she choked out a question. "The Pendletons?"

Her father spoke softly. "He apologized. Said his wife needed to go home."

"And Jack?" Her dismay increased.

"Said he had work to do at the farm." Gently, Kemper placed his hands on her shoulders and drew her to him, his voice yet softer. "Would you like to tell me what's wrong?"

All at once the full weight of the evening's catastrophe descended upon her. She buried her face in her father's chest. "Oh, Dad, I've really torn it." She broke into sobs. "I've lost us every friend we have in town."

Chapter 21

After leaving Lisa's house, Jack drove south toward Shipley. His teeth were clenched and anger churned in his stomach.

So that was Lisa's Indiana boyfriend! A blowhard, a self-appointed expert on everything! Jack had met a hundred like him in the service, and he had no use for any of them. But Alex *was* a handsome rascal, he conceded. Handsome, but greasy. Jack struck the steering wheel. How could a girl like Lisa fall for such a jerk?

And she must be drawn to Alex, Jack concluded. No matter how rude the man was to her guests, Lisa showed no disapproval. She was as gracious toward Alex tonight as she'd been toward Jack last weekend.

Of course she was, said a voice within. *He was her guest, too.*

That's no excuse, argued his anger. *He was way out of line.*

The more Jack brooded on it, the more his resentment grew. Even two days ago in the drugstore, Lisa had been particularly friendly. So friendly he thought she held special feelings for him as he was beginning to hold for her. Then, SLAM! Tonight she appeared to show the same "special feelings" to Alex. To a loudmouthed boor. How could she?

What did she say last Saturday? "I'll have as many friends as I like." A charming independence and spunkiness, he'd thought then. But now, with Alex included, she seemed to want things all ways at once.

Alex's condescension toward the people of Beneficent made Jack's blood boil. He'd suffered it tonight out of courtesy for Lisa and her father, but enough was enough. While Alex was out of the room and Lisa was in the kitchen, he decided it was time to go. He had to get out of there before his temper exploded. Harry Pendleton must have felt the same, for he and his family were leaving as Jack drove away.

At Shipley, Jack turned around and drove home. The phone was ringing when he arrived. He let it ring.

His anger subsided into chagrin. He mustn't see Lisa for a while. He'd skip church tomorrow and prayer meeting on Wednesday. He didn't want to see her even from a distance.

He undressed, turned out the lights, and went to bed. He'd been a fool to think a girl as sophisticated as Lisa could be attracted to him. As it said in the song she'd played on the juke box, that *was* "the craziest dream." The memory hurt. Hoping for more, he'd been a fool.

The telephone rang again, but he refused to answer. After the tenth ring, it stopped.

Jack turned his face to the wall. Tonight he didn't want to talk to anyone.

***

Sunday, February 8

In church, Lisa clasped the hymn book tightly in her lap. She knew everyone must be staring at her. In spite of Rose's arm around her shoulders, she felt more out of place than ever. Lost sleep didn't help, for last night's frenzied activity had kept her and her father up late.

Stephen Kemper had acted quickly when he learned what Alex had done. The young man had scarcely stanched the blood from his cheek when Kemper, accompanied by Lisa, grilled him about his pass at Precious. When Alex admitted making the pass but regretted nothing except getting scratched, Kemper gave him brief but pointed instruction on the rules of hospitality and told him his presence was no longer welcome.

"The train doesn't leave till tomorrow night," Alex protested. "What am I supposed to do all day tomorrow with my face messed up like this?"

"You aren't taking that train," Kemper replied. "I'm driving you to Memphis tomorrow morning and buying you a ticket on the first train to Chicago."

Alex glowered at Lisa but did not argue.

Kemper telephoned Harry Pendleton with apologies. These were accepted but, Lisa could tell, accepted with cool courtesy. Lisa then talked with Precious, who said she didn't see what all the fuss was about. Kemper phoned each of his other guests, apologizing for Alex's rudeness but not mentioning the incident with Precious. He spoke with everyone except Jack and gave up on him after the third try.

Alex's early departure had to be explained to Rose, of course, so Lisa accomplished that in person. Rose made no comment about Alex, but leaped ahead to Lisa's next problem. "With your car gone, you'll need a ride to church with us." When Lisa looked away, she added, "You mustn't stay home tomorrow. Lord help us when we have to use church for something besides worship, but you need to make tomorrow look like any other Sunday. Sooner or later, Precious or someone will let it slip about Alex, and everyone will know. When that happens, they mustn't think you acted guilty or ashamed."

So now Lisa sat in church feeling more than ever the outsider, scarcely conscious of what went on during the service. She kept looking for Jack, but he never came. Could he have heard about Precious? The beautiful girl herself wore her usual bored expression and occupied her usual place in the choir.

After church, Lisa sought out Honey Pendleton and whispered, "I'm sorry about last night. Alex wasn't like that when I dated him last year."

"You couldn't help it," Honey said. Her words were soft, but her formulated smile conveyed a definite coolness.

At home after church, Lisa's low spirits sank deeper as she wondered how last night's disaster would affect her father's standing in town. She worried about something else, too. She'd been praying for certainty, but after last night she felt more uncertain than ever.

When Stephen Kemper returned from Memphis, Lisa apologized to him again and confessed, "I've really made a mess of things."

"Nonsense." He patted her shoulder. "No one in his right mind could blame you. The question is whether people are in their right minds." Still, he didn't sound happy.

Soon afterward, the phone rang. "A meeting up there on Tuesday?" Kemper asked. "That's mighty short notice." During the pause that followed, Lisa gathered there were explanations but no concessions. Kemper asked, "How many days?" After another pause, he added without enthusiasm, "All right. I'll get on the road in the morning."

His lips tightened into a thin line as he hung up. "They've called a meeting with the heads of all outlying factories," he explained. "With any luck, I'll be back Friday. I always hate to leave you here with no car, but particularly right now."

Inwardly stricken, Lisa put on an optimistic face. "I'll be all right, Dad. Everything I need is within walking distance, and Rose is always right next door."

Kemper tried to phone Jack about his forthcoming absence, but he again got no answer. Finally, he settled for sending a note, which Ralph McKenzie agreed to drop off at the construction site.

Alone in her room that night, Lisa felt overwhelmed by uncertainty and an increasing sense of isolation. For the first time since her mother's death, she cried herself to sleep.

***

Monday, February 9

His business in Jackson completed, Ben Patterson returned early to Beneficent. Surprisingly, he felt glad to be back.

"Welcome home, Ben," Sheriff Rainwater said. "Mrs. Telebit's been asking if you'd skipped town to get out of paying your bill."

"So that's why she was glad to see me!" Patterson sniffed. "You know what she asked me? She wanted to know why I always wear a blue-checked suit."

Rainwater pulled at his ear. "What'd you tell her?"

"I said it was 'cause they don't make 'em in neon."

The sheriff laughed. "You should've said it was 'cause I'd lock you up if you went naked. What did you find out in Jackson?"

"You won't like it." Patterson eased his bulk into a chair. "Your tramp has an ironclad alibi for the night of the murder."

"Claimed he was working on the roads," Rainwater said, "but the Jackson police couldn't find a construction firm that ever heard of him."

"For good reason," Patterson explained. "His name isn't Abraham Martin. Down there they know him as Martin Abrams. And he didn't work for a construction company. He worked on the roads for Rankin County while he was doing thirty days for petty larceny. They let him out three days after Callie was killed."

Rainwater snorted. "There goes our last outside suspect. I've always thought somebody local must have killed Callie, but I hoped I was wrong. Oh, I almost forgot." He took a file from a desk drawer. "Here's a copy of Jack Davis's Army record."

Patterson took the file and studied it.

"What do you think?" Rainwater asked.

"Enviable record," Patterson said. "It shows guts and good character, but it doesn't prove his innocence."

"I thought you'd like it." Rainwater ignored the implication and changed the subject. "Well, we still have one lead I'd like you to follow up."

"What's that?"

"You remember Ronnie Parker passed two westbound cars while he drove back into town? The driver of one called in. He lives in Crystal Creek, down in the Delta. Claims he didn't know about the crime till he heard people jawing in a barber shop. Almost had a fit, he said, when he realized we was looking for him."

Patterson made a face. "The 'sincere innocent,' huh?"

"Prob'ly. He's a milksop sounding sort of a guy, name of Clarence Millbar. He sells dental supplies in a three-state area. He'd been in Alabama that week and came through here late Friday night on his way home."

"That gravel road isn't exactly a main highway."

"He said it was a shortcut. Looks reasonable enough on the map."

Patterson nodded. "Okay. How do I contact him?"

"I got his address and phone number. He's selling in Arkansas this week, poor fellow. Should get home around noon Thursday. He'll be expecting you."

Outside, Patterson walked around the block to stretch the travel out of his legs. As he turned a corner, he saw Vesta Childress enter the drugstore.

That was a mighty-fine-looking woman going to waste, and he had time to spare for all the good he was doing on this case. Why not tackle both problems at once?

After a discreet interval, he followed her into the store. He spoke to Mrs. Harding and then let his eyes look around for Vesta. He found her seated at one of the marble-top tables, sipping a fountain Coke through a straw. Her brown hair was combed straight back and rolled tightly in a bun, though the usual unruly wisp hung loosely across her forehead. She looked up as Patterson advanced on her.

He put on the expression he called his 'serious smile.' "Miss Childress, I'm Ben Patterson from the State Police. I wonder if I could talk to you for a minute."

The question on her face changed to apprehension. "I'm sure you may, but I doubt I can help you."

Patterson shifted from one foot to the other, uncomfortably aware that he hadn't been asked to sit down. "I'm looking into all aspects of the Callie Rakestraw case, and I thought maybe some of you teachers could give me a line on her."

Vesta's hands on the table tensed into fists. Her gaze dropped downward. "I'm a librarian, not a teacher. I didn't have the close contact with Callie that a teacher would."

Patterson noticed that Mrs. Harding had moved to a position within earshot, but he didn't let that stop him. "Well, it's possible you saw something and didn't recognize its significance, like maybe Callie was keeping doubtful company."

Vesta's gaze remained fixed on the table.

"Sometimes . . ." Patterson licked his lips and blundered on. "Sometimes a girl and boy get into something they shouldn't, and then they get scared somebody's going to find out—"

He stopped as Vesta's face showed something close to panic. Her lips moved without words. Then she stammered, "I . . . I don't know anything like that about Callie." She stood up and seized her purse. "I don't know why you think I would. I have to go now."

She hurried out, her Coke left unfinished on the table.

Patterson stared after her with his mouth open. He turned to meet Mrs. Harding's eyes as she stood with hands on hips. He swallowed once and mumbled, "I wonder what got into her?"

Mrs. Harding's voice carried a distinct edge. "Maybe she doesn't like blue-checked suits."

***

That same morning found Lisa feeling more isolated than ever. Not even Rose's efforts over coffee could lift her spirits. She hoped for a brief respite that afternoon when Buddy Robinson came to trim the hedges, a planned task that weather had postponed. But no respite came, for today Buddy's bubbly volubility expressed only wholesale resentment of adults.

"Do you mean all adults, Buddy?" Lisa asked after the boy's fourth bitter comment. "You have to remember that I'm an adult."

"No, ma'am. You can't be." Buddy shook his head vigorously. "You never made me do anything I didn't want to."

Perplexed by that definition, Lisa completed the project with as little comment as possible. Still, the incident placed a barrier between her and the boy she had thought of as a friend.

When Lisa worked her stint in the library on Tuesday, the other students' customary friendliness lifted her gloom a bit. Her day took a definite upturn when Precious asked if she'd like a soda at the drugstore.

"Daddy's still mad," Precious confided as she sipped her cherry soda, "but he'll get over it in a week or two." A look of bewilderment came over her face. "What's the big deal? All Alex did was wrestle me around some."

Lisa's curiosity got the better of her. "Exactly what did he do?"

The blank look returned to Precious's face. "I'd filled the punch pitcher and set it on the cabinet. Then he showed up and asked some silly question about 'hot little Southern girls.' I told him I reckoned we came in around ninety-eight point six degrees Fahrenheit, the same as everyone else. Next thing I knew, he pinned me up against the cabinet and said some dumb thing about checking my temperature."

Her blank look changed to resentment. "I tried to push him away, but he twisted my arm up behind me till it hurt. I saw he was going to kiss me, and I got mad 'cause I hadn't had time to eat raw onions like Mama said. I could have yelled, maybe, but I didn't want to spoil your party."

A sweet smile replaced the resentment. "Then I realized I had one hand free, so I scratched his face, and he turned me loose. I didn't break a single nail, and it's a good thing 'cause I'd done them all just that afternoon." Her face grew earnest. "I worried that maybe I'd hurt him too much, so I came and told you he needed help."

"That was thoughtful of you, Precious. He didn't deserve any consideration." Lisa tried a gentle question. "Haven't any of the local boys ever tried anything like that with you?"

Wide-eyed, Precious shook her head. "They all know about Daddy's temper."

Lisa frowned. "I wouldn't have thought it. He's been so gracious to my father and me."

"Most of the time he's real nice. He almost *never* gets mad, but he's a holy terror when he does."

"I guess we all are, sometimes." Lisa decided to change the subject. "Have you done any more reading?"

"I finished *Pride and Prejudice*. You were right about Darcy. By the end of the book he'd come off his high horse and treated people right. I've started on *Wuthering Heights*." Her eyes sparkled. "I like Heathcliffe. Did I pronounce his name right? Long *e* or short?"

Lisa smiled, her cares pushed back for the moment. "You said it right. Long *e*. He's an intriguing fellow, but don't get too hooked on him before you find out everything he does."

That evening, though, Lisa's bleak mood returned. Nor could she banish it by reminding herself that, with the exception of the Pendletons, no one's treatment of her had changed. Except maybe Jack's. Her father's unanswered phone calls left a question in her mind. That question stayed with her through Wednesday as her blue mood threatened to slide into black. I'll see him at prayer meeting, she told herself. Then I'll know, one way or another.

But Jack was not there. Buddy Robinson and an unusual number of teenage boys were. Lisa heard surprised comments about their presence. Unable to focus on the meeting, she spent most of the time in silent prayer to understand her plunge into dejection.

Returning home as despondent as before, she realized for the first time that Alex's visit was not the only cause of her melancholy. Much of it came from simple loneliness. *Loneliness for what? Or whom?* She considered every person she knew in town and found that, more than anything, what she wanted—no, needed—was a telephone call from Jack Davis.

But no call came.

Chapter 22

After prayer meeting, Buddy Robinson and his newfound friends again headed toward the east side of town. This time, though, they left the dogs alone and moved quietly with a definite purpose.

Being accepted in a group was a new experience for Buddy. It went to his head like strong wine. He liked the usefulness of prayer meeting, too. It gave him a good excuse to get out of the house. His mother grew suspicious when he asked, but what parent could refuse a son's sudden impulse toward piety?

By agreement, the other boys had told their parents the same thing. Their showing up at prayer meeting raised questions but, Buddy's sharp ears told him, several adults said it proved people in Beneficent were raising their children right. Jed Stoddard gave The Old Folks further evidence by volunteering to lead in prayer. He made a good job of it, too.

Jed's prowess in prayer was surpassed by his mastery of mischief. He'd planned tonight's operation carefully, like one of those commando raids in the movies. From under a bush near Mr. Ricketts' house, he took a long length of plow line he'd hidden there earlier. Then he sent Buddy forward as a scout.

Buddy found everything in order. Mr. Ricketts' house was dark, but the streetlight on the telephone pole still illuminated the yard. Old Shep might be lurking behind his fence, but for the moment he remained quiet. The heavy wooden lawn furniture sat under an oak tree on one side of the yard. On the other, a new feature had been added. Chained to an iron stake, a young calf grazed contentedly on what was left of the grass. They hadn't expected to find the calf there, but it wouldn't affect their plans.

When Buddy reported back, Jed gave the order to proceed. Accompanied by two younger boys, Jed carried the rope directly to the telephone pole. The boys boosted him up to the lowest of the pole's climbing spikes. From there, he made the climbing look easy.

On tiptoe, almost soundlessly, the other boys ran forward and carried the heaviest lawn chair to the pole. By that time, Jed had looped the plow line over the highest spike and dropped both loose ends to the ground. They hit with a *splat* as the boys arrived with the lawn chair.

The noise alerted Old Shep, who erupted into a fierce fit of barking and leaped savagely against the fence.

Hurriedly, the boys tied the lawn chair to one end of the rope, careful to use the half-hitch knot Jed had taught them. Then they seized the rope's free end and hoisted the chair up to Jed. The plow line slid over the top spike as easily as if it had been a pulley.

"A little higher," Jed called softly.

At the sound of his voice, Old Shep redoubled his barking, and the fence shook ominously. A light came on toward the rear of the house. The boys strained on the rope.

Jed guided the cross brace of the chair back onto the next-highest spike on the pole. "Now ease it down," he called, and a few seconds later, "that's good."

He worked feverishly with the knot for a moment. Then the rope came free and fell to the ground with another *splat*. Jed shinnied down the pole while his cohorts gathered up the rope.

A voice from the dark porch shouted, "Hey! What are you boys doing?"

Jed's feet hit the ground running, and the rest of the group joined him in flight. Buddy could hear Mr. Ricketts cursing on his front porch and Old Shep barking behind the fence. Neighbors' dogs joined the chorus as they had on that earlier night.

After a block, the boys stopped to laugh. As before, they laughed until their legs couldn't carry them. Then they sat down in the street and laughed some more. That would teach Mr. Ricketts to interfere with their fun!

"Okay, that's enough," Jed said when the laughter subsided. "Let's split up. Everybody go home."

As before, Buddy turned north to the road behind Miss Childress's house. It was deserted, as he knew it would be. He laughed again. He'd like to see Mr. Ricketts get his chair down! They'd showed *him*. And just wait till next time!

He looked toward the dark, wooded hill between the road and the back of Miss Childress's house. Was something moving there in the darkness? He stopped and looked more closely.

He saw nothing.

"Imagination," he whispered to himself. "No one ever goes there."

A chill ran up his back. He shivered and hurried home.

"How was prayer meeting?" his mother asked.

Buddy gave her his brightest smile. "It was real good, Mama. I think I'll go again next week."

***

Later that evening, Vesta Childress listened as her back screen banged shut. Jimmy had departed as abruptly as he'd arrived. Lying still in her bedroom, Vesta heard his unsteady progress through the woods behind her house. He should know it well by now, but tonight his drinking made him clumsy.

She heard him blunder into something and fall, but at least he made little noise. She'd made her demand for secrecy quite clear. Thus far, he'd honored it. Presently she heard his truck engine start, quietly, beyond the hill. No truck door slamming. Only the engine starting, then fading into the night.

The low flame in the gas heater gave her room an eerie blue light. The flame popped and flickered yellow, subsided again into blue. The air remained hot and dry to push back the cold dark outside.

Her affair had brought the passion she'd longed for, but she hadn't yet come to grips with its aftermath. This strange emotional null: Was this the satisfaction she'd heard about? Or only emptiness?

The image of Ben Patterson appeared in her mind. Two days ago she'd panicked when she feared he'd discovered her secret. Now she realized he hadn't, that his questions were an attempt to get to know her. Probably a good man, she thought, for all his brusqueness. If she'd met him before she accepted Jimmy . . .

Vesta rose from the bed and opened the taps on the bathtub. While it filled, she revisited the rooms she and Jimmy had used, putting out bowls of vinegar to take up the whiskey smell. It turned stale so quickly . . .

She bathed in water as hot as she could stand, trying to wash away the emptiness. Then she paused before the mirror, combing the rich brown hair that fell loosely onto her bare shoulders. It had become tangled. She fought unsuccessfully with the tangles, but abandoned the effort. She'd deal with them tomorrow.

Lovingly, she put on a long-sleeved nightgown. It was the special gown, white batiste adorned with lace and frill that she'd bought years before for the honeymoon that never happened.

Too restless to sleep, she moved to the oak secretary. It no longer carried the photograph of William Bradley but, as before, the dowels' shadows formed a pattern of bars on the wall above her.

Vesta always cheered herself with reading when low moods troubled her, but tonight's drab sadness was the worst she could remember. It wasn't dramatic and poignant like grief, where one could name a specific cause. She'd learned long ago how to deal with that. This was much more terrible, an all-encompassing sense that someone had let the air out of everything.

What reading could assuage that dread feeling? Robert Browning, perhaps? He was such an optimist. Taking the book from the shelf, she looked for the right poem. No, not "Love Among the Ruins." Not tonight. She opened the book at random and read:

Grow old along with me!
The best is yet to be,

The last of life, for which the first was made . . .

No, not that one, either. That hope had died years ago on Tarawa with William Bradley. She flipped the pages again. Ah! Here was a lively one about Mardi Gras in Venice!

She surrendered to the poem's vigorous rhythm and sensuous images:

Did young people take their pleasure when the sea was warm in May?
Balls and masks begun at midnight, burning ever to mid-day . . .

Exactly what she needed, Vesta thought. Now smiling, she read on:

Was a lady such a lady, cheeks so round and lips so red,—
On her neck the small face buoyant like a bell-flower on its bed,
O'er the breast's superb abundance . . .

Wonderful, she thought, the very promise of passion. But . . . but why must the poem grow so grim? Her smile died as she forced herself to continue:

As for Venice and its people, merely born to bloom and drop,
Here on earth they bore their fruitage, mirth and folly were the crop.
What of soul was left, I wonder, when the kissing had to stop?

The flame in the gas heaters sputtered, flickered yellow, and returned to deep blue. The air continued hot and dry. Deep-lined shadows of the dowels grew darker on the wall.

As she had done so many nights before, Vesta Childress sank forward upon the book, rested her head upon her arms, and wept.

Chapter 23

Later that night, Jack sat alone in his kitchen and tried unsuccessfully to read. He had moved the table and lowered the shades so he wouldn't present a target to the unknown sniper. He'd lived with the consciousness of danger for days, but that wasn't what bothered him now. Nor was it the sense of isolation he felt after skipping church on Sunday and prayer meeting tonight. Cutting himself off from the community he loved was inconvenient, but it still wasn't what bothered him. What did, eating into his insides like acid, was his inability to banish the image of Lisa Kemper from his mind.

He'd been thinking of her on Monday when Ralph McKenzie brought him a note saying her father would be gone most of the week. At first, Jack was glad. Kemper's absence meant he wouldn't have to pretend a civility he no longer felt. Better yet, he wouldn't be reminded of Lisa. But no matter how he fought them, his thoughts kept returning to her with regret that she'd smashed his half-formed dreams for their future.

For three days now he'd sleepwalked through his work, haunted by the memory of her smile, her quick wit, and her courage in the two dangerous situations they'd shared. Why would a girl like that waste herself on a boor like Alex?

The drone of a motor vehicle approached on the road below his house. It grew louder, then disintegrated into a series of scrapes and crunches followed by silence. Had someone driven into the ditch? Throwing on a jacket and grabbing his truck keys, Jack ran outside. Yes, he saw a pair of headlights down on the road, but he heard no engine. Someone had trouble.

Hurriedly, Jack drove his own truck to the scene. A dark-colored pickup, westbound, sat canted at a forty-five degree angle, its left wheels sunk in the left-hand ditch and its right wheels suspended in air.

Jack left his own truck, climbed onto the tilted vehicle's running board and yanked on the passenger door handle. The door did not budge. He played his flashlight beam through the window and saw a man crumpled against the driver's door, his face covered with blood. Hastily, realizing he had to lift the heavy door against the force of gravity, Jack tried again. This time he grasped the handle with both hands, squatted with his feet planted on the side of the tilted vehicle, and thrust upward with the full strength of legs, arms, and back.

The door came open, but its weight kept trying to force it closed. Jack removed his jacket and used it to wedge the door partially open. He slid into the passenger seat and again played his light on the driver. Only then did he recognize Jimmy Fletcher.

"Jimmy!" Jack shook his friend's shoulder. "It's Jack. Are you hurt bad?"

Jimmy opened bleary eyes and squinted against the light. "Panther," he mumbled. His right hand grasped for a handshake that wasn't there, then flopped back to his side. The smell of whiskey filled the cab. "Teammates," Jimmy muttered, his speech slurred. "Only worthwhile thing in town."

Was Jimmy badly hurt or only drunk? Examining his friend's head, Jack found a single split in the skin of the forehead. The bleeding had stopped. He could find no other injury.

"Come on, Jimmy. We have to get you out of here." Jack shook his friend awake again, then half-coaxed and half-lifted him outside and into Jack's truck. Inside, Jimmy dozed off again.

Jack left him there while he decided what to do about Jimmy's truck, now a danger to any car that happened along. In the end, he put out railroad flares as a warning and left the truck's lights on. Caring for his friend came first.

At the house, Jimmy woke up enough to help Jack get him inside and into a kitchen chair. He managed to sit more or less still while Jack cleaned and dressed the head wound.

"What happened, Jimmy?" Jack finished taping the bandage on.

"Road slipped out from under me," Jimmy mumbled, his eyes unfocused. "Never did that before."

Jack thought for a moment. All the bootleggers he'd heard of operated well west of town in Branch Bottom, near Jimmy's own place. Yet Jimmy had obviously done his drinking in town or near it, and was headed home.

"Where had you been?" Jack asked. If a bootlegger was conducting business near his farm, he wanted to know.

Jimmy's eyes closed and a sly grin spread across his face. Seeing that further questioning was futile, Jack stripped off Jimmy's jacket and muddy shoes, carried the larger man's dead weight into the bedroom, and laid him on the bed.

"Where?" Eyes still closed, Jimmy muttered vague syllables: ". . . dried-up . . . li . . ." followed presently by something that sounded like "very . . . um-m-m-m-m." His voice dwindled into silence.

Jack ignored the words and turned to the matter of Jimmy's truck. Not too difficult a task for a farm boy who'd grown up solving his own problems. He checked Jimmy's pockets for the ignition keys but did not find them.

He shook his friend's shoulder. "Where are the keys, Jimmy?" No answer. He shook him again and shouted in his ear, "The keys!"

Jimmy roused enough to whisper "Truck," then sank back into sleep.

Jack kept a tow chain in his own pickup. With this, he soon had Jimmy's truck back on the road. One of Jimmy's fenders had been crushed onto a tire, but a few minutes' work with a crowbar moved it enough to make the vehicle driveable. Now all Jack had to do was move both vehicles up to the farm.

Jimmy's first. In the cab, he found no keys in the ignition lock. Using his flashlight, he made a hasty search about the seat. No keys. He slid over to the passenger seat and opened the glove compartment. What he saw there made him gasp.

He found the keys. But among the clutter of the ill-kept compartment, his flashlight beam reflected from the coppery jackets of two .30 caliber rifle bullets.

***

Thursday, February 12

Jack woke suddenly after a night of troubled sleep, surprised to find himself in his parents' bedroom. Then he remembered. He'd given his own room to Jimmy Fletcher. He dressed hurriedly, then checked on his teammate. He found Jimmy peacefully asleep, the corners of his mouth turned upward in what seemed a secret smile.

Jack shaved and put the coffee on, then shook his friend awake.

Jimmy woke with a frown that dissolved into a grin. "Hello, Teammate. How'd I get here?"

"You drove your truck in the ditch. I didn't think you'd want to spend the night there."

Jimmy's grin widened. "You're right about that. How bad is the truck?"

"It's driveable. Barely. Let's have some breakfast, and you can look at it."

"I'll settle for coffee." Jimmy made a face. "I don't feel hungry."

Regardless, Jack cooked bacon and eggs for two. Jimmy struggled with the first few bites but then dug in like a lumberjack. Jack marveled at his friend's appetite after being so thoroughly drunk. Jimmy must have the stomach of a goat.

When they finished, Jack reluctantly broached the subject he'd often discussed with Jimmy before. "Teammate, you can't go on like this. You need to sober up. Get a job. Make yourself a place in the community." He didn't yet mention church. With Jimmy that was opening a hornet's nest.

Jimmy showed an irreverent grin. "I came out of Branch Bottom—bootlegger country. This town will never forget that. Our team is the only thing I've ever been a part of."

"People change, Jimmy. Jacob Weaver used to be a bootlegger in Branch Bottom. Now he's a respected businessman and a deacon of the church. You can do the same. Besides, you need the Lord's help to find a purpose in life. Once you do that and get a steady job, you'll become part of the town."

Jimmy's eyes blazed. "Lord or no Lord, job or no job, I still live in Branch Bottom. There's no way they'd ever let me be a deacon." The anger suddenly vanished and the grin returned. He pushed back his chair and stood. "Besides, I'm having fun. Did you say my truck was driveable?"

"More or less." Jack pointed toward the two bullet holes high on the wall. "You haven't noticed the new ornaments for my kitchen." Getting this point across would be ticklish.

Jimmy eyed them without expression. "Looks like somebody helped you decorate."

"More than I needed. If he comes back, I'll have to pay the bill with interest."

Jimmy lifted one shoulder in a gesture of dismissal. "Be careful, Panther. I'd hate to lose a teammate over something foolish like that."

Jack let a smile soften his words. "I'd hate to lose a teammate over *anything* foolish. Try staying sober. And be careful where you drive."

They exchanged the ritual handshake. With a laugh, Jimmy was gone. Sadly, Jack listened to the sound of his friend's truck fading into the distance. He'd failed again to persuade Jimmy to become part of church and community, and he was no closer to solving the mystery of the sniper. The cartridges in Jimmy's truck proved nothing.

Something heavier and more puzzling nagged at his mind, too. Logically, his recurrent nightmare should be related to his endangerment by the sniper—a subconscious warning, perhaps. Yet his instincts found no connection. Perplexed, he put the problem aside and set about the day's work.

After getting things started at the plant, he drove into town and stood uncomfortably before Sheriff Rainwater's desk. "The sniper business . . ." he began. "I don't know if this means anything . . ." He waited for some response from Rainwater but received only a deadpan stare. "I found two cartridges for an M-1 rifle in the glove compartment of Jimmy Fletcher's truck."

Rainwater stroked his chin. "An' why was you poking around Jimmy's truck?"

"He needed me to drive it for him. I was looking for the keys." Jack's discomfort grew as he realized how lame it sounded.

The sheriff squinted, but the stare remained. "So you think maybe it was Jimmy what shot at you? I thought you teammates was thick as flies at a outdoor bake sale."

"I thought so, too," Jack said. "Now I don't know what to think. None of it makes sense."

"None of what? Something more than two cartridges?"

"Nothing concrete, except—"

Rainwater's eyes grew hard. "Except what?"

Jack felt his face redden. "Jimmy has too much money. He hasn't worked since he got back from the war more than two years ago. He couldn't have saved that much money in service. Maybe we ought to find out what he actually did in the Marines."

Rainwater lifted one shoulder. "I figgered he was bootlegging like his ol' man did. But come to think of it, I never heard nobody say so." His gaze shifted to the wall above Jack's head. "I guess Jimmy'd know your place well enough to get away from you twice on it."

After a long silence, his gaze returned to Jack. "Well, I got nothing else to go on. Let me fiddle with this an' see what I can come up with."

***

Lisa's spirits sank lower as the week progressed. The cold, wet weather sent a chill through her bones, and on that Thursday morning two more dead squirrels appeared on her porch. Someone must really have it in for her. Or her father. She wondered why.

"What's wrong, Lisa?" Rose asked over coffee that morning. "You've been sunk in the glums all week."

"The weather, I guess." She knew it was a trite excuse, but her father wanted to keep the squirrel problem quiet while the sheriff worked on it. Besides, there must be other reasons for her depression if she could only find them. "Maybe I'm just lonely without Dad. I worry about him when he's away on business, and he hasn't called."

"Has anyone made trouble about Saturday night?"

"Not really." Lisa welcomed the change of subject. "Mrs. Pendleton acted cool, but Precious was the same as always. Everyone else seems the same. Maybe no one but the Pendletons knows about Alex and Precious."

"They won't if Honey Pendleton has her way."

Lisa glanced downward. "I've never been so embarrassed. Alex had changed so much since last spring, and all for the worse."

Rose's tone was reassuring. "Everyone knows he embarrassed you. All evening long you looked like someone waiting for the other shoe to drop."

Lisa showed a rueful smile. "I expected the other *one* to drop, but I didn't expect Alex to be a centipede."

Rose chuckled. "Or an octopus, either, I suppose. Have you talked to all of your guests?"

"All but Jack." Lisa felt blood rush to her face and hoped Rose wouldn't notice. "He didn't answer his phone. That's why Ralph had to take him the note about Dad's being gone. He wasn't at church Sunday or prayer meeting last night."

"That isn't like Jack." Rose pursed her lips. "He's almost always there. Something to do with his parents' death, I've always thought."

Lisa's interest surged. "What really happened to his parents? All I've heard is that they died in an accident while he was overseas."

"A horrible accident. I didn't see it, but I've imagined it a hundred times. Some nights I still dream about it."

They sat in silence for a few moments. Then Rose began her story.

"Sarah Davis and I came here to teach in the same year—Sarah Boyd she was back then. We roomed with a family named Quincy in a house that used to stand where the gym is now. We spent many a night in front of the fireplace, talking and watching the coals burn down to embers. That was before butane gas came in."

Rose sighed. "We talked about our dates in the first two years and our wedding plans in the third. By then I was engaged to Ralph, and Calvin Davis had convinced Sarah to marry him. Not that it took much convincing. I kept on teaching after marriage, but Sarah gave full time to Cal and the farm."

Lisa felt drawn into Rose's memories. "Did you stay close friends?"

"Cordial, but not close. We talked to each other at church functions. Ralph and Cal swapped techniques of farming. We always said we'd take a two-family vacation together, but we never got around to it. Now it's too late."

"What actually happened?"

"It was a Monday afternoon in December, 1944." Rose looked again into the distance. "The morning began cold, with frost on the ground, but by noon it seemed warm as spring—you know this Mississippi winter. Sarah and Cal had been gone a week, something about a funeral in Arkansas. That part has never been clear to me. People saw them in town that morning, but they were back at their farm by noon. That's when Mr. Miller came over to borrow some bales of hay for his cows."

Rose blinked back a tear. "Mr. Miller was already getting frail, and afterward he regretted letting Calvin do the sweaty work with the bales. He said Cal was happy as a duck in a corn crib. Cal talked about celebrating something, but Mr. Miller didn't get it straight 'cause he had his mind on the hay.

"That's the last time anyone saw the Davises alive. Late that afternoon, on the Shipley highway, they got tangled up with a gasoline truck. No one knows how. People came when they saw the fire, but it was too late to help. Sarah and Cal and the truck driver were burned beyond recognition."

Rose shuddered. "It took dental records to make the identification. That was a long time ago, but it's still gruesome to remember. Sarah was so soft and feminine."

Lisa felt a pang of guilt for making Rose relive a sorrow, but curiosity drove her to press further. "Jack didn't come home for the funeral?"

"The Army couldn't find him. The Battle of the Bulge had begun, and somehow they lost him for a month or more in the confusion. When they did find him, there wasn't much he could do. He wrote the church and asked if the deacons would find someone to sharecrop his farm till he got home. They did, of course. Harry Pendleton was a real prince about it."

Lisa hoped for more detail, but Rose had other ideas.

"Enough of that sad stuff," she said, wiping a tear with her handkerchief. "You said you were going to try Brother Smallwood's ideas about prayer. Are they working out?"

Lisa hoped she didn't look as helpless as she felt. "No results. Everything feels just the same." Actually, it felt worse. The sadness of Rose's story pushed Lisa deeper into depression.

"You have to keep at it," Rose counseled. "Like Brother Smallwood said, the effects of prayer are cumulative. And some are very subtle. For me it's like part-singing in a choir. You get a deep pleasure of . . . of *rightness* . . . just from being in harmony, from *living* in harmony. And you reach a point where you know instantly when you're not."

"You make it sound wonderful." Lisa felt a twinge of envy. "I'll keep trying, but I'm not getting any answers. I'm as uncertain about everything now as I was when I started."

Rose's eyes twinkled. "Are you still uncertain about Alex?"

Chapter 24

Friday, February 13

Ben Patterson returned to Beneficent at noon, surprised again that he was glad to be back.

"It's turning cold out there," he announced as he walked into the sheriff's office.

"S'posed to drop below freezing tonight," Sheriff Rainwater said. "I hope you brought your long johns."

Patterson laughed and eased into a chair. "I'm never without them in winter. I hope Mrs. Telebit paid her gas bill."

"Yep. What'd you find down there in the Delta?"

"Flat country." Patterson avoided a smile. "It makes ant hills look like the Alps."

Rainwater did not take the bait. "Find Crystal Creek okay?"

Patterson jerked a quick nod. "I found a town by that name. After a two-hour search I found the creek, which wasn't as big as a self-respecting irrigation ditch. Hardly enough water to make good mud. The only crystal was a busted RC Cola bottle somebody'd thrown in it."

"Did you talk with Mr. Millbar?"

"I talked with him." Patterson snorted. "Odd kind of fellow. About five feet four and so fat he walks like a walrus. Round head, bald on top with fringe on the sides and back. Nose like the knob on a dresser drawer." He took a deep breath and leaned back. "Would you believe he wears a neatly trimmed, thin little mustache like Errol Flynn in the movies?"

Rainwater's expression did not change. "Maybe he's just staying in character as a traveling salesman. What did he have to say?"

"Volumes. Encyclopedias. Gave me a travelogue of his territory and told me how to sell to five different kinds of dentists. Seemed disappointed that all I wanted was what he saw between Beneficent and Cherry Grove on January ninth."

"Well, what did he see?"

"One vehicle, car or small truck, just outside Beneficent, headed east. No pedestrians and no other traffic before Cherry Grove. We can depend on it because when Millbar's on the road he plays a game with himself, counting traffic. He remembers that night because he almost never sees just one car between towns."

"That one vehicle would be Ronnie Parker headed back to town after Callie decided to walk home. Did Millbar see her or any sign of the other westbound vehicle Ronnie saw?"

"No sign of either. He said the road was so empty he thought maybe the Rapture'd come and he'd been left behind."

Rainwater grunted. "If it had, he'd have had plenty of company out in Branch Bottom."

He squinted and thoughtfully rubbed his chin. "Ronnie Parker said he saw two cars headed west. If he and Millbar are both telling the truth, Millbar was driving the second vehicle. Somebody in the first had already picked Callie up, carted her off the road, and prob'ly killed her before Millbar come along."

He cast a sad gaze at Patterson. "We've been on this case five weeks tonight an' we still don't have no idea who that somebody is. I'm as confused as a real estate salesman in a sandstorm."

Patterson stirred in his chair. "You've said it has to be somebody local, or Callie wouldn't have accepted a ride."

"That narrows it down to the eight thousand four hundred and fifty-six people who live in Coosa County."

"You can narrow it again." Patterson ticked off the possibilities on his fingers. "Count out the Negroes, about forty-three percent of the population. Right or wrong, Callie wouldn't have gotten in the car with one of them. The same applies to the Gypsies, so you can count out most of them. Callie would have put up a fight if she'd been abducted, but there were no marks on her body. That brings it down to maybe a couple of hundred people she knew well enough to trust."

Rainwater wrinkled his nose. "That puts us right back where we started five weeks ago. We've questioned everybody west of town twice already, and we still don't have a clue. If the weather turns as bad as they say, we'll be too busy to question 'em again for another week. You got any ideas?"

Patterson spread his hands, palms upward. "There's no statute of limitations on murder. We have time whether we like it or not. What we have to do is keep our eyes and ears open." After a long pause, he added, "And pray for a break."

***

Just after noon as the temperature dropped and black clouds swirled in from the northwest, Jack sent his construction crew home to prepare for bad weather. At his own farm he found a note on the door.

Jack: I put two horses in your barn in case the weather turns real bad. Remember what your father and I did in '40?

Yours truly,
Hiram Rakestraw

Jack remembered vividly: the first significant snow of his life, a whole six inches of it. In Mississippi, snows that deep came only once or twice a decade. Coosa County, then and now, kept no snow removal equipment, nor did motorists bother to buy snow tires or chains. It cost less to shut everything down for a few days until the snow melted.

The downside was that some families, especially the poor without radios or telephones, would be caught unprepared. Some lacked adequate clothing and had to huddle by their fireplaces until the weather broke. In 1940, when snow-covered roads rendered automobiles useless, Hiram Rakestraw and Calvin Davis had gone on horseback to see to their neighbors' needs.

Jack phoned Hiram and thanked him. "I remember what you and Dad did," he said, "but not how you divided the territory."

"I'll check on everyone from Branch Bottom to your place," Hiram said. "You look to everyone from there into town."

"The forecast isn't that bad, but I'll be ready just in case."

After hanging up, Jack moved his own small herd into the barn and sorted them out into stalls separate from the two horses. As he forked hay for them, he was glad he'd converted two stalls into a ground-level hay bin. That freed him from storing bales in the barn's old hayloft and retrieving them with block and tackle, an operation too cumbersome for one man.

A cold drizzle was falling when Jack left the barn, and ice had already formed on the trees. Later, from his porch, he watched the sad spectacle as winter-black tree limbs turned to leaden gray and bent low under their burden of ice. He would lose timber before this was over.

A snapping sound from down on the road drew his attention. An electric wire fell from its pole. For a few moments it writhed on the ground, hissing and exuding a profusion of sparks. Then all was quiet. Inside the house, Jack confirmed that the electricity was off. Wires would be down all over the county. He wondered how Lisa and her father would fare. They'd be used to cold weather, but only in an area equipped to handle it. Here, they'd be on their own. Kemper was Jack's boss. Maybe he ought to call and report on things at the plant. But Lisa might answer.

Her tolerance of Alex stung Jack again. He hesitated before the phone in the hallway. Determined not to give in to jealousy, he lifted the phone's earpiece from its cradle.

The line was dead. He could have saved himself the argument.

Jack cooked a quick supper and ate by candlelight, then turned off the gas burners and went to bed early. In the quickly chilling darkness, he wondered again about Lisa. How would she fare in this weather?

She'll do just fine, his resentment said. *So sophisticated and sure of herself.*

But she's in a strange land here, his reason argued back.

His mind drifted in half-sleep. Lisa, solemn and sympathetic over his parents' graves . . . laughing and playful at the juke box in Shipley . . . spunky and game as could be, making jokes under sniper fire . . . fiercely independent at the suggestion Hollis Wilson might have a claim on her. Her variety of moods and her quick wit would keep any man fully occupied for a lifetime.

What a crime to waste it all on a jerk like Alex!

After a dreamless night, Jack woke to the cold darkness of his room, thankful again that his nightmare had not visited. But what had wakened him? From long habit, he lay still and listened. Not a sound. No cars on the road. None of the bird songs that usually accompanied his waking. Not even a whisper of wind.

False dawn faintly distinguished the windows from the greater darkness. Why this complete silence? He arose in the cold room and lit the gas heater, comforted by its reassuring hiss. He dressed quickly by candlelight, careful to layer the clothing as he'd learned in the Army, then pulled on calf-high leather boots he hadn't worn for years.

Only then did he venture onto the porch to check the weather. In the dim pre-dawn light he saw nothing but white, a landscape buried beneath at least six inches of snow. That explained the silence. For a moment, he stood in awe at the sheer beauty of it, so rarely seen in Southern climes. Then the damage made itself evident: a huge limb broken from a great oak and several young pines bent over to the ground.

The trees had received a coating of ice and then the added weight of snow. He'd lose more of his timber than he'd thought, and Coosa County would count its losses in millions. But he couldn't worry about it now. He had work to do.

The gray gloom that passed for full daylight found him with both horses prepared, the big paint saddled for riding and the bay mare fitted for cargo. His territory included thirteen families, both black and white, in houses and cabins scattered along trails and paths that branched off from the county road. Their needs might well add up to a full load for the mare.

No snow was falling, but the temperature held well below freezing. The horses' breath steamed in the frigid air, and the chill stiffened the skin on Jack's cheeks. He snugged his wool Army scarf tighter around his neck and pulled his hat lower. He'd soldiered through worse in Europe, but that didn't make today's weather any more pleasant. Grasping the lead rein of the bay, he dug his heels into the paint's sides and urged him toward the road.

The big animal moved sure-footedly on the snow, which packed under his feet and shielded him from the slippery ice underneath. Jack held him to a cautious walk at first, then allowed freer movement as horse and rider gained confidence in the unfamiliar conditions. The unbroken snow bore witness they were the morning's first travelers.

Ten minutes later, Jack hallooed the first farmhouse on his route. The family was surprised to see him and happy to be spared the trouble of a supply run into town.

"Don't know if my mule'd make it," the farmer said. "Snow's got him flusterated. He keeps trying to eat it in place of hay, an' he kicks like fury when it don't satisfy."

Jack listed the family's needs and proceeded on his route. Some families had few needs and some had many, but all thanked him for coming. Noon found him delivering their lists to stores in town, all of which readily extended credit.

No cars could be seen on the downtown streets, and the number of horses and mules tethered there took Jack back to pre-war days. While the stores filled his orders, he tied his horses in front of the drugstore/café and stopped in for a hamburger. The air inside was warm from the gas heaters, and oil lamps cast a soft light over everything.

"We haven't seen you for a while," Mrs. Harding said when she took his order. "Where've you been hiding?"

"Just busy." Jack kept his voice matter-of-fact. "How're things in town?"

"No electricity and no phones, but otherwise okay. You know Beneficent: Everyone's helping everybody else. Jed Stoddard organized some young folks to carry water for people whose pipes burst." She laughed. "Buddy Robinson staggered around with a tub of water as big as he is."

"Can the delivery trucks get through?"

"Not yet, but most of the stores can run four or five days with what they have in stock." She looked toward the front door, which opened to admit Mrs. Telebit. Mrs. Harding's facial expression froze and she called toward the kitchen, "Martha!" She disappeared into the pharmacy at the rear of the store, leaving Mrs. Telebit standing at the front counter. Martha, the Negro cook, brought Jack's hamburger and coffee from the kitchen, then waited on Mrs. Telebit.

Jack chewed his lip in frustration. *Same silly feud. Won't they ever call it off?*

Mrs. Telebit paid for her purchase and left. Mrs. Harding returned to the front counter. Soon afterward, Ronnie Parker entered, cheeks rosy from the cold.

"I got the information about the Army for you," Jack said. "They want you to finish high school before you join."

Ronnie absorbed the news stoically. "I knew what they'd tell me, but I didn't want to hear it. Things aren't getting any better either at home or in town."

"I know it's tough," Jack said, "but you can stick it out. After what you're going through, Army training will be a cinch."

Ronnie left and Jack approached the counter to pay his bill.

"How is Lisa doing in this snow?" Mrs. Harding asked. "It ought to be old stuff for her."

"I haven't seen her in a week." Jack's voice sounded more harsh than he intended.

Mrs. Harding didn't seem to notice. "She sure shipped out that Alex creature in a hurry. He came for a week's visit on Saturday and she sent him back to Yankeeland on Sunday morning. Good riddance, I say."

Joy flooded through Jack's veins, but he refused to let it show in his voice. "Oh? I hadn't heard."

Outside, the weather seemed colder and a rising wind chilled his cheeks. Jack snugged his scarf again and, as he collected his orders from the stores, pondered Mrs. Harding's news. Should he visit Lisa?

No, he told himself. He'd allowed his hopes to outpace reality once. He wouldn't do that again.

His supplies loaded, he guided his horses toward the westward road. For the first time, they seemed reluctant. Or was he the one who was dragging? He was sure he'd made the right decision. Let Lisa wait.

He reached the street that led northward to her house. The horses stopped. Jack's irritation grew as he hesitated, questioning himself and becoming more conscious of the cold.

"All right," he said to the horses. "Maybe you know something I don't." He headed them north, turned into Lisa's yard, and hitched their reins to a shrub. Mr. Kemper's Frazer was not in the driveway. With growing misgivings, Jack mounted the porch, removed his hat, and knocked on the door.

At length, Lisa answered, her face solemn. Sad or not, though, she looked stunning in black wool slacks and sweater with a blue kerchief tied at her neck. She held the wooden door open as she had on Jack's first visit, leaving the screen door latched. It seemed like a steel barrier between them.

He found himself stammering. "I . . . uh . . . is your father here? I thought I'd tell him how things are going at the plant."

Lisa's face remained unchanged. "He's still in Indiana. Iced in. He called yesterday before the phones went out."

"When he calls again," Jack said, "would you tell him we're almost finished? I think three days will complete the job."

"I will tell him." Her voice was flat.

An awkward silence followed. "Do you need anything?" Jack motioned toward the horses. "I have to take these things to my neighbors, but I can bring you anything you need from town."

"Thank you. I walked down this morning and got what I needed." Her gaze held his as if something were left unsaid.

Jack shifted his feet. "I guess I'd better get started." He stepped backward, then turned to go.

"Jack, I'm sorry about Alex." Lisa spoke as if each word brought pain. "He wasn't like that last year. I couldn't believe he was so rude to all of you Saturday night. Dad called to apologize, but you didn't answer."

Chagrin, relief, and hope mingled in Jack's emotions. "It's all right," he said. "You couldn't choose his words for him."

A smile brightened her face. "I didn't know you kept horses. I enjoyed the riding classes back at school."

Jack returned the smile with enthusiasm. "Hiram Rakestraw lent them to me. Say, things ought to be under control by Monday. If you'd like, we could make a horseback tour of the farm. It's really beautiful in the snow."

"I'd love to, Jack. But what about the sniper?"

"He won't dare show up. He can't cover his tracks in the snow. Would nine-thirty be too early?"

"That will be fine."

Jack mounted the paint and pointed it toward home. He paused at the street and looked back. Lisa still stood in the doorway. She lifted her hand in a brief wave.

Jack returned her wave and nudged his horses into a trot.

The wind had grown sharper, but he did not feel the cold.

Chapter 25

Monday, February 16

For Lisa, the weekend had seemed interminable. Happy to be back on good terms with Jack and delighted at the prospect of a ride through the snow-covered countryside, she chafed at the slow passage of hours.

Church on Sunday morning had brought some respite. The small group of worshipers who walked to church through the snow made up for its size by enthusiasm. Dark clouds hid the sun and left the unlighted sanctuary too deep in gloom for anyone to read a hymn book, but the song leader led the congregation through medleys of hymns everyone knew by heart. Brother Smallwood topped it off with a rousing sermon on perseverance in the face of adversity.

Afterwards, though, time resumed its snail's pace. In the empty house, Lisa wondered if she expected too much from Monday's ride. Jack had seemed terribly reserved. She cautioned herself not to expect anything from him. The ride itself would have to be enough.

Monday morning, she dressed in boots, black wool slacks, and a light gray sweater set off by a rose kerchief. Near the front door she laid her outer wear from Indiana: red mittens and a black weatherproof jacket with a hood. Not normally vain, she nevertheless checked her appearance three times in the full-length mirror before Jack knocked on the door.

He wore the same boots and jacket he'd worn on Saturday, and he again held the broad-brimmed hat in front of him. A gusty wind tousled his sand-colored hair. His approving look rewarded Lisa for her efforts in front of the mirror.

"You look great," he said. "Still game for a ride?"

"To anywhere," she said, happy simply to get out of the house. "I don't care if we ride all the way to Spain."

Jack's slow grin did not reveal his thoughts. "These horses can't last beyond Bermuda. But if we take the western route, maybe we can get fresh ones in Hawaii."

She laughed at his jest, but to hide her increasing consciousness of him, she rushed ahead toward the horses waiting in the driveway.

"I thought you'd like the bay mare," Jack said. "Her name is Priscilla."

"She'll do fine," Lisa said, pleased to find the stirrup height had been adjusted exactly right for her. She felt even more gratified at how easily the animal responded to the reins.

"She's well-trained," Lisa called to Jack as they cleared the town and cantered westward.

Jack threw her an approving look. "Be sure to tell Hiram Rakestraw. Training horses is a point of pride with him."

Lisa made no reply, but surrendered to the pleasure of the ride—the beauty of snow-covered landscape, the exhilarating chill of cold air on her cheeks, and her joyful sense of the powerful but well-controlled animal moving beneath her. Most of all, she enjoyed a sense of freedom after several days of being almost housebound.

The road had been well traveled by horses, but there were no vehicle tracks. Too much snow for cars without chains, Lisa guessed. Then the storm damage drew her attention and limited her feeling of exhilaration. Many white-encrusted trees, somber beneath dark clouds, had lost limbs to the weight of ice and snow. A few had toppled over and lay with their earth-entangled roots thrust upward through the snow's white mantle.

No beauty without pain.

The ice-coated power lines beside the road showed many breaks. No wonder Beneficent had no power! Entire new lines must be strung, and the larger towns would undoubtedly come first.

Turning into Jack's driveway, Lisa saw that a number of his trees were damaged. As they walked the horses toward the house, she watched Jack's face to discover his response to the damage. He showed none. Indeed, he seemed more at ease than usual as he reined in beside the house. Whistling, he dismounted, broke the surface ice from a tub of water that stood under a hydrant, and let the horses drink.

Jack's glance at Lisa seemed completely carefree. "Do you need a rest, or are you game for more riding?"

"Still game." Her sadness at the storm damage vanished before his enthusiasm. "What's next, maestro?"

"We'll follow the same route we walked on your last visit," he said, remounting. "For openers, ride past the corner of the house and tell me what you see." His face showed the smugness of someone who knew a secret but wouldn't tell.

She raised an eyebrow but complied with his directions, reassured only slightly by his following close behind. Passing the corner, she scanned the immediate surroundings. She saw nothing unusual. Then, lifting her eyes, she caught her breath as she suddenly understood Jack's secret.

The snow-covered landscape held a pristine beauty no painter could hope to capture. Immediately before her, the land sloped down into the pleasant valley where Jack hoped to build a lake. The valley itself lay quiescent as if asleep beneath its cover of white. On the ridgeline beyond, snow-filled trees blended with the darker gray of low clouds scudding swiftly across their tops. Between trees and clouds, a solitary hawk beat back against the wind, then turned and glided with it, disappearing beyond the trees. An austere, almost audible silence hung over everything.

"It's beautiful, Jack," she murmured. "Absolutely perfect."

"I thought you'd like it." His face showed pleasure akin to hers as he reined in beside her. Still, he seemed to be holding something back.

Lisa gazed at the valley again, searching now for some hidden detail. She saw nothing she hadn't seen on first viewing. She looked to her left, where at a distance the barn's black roof thrust up into low clouds. A multiplicity of tracks between house and barn attested to Jack's care of his animals.

Tracks! That was it! The snow to her front showed no tracks at all. Her mind raced with that fact's implications, which suddenly coalesced into delight.

"Jack, there are no tracks out there. That means . . . did you . . . ?"

"I thought you'd enjoy seeing it like that."

"But you know your timber has been damaged. You haven't even checked to see how much?"

The easy smile again played about his face. "The damage is already done. I can't change it or clean it up till the snow clears. So why track up a good view for nothing?"

"Why track it up now? Why not keep it till the snow melts?"

"It's there to be used. I'd like you to be the first."

Thrilled at the compliment, Lisa looked for words but didn't find them. In the end, she only said "Thank you" and urged the bay mare forward into the virgin snow.

The cares and tensions that had plagued her for the past week fell away as she and Jack crossed the valley and climbed the next ridge. The snow there remained undisturbed except for tracks of small animals. Seen from that ridge, Jack's new land lay blanketed under solid white. They viewed it in silence, then turned into the timbered area he was thinning to convert into pasture. Among the ice-laden trees, every fourth or fifth had lost limbs. Some were almost stripped.

Jack viewed the damage without emotion. "Looks like the weather did some of my work for me. I'll have to get a crew in here before summer to finish the job."

In silence, then, they rode to the place where the sniper had targeted them. Strangely, that frightening incident took second place in Lisa's memory to Jack's pointing out the roof of his house—their sudden intimacy and her doubts about his intentions.

"I can see your house this time," she said. "I guess it's easier to see from horseback. I haven't forgotten what you said about the view from the barn loft, either."

"We need a clear day for that. All you could see from it today is the inside of a cloud." He nodded toward the farmhouse roof that showed above the trees. "Shall we ride back and have lunch?"

"Okay, podner," she said, mimicking the dialect of a western movie. "If I get any hungrier, I'll go 'on the prod.'"

Mischief danced in Jack's eyes. "Don't do that. The Bible says 'prod goeth before destruction.'"

She shook her finger at him. "The word is *pride*, Jack Davis. You don't have *that* much Southern accent."

They laughed together and rode to the barn. Jack stabled the horses and rewarded each with a feedbag of oats. "We usually feed them twice a day," he explained, "but today they need an extra meal. They still have eight miles to go."

The two-hundred-yard tramp from barn to house presented no difficulty, though the wet snow clung heavily to their feet. On the kitchen porch Lisa bent to remove her boots and leave them outside, but Jack opened the door and motioned for her to enter.

"I'll get your floors wet," she protested. Nevertheless, she stepped through the door. She found herself standing on a rag throw-rug that had not been there on her previous visit. "I might have known you'd think of that," she said, and moved to one end of the rug so Jack could enter.

He chuckled. "It's not a new problem, but we usually have mud instead of snow."

As she took her boots off, he disappeared into the adjacent room. He emerged a moment later and handed her a pair of fur-lined bedroom slippers. The linoleum floor was ice cold, but the slippers felt warm, almost hot, on her feet. Jack must have left them all morning in front of a heater. Surprisingly, they almost fit.

"You think of everything," she said. "Where did you get these? They wouldn't fit you."

"They did once. I found them tucked back in a drawer."

"You still had to think of looking for them."

"My mother said we should always prepare for company." Looking uncomfortable, he shifted subjects. "I have to change shoes, too. I'll only be a minute." He unlaced his boots and left them on the rag rug, then tiptoed sock-footed back into the bedroom.

Lisa moved to the kitchen window and, in contemplative mood, surveyed the snow-covered valley. Its crystalline beauty spoke to her in poignant language more profound than speech. She felt . . . yes . . . almost as if she and the landscape were blending into each other. Tears of something beyond pleasure rose in her eyes.

It was like—what had Rose said?—like *singing in harmony*. In this case, harmony with everything around her: with the landscape, with this comfortably lived-in house, even with Jack. But Rose had been talking about her relationship with God. Was it sacrilege to feel that way about anything else?

Jack's footsteps sounded behind her, but she held her gaze on the valley, unwilling to let go of the moment.

"I've always liked that view," he said. "Are you looking for anything in particular?"

For certainty, as always. But she said, "I was trying to find the place where you'll build the dam for your lake." With her slight falsehood, the harmony wavered.

"It's hard to see from this window." Jack touched her arm, moving her to the left, then pointed over her other shoulder. "There. Down where the two ridgelines bend toward each other and almost touch."

"I see it now."

The sense of living in harmony came back with a rush, stronger than before. Jack's pointing hand returned to rest on her shoulder. He stood quite close, his other hand still lightly touching her arm. Idly, she noticed that he smelled like soap, a clean smell so different from Alex's aggressive aftershave. And this time—yes, she was sure of it—Jack's lips *were* brushing the back of her hair.

She turned to face him, and her inquiring gaze met his. They stood for a moment in silence. Then his lips descended toward hers.

She gave herself to the kiss, fully confident now as her awareness of exquisite harmony continued undiminished.

Chapter 26

Jack's lips were firm on hers: questing, not demanding. She answered his quest, conscious of the strength and force of him but conscious also of his holding that force in control. Presently they drew apart, still half-embracing, each one's eyes questioning the other's.

"Jack," Lisa said, searching for words. "What . . . what are we doing?"

Mischief returned to his eyes. "It's called kissing."

She gave an involuntary laugh. "I know that, silly." She grew earnest again. "But what does it mean?"

"It means I like being with you and . . . and I think I'd like to be with you always."

She scanned his face. "Is that a proposal?"

He looked surprised, then thoughtful. "I guess . . ." His jaw clamped tight. "Yes . . . yes, it is."

Now it was Lisa's turn to be surprised. She searched again for words but found none.

He broke the silence. "I didn't plan it. Certainly not this way . . . so sudden. But is there a chance?" Anxiety in his face spoke the depth of his sincerity.

She chose her words with care, knowing she must be completely honest about her feelings. "It *is* sudden. And I *am* surprised." She found herself smiling. "I . . . I think I'm most surprised that I'm not saying no. Right now I'm more awed than anything else."

He nodded gravely. "It *is* awesome. I hadn't thought this through, and now all at once we're talking about the rest of our lives." He looked past her for a moment, then met her gaze. "For both our sakes, we have to get it right. It won't do to rush into something we'll regret later."

Lisa paused. Everything about this felt right. Yet how could she say so without giving Jack a hope that she might have to disappoint? "We do have to take time to be sure. This sounds terribly unromantic, but can we let it be an open question?"

Jack gave her shoulders a gentle squeeze, then released her. "An open question means we have to keep seeing each other. What's unromantic about that?" He smiled. "Speaking of things unromantic, would you like to wash your hands while I fix lunch? You know where the towels are."

"I remember." She welcomed that relief from their emotional intensity, yet at the same time she hated to let go of it.

Thoughts crowded her mind as she crossed the bedroom toward the mahogany chest of drawers: Alex's near-proposal last spring and her apprehension about it, feeling flattered but knowing she wasn't ready for a life-changing decision. In retrospect, she realized some inner dissonance had warned that Alex was not right for her.

Things were so different with Jack. She felt no dissonance. It was her head, not her heart, that told her to slow down—that their backgrounds were too different, that difficult problems must be solved. She knew both cautions were true, but still she gloried in that quiet but wonderful sense of singing in harmony—and the fact that it hadn't departed during the warmth of Jack's kiss.

She paused before the mahogany chest. Towels. Which drawer? Upper right or upper left?

Upper left, she thought, and opened the drawer. Instantly, she knew she was wrong. She looked guiltily away and shut the drawer, but its contents had already imprinted themselves on her memory. A certificate bearing the words *Silver Star Medal* and the name *1st Lt. Jachin Davis*. Beside it, the brass eagle collar emblem signifying an honorable discharge. And nearby, partially hidden under an olive drab handkerchief, a medal she recognized as the Purple Heart.

A weight of guilt formed in her stomach as she opened the top right drawer and took out a bath cloth and hand towel. The guilt remained as she washed hands and face. It diminished her pleasure at noting, this time with a warm sense of companionship, Jack's everyday personal items remembered from her first visit: the safety razor, the cup of shaving soap with brush handle protruding, the hairbrush she'd borrowed to brush sand from her hair. And all the while she wondered what to do about her intrusion—yes, *intrusion*—into Jack's privacy.

Back in the kitchen, she found that he had lunch ready: bacon, scrambled eggs and toast, the same menu he'd prepared for them before. But this time he'd chosen chocolate instead of coffee. Hers with two marshmallows, his with none.

On the table he'd placed two oil lamps. Their flickering light shone in a circle of soft gold that seemed to shield them from the gray gloom of winter. "We used lamps before we had electricity," Jack explained. "Not romantic like candlelight, but they'll have to serve."

"They'll do fine." Her prosaic words failed to express the depth of her approval.

They ate hungrily, but conversation lagged as a new constraint hung between them. A solemnity, Lisa thought, from the magnitude of their changed relationship.

"We're a fine pair," Jack said as he pushed back his plate. "Before I proposed to you, we chattered like mockingbirds. Now we don't say a word. We should be talking our heads off—discussing, questioning, maybe even fussing."

"Not fussing." Lisa tried to smile, but tears rose in her eyes. "There's something I have to tell you. I know you've always avoided questions about your military service. I didn't mean to intrude, but I opened the wrong drawer. I found your decorations."

"Nothing to cry about." Jack reached across the table and took her hands. "I've proposed to you. You have a right to know."

"I'm sure you had good reasons for not talking about it."

He released her hands and ran one of his through his hair. "Two that seem good to me. First, most people aren't really interested and wouldn't understand if I tried to explain. It's a lot simpler to keep quiet."

"And the other reason?"

"I'm sick of the people I call 'professional veterans,' the ones who brag about what they did. They act like people owe them a living because of it. We just did our job. That's all."

Images of Alex's boasting flitted through Lisa's memory. "I think I understand. Sometime when you're ready, I'd like to know as much of it as you want me to."

"You're welcome to ask anything."

"Well, I've wondered why they couldn't find you after your parents' death. You said things got confused, and Rose blamed it on the Battle of the Bulge."

Jack laughed softly. "The Bulge was well north of us, but we had our hands full, too. Mostly, my situation changed faster than the message could follow. When my parents died, I was executive officer of an Infantry company. Shrapnel in the legs put me in the hospital for a few days, so my unit forwarded the death message there. When it arrived, I'd been released. My regiment sent me as a liaison officer to the unit on its flank, and things really got mixed up."

"Wait a minute," Lisa said. "I'm confused about companies and regiments."

"Companies do the real fighting. Each one has about two hundred men. Companies make up battalions, about a thousand men each. Three battalions and support units make a regiment—maybe four thousand people, all told. A regiment exchanges liaison officers with the units on its flanks to keep them posted on each other's operations."

"I'm with you, so far." Lisa hoped she was.

"It gets worse." Jack's frown attested that it did. "When the unit I was liaison to lost communication with one of its forward elements, I said I'd go up and try to make contact. That wasn't part of my job, but my sergeant could handle things temporarily and my host unit was running out of people."

"Does that mean they'd been killed?"

"Or wounded."

Lisa was horrified at the thought, but Jack continued in a matter-of-fact voice. "The communication problem wasn't much, just green troops who didn't know how to calibrate a radio. But the unit had lost all its officers, and that made me responsible. Then the Germans counterattacked."

"You did have a mess on your hands."

"A real mess. We held our position, but we were cut off for four days. When friendly forces got through to us, we went on the attack again. Somewhere along there the death message reached me, but by then I felt closer to my men than I did to my parents. That sounds harsh, but it's the way things happen in war."

Jack turned his palms upward. "My parents would have been buried by that time, and other things didn't seem important. When my new unit finally came off the line, I wrote the church and asked the deacons to manage the farm till I got home."

"Did you ever get back to your original unit?"

"It agreed to my transfer, and the orders finally made things official."

Neither spoke as they regarded each other in the soft lamplight. Jack had evidently finished his story, and Lisa was trying to make sure she understood it.

"You left out a lot," she said. "All of that happened in the dead of winter, but you never mentioned how hard the weather made things for you. You never said what the Germans tried to do or what you did to stop them. What you did could have gotten you killed or maimed, yet you talk about it as calmly as if it were spring planting."

Jack shrugged. "I didn't get killed. The rest is just a bunch of facts. History. No use getting worked up about it now. If you let yourself get excited, you can't think straight."

"That's . . . that's one way of looking at it. Is that how you got through the war?"

"Partly." Jack spoke almost as if to himself. "I hope this doesn't sound like bragging, but . . . well, whatever came up, it seemed I could find a way to handle it. I guess that's the basic idea I live by. My hope for Beneficent, too. Good people in a good town, leading good lives and not wishing anyone harm. If we all work together, we can make things even better."

"That's quite a utopian idea." Lisa kept her voice neutral, though warning flags were flying. Callie's death and the sniper's malice had to mean *something*. So did the dead squirrels on her porch.

She decided to change the subject. "Two more questions. Your name, first: I assumed that *Jack* was a nickname for *John*, but the citation called you Jachin."

Jack made a face. "Not many people know that's what my parents named me. It means 'God establishes.' They thought people would shorten it to Jake, so they started calling me Jack. What's the other question?"

"Someone told me you enlisted, but you said you were a liaison officer. Isn't that a contradiction?"

Jack showed an easy smile. "Not really. We'd worked our way through Italy and southern France. If you hang around long enough, you get promoted. I'm still in the reserves, but inactive. I don't get called back unless we have another war." He looked at his watch, then stood. "We'd better be moving if we're going to get you home and me back here before dark. I don't want to. I'd like to keep talking."

He put out the oil lamps, and the charmed circle around them disappeared. Lisa felt the regret she'd felt as a child when her parents turned off the Christmas tree lights. But this time her inner warmth remained.

"I'd like to keep talking, too," she said, "but we'll find other times. We'll have a lot to talk about."

The understatement drew a grin from Jack. "Then it's still an open question?"

"Very much so." The joy of first discovery thrilled through her again. Her heart pleaded with her to hoist full sail and run before the wind, but her mind still counseled caution.

In a near-daze, she forced herself to the door and struggled into her boots. Jack held her coat and, as she turned and slipped her arms into it, her eyes for the first time focused on the two bullet holes high in the kitchen wall.

She froze. "Jack . . . the sniper . . . are those the bullet holes? I can't believe I sat there that long and didn't notice them."

"You had your mind on other things." The glimmer in his eyes gave the words special meaning. "I didn't want to break the spell, so I put you with your back to them."

She stamped her foot in mock anger. "While you were in Italy, you must have learned a few tricks from Machiavelli."

He feigned ignorance. "MacWho? I always thought he was a Scotsman."

Gently, Jack lifted the hood of her coat to cover her hair, then brushed a kiss onto her forehead. "That's for the open question."

"It felt more like an exclamation."

"It wasn't." He took her shoulders as if to draw her to him. "An exclamation is more like—"

"Jack!" She stopped him with a hand on his chest. "We can discuss punctuation some other time. Right now we have to go."

Laughing together, they walked through the snow to the barn and remounted their horses. Skies remained darkly overcast and the day had grown colder, but within her heart Lisa felt a roseate warmth of rightness—that now-familiar sense of singing in harmony. She wasn't jubilant, yet never before had she been so enveloped in happiness. If she kept feeling like this, Jack's question wouldn't remain open very long.

Jack led the way down the driveway toward the main road. Suddenly, his horse neighed and shied. Jack controlled him, patted his neck, and spoke soothingly to him. Lisa eased her mount forward to see what the problem was.

In the middle of the driveway, where nothing of note had been when they passed before, a patch of red blood defiled the white snow. Small animal tracks, scuffs and pits in the snow nearby gave evidence of a brief but savage struggle. At the edge of the bloody patch lay the tail of a raccoon, roughly slashed off at its root.

Lisa stared at the blatant red stain as its meaning swept through her with stunning force. The same hour that brought her and Jack their quiet discovery of love had led this small animal to a violent fate. The world that had overwhelmed her today with happiness and harmony could, without warning, deliver pain and death.

Chapter 27

With the coming of ice and snow, Beneficent seemed to leap fifty years backward in time. Oil lamps emerged from attic trunks where they'd been stored in the decade since the Tennessee Valley Authority brought in electric power. Horses and mule-drawn wagons replaced automobiles on the streets, and neighbors accustomed to visiting by telephone trudged through snow to check on each other in person. Telegraph lines were down briefly, but quickly restored. Then for several days, telegraph and railroad became the town's only contacts with the outside world.

Beneficent's apparent time-travel was only an illusion, though, for modern capabilities did exist. Mayor Shiloh Simpson and the town council considered clearing the streets with the town's one bulldozer, owned by Mr. Ricketts. However, Jacob Weaver's hasty cost estimate for repairing street damage by the bulldozer showed them the wisdom of waiting for the snow to melt.

On Monday, Sheriff Rainwater sent mounted deputies north and south along the highway. They persuaded tractor-owning farmers to break a trail into town. The tractors' mud tires worked well enough in snow, and by Tuesday evening their well-defined ruts opened the highway for travel. Delivery trucks began arriving on Wednesday, and those that replenished home supplies of butane gas were particularly welcome. Clouds still threatened, but temperatures rose and trickles of water appeared in ruts and gutters.

That afternoon, Sheriff Rainwater squinted in the dim lamplight of his office as Ben Patterson entered.

"Hello, Ben," the sheriff said. "I almost didn't recognize you without the blue-checked suit."

"It's there," replied the detective, "somewhere under this overcoat."

On second glance, Rainwater noticed a flash of blue-checked trousers between the black overcoat and the tops of new black boots that looked at least a size too small.

"It's cold enough to freeze the ears off a cornstalk," Rainwater continued. "You been keeping warm?"

"I've mostly been hugging the gas heater. What's new?"

Rainwater leaned back and clasped his hands on his paunch. "Not much. You prob'ly knew school'd been canceled 'cause the buses couldn't run. So we re-questioned the town kids and their parents about who Callie Rakestraw's friends was and where they was the night she was killed. We didn't turn up nothing helpful."

Distractedly, Patterson tapped his knuckles together. "How about people along the road where she was killed?"

Rainwater sniffed in disgust. "Snowed in. We'll question 'em again soon's the weather breaks."

Both men looked up as Deputy Brown entered with a worried look, his face redder than usual from the cold. He wore a pile cap with the ear flaps pulled down and tied under the chin.

"Sheriff," he asked, "is there really a place named Tarnation?" He removed the pile cap, allowing half-combed hair to fall disheveled onto his forehead.

"Um-m-m." Rainwater tiptoed around the question. "Why d'you ask?"

Brown's worry deepened. "You know that little church on the south edge of town? Last Sunday the preacher preached on Christ in Tarnation, and I can't find the place on my Bible maps. It ain't in the concordance, either."

Patterson cleared his throat and spoke softly. "The word he used was probably In*car*nation. It means Christ came to earth and took human form—lived in a human body."

"Heck, any fool knows He did that." Brown threw a suspicious look at the sheriff. "Is this guy pulling my leg?"

"Nope. It's Gospel truth."

Brown slapped his pile cap on a chair back and made his exit muttering "Always thought a carnation was a flower."

Rainwater and Patterson eyed each other, tight-lipped until they heard the outer door slam. Then they burst into laughter.

"You see what I got to work with?" the sheriff asked.

Patterson nodded but said, "He does a good job of interrogation."

"He's okay as long as he don't have to plan nothing." Rainwater gave his visitor a sidelong glance. "How're you liking Beneficent now that you been here a while?"

The detective looked uncomfortable. "It's a nice town, I guess. Why do you ask?"

"I'm getting no younger. Fifty-five last month. Maybe two, three more years an' I better call it quits." He looked earnestly at the younger man. "My deputies is okay, but none of 'em can handle the complete job as sheriff. You'd be a natural for it, if you took a notion."

Patterson rubbed his chin. "I already have a job in Jackson. Thanks for the compliment, though."

"Think about it. Someday you'll get tired o' being sent to odd corners of the state to solve tough cases."

"I'll keep it in mind. Speaking of cases, I heard you were checking up on this Fletcher character."

"Jack Davis thinks Jimmy might be the one what shot at him, but there's nothing definite." The sheriff wrinkled his nose. "Jimmy don't work but spends money like he did. Last Friday before the snow fell, he drove up in a new Ford truck with dealer tags. Got it Thursday in Cherry Grove. Traded in an old one with banged-up fenders, paid cash for the difference. He always pays cash. No bank account. Postmaster says he don't receive no gov'ment check, neither."

"Sounds like a real ghost. Think he's bootlegging?"

"The usual sources ain't heard about it. Jimmy tells it that he saved money in the Marines and got lucky at poker. I've asked for his service record, but got no word yet."

"Anything suggest a connection with Callie?"

Rainwater sighed. "Teammates with her brother, the one got killed in the war. Nothing to connect Jimmy with her murder, nothing to rule him out. I was working on the sniper thing."

Patterson heaved his own sigh. "So we're still dead-ended about Callie."

"Yep." The sheriff stared at the wall. "We'll work on the western road folks again when the snow melts."

***

After Jack took Lisa home that Monday afternoon, he discovered the meaning of loneliness. The old farmhouse had always satisfied him before, but now it seemed empty. The only thing that could fill it, he knew, was Lisa's presence. Without her companionship, his life would never be complete.

An open question, they'd agreed. But his answer had been decided the moment Lisa asked the meaning of their kiss. He'd known that some force drew him strongly to her, but until her question he hadn't realized its full implications. In that moment, everything fell into place. He wanted to spend the rest of his life loving her, caring for her and enjoying her company. Her image haunted him for the rest of the day, and that night it filled his last thought before he slept.

But if he fell asleep in the warmth of love, he woke in the cold sweat of nightmare. The same dream again: the tranquil forest area he could never quite identify, the same mortal terror as he stared down the barrel of his enemy's pistol. This time, as he woke, he even thought he heard the shot. Fully awake on the instant, he forced himself to lie still and listen.

He heard nothing.

He eased out of bed and listened again.

Still nothing.

Silently, he explored the darkness of the house. All was in order. What, then, had he heard? He found no answer.

He padded back to the bedroom, now conscious of the cold floor beneath his bare feet. He struck a match. Five o'clock. Might as

well get on with the day. He lit the heaters and a lamp, made coffee, and cooked breakfast, still brooding over his dream. He asked himself again if it could be a subconscious message warning him about the sniper. That seemed logical, yet his instinct still denied the connection. In the end, he fell back on his previous opinion that the dream must be a relic from the wartime past that had no part in his present life.

Or did it? He would have to tell Lisa about the dream before she made a commitment to him, and he would have to tell her in a way that left her free to make her own judgment. He must do that at their next meeting.

In the gray light of another clouded day, Jack checked outside the house for signs of any intruder. Finding none, he decided that whatever he'd heard was part of his dream. He cast the matter aside and spent the day catching up on as much farm work as weather permitted. That night, tired but satisfied, he slept without dreams.

Noon on Wednesday found him thinking more and more about Lisa. After lunch, he rode the paint into town, anticipation growing with each beat of the horse's hooves. Two o'clock found him knocking on her door.

There was no answer. His heart fell. He knocked again and yet again. Still no answer. After the fourth knock, he turned from the door in disappointment.

"Jack."

The call came from the house next door, and he turned to see Rose McKenzie standing on her porch.

"If it's Mr. Kemper you want," she said, "he's stranded in Indiana. If you're looking for Lisa, I saw her heading downtown with Preciou Pendleton."

"Thank you, Mrs. McKenzie." He felt the rush of pleası overflow into his face. "I'll look for her there."

Without further words, he urged the paint into a ca Something of value might yet be salvaged from this day.

Chapter 28

Lisa had returned from her Monday-afternoon visit to Jack's farm feeling contentment mixed with concern. Her sense of the rightness of their words and actions persisted, but Jack's proposal raised more questions than the one they'd left open. What about her plans for graduate school and hopes for a career? She couldn't follow those if she married Jack. And how could she adjust to living on a farm? Living eight months in a town she didn't like could be tolerated. But embracing that town permanently was quite another matter—even if she didn't dislike it as much now as she had at first.

She needed to talk to Rose about it, but the snow was keeping Ralph McKenzie at home, and Lisa didn't want to intrude. Her father remained absent, nor could she talk to him by phone while the lines were down. In the end, she realized she'd have to worry matters through by herself.

Her memory of the bloody snow and amputated raccoon tail also darkened her mood. Jack thought he recognized bobcat tracks at the scene, though none of the beasts had been seen locally since he was a boy. She accepted his explanation. Still, the incident and storm together were reminders of the savagery inherent in nature. That in turn brought thoughts of Callie's murder and the dead squirrels, clear evidences of the savagery inherent in man.

On Tuesday morning, Buddy Robinson knocked on Lisa's door and offered to shovel snow from her walk and driveway for a fifty-cent fee. She agreed, more to make him feel useful than for any need of her own. When he finished, she had a mug of hot chocolate waiting for him in the kitchen.

"Miss Kemper," he asked, his face earnest, "did you ever play pranks when you were a teenager?"

"What kind of pranks?" Lisa knew better than to commit before she found out what Buddy was getting at.

His fingers twiddled with the mug. "You know—just pranks." His gaze slid away and focused on the wall.

Lisa remembered Buddy's unexplained anger toward adults. His question must have something to do with that. Since graduation, Lisa had worn her adulthood as joyously as a new dress for Easter, but now it felt like an overcoat of lead. She had to find the right answer, and it mustn't sound preachy.

"I probably did play pranks," she said, "but mainly I remember that they weren't a smart idea. When you play a prank on someone, he gets even with you. Then you retaliate, and so does he. The game gets rougher and meaner until someone gets hurt. It's wiser not to get started." Images of dead squirrels flitted through her mind. "Were you thinking of anything in particular?"

Buddy continued to study the wall. "No, ma'am. Some of the boys was talking about it."

She decided to close the subject. "My advice is not to get involved. Pranks may be fun for a while, but they end in big trouble."

Buddy said nothing, but finished his chocolate and left. Lisa wondered if she'd helped him or only lost a friend. Being an adult was proving a greater burden than she'd imagined during college. She added Buddy to her list of things to pray about, giving him priority almost equal to her quest for certainty.

Wednesday afternoon brought another knock on Lisa's door. This time, Precious Pendleton asked if she'd like to walk to the drugstore. Lisa accepted gladly.

"I'm going nuts at home," Precious confided as they neared the store. "I've read my eyes out by lamplight, and you can only do your nails and makeup two or three times a day. Say, have you noticed a change in Miss Childress lately?"

"Should I have?" Had Lisa been so caught up in her own problems that she'd failed to see Vesta's?

"I don't know." A frown creased Precious's doll-smooth forehead. "She's always looked sad, but lately she's been . . . well . . . absentminded or something. Sometimes when you're talking to her she'll be staring off into space, and then it's like she brings herself back and doesn't know a thing you said. I thought you might have noticed."

"I hadn't, but I know she's been worried about several things in the library." The statement was true, Lisa told herself, and would continue to be true on any day of the year. But it didn't explain a change in Vesta's conduct, if there really had been one. Lisa would have to watch and form her own opinion.

Cloudy skies kept the drugstore's interior gloomy, but Mrs. Harding carried an oil lamp to their table. For Lisa, it evoked memories of the golden circle in Jack's kitchen. She and Precious ordered the same drinks they had on their last visit: lemon coke for Lisa and cherry soda for Precious.

"How are your parents getting on with this snow?" Lisa tried to steer the conversation away from Vesta.

"The snow's no problem, but Daddy's still mad about Alex."

Lisa had hoped not to bring that up again. "I can't blame him. Alex was out of bounds by any standard."

"Yeah, but Daddy doesn't have to show his temper to me. It's not like I made Alex do it."

"You certainly didn't," Lisa agreed. "You said you'd been reading?" *Anything to change the subject.*

"I finished *Wuthering Heights.*" Precious made a face. "Heathcliffe turned out to be a real stinker. I didn't think much of Cathy, either. She was too proud of her family's place in the community to let herself love Heathcliffe. If she hadn't been so stuck up, they might have worked something out."

Lisa chose her words with care. "People and families often think more of themselves than they should. It keeps them from making normal friendships with the people around them."

"That couldn't happen in Beneficent," Precious said, missing Lisa's point completely. Her face lighted up. "I've been reading *Idylls of the King*, too. Talk about pretty! Some of the words sound so beautiful, you don't care if they mean anything or not."

"What part did you like best?"

"I *loved* the one about Gareth and Lynette, but everything in Camelot seemed to go downhill after that. The Holy Grail story was good, though. Specially when Lancelot's sin and noble deeds got so mixed up together that he couldn't separate them. I didn't understand that part, so I asked Daddy."

"What did he say?"

The girl's enthusiasm faded into a frown. "He said it was hogwash. But I guess it *could* happen if someone sinned and didn't want to admit it." She brightened again. "I said, 'Okay, Daddy, but I bet nobody ever washed a hog in prettier language.' He'd already walked out, though."

Lisa couldn't find a reply, and Precious bounced on to a new subject. "I'm singing in church again. Not this Sunday but the next." She finished her soda and made slurping sounds with the straw as she tried to suck out the last few drops. The uncouth action clashed with her immaculately made-up beauty.

Lisa watched in fascination, vaguely conscious of soft hoof beats stopping outside, followed by the opening of a door. When she looked up, she saw Jack approaching their table.

He only said "Hello," but his voice gave the word special meaning. Flickering lamplight tinged his face with gold. There was no mistaking the pleasure she saw there, and his eyes were fixed on her.

Their assurance made her heart beat faster, but she matched the simplicity of his greeting. "Hello. Won't you sit down?"

Precious regarded each of them in turn. With a knowing expression, she jumped up and exclaimed, "I have to go see Daddy at the bank. Lisa, this time it's my treat." She banged fifteen cents onto the table and headed for the door, calling "Bye, Jack," over her shoulder.

"What's got into her?" Jack followed Precious's progress with an incredulous expression.

Lisa said nothing, shocked to learn how much their faces had revealed about their hearts.

Jack's gaze returned to Lisa. "I've missed you."

At any other time she would have teased him that it had been only two days, but the intensity of his eyes stopped her. "I've missed you, too. I'm glad you came."

A loud *harumph* announced Mrs. Harding's arrival. She wore the expression of one who knew a secret but wasn't about to tell. "Are y'all going to order or just sit here and enjoy the lamplight?"

"Two chocolates, please." Jack's deadpan expression could have passed for Sheriff Rainwater's. "Lamplight doesn't do much to quench the thirst."

"That depends on what you're thirsty for." Mrs. Harding departed toward the kitchen.

Jack and Lisa exchanged an embarrassed glance.

"Are we that obvious?" he asked.

She showed him a rueful smile. "I'm afraid we must be. I don't suppose we can stop rumors from spreading?"

Jack laughed. "Not with the Maginot and Siegfried lines reinforced by Boulder Dam."

"So what must we do?" Lisa's status as an outsider flared up in her consciousness.

"Not much we can do." Jack looked intensely serious. "If we're seeing each other—dating—they'll be talking about it." He blinked, then grinned. "It just occurred to me. I guess we will be dating as long as that 'open question' remains open."

He paused as Mrs. Harding delivered the chocolates, Lisa's with two marshmallows and Jack's with none. She made a show of avoiding their eyes and withdrawing beyond earshot.

"You were saying that we'll be dating." The idea gave Lisa a warm feeling.

"Like I said at the farm," Jack continued, "we're talking about lifetime commitment, nothing less. If we remember that—regardless of which answer you give—most people will know we have nothing to be ashamed of."

"I like that idea." Lisa felt grateful. Jack was making it possible for her to turn him down and walk away without damaging her reputation. The thought of walking away wrenched her heart, and she realized again how powerfully she felt drawn to Jack.

Slow down, she told herself. *Even if everything feels right, you still have problems to work out.*

They drank their chocolate in silence, occasionally exchanging meaningful glances. Lisa felt content at their being together in the lamplight and judged Jack must feel the same.

"I'll walk you home," he said when they finished.

Outside, he checked his horse's tether and patted its neck. "Be patient," he told it. "I'll be right back."

He and Lisa turned toward her house. The crusted snow crunched under their feet as trickles of water underneath it revealed the continued melting. With the footing uncertain, it seemed only natural that Jack held her hand.

"While you're considering that important question," he said, his face solemn, "there's one thing you have to know."

She couldn't help smiling at his seriousness. "Only one?"

Jack laughed. "Dozens, probably, but this one is important." Intensity returned to his face, and he explained his recurrent dream.

With each detail, Lisa grew more appalled. From childhood, she remembered the terror that nightmares could bring. To think that Jack suffered them wrung her heart. "That must be horrible for you, Jack. Horrible."

"It's just another fact of life. I always wake up none the worse."

Realization dawned on Lisa. "At the jukebox in Shipley—that's why you looked so surprised when the song I chose was 'I Had the Craziest Dream.'"

"I thought you must be clairvoyant like Marlene Dietrich in the movie."

"There has to be a reason for your dream," Lisa mused. "Could it be a . . . a subconscious warning? Maybe about the sniper?"

Jack shook his head. "I thought of that, but somehow the two don't seem to match. It's probably baggage left over from the war. To be truthful, though, I don't feel a connection there. At any rate, I thought you ought to know."

"I'm glad you told me, but I don't see that it makes any difference about The Question." Her mind capitalized the words without conscious effort. "I'm only sorry you have to go through anything so unpleasant."

On the front porch of her house they paused, facing each other as Jack clasped both her hands.

"Father isn't back yet," she said. "I can't ask you in."

Jack nodded. "I understand. That's part of our doing everything right." He kissed her lightly on the lips. "I guess that's the right way for now."

She watched him depart, striding sure-footedly through the crusting snow until, with a wave, he disappeared around a corner. Only then did she look inward to examine what she was feeling: contentment at being with Jack, contentment in the knowledge of his love. And beneath the contentment, solid as granite but vibrant as life itself, that now-familiar sense of rightness and singing in harmony.

She knew she could depend on these perceptions. Yet swirling on the surface above them were Jack's nightmares, the hidden malice of the sniper, and the dead squirrels on her porch. These shouted that malevolent forces were directed toward her and Jack. Against anything so powerful, could rightness and harmony prevail?

Chapter 29

As the snow melted during the next few days, Beneficent slowly returned to normal. Thursday saw electric power and telephone service restored, and a farm tractor made enough ruts in the westward road for a few pickup trucks to creep into town. With the phones working again, Jack rounded up a crew and completed a full workday at the chemical plant on Friday.

Stephen Kemper arrived home that day, and Lisa wasted no time in telling him of her changed relationship with Jack. His face showed the first real pleasure she had seen there since her mother's death. Kemper swept her into a father's embrace and rocked her back and forth. "Jack is solid and dependable," he told her. "With him, you can afford to follow your heart."

"I know where my heart is," Lisa replied, "but we've decided to take things slowly. We don't want to make a mistake."

Kemper nodded and said, "Good strategy." His happy expression unchanged, he moved to the phone and dialed Oleta Brooks's number. "Stephen Kemper here," he said. "My company has approved a one thousand dollar grant to buy lab equipment for your school. Can we get together soon and talk about it?"

He winced and jerked the phone away from his ear. From the receiver, an excited, high-volume female voice reverberated down the hall. The appointment made, Kemper visited the plant and found Jack's crew rapidly closing in on completion.

Though skies remained cloudy, the snow continued to melt. On Saturday, the school administration announced that school would resume Monday morning. On Sunday, church attendance returned to normal. Jack's joining Lisa and her father at morning worship sent a ripple of whispers through the congregation, and Mrs. Telebit hardly took her eyes off of them during the service.

Work continued at the plant on Monday, and that afternoon Stephen Kemper and Oleta Brooks began preparing their want list for the school laboratory. Lisa worked her usual stint at the library on Tuesday, and at mid-afternoon that day, Stephen Kemper and Jack conducted a joint inspection of the plant and pronounced Jack's part of the project finished.

"I can't thank you enough," Kemper told him. "I was lost on the construction work, but now I'm on familiar ground. My company will send a crew to install equipment and train workers. We'll be in business within a month."

By evening that day, the last of the snow melted from the roads, and Beneficent settled again into its placid way of life.

**

Wednesday, February 25
"Something has given you a new Lisa on life." Rose McKenzie's eyes twinkled in enjoyment of her pun.

Lisa laughed aloud and responded with one of her own. "You Rose to that occasion. Yes, things look better now."

They sat in Rose's kitchen on Wednesday morning, sharing coffee for the first time since the snow had kept Ralph McKenzie from work. He'd been prowling the house like a caged bear, Rose said. When this morning brought the first clear skies in almost two weeks, he went to assess the damage on his farm.

Rose herself was all smiles. "You certainly look better. Would Jack Davis have something to do with it?"

Knowing Rose would keep her confidence, Lisa told of Jack's proposal and their agreement to postpone a definite decision.

"What would your answer be if you had to give it today?" Rose's soft voice took the sting out of her question, but her directness forced Lisa to face the issue.

"When I'm with Jack it always seems like 'yes.' But when I'm away from him, other questions come up."

"What kind of questions?"

"Not going to graduate school. Whether I could adjust to living on a farm. I'd never considered that."

Sipping her coffee, Rose gave a kindly glance across the cup. "In time, questions like those tend to answer themselves. Do you have any reservations about Jack himself?"

"I don't think so, but I worry about overconfidence. He has an idea that he can handle any situation if only he keeps his head. It's mixed up with his idea about Beneficent, that good people working together can make an ideal town. He knows there are bad things in the world, like the sniper that shot at us, but Jack sees them as something brought into Beneficent from outside. He knows they exist, but they seem to bounce off of him as if they didn't."

Rose thought a moment. "I understand his confidence about handling anything. He did it all through school. He never talked much, but when something needed to be done, he did it. And he's not alone in exaggerating Beneficent's virtues. That's why our sign on the highway has that silly motto. Has it occurred to you that Jack and Alex have something in common?"

"It certainly has not!" Lisa felt her temper rising.

Rose smiled. "So quick to defend Jack? Hear me out first. He and Alex share an overconfidence in human action. As a socialist, Alex thinks an elite group of intellectuals can make the country run the way it should. With Jack, human goodness within the Christian faith defines the elite group."

Lisa's anger receded. "I never thought of it that way."

"The problem is that we humans can't ever be that smart or that good," Rose continued. "Corruption always sets in. Give socialists the power they want and they run over anyone who gets in their way. When we Christians work up enough virtue to be conscious of it, we get proud of ourselves. And when pride comes in one door, virtue goes out another. Ever since Eden, that's the way things are. In Beneficent and everywhere else."

The words struck deep into Lisa. Hadn't she begun to take pride in that feeling of singing in harmony as if it were something she'd invented? So she asked, "What's the solution?"

Rose shook her head. "Collectively, there is none. It has to happen individually through humility and constant prayer. And we can't do it by ourselves. Like the psalmist says, 'Except the Lord build the house, they labour in vain that build it.'"

A knock sounded at the front door. Stephen Kemper's voice called, "Lisa, Jack wants you on the phone."

"I'll be right there." Lisa squeezed Rose's hand. "Thank you. You've given me a lot to think about." In her own house, she checked her watch as she picked up the phone. Nine-thirty.

"Are you free today?" Jack asked. "It's a perfect day to take in that view from the barn."

"I'd like that." Lisa tried not to sound too eager. "What time?"

"Two choices," he said. "I have to do a tune-up on the truck. Should be finished by eleven. If you have a car, you could drive out about then. If not, I can pick you up around one."

"I'll drive out. My father says he'll be buried under paperwork all day."

Jack laughed. "My condolences to him. I had the easy part of getting the plant started."

Later, as Lisa drove past the familiar landmarks toward Jack's farm, her pensive mood from the visit with Rose dissolved into euphoria. When she parked beside Jack's house, she found him fastening the hood on his truck.

He held his hands up for inspection, then opened her car door. "All cleaned up before you got here. But I couldn't resist a last look at the engine."

She showed a mock-frown. "Are you hiding your other girlfriend in there?"

He put on a discouraged look. "She wouldn't fit. Guess I'll have to be faithful to you."

She matched his sad countenance. "A horrible fate."

Laughing together, an act that now seemed as natural as breathing, they hiked toward the barn, their breath frosting in the cold air. Lisa felt glad she'd worn her jacket and mittens, and Jack soon put on the gloves he'd stuffed into his coat pockets.

As Lisa remembered, the barn stood on the highest ground in the area, some two hundred yards from the house. The peak of its hayloft towered half a story above the surrounding trees and promised a spectacular view. Once inside, they paused beside a wooden ladder built onto an interior wall.

"Do you take all your girls up to the hayloft?" Lisa teased.

Jack grinned. "Only the pretty ones. Actually, I haven't been up there myself since I got back from the Army. No telling what shape it's in. Watch out for cobwebs."

"Cobwebs?" Lisa pretended surprise. "Don't tell me you store corn up there, too."

Jack waggled a forefinger. "Don't pull that sweet and ignorant act on me. I know what part of Indiana you come from."

Laughing again, Lisa climbed the ladder in a state approaching bliss. It wasn't that anything particularly exciting was happening, but whenever she was with Jack that sense of harmonious rightness returned, and all the things she worried about faded into nothingness.

"I see what you mean about cobwebs," she said as she reached the hayloft. In fact, the light was too dim to see much else.

Jack stood close behind her. "It's worse than I thought," he said. "Sorry. I should have cleaned it up before you came. Wait here." He picked up a short length of two-by-two that lay nearby, stepped around Lisa, and cleared a path through the cobwebs. She lost sight of him in the dim light, but heard him fumbling with something that sounded like a latch. Then double doors at the front of the loft swung open, admitting a blinding flood of sunlight.

At Jack's signal she came forward, squinting into the glare as her eyes gradually became accustomed to it. Holding the door frame, she sat in the doorway and dangled her feet outside. Jack eased into position beside her.

The view was all she could have wished. The silent land lay spread out before her like a map. Isolated patches of snow remained, but elsewhere the earth had returned to its winter color of dun. Wooded areas revealed dark evergreens interspersed with stark black limbs of hardwoods. Eastward, the dark, fertile soil of Jack's new acreage showed through the green of its winter cover crop. Beyond, an ebony thread of highway snaked away northward, with cars no larger than fleas creeping along it. Beside it lay the railroad and, far to the north, a string of coal cars stood idle on a siding while, in miniature, a mile-long diesel freight slid slowly southward.

Lisa again felt herself in harmony with all she saw, and with its Creator. "It's more than beautiful, Jack," she whispered. "It's like . . . like looking into eternity itself."

"It's always given me that kind of feeling," he replied, "but I could never put words to it."

They sat in companionable silence for perhaps a quarter-hour until a sharp wind rose, chilling their faces and raising tears in their eyes. Jack moved back from the door and stood, then helped Lisa up.

"We'd better go before we're too stiff to climb down," he said. "I'll keep these doors open till you reach the ladder. Otherwise it'll be too dark to see."

Lisa turned to comply, but the light from outside revealed something that had escaped her notice before the doors were open. Something dark and leathery-brown hung from a nail on an upright brace near the ladder. She might have missed it even then if it had not wavered in a gust of wind.

"What's this, Jack?" She lifted it from the nail and shook the dust from it. "It looks like a jacket."

Jack left the doors open and arrived beside her in one bound. He took it from her hands and examined it. When he spoke, his voice was filled with wonder. "It's my father's leather work jacket. I never found it when I sorted through his things. This and his Sunday suit were missing." He looked off into space. "I'd figured he was wearing the jacket when he was killed, and that someone made off with the suit before I got home."

"I'm glad you found it." Lisa touched his arm. "I can tell it means a lot to you."

"He wore it so often it seemed like part of his skin." Idly, Jack ran his hands through the pockets. "What have we here?"

He withdrew a slip of white paper that unfolded into an oblong rectangle. He held it up to the light for his and Lisa's inspection. Lisa immediately recognized it as a numbered receipt. In a single flash, as quickly as the citations for Jack's decorations had stamped themselves on her memory, its words and numbers embedded themselves in her consciousness.

On December 18, 1944—the day Jack's parents were killed—Calvin Davis had made a payment of four thousand dollars to Beneficent National Bank. The receipt was signed by—the name struck Lisa like lightning—Harry Pendleton.

"Jack . . . What does it mean?" She glanced at Jack, whose face reddened even as she watched. His breath came short and fast.

"I can't believe—" The words forced their way through Jack's clenched teeth. "He couldn't—" His eyes grew hard, harder than they'd been the night he routed the two toughs in Shipley. He moved mechanically toward the ladder, his gaze fixed straight ahead.

Cold fear gripped Lisa's heart. "Jack, answer me. What does it mean?"

He looked at her like one hypnotized. "He has to explain." His voice had a faraway sound. "I have to make him tell." Still gripping the jacket and the receipt, he started down the ladder.

Lisa called after him. "Jack, listen. The other day you talked about not losing your head, but you're losing it now. Stop and think."

Jack spoke as if to himself. "Harry has to answer me."

He reached the bottom of the ladder and ran from the barn.

Lisa scrambled down as quickly as she could and tried to follow, but she was no match for Jack's speed. He reached his truck a full hundred yards ahead of her. With a clash of gears and a shower of flying gravel, he wrestled the vehicle through a tight circle and roared down the driveway. By the time Lisa reached her car, his truck had disappeared onto the main road.

Out of breath and trembling, Lisa managed to fumble her key into the ignition. Panic clutched at her heart. But even as she fought through its near-paralysis, she knew her fear was for Jack rather than herself. Whatever that receipt meant, it had driven him beyond the self-control that had carried him through the war. Whatever consequences his recklessness might bring, her love demanded that she face them beside him.

She turned the car toward town, driving with a newfound certainty of which she was not yet aware.

***

The moment Jack saw the receipt, he knew he'd been cheated. Four thousand dollars! Not a penny of it showing on the bank records he'd examined! Violent, white-hot rage rose in him. Cheated! By a man who pretended to be a friend!

Vaguely, he heard Lisa's voice, but no words penetrated his rage. He made some mindless answer, but his consciousness fixed on one thought: confront Harry Pendleton and—his mind went blank except for a single idea. *Confront and demand.* Demand what? Another blank. *Confront and demand.* That was enough.

Without knowing how he got there, he found himself at the bottom of the ladder. He heard Lisa's voice calling from the loft, but his fury demolished her words before they reached his mind. *Confront now*, his mind commanded. He broke into a run toward his truck. With each step, his mind hammered the same words. *Confront now. Confront and demand.*

There must have been another break in his consciousness, for he was in the truck and gunning it through a one-hundred-eighty degree turn and down the drive toward the road. Another break, and he was rawhiding toward town with no care for speed or traffic. Strangely, he saw only what lay straight ahead, and that as if through red-tinged gauze.

Painful images flashed through his mind, a montage of his life these three years since the war: the constant, brooding burden of debt he carried in every waking moment and the thousand-odd tasks he'd done to chip away at it . . . all of the crops he and his workers had raised . . . all of his gambles on crop rotation and artificial fertilizer . . . the late-night extra hours he'd worked, alone, to spare himself the expense of hiring even one more hand . . . all the backbreaking piece-work drudgery he'd labored through in off-season construction jobs, doing his farm chores early and late, day after day, and falling into bed exhausted at midnight.

And with each remembered image, his anger grew. *Cheated!* His mind throbbed with the word:

Cheated! Confront and demand.

The road-sounds changed from the crunch of gravel to the hum of pavement as he barreled into town. A creeping, mule-drawn wagon loomed ahead, partially obstructing the road. Without thinking, he swept around it, tightwire-walking his wheels along the edge of the ditch and leaving the frightened mule bucking in its traces. Tires screeched as he skidded to a stop before the bank.

The same words again thundered in his mind. *Confront and demand!*

Inside the bank, he dodged the customers waiting at teller windows, ignored a teller's greeting, and barged through the rear door into Harry Pendleton's office.

Seated at his desk, Pendleton wore his usual worried expression, but he looked up with a smile. The smile faded as he saw Jack's face, but his voice remained calm. "What can I do for you, Jack?"

"Explain this." Jack's voice was hoarse with anger as he charged the desk and held the receipt before Pendleton's face.

Fear showed first in the banker's eyes, followed by craft. "Let me examine it," he said, reaching for the receipt.

Jack snatched it back. "You know exactly what it is. Your signature says my father paid you four thousand dollars on the day he was killed. What happened to it?"

"That's easily explained." Pendleton smiled. "I have the documents right here." He opened the upper right-hand drawer of his desk and fumbled within it.

The man's deliberate calm made Jack stop and think. The film of red gauze fell from his vision. Could he be wrong? Could there be some explanation other than the damning one he had imagined? Pendleton seemed to take forever to find the documents. Little by little, Jack's peripheral vision crept back. He became aware of the richly flowered wallpaper to his right and left. Surely, his conscience whispered, a man with such taste for beauty could not be capable of cheating anyone. His anger ebbed under the pressure of self-doubt. Had he leaped to the wrong conclusion?

Jack lifted his gaze to the green woodland pictured on the wall behind Pendleton's desk. Its cool shade further dampened his anger, leaving him weak and empty. Yet there was something familiar about those woods. Danger signals inside him whispered, cried aloud, and finally screamed a warning. There was something he had to remember.

"Ah! I knew I'd find them." Harry Pendleton's voice remained calm. He stood, but his hand held no documents. It held a Colt .32 caliber pistol, the smaller brother of the Army's standard Colt .45. The banker's eyes burned with murderous intent.

As suddenly as a stroke of lightning, all the pieces fell into place for Jack. The woodland scene image behind Pendleton's desk was the familiar woods he had seen so often in his nightmare. Harry Pendleton was the enemy who lurked there. And, as in the dream, that enemy now held a pistol pointed with deadly malice directly at Jack's heart.

Chapter 30

Immobilized and in shock, Jack knew what was happening but could not make his body respond. The elements of his situation flashed through his consciousness, stunning him like blows to the head. For three years he'd been cheated. *Swindled!* Swindled by a man who posed as his friend, a man whose apparent goodness formed the cornerstone of his faith in Beneficent and its people. Images from his nightmare raced through his mind. Warnings, he suddenly understood, warnings of the life-threatening reality that now confronted him.

He knew all these things, knew he must act or die, and yet he could not move. He stood paralyzed by a single realization: Pendleton's betrayal spelled destruction of the faith in human goodness that had sustained him through the war. For, in the darkness of a world dominated by evil, Jack had treasured Beneficent as a tiny candle of righteousness, a blessed community radiant with the Christ-like virtues of its citizens.

He had known that Callie's murder and the sniper's malevolence held potential threats to this vision, but he'd hoped outsiders were the bringers of evil. The slender receipt in his hand, though, brought proof of perfidy by a trusted citizen. With that proof, Jack's edifice of faith in human goodness came crashing down.

Its destruction stunned him. He could not move.

"Give me that receipt." Harry Pendleton's eyes blazed. His hoarse voice quivered, but his gun hand held steady.

Instinctively, unthinking, Jack clutched the receipt more tightly against his chest.

"Give it to me," Pendleton rasped. "Give it to me or I'll kill you. No one will blame me for shooting a crazy veteran who attacked me in my own office."

"They . . . they won't believe you." Jack's voice returned as a whisper he hardly recognized. His mind was beginning to work again, too. His body still felt numb, but he managed to force it into a half turn to the left. If Pendleton's claim of an attack were to be believed, his attacker must be shot from the front. Jack's turning his body forced the banker to come out from behind his desk to reestablish the necessary angle. That meant he had to face Jack across an open space.

"They will believe me." Wild-eyed, Pendleton circled the desk. But to Jack's dismay, the man stepped backward, increasing the distance between them and removing any possibility of disarming him.

The banker's eyes narrowed. "I've gotten by with this for three years. Once I have that receipt, no one will ever know."

The pistol again pointed at Jack's heart.

***

Frantic with fear for Jack, Lisa drove the rough gravel road as fast as she dared. Even so, she knew she was falling farther behind, for the car's soft springs made it harder to control than Jack's truck. Lisa's eyes concentrated on the erratically banked curves of the twisting road, but her mind kept repeating a single prayer. *Don't let Jack do anything he'll regret, Lord. And please keep him safe.*

Her anxiety remained, but the near-panic she'd felt earlier now receded. As it did, she felt an unaccustomed detachment form deep down beneath it. This had nothing to do with the adrenaline moments caused by the speed of her passage. An oncoming car, turning too wide on a blind curve, sent her skidding in loose gravel. Unassisted by thought, her hands whipped the steering wheel into the skid. The car hovered on the brink of the ditch, steadied, and came back under control.

Fear shot through her, and her tension ratcheted a few notches higher, but the underlying detachment—an almost surreal calm—held steady. She could reach down inside herself and touch it. Years before, she'd learned to swim in the shallow waters of a lake. Whenever her strength failed, she could reach down and touch bottom with her feet. This detachment, this bedrock of calm beneath her tension, reminded her of that.

The pavement beginning at the city limits allowed her to drive faster, though she still had to dodge potholes. The tires screeched as she turned into the main street. A few startled pedestrians stopped in mid-stride to watch her pass.

Now she saw Jack's truck parked haphazardly in front of the bank, the driver's door open and the engine running, more evidence that Jack had lost his normal control. Fear raced through her again as she imagined what might be happening inside the bank. The same prayer throbbed through her mind. *Don't let him do anything he'll regret, Lord. And please keep him safe.*

Lisa braked to a stop beside Jack's truck and leaped from the car, in her haste leaving the door open and the engine running, as Jack had. From the corner of her eye she saw, across the street, the scarecrow-thin form of Shiloh Simpson. The mayor stood watching from the door of his laundry, a look of alarm on his face. She ignored him and ran to the bank's side door that opened directly into Harry Pendleton's office.

Without knocking, she opened the door and thrust herself inside. The sight she saw stopped her in her tracks.

Jack stood with his arms at his sides, half-turned from Pendleton's desk and motionless as a bird charmed by a snake. Harry Pendleton held his pistol aimed at Jack, his face contorted in rage. As Lisa watched, the banker moved around the desk until he faced Jack squarely. The muzzle of the weapon never wavered. As if from a great distance, she heard the words, "No one will ever know."

Their meaning crashed into her consciousness like a blow to the head. Some way, somehow, she had to get the banker's attention away from Jack.

"It's too late, Mr. Pendleton," she heard herself saying. "I know, and others will."

"Others?" For a moment, doubt clouded Pendleton's face. Then anger and determination returned as his attention shifted from Jack to Lisa. His voice was flat. "No, Miss Kemper, they will not. I'll see to that." He swung the pistol to aim at Lisa. Wildness flamed in his eyes.

She recoiled from the sight of such malice in a human face. Terror grasped at her heart as she saw death a split-second away, needing only one twitch of a finger to slam it home. Yet beneath her terror, the underlying calm held firm.

She fixed her gaze on Pendleton's. "The sheriff knows," she lied. "I told him before I came."

Jack must have made some movement then, for the banker jerked the weapon back toward him and commanded, "Don't move."

Jack froze, then slowly lifted his hands in surrender. "Let her go, Harry," he pleaded. "She has no part in this."

The two men stared at each other. Pendleton sucked in his breath and seemed to steel himself for action.

Lisa searched frantically for a way to stop him. "I *do* have a part in it," she cried. "So does the sheriff. I've told him everything. He'll be here any minute."

Doubt returned to Pendleton's eyes as he glanced from Jack to Lisa and back again to Jack. The muzzle of the pistol wavered.

Lisa pressed her attack. "It's too late, Mr. Pendleton." The firmness in her voice surprised her. "The word is out and you can't stop it. Anything you do now will only make it worse."

For a few moments the three of them stood motionless as if in tableau: Jack most obviously because the weapon remained pointed at him, Lisa because she feared any movement might tip the banker's indecision into a deadly result. In horror, she realized the next few seconds would determine the kind of future she and Jack could share. Indeed, those seconds would determine if they would have a future.

As she watched, the pistol wavered again. Then Pendleton's gun hand slowly sank to his side, the weapon pointing uselessly at the floor. Something like a sob sounded in the room. Harry Pendleton's shoulders slumped as he shuffled back behind his desk and dropped into his chair.

He sat with head resting on one hand while the other lay loosely on his desk on top of the pistol, his finger no longer on the trigger.

Without bodily movement, Jack and Lisa exchanged glances. His gaze moved from her eyes to the pistol, which rested on her side of the desk but still under Pendleton's hand. Jack's glance returned to Lisa's. With an almost imperceptible motion, he shook his head. *No, don't*, he seemed to say. She was not to move. There was danger as long as the banker's hand remained on the pistol. Hardly daring to breath, she focused on the man behind the desk.

Pendleton's crying began quietly, then grew to great sobs that wracked his entire body. The sight mitigated Lisa's fear and loathing with pity. Caution prevailed, though, and she held herself motionless.

Then Pendleton's hand left the pistol and joined the other in covering his face. Without waiting for a signal from Jack, Lisa stepped forward and scooped the weapon up, holding the butt of it gingerly between two fingers and thumb.

Jack nodded his approval. Lisa surveyed the weeping Pendleton once more, and another wave of pity swept through her. He needed help that neither she nor Jack could give. Still holding the pistol with one hand, she used the other to un-cradle Pendleton's telephone and dial Shiloh Simpson's laundry.

"Mr. Simpson?" The strength of her voice again surprised her. "This is Lisa Kemper. Get Jacob Weaver and come to Mr. Pendleton's office. He needs you right now."

She hung up without waiting for an answer, then crossed the room and put her free hand on Jack's shoulder. "It's over, Jack," she whispered. "It's going to be all right."

He nodded again, but gazed dully beyond her into space. The crisis past, he seemed to slide back toward the state of near-hypnosis that had possessed him as she entered.

Finally, he spoke. "I've been a fool, Lisa." He collapsed into a chair and, like Pendleton, put his head in his hands. "I went off half-cocked and almost got both of us killed."

"It's over now," Lisa repeated. "It's going to be all right."

Neither said anything more. From the front of the bank, sounds of routine business penetrated the office, a reassuring counterpoint to Pendleton's quiet weeping.

Shiloh Simpson and Jacob Weaver entered the side door, breathless, their faces reflecting shock as they saw the pistol in Lisa's hand.

"The gun is not the problem," she said. "This is." She took the receipt from Jack and held it up for their examination. Their faces showed momentary unbelief, then comprehension.

Lisa looked again for some signal from Jack, who watched listlessly from his chair. All the energy seemed to have drained out of him. This wasn't the Jack that she knew. When he showed no inclination to speak, she continued.

"We found the receipt today in a pocket of his father's jacket. When Jack came to get an explanation, he faced this." She held up the pistol. "I think Mr. Pendleton has something to tell you."

The banker raised his head from his hands, his eyes now red with tears rather than anger. "It's true." He choked out the words. Then his voice fell to a whisper. "I . . . I took the money." He hid his face again.

Simpson and Weaver stared at Pendleton, then returned their gaze to Lisa as unwelcome acceptance spread over their faces. Without comment, Weaver took the pistol from her and ejected the magazine, then cleared the last round from the chamber. He slipped both pistol and magazine into his pocket. Simpson reached as if to take the receipt from her, then appeared to think better of it.

"You're right," she said. "This piece of paper nearly cost Jack his life. I'll keep it for him until he's ready."

Increasingly worried by Jack's passiveness, she crossed to his chair and took his hand. "Come on, Darling," she said, blood rushing to her face at her first use of that endearment. "It's time for us to go."

Slowly, as if waking from a deep sleep, he rose and collected himself. His jaw grew firm again and some of the customary animation returned to his eyes. Deliberately, he surveyed the broken banker weeping at his desk and the still-amazed faces of the newcomers. Then his gaze returned to Lisa and softened.

"I heard what you called me," he said.

Suppressing tears of joy, Lisa put on a stern face. "I'll call you more than that if you don't come away with me right now."

Still holding his hand and gratified by his response, she led him to the door. But a grim suspicion tempered her joy. They had survived a deadly encounter. Yet instinct warned that the battles that lay ahead might prove more dangerous than the one that lay behind.

Jack retrieved his keys and shut his truck door before joining Lisa in her car. Neither spoke until they parked in her driveway. With a sigh, he took her hand.

"Can you forgive me, Lisa? I lost my head and put you in danger. You kept yours and saved my life."

"It was my turn. You've rescued me twice." She squeezed his hand before disengaging hers. "Come inside." The crisis past, she felt her self-control slipping.

In the living room, she rushed into his arms and burst into tears. For a long while they simply held each other as she cried. When her voice returned, she whispered, "I couldn't stand the thought of losing you, Jack. It took me twenty-two years to find you, and I wasn't *about* to let anything take you away."

"In the future I'll hold you to that," Jack said. "Right now I'm content just to hold you."

From the hallway came the sound of a throat being cleared. "I don't have to ask what's got *hold* of you two," said Stephen Kemper, "but I would like to know what's going on."

Lisa faced her father but kept one arm around Jack. "I think I just said 'yes.'"

Kemper raised both eyebrows. "I'm delighted, of course. But why all the tears?"

In a rush, Lisa told what had happened. Kemper's deepening frown showed his grasp of the danger they had been through.

"She's letting me off too easy," Jack said when Lisa finished. "I went off half-cocked, and when he pulled the gun I couldn't react. Lisa's quick thinking saved us."

Footsteps on the porch forestalled Kemper's answer. He opened the door, and Shiloh Simpson entered.

"Harry Pendleton has promised restitution," he said to Jack. "He's asked Jacob Weaver and me, together with anyone you name, to figure out what he owes. That could get complicated. The money has been working three years and you've been making payments, too. We have no idea how it will work out." He gave Jack an anxious look. "Who would you like to represent you?"

Jack seemed withdrawn. "I don't know. I haven't thought. Unless . . . Mr. Kemper, would you have time to help?"

"I'd be honored." Kemper's nod affirmed his words. "The installation crew for the plant doesn't get here till next week."

Jack turned back to Simpson. "Mr. Kemper, then. Hollis Wilson if he's in town. If not, Otis Hahn."

The team of 'forty-two again, Lisa thought. The strength of that bond still surprised her, but she was proud Jack had chosen her father along with his teammates.

"How about all three?" Simpson's lean face showed concern. "For years, people have said Harry and Jacob and me are thick as thieves. Now Harry's made that a little bit too close to the truth. Folks won't trust our decision unless your people can outvote us."

"All three, then." Jack's voice grew decisive again. "But I don't want any contact with this till you have it worked out."

"All right." The mayor ran his hand over his brow. "Two other things: Because of this . . . uh . . . problem, a team of auditors will examine the bank's records beginning tomorrow, and Harry plans to make a public confession in prayer meeting tonight."

Jack's voice was hard. "I'll pass on that. I don't want to see him. Maybe not ever. Not for a year or two, anyway."

"I can understand that." The mayor's eyes searched Jack's. "But the whole church and town are involved. For everyone's sake, we need to settle this quickly. If you're not there tonight, no one will believe Harry has told the full truth."

Jack's eyes closed and he took a deep breath. Lisa thought she could actually see the weight of responsibility descend on him. When his eyes opened and he spoke, every syllable showed fatigue and resignation. "I guess I have to be there."

"Good." Simpson visibly relaxed. "Now I have to speak to you as a deacon. There's the matter of forgiveness—"

"Forgiveness?" The word exploded from Jack's mouth. "How do you *dare* mention forgiveness? The very day my father was killed, that man stole his money. While I served overseas, he stole from me. Today he came within half a second of murdering Lisa and me. And you talk of forgiveness? Forget it."

Simpson took a step back. "You have a long life ahead of you, Jack. Can you carry that burden all the way to the end?"

Lisa, Jack, and her father sat in brooding silence long after Simpson left. She felt emotionally drained. Jack appeared to feel much the same, while Stephen Kemper seemed content to follow their lead.

Was it today's close brush with death that determined their mood? Lisa wondered. Or was it the lifelong implication of the mayor's probing question?

Chapter 31

Lisa knew the Wednesday night prayer meeting usually drew about thirty people, but the packed church showed that the news about Pendleton had spread throughout town. She, Jack, and her father found seats near the back, but her hope of remaining inconspicuous proved vain. Everyone seemed to be staring at them.

"Stare back at them," Stephen Kemper advised. "Show them more brass than John Philip Sousa."

When Lisa did, most people looked away. As she glanced around, she saw new faces among the usual church crowd. Of course. People from other churches also had business with the bank. She wondered how they would go about merging their knowledge of Pendleton's crime with their image of Beneficent. It seemed like a painful adjustment.

The Pendleton family sat in the front row, isolated except for Brother Smallwood and Shiloh Simpson. Honey Pendleton and Precious sat hunched forward with heads down. Lisa admired their courage for appearing, and her heart went out particularly to Precious. The girl's self-image was built on her family's community standing. Her father's crime must have dealt it a crushing blow.

Brother Smallwood welcomed the church's guests and opened with prayer that the Lord would guide everyone's heart during the meeting. After the 'Amen' he said simply, "You all know Brother Pendleton. He has something to tell you."

The Harry Pendleton who ascended to the pulpit was totally unlike the crazed banker Lisa had seen earlier that day. His shoulders slumped, the flesh around his eyes showed red and puffy, and defeat was written in every line of his face. Yet his gaze remained direct as he faced the congregation.

"Today," he said, his voice husky but strong, his tone as matter-of-fact as if he were announcing a church picnic. "Today I resigned as president of Beneficent National Bank and submitted my resignation as a deacon of this church. The reason is that I have been caught embezzling four thousand dollars that Calvin Davis paid to the bank on the day he was killed."

He paused as a murmur passed through the congregation.

"Because of my crime," he continued, "auditors will examine the bank records beginning tomorrow. Those of you with accounts there may rest assured they will find no irregularities except for my one theft."

A few relieved sighs could be heard. Then Pendleton spoke again, his voice soft and reflective. "You've been my friends, and I've wronged all of you. More than that, I've wronged my wife and daughter, my dead friend Calvin Davis and his son Jack, and that lovely newcomer in our midst, Lisa Kemper. But most of all, I have wronged my Lord."

With these words his voice broke. Lisa felt blood rush to her face as a multitude of eyes focused on her and Jack. She felt his tension beside her, but he showed no notice of the stares. She tried to ignore them, too.

The Congregation's gaze returned to Pendleton as he gathered himself and continued. "I have no excuses, but I'd like you to know how this happened. You'll remember that for years I've supported the state's Balance Agriculture with Industry program. In autumn of 1944 I'd been looking for small industries we could bring into Beneficent at moderate cost, like that man from Chicago—the Russian refugee—is doing with the furniture factory over in New Albany. A Memphis man and I hatched the idea of setting up the shirt factory. By December I'd put a lot of money into it, and I thought everything was falling into place.

"Then the other man pulled out and left me holding the bag. I had to find five thousand more dollars right away or lose the factory and all the money I'd already put up."

A haunted look came over the banker's face. "That's where I made my first mistake: I was so obsessed with raising money that I forgot to ask the Lord about it. When He lived on earth He said, 'Watch and pray, that ye enter not into temptation.' That's a command I failed to follow. Maybe the Lord didn't want us to have the shirt factory. I don't know what He'd have said if I'd asked, but I'm certain He wouldn't have told me to steal four thousand dollars.

"Looking back, I can see that my efforts didn't have His blessing. In three frantic days of calling in every chip I could think of, the most I could come up with was fifteen hundred."

Pendleton took a deep breath. "That's how things stood on December the eighteenth, 1944, when Calvin Davis walked through the side door of my office with one of the wildest stories I ever heard. He and Sarah had just returned from burying an eccentric aunt of his over in Arkansas. The lady had gotten married and moved away when Cal was still a child. He had no memory of her except for hearing people say she was odd. She and Cal's parents exchanged Christmas cards every year, and after they died Cal kept up the practice out of respect for them.

"The aunt had no children. Cal wasn't sure when she lost her husband, but she was already a widow when they began exchanging cards. Every year she'd write him about how she'd enjoyed playing with him when he was young. So when word came that she'd died, he and Sarah thought the least they could do was go to her funeral."

Pendleton gave a sad laugh. "I never asked how they found the extra gas ration for the trip, but they got there and saw the good woman laid to rest. After the interment Cal said a fellow came up and asked if he was Calvin Davis. The man turned out to be a lawyer and a neighbor of the deceased. He took Cal to his office and then to a bank where the aunt had a safe deposit box."

Beside Lisa, Jack gave a sharp intake of breath and leaned forward, intent on the banker's words.

"In the box was an envelope with Cal's name scribbled in shaky handwriting, along with a message, 'In memory of the pleasant times we had together.' That was all. Cal tucked the envelope in his pocket, thanked the man, and asked if he owed him anything. The man said no, it was a neighborly thing, so Cal left and went back to the car.

"He and Sarah were halfway home when she asked what happened in the bank. When he told her, nothing would satisfy her except to stop and see what was in the envelope. So they did. They found a child's crude drawing of a lopsided wagon pulled by a three-legged horse. But wrapped in that drawing they found four thousand dollars in cash."

An awestruck gasp rippled through the church.

"When they got home, Cal came in the side door of my office and laid four thousand dollars on my desk as partial payment on the six thousand he'd borrowed to buy new land. I was busy with the factory problem, so I wrote him a receipt and put the money in a desk drawer till I had time to take it in to a teller."

Sadness swept over Pendleton's face. "A couple of hours later, someone ran in and said there'd been an accident on the highway. By then I'd forgotten about Cal's money, so I locked up and drove down to see what had happened.

"I guess it was next day when I heard they thought it was Cal and Sarah that had burned to death. Then I remembered the four thousand dollars, and I wondered if Cal's receipt had burned up with him. Right then, temptation took up residence in my stomach like a hot, live worm. I'd had no luck raising money, and suddenly I saw a chance to redeem my investment and bring in the factory I thought the town needed. So I said nothing about Cal's money. I just let it lie there in the desk drawer."

Pendleton mopped his brow with a handkerchief. "I told myself I hadn't done anything wrong yet. I'd wait and see if Cal's receipt turned up. If it did, I'd apply his money to the loan. If it didn't . . . well, you know what happened.

"People said I was generous in giving so much time to settling Cal's estate and property. But I wasn't generous. I was looking for that receipt and feeling mighty glad Jack wasn't around to make things difficult. I was glad, too, when the Army couldn't find him. The longer it took, the better I liked it."

Pendleton's eyes closed. He made a choking sound, then recovered and his eyes opened. "I thought how convenient it would be if they never found Jack, or if they found him dead. Most of the time I didn't wish it, but there were times when I did. That was my low point: thinking those thoughts about a man who was risking his life to defend his country.

"I felt relieved when Jack wrote and asked the deacons to manage his farm till he got back. You can bet I was glad to help. That gave me more excuses to search through Cal Davis's papers. And I kept remembering how Jack might yet manage to get himself killed before the war ended."

Pendleton let his breath out slowly and looked down. "Somewhere in there I decided the receipt had burned up with Cal. So I tore the carbon copy out of the receipt book and destroyed it. I mixed that book in with some the tellers used. You may remember that the auditors found a numbered receipt missing that year. They couldn't connect any money with it, so they logged it as a minor irregularity and let it go.

"About then I noticed a change in my face. Every morning when I shaved, I'd see the worry lines grow deeper. I passed it off that I was concerned about the war, and later about the Russians, but the cause wasn't anything that noble." His voice fell almost to a whisper, yet each word carried throughout the silent church. "It was nothing more than guilt, compounded with hardcore selfish worry about getting caught."

He raised his palms in a gesture of helplessness. "It was also about then that the Lord stopped accepting my prayers. They seemed to bounce back at me off the ceiling. So I tried to compensate by doing good works. It was no use. There's an irony in this. You all gave me credit for being some kind of saint, but the Lord knew better. Now I understand a hard truth: Even without the kind of sin I committed, we can't ever be good enough to become acceptable to God. The only way we can do that is through wholehearted surrender. The only prayer God would accept from me was one of repentance, and that was the one prayer I wouldn't make.

"By then, the time had passed when I could put the money back and juggle the books to cover it. I'd condemned myself to live with my crime. What was worse, the shirt factory flourished. It brought new workers and new money to the bank and the town, and my reputation grew in the church and the community. People said I was a financial wizard.

"They also said I was favored of God. But the truth was that He used prosperity to punish me. I spent the new money as if it would never stop. I bought a second car and new furniture, decorated my office at the bank with fancy wallpaper, dressed my wife and daughter in the expensive clothes I thought my position in the community required. But my pleasure in those things was cankered by knowing that my life was a sham. Deep inside, I knew how I'd gotten them and knew they'd be gone in a minute if my crime ever became known.

"So I lived these past three years in constant fear of discovery. Today, without warning, that discovery came. I don't know where the receipt had been, but Jack found it. He came into my office and demanded an explanation. He couldn't seem to believe I'd robbed him, even when he held the proof in his hand. And while he hesitated, I came close to committing the worst sin of all, except for unbelief: the sin of murder."

His sad gaze wandered over the congregation. "Yes, murder. My fear of discovery flamed up into anger. I knew if I didn't kill Jack Davis, everything I'd worked for would go smash. I've always had a bad temper, but this level of rage was completely new to me. I felt possessed by something I couldn't control, but at the same time I knew I *could* control it and *ought* to control it. Yet, knowing that full well, I made a conscious decision to kill Jack and justify my crime by saying he'd gone berserk and attacked me. I knew people would believe me because of my reputation and because he was a war veteran.

"When Miss Kemper showed up and said she knew about the receipt, I would have killed her, too. Something wild inside me said people would believe she helped Jack attack me. They'd believe me because she was a Northerner—not one of *us*. So I was ready to commit two murders to cover up my crime.

"I would have done it, too, if Miss Kemper hadn't told Sheriff Rainwater about the receipt before she came to my office. Thank God she did. When she said the sheriff already knew, I saw it was no use to pretend any longer. I wouldn't be believed."

Lisa's heart gave a glad leap. *He still doesn't know I lied.* Jack touched her arm and followed with a wink. She understood. Her lie would remain a secret between them.

Pendleton lifted his gaze toward the back of the church. Everyone followed his example, and Lisa saw for the first time that Sheriff Rainwater occupied an aisle seat on the back row, his florid face as expressionless as ever.

"So here I am, Sheriff." Pendleton's voice drew people's attention back. "I confess to embezzlement, endangerment, and Lord knows what else. You can arrest me whenever you like."

He again surveyed the congregation. "I've promised full repayment to Jack. But we all know there can be no repayment for what I've done to him. Or to Miss Kemper. Nor can I ever atone for the wrong I've done to everyone in bringing shame to our church and our town." He looked downward. "For all of these wrongs I ask your forgiveness, though I don't deserve it."

He paused again and stood, eyes downcast and hands at his sides as if waiting for something to happen. The silence in the church became almost unbearable. At length, Pendleton seemed to sense the need to make an end. Awkwardly, he took two steps away from the lectern and mumbled, "I guess that's all I have to say."

He looked again toward the back of the church and added, "Here I am, Sheriff. Come take me to jail." Slowly, then, his expression changed from sadness to bewilderment. Like everyone else, Lisa turned to see what Sheriff Rainwater would do.

The seat the sheriff had occupied was empty.

The congregation's silence dissolved in a general murmur.

In the pulpit, Harry Pendleton glanced around in confusion, then slowly descended to sit beside his family. Honey Pendleton held a handkerchief to her face, her body wracked with quiet sobs. Lisa's heart ached for Precious, who sat staring at the floor.

The murmur in the church grew louder, and the congregation seemed as confused as Pendleton.

Lisa whispered to her father, "What do you think happened to the sheriff?"

"Took the gracious way out," Kemper answered. "He can't make an arrest unless the bank files a complaint. He probably thought it was easier to leave than explain."

The noise level in the church increased until finally, Brother Smallwood asked for silence and closed the meeting with prayer. His words were lost on Lisa, who was trying to sort out her conflicting emotions. She did not succeed and was grateful to hear the pastor's final "Amen."

The people in the church seemed more stunned than they had at Callie's funeral. They broke into groups and stood in conversation among the pews and in the aisles. Mrs. Telebit spoke angrily to a woman Lisa did not know. On the front row, the Pendletons remained isolated except for the pastor and Shiloh Simpson. Then Rose McKenzie pushed her way to them through the crowd. She put her hands on Honey Pendleton's shoulders and bent to speak into her ear. She did the same with Precious, then disappeared into the crowd. No one else came forward.

I must go talk to Precious, Lisa thought. A light squeeze on her shoulder made her conscious of Jack's arm around her. *How long had it been there? How could she not have known?* His face showed a somber expression compounded by fatigue. Suddenly, Lisa's own fatigue closed in. She wondered if she looked as washed out as Jack did.

"It's been a rough day," he said. "I feel like the sky fell on me with a few planets on top of it, but I want you to know nothing has changed between us."

"No, it has changed." Lisa hoped her smile didn't look as tired as it felt. "The Question is no longer open. I said 'Yes.'"

Jack's own tired smile was all the answer she needed.

As they moved to the aisle, Lisa saw that the Pendletons had left the church. *I must talk with Precious soon. She'll need all the support I can give.*

Outside, Jack placed gentle hands on Lisa's shoulders and asked, "Would you mind too much if I don't take you home? I have some serious thinking to do."

"I'll be fine," she said, "and you'll think much better after you've had some sleep."

"I'll think about that, too," he said, tired eyes sparkling to signal his wordplay. He bent forward as if to kiss her, then dropped his hands to his sides as he became conscious of people watching. He turned to Stephen Kemper. "Thank you again for representing my interests."

"Glad I can help." Kemper took Lisa's arm.

Father and daughter stood a moment, watching as Jack strode away into the darkness. Lisa again felt the familiar loneliness at his departure and wondered if her absence affected him the same way. Beyond the loneliness, though, she worried about Jack's grim countenance. What were those "serious things" he had to think about? And how would they affect her newly acknowledged love?

Chapter 32

As Jack drove home, the dark western road matched the darkness of his mood. He'd been wrong today, terribly wrong. After years of keeping an iron lock on his emotions, he'd let them slip. That had almost cost his life and Lisa's too. He couldn't have done worse if he'd tried.

Yet he had done worse, he chided himself as he turned into his driveway. Much worse.

He entered the house and, without turning on a light, sank into a chair at the kitchen table. There in the darkness he forced himself to face his errors. The most catastrophic was his vision of Beneficent. It *was* a good town, but not the heaven-on-earth his imagination made it out to be. With that concession made, some mental barrier fell away and released a flood of understanding.

For years, he'd built his hopes and dreams on a false vision, one that Harry Pendleton had smashed today when he drew his pistol. The mere thought of it ignited Jack's anger. With an effort, he suppressed it and forced himself to think unemotionally. And though he loathed the very thought of Harry Pendleton, the man had spoken one sentence tonight, apparently as a casual aside, that had struck Jack's heart like a bolt of lightning.

Then he remembered the lightning on the night he found Callie's body. He knew it brought destruction somewhere, but its light on the dark road let him see things he would have missed without it. *In the same way tonight*, he thought, *it's the sudden strokes of destruction that let us see the truths our inner darkness has hidden.*

In that burning light, he saw that he'd let his false myth of Beneficent's virtues gain precedence over worshiping the God who created those virtues. By fixating on human goodness and good works, he'd built a false parody of Christianity.

The words of the prophet Jeremiah flashed into his mind:

> *Thus saith the Lord,*
> *"Cursed be the man that trusteth in man*
> *And maketh flesh his arm,*
> *And whose heart departeth from the Lord."*

Nothing could better describe what Jack had done. He'd let human observances like church attendance, fellowship, and good works crowd out the inner reality of true worship. In his own mind he'd created an idol as false as any described in the Old Testament and much like that of the Pharisees in the New.

So he'd been terribly wrong. And, in an ultimate irony, it was his betrayer, Harry Pendleton, whose words had showed him his error. "Tried to compensate by doing good works," Pendleton had said, "but it was no use. We can't ever be good enough to make ourselves acceptable to God. The one way we can do that is through wholehearted surrender."

Pendleton had been right. There was only one way. With that confession, Jack laid aside the last vestige of false mythology and, on his knees, sought acceptability before his Lord.

***

As soon as prayer meeting ended that night, Buddy Robinson joined Jed Stoddard and four other boys on a street corner. All wore solemn faces after hearing Harry Pendleton's confession.

"Phew! That was heavy stuff." Jed pretended to wipe sweat from his brow. "Let's do something to lighten up."

"Maybe throw rocks at streetlights?" asked another boy. He bounced a few pieces of gravel in his hand.

Jed snorted. "That's kid stuff. I got a better idea."

The boys huddled while Jed explained. All nodded in agreement. Buddy and two others laughed out loud.

"Cut that noise," Jed commanded. "Remember how easy Ol' Shep gets riled up."

That quieted them, and Jed made the assignments. They crossed without further comment to the east side of town and stopped where they could observe Mr. Ricketts' house. The windows were already dark, the yard illuminated only by a streetlight on the telephone pole where they'd hung the lawn chair. The chair still hung there, like a towered sentinel watching over his companions below in the front yard. With the snow gone, the half-grown calf was again tethered to graze in the side yard.

On Jed's signal, Buddy went forward and loosed the calf's chain from the iron stake that held it. Another boy seized the calf's end of the chain and led the animal to the front steps. Buddy followed. Stealthily, Jed and the other three joined them there, each assigned to one of the calf's legs.

At that point, the plan developed a hitch. When the boy holding the chain loosed it from the calf's neck, he dropped it. The chain made a loud *CLINK* when it hit the sidewalk. In the back yard, Old Shep erupted into a paroxysm of barking. In the rear section of the house, a door slammed.

"Quick," Jed whispered, "All together . . . *up*."

The four boys lifted the now-bawling calf by its legs and staggered up the steps onto the porch. Buddy skittered ahead to hold the screen and front door open. The calf's hooves sounded like bricks landing on the wooden porch. The din reached greater heights as the boys pushed the awkward beast, bleating and kicking, into the house. Buddy shut the two doors behind it, and everyone ran for the safety of darkness beyond the streetlight. As they cleared the porch, a hideous crash echoed within the house.

At the next corner the boys collapsed with laughter, rolling in the street as they had after their other pranks.

Their laughter was short-lived. A ferocious bark from Mr. Ricketts' front yard announced that Old Shep had finally broken through the dilapidated fence. Buddy looked up to find the huge German Shepherd bounding toward the group, snarling as he came.

"Run," Jed ordered—uselessly, for his platoon of pranksters had already dispersed in all directions.

As before, Buddy ran north to the road behind Vesta Childress's house, but now in terror rather than mirth. For the first time since the pranks began, he realized he might actually have to face Old Shep.

"Lord, don't let him get me," Buddy prayed. In desperate bargaining, he swore an oath never to play another prank. For insurance, he promised a greater catalog of good deeds than he would ever remember. As he turned the corner toward Vesta's, a backward glance revealed no pursuit, though continuing sounds of Shep's ferocity told that others had not fared as well.

"Thank you, Lord," Buddy whispered in true gratitude. Maybe there was something to this prayer business, after all. Now, if he could just get home without being seen . . . He slowed to a trot, thankful that the road was rarely traveled.

When he passed behind Miss Childress's place, though, he saw the headlights of a car turning into the road up ahead. Was Mr. Ricketts chasing them? Quickly, before the lights could catch him, Buddy leaped from the road and ran into the woods. He caromed off a tree before he realized how dark it was. Slowly, then, one hand held in front, he groped through the darkness.

Almost far enough. Surely he can't see me now.

Suddenly, his hand touched something that shouldn't be there. Something made of metal. Warm metal.

Instinctively, Buddy crouched and listened. Fear gripped him again. This time, fear of the unknown. He heard the car pass on the road. Its headlights did not penetrate the woods. The engine drone and the scrunch of tires on gravel faded in the distance.

Buddy listened for a long time. He heard nothing, not even wind in the trees. Certain now that he was alone, he took out one of the kitchen matches he was forbidden to carry and struck it on the sole of his shoe.

The flickering light revealed the radiator grill, front bumper, and license tag of a pickup truck. *This shouldn't be here.* By instinct, he memorized the six white numbers that stood out against the black background of the license.

Then he remembered: Once before, after a prank, he'd thought he saw movement in this woods. As it had then, a chill ran up his back. He shivered once, then stealthily groped his way back to the road. Without stopping, he ran all the way home.

**

Inside her house, fully clothed, Vesta lay on her back and stared at the ceiling. The wooden floor felt cold beneath her head, but her body did not feel it. She willed her body to move, but it did not respond. Then she understood.

Her neck was broken.

That meant she was going to die. Not out there at some indefinite time in a dimly imagined future. But here, in this familiar living room, within the next few moments.

Strangely, she did not mind dying. Nor could she have chosen a better place. What better than this house she'd always called home, with the gas heaters' low hiss as undertone and their blue flames occasionally flickering into yellow.

Better to die here than in a watery ditch on someone else's land, like Callie Rakestraw. And it was Callie's death that had brought Vesta the fatal knowledge that now caused her own.

For last night Jimmy Fletcher was already drunk when he arrived. Not bragging drunk or mean drunk, but steeped in the sadness of alcoholic remorse. Seated on the floor beside her chair, he had cried with his head in her lap as if she were his mother instead of his mistress. And between fits of weeping, he told how he'd killed Callie.

He hadn't meant to, he said. His temper had done it. He'd always had a bad temper. On the ball court, Jack and Hollis and Otis Hahn had to keep him cooled down, and in the Marines his temper had gotten him into real trouble. Jimmy did not explain how, and Vesta dared not ask.

He'd only meant to make out with Callie when he found her walking home on the western road. But when he put his arm around her shoulders and caressed her earlobe with the other hand, she hit him in the ribs with her elbow. It hurt like fury. His temper exploded and his arms simply reacted. The next thing he knew, there she was with a broken neck.

What could he do but dump her and drive home? The worst part was, she was the sister of his dead teammate, Clyde Rakestraw. That was the thought that sent Jimmy into remorse. He'd betrayed a teammate, a member of the only group where he'd really belonged.

So Jimmy wept in Vesta's lap and she tenderly stroked his head while the horror of his confession tore at her heart like a hawk with icy talons.

When he finally fell into a drunken slumber, Vesta eased his head from her lap and laid him out on the floor. Then, quickly, she moved to the nearby secretary, recorded all she had heard in her diary, and secured it in the secretary's one locked drawer.

She did not sleep that night, nor could she decide what to do. Well before dawn, though, she woke Jimmy up and cajoled him into drinking half a pot of black coffee. Still half-drunk, he seemed to have no memory of confessing. Vesta helped him out the back door and felt relief as she heard his truck depart.

The problem troubled her all day, and late that afternoon she made her decision. Tonight Jimmy came back, soon after dark while most people were at prayer meeting. This time he was cold sober, though more taciturn than usual. He listened respectfully while she told him he must go to Sheriff Rainwater and confess. At first his eyes grew hard, but they softened as he promised to go first thing in the morning. He even gave her a hug in gratitude for leading him to the right decision.

The hug became her undoing. The arm around her shoulder suddenly locked with the other around her neck. There was a sharp pain and violent popping sound that she felt as much as heard. Then the pain stopped, and she was lying on her back feeling nothing but the cold floor under her head and knowing that in a few moments she would die.

Beyond the range of her sight, she heard Jimmy cursing as he rifled papers in the secretary. How did he know? Had she told him about the diary? She couldn't remember. Another curse, a crash and a splintering of wood, followed by silence except for Jimmy's heavy breathing and the hiss and pop of the gas heaters.

Then he was standing above her, not the childlike penitent of last night but fierce and feral, taller, broader, and more powerful than she remembered. His right hand gripped the diary where she'd recorded his confession. With a grin of triumph, he held the book in front of her face, shook it three times, and departed without a word.

Then, more than ever, the magnitude of her failure filled her with bitterness. As if a veil were lifted, she saw the impossibility of her fantasy about marriage to Jack. With newfound clarity, she saw the futility of her affair with Jimmy. Its momentary pleasures were worthless counterfeits of the happiness no affair could provide, counterfeits that had left her emotionally bankrupt. She had failed in every way she could imagine: failed the memory of her one love, William Bradley, and failed the woman of strength and character that she should have been. Most of all, she now understood, she had failed her Lord.

For the first time in weeks, she turned to prayer, unable to speak but mentally pronouncing each word, enumerating each sin in turn and asking God's forgiveness. As she prayed, the bitterness drained away, replaced by an inward flow of peace.

How foolish we are. His peace is always there for us if only we're willing to accept it.

Her breathing grew ragged, with long intervals between breaths, each delayed inhalation a gasp that might be her last. She felt no bitterness now, only tranquility and peace. Yet there remained a troubling sense of something left undone. She searched her dimming consciousness to find it. Then another veil seemed drawn away, and she understood the all-important act she had neglected.

In a final effort of mind, she forgave Jimmy Fletcher and prayed for his salvation. Her peace became complete. Enveloped in its loving warmth, she entered the presence of the One from whence it came.

Chapter 33

Thursday, February 26

For Lisa, the day began in apprehension and ended in horror. She wondered what caused the apprehension. The sniper? The dead squirrels? Callie's unsolved murder? Could it be threats of another war brought on by yesterday's Communist takeover in Czechoslovakia? Yet none of these seemed to connect. Perhaps she was only tired from yesterday's frightening events. Tired or not, though, she had work to do. Nine o'clock found her at her library volunteer job and with no further opportunity for introspection. Vesta Childress was not present in the library, and bedlam reigned. Lisa put the students to studying or working on projects, then sent a girl to the principal's office to ask about Vesta.

No helpful information came back. The principal had gone with the basketball team to the regional tournament. The secretary was busy, but said she would phone Miss Childress when she got a chance. The tiny school had no reserve personnel to inquire further. Increasingly worried, Lisa resigned herself to handling the library alone.

She had hoped to see Precious, but the young beauty was absent. Given Harry Pendleton's disgrace, Lisa wasn't surprised. She resolved to call the girl after school. Buddy Robinson appeared in the library at eleven, but avoided meeting Lisa's eyes. Had her counsel against playing pranks cost her his friendship?

At noon, Lisa sent out for a sandwich and dug in for an afternoon much like the morning. More inquiries at the office left Vesta's absence unexplained and Lisa more apprehensive. To her surprise, Ronnie Parker entered the library.

"I thought you were playing in the regional tournament," she said.

Ronnie squinted and made a face. "We played this morning," he said. "Baldwyn beat us. They double-teamed Jed Stoddard, and the rest of us couldn't hit a bull with a bass fiddle. Everyone says Baldwyn will win the state championship."

So the record of the team of 'forty-two remains intact, Lisa thought. But she said, "I'm sorry, Ronnie. Can I help you with anything?"

The boy shook his head and wandered off to an unoccupied corner, ostracized by his fellow students even in the team's defeat.

Lisa's apprehension grew as the hours passed. When school dismissed at three, she met her father and Oleta Brooks in the hallway.

"Do you know anything about Vesta?" Lisa asked Mrs. Brooks. "She's been absent all day. The secretary says she doesn't answer her phone."

Mrs. Brooks's sharp features twisted into a frown. "That's not like Vesta. I'd better check on her. Stephen, would you mind waiting thirty minutes for our conference?"

"Why don't I go with you, Oleta? If something's wrong, you may need an extra hand."

When Mrs. Brooks agreed, he handed Lisa his car keys. He and the stocky science teacher walked toward her car. Lisa drove home, curious that her father and Mrs. Brooks had progressed to a first-name basis. In front of the bank she saw several strange men in business suits. The auditors, she supposed. She wondered what progress her father and the others had made that morning toward deciding Jack's compensation from Harry Pendleton.

At home, she opened a frosty Coke and tried to phone Jack. He did not answer. Probably working somewhere on the farm, and probably working hard so he wouldn't brood about yesterday. Restless, she sipped the Coke and tried not to brood about yesterday herself.

A knock sounded from the front door, and she opened it to Precious Pendleton. The girl had been crying. She wore no makeup and her hair hung only half-combed, yet she remained surprisingly beautiful. Lisa immediately swept her into an embrace. They held it for a long time while the girl buried her face in Lisa's shoulder and sobbed.

"I had to talk to somebody," Precious said after regaining her composure. "I couldn't face anyone at school and it's like a tomb at home. Mama's cried all day and Daddy just stares at the wall."

Lisa guided Precious to the sofa and sat beside her. "It takes time to work through something like this."

Precious burst out, "How could he do that to us? I won't ever be able to hold my head up in this town."

You've held it too high for too long, Lisa thought. But she said, "Everyone knows you had nothing to do with it."

"They won't say anything to my face, but they'll talk behind my back. Whenever I get a new dress, they'll whisper about where the money came from."

"Most people aren't that spiteful." Lisa hoped it was true.

"Not that there'll be many new dresses," Precious lamented. "Daddy's finished at the bank, and he thinks he'll lose the shirt factory, too. He'll probably go to jail. Even if he doesn't, no one will hire him. We don't know how we're going to live."

Lisa squeezed the girl's hand. "You can't find all the answers at once. Working things out will take months. Your parents will solve one problem here and another one there, and eventually you'll get through it. In the meantime, you have to find the faith and strength to persevere."

Precious gave her an incredulous look, but one that cried out with desire to believe.

"The Lord will not abandon you," Lisa said, self-conscious at sounding pious even when she believed God's promise with all her heart. "King David did something far worse than your father did. David misused the authority God had given him and ordered Uriah killed. But he repented and asked forgiveness. The Lord gave it, and David is remembered as the greatest king Israel ever had. Your father has repented, too. God isn't going to forsake him."

"I feel like He's forsaken *me*," Precious wailed. "I'm supposed to sing in church Sunday, but I can't. I'm too ashamed."

"Precious, listen to me." Lisa said a silent prayer for the right words. "We all get knocked down by life. You have to decide whether you're a person who stays down or one who gets up and puts things back together. People will be watching to see which kind you are. With the Lord's help, you can give them and yourself the right answer."

Precious yanked her hand from Lisa's and jumped up, her face red with anger. "I *can't* sing. And you're no help. I bet you want me to forgive Daddy, too. But I *won't*."

"You'll have to sooner or later. Or else grow bitter."

"I suppose you've forgiven him for holding a gun on you!" The girl's hands doubled into fists.

Guilt struck at Lisa's heart. She'd been so focused on Harry Pendleton's threat to her life that she hadn't really thought about forgiveness. "No," she began, "I haven't—"

Precious cut her off. "Then don't ask me to do something you won't." Sobbing again, she ran for the front door and slammed it behind her.

Lisa followed more slowly. It was too late to tell Precious her next words would have been, "But I'll have to try." Much as she abhorred the idea, she knew her faith required it.

From the doorway, she watched Precious's retreating form. Out on the street, Buddy Robinson stood and stared. Lisa couldn't tell if he stared at her house or at Precious. When the boy saw her watching, he dropped his gaze and moved on.

Something is really biting him.

Lisa turned from the door and went back to her Coke. It had gone flat. She poured it out, berating herself for failure with Precious. When she half-succeeded in pushing that out of her thoughts, she confronted again the nameless foreboding that had plagued her all day. She tried again to call Jack, but he still did not answer.

Presently, she heard a car pull into the driveway. One car door closed, then another. Lisa's apprehension grew. Her father had planned a lengthy conference with Oleta Brooks. *Why would he come back so early?*

She rushed to the door as Stephen Kemper and Mrs. Brooks entered, their faces ashen.

"What's the matter, Father?" Lisa cried. "What's wrong?"

He turned sad eyes upon her.

"It's Vesta," he said. "She's dead. Murdered."

Chapter 34

Friday, February 27

At sunrise, Sheriff Rainwater and Ben Patterson revisited Vesta Childress's house to check with the two deputies the sheriff had stationed there. When they reported no activity, Rainwater drove to his office while Patterson stayed to reexamine the crime scene.

As Rainwater waited for Patterson's report, he reviewed Jimmy Fletcher's Marine Corps record. He'd begun reading it the day before, but the report of Vesta's murder made him drop that and everything else. Jimmy's record made Rainwater cringe. He'd thought all the local boys had done well in the war, but this one hadn't. Stationed in San Diego, Jimmy had received three convictions by court martial in six months: one for drunk and disorderly, two for assault. The last one cost him a year in confinement and a dishonorable discharge.

Jimmy's sentence ended with his discharge in December, 1943. That left two years unaccounted for before he returned to Beneficent sporting a military field jacket and a brass pin that claimed the honorable discharge he hadn't earned. Two years, then, for him to find profitable war production work in labor-starved California. No wonder he'd come home flush with money! The service record didn't convict Jimmy of any new offense, but it said he'd qualified as an expert with the M-1 rifle. That made him a good suspect for the sniper case.

Ben Patterson charged in, grim-faced and fiery-eyed. "You were smart to post a man behind Vesta's house. Someone paid her regular visits on the sly. Lots of tire tracks and footprints there in the woods. We preserved all of 'em in plaster. Your stake-out makes it good evidence."

Rainwater grunted. "Glad we did something right. What else you got?"

"Fingerprints of three people. Mister Kemper's where he said they'd be: front and back doorknobs and the telephone. Miss Childress's on almost everything. The third set is probably the murderer's. Fresh prints all over that desk with the broken drawer." He gritted his teeth. "We found that third party's prints in the kitchen and bedroom, too. Old prints as well as new. He was no stranger in the house."

Rainwater scratched his head. "I never heard of Vesta having anything to do with men since before the war. You knew the man she was engaged to got killed?"

"I heard." Patterson ground his teeth again. "But like I said, this fellow paid regular visits. Including the bedroom."

"No use getting steamed up about it. What else do you know about him?"

With a visible effort, Patterson calmed himself. "Big fellow. Footprints say he wears maybe a size thirteen shoe. His size would make him strong enough to break Miss Childress's neck. And Callie's. I'm betting he killed them both." Patterson grimaced. "We've got plenty of evidence. What we don't have is a suspect to match up with it."

"Patience." Rainwater waggled a finger. "The fingerprints will identify him if he's got a prison record or served in the armed forces. Meanwhile, we'll ask if the neighbors saw Vesta with a big man. But it's early times yet. We don't even have a coroner's report."

Patterson sniffed. "We don't need a coroner's report to diagnose a broken neck. Speaking of which . . ." The big detective's hands made a choking motion. "If I ever catch that guy—"

Rainwater slapped the desk so violently that Patterson jumped. "I said be patient. Callie and Vesta are my people. Their murderer is going to fry in the electric chair, and nobody—*nobody a-tall*—is going to shortcut justice in my jurisdiction."

In the quiet office, the two men glowered at each other.

***

Mid-morning found Lisa with contradictory moods. Vesta's murder had shocked her deeply, and her apprehension from the day before had grown to a haunting sense that even greater horrors lay ahead. Disturbing as those feelings were, their turbulence did not reach beneath the surface of her consciousness. Deeper down, the underlying calm she'd received during her frantic drive to the bank remained, a bedrock assurance untouched by the flux of day-to-day uncertainties.

Yesterday it had kept her functioning through a stressful evening. Oleta Brooks, shaken by discovering Vesta's body, feared to stay in her house alone. Stephen Kemper invited her to visit with him and Lisa until her son could drive back from Ole Miss. They passed the hours in desultory conversation, mostly about Vesta, until the son arrived. In spite of the sad occasion, Lisa was pleased to see friendship develop between her father and the chemistry teacher.

Lisa was alone in the house this morning, for Stephen Kemper was helping Shiloh Simpson, Jacob Weaver, Hollis Wilson, and Otis Hahn calculate Harry Pendleton's repayment to Jack. They hoped to reach a final figure today.

At midmorning, Buddy Robinson knocked on Lisa's door. He looked even guiltier than he had the day before.

"Shouldn't you be in school?" she asked.

"No, Ma'am." Buddy showed a sad smile. "They sent us home because of Miss Childress."

Lisa seated him in the living room.

"I've got a problem that's really bugging me," he said. "I thought maybe you could help me with it."

Lisa tried an encouraging smile. "What's bothering you?"

Buddy's eyes focused on the wall above her head. "I . . . uh . . . well . . . it's like—"

Lisa laughed. "Buddy, just tell me about the pranks and get it over with."

"They wuz fun." His face lit up. "Like after prayer meeting Wednesday when we put the cow in Mr. Ricketts' house."

With an effort, Lisa held back laughter.

"We planned it like a real commando raid." Buddy beamed with pride. "It went 'xactly like we planned, too. Leastwise, till afterwards when Mr. Ricketts' dog got after us."

"I'll bet that was a merry chase!" Lisa relaxed to enjoy the story. "Did he catch you?"

"No, Ma'am." Buddy's sheepish grin drained from his face. "But while I wuz running away, I saw the truck."

Lisa's amusement evaporated, replaced by a chilling premonition. "What truck? What are you getting at, Buddy?"

"The truck parked in the woods behind Miss Childress's place. After we put the cow in the house, I wuz running down that road an' a car come along. I thought it might be Mr. Ricketts, so I dodged into the woods to keep from getting caught."

"What did you see?" Lisa held her breath.

"Not much of anything." Buddy's voice cracked, but he stammered on. "It—it was too dark. I ran into the truck before I saw it. I struck a match, but I only got the license: a Coosa County tag, number two-oh-oh, one-four-five."

"Are you certain of the number?"

"Yes'm." Buddy swallowed hard. "I didn't think much about it till I heard Miss Childress had been killed. Then I thought I'd better ask you what to do."

Why me? Lisa thought. But she said, softly, so as not to frighten Buddy off, "You must tell the sheriff."

"What if it gets somebody I know in trouble?"

Lisa gave him a straight look. "Do you know whose truck it was?"

Buddy's eyes met hers and he answered without hesitation. "No, Ma'am."

"The truck's owner will have a chance to explain what he was doing there, but you have to tell everything you know. We all have a duty to help find Miss Childress's murderer. Would you feel better if I go with you to the sheriff?"

Buddy scowled. "Will I get in trouble for putting the cow in Mr. Ricketts' house?"

"I don't think so. The sheriff has too many other things on his mind." Lisa hoped she was right.

The boy's face brightened. "Then I guess I'll go."

As he and Lisa stood, the phone rang. Lisa ran into the hall to answer. Her heart gladdened at the voice she heard.

"I'm glad you called, Jack. It's so horrible about Vesta . . ."

His voice grew somber. "Yes, it's terrible. Can I come over? I want to talk to you about that and several other things."

While Lisa listened, she scribbled the license number Buddy had given her on a page from a scratch pad and stuffed it into her jacket pocket.

"Can you come now?" she asked. "I need help with something." She would feel more confident if Jack went with them to the sheriff.

"I'll be right there. I'm at the bank now. Shiloh Simpson says the loan on my farm is paid and Mr. Pendleton still owes me money, but he's not solvent enough to pay." His voice showed distaste. "They're offering me a sixty percent interest in the shirt factory. I don't want that, not with Harry as a partner. Besides, there's no one to manage the factory. I certainly don't know—"

Increasingly anxious about Buddy, Lisa interrupted. "Jack, I can't talk now. Please come quickly."

"I'm already there." He hung up.

Lisa headed back to the living room. "Buddy, I'm sorry to be so long. Jack Davis will go with us—" She broke off.

The living room was empty.

She ran to the door and looked out. Buddy was nowhere in sight.

Had he gone to the sheriff on his own? Had he changed his mind and gone home? Should she call the sheriff and tell him to expect Buddy? That might smooth the way for the boy, but he might resent her interference. What if he changed his mind? Her anxiety skyrocketed as she imagined the possibilities.

Then she reached down and touched the now-familiar layer of calm beneath the anxiety. If Buddy decided not to tell the sheriff, she would track him down and convince him that he must. Jack would help. The boy would be more likely to listen to him.

When Jack's pickup rolled into the driveway, Lisa grabbed her coat and ran to meet it. "Take me to the sheriff's office," she said as she climbed in.

Her face must have showed her seriousness, for Jack put the truck in motion without a word. While they drove, Lisa told Jack what Buddy had seen. When they entered the sheriff's office, Sheriff Rainwater and Ben Patterson looked up with tired eyes.

"Has Buddy Robinson been here?" Lisa asked.

"No, Ma'am." Rainwater squinted as he seemed to read her concern. "Is he in trouble over something?"

"He saw a truck parked in the woods behind Vesta Childress's house Wednesday night. He got the license number. I sent him here to tell you."

Rainwater opened his mouth to answer, but Patterson's bellow cut him off. "Did he give you the number?"

Lisa recoiled from his ferocity. "Yes." She took the hastily written note from her pocket. "It's from Coosa County. Two-oh-oh, one-four-five."

Patterson ran into the next office. Lisa heard sounds of a telephone furiously dialed, then the unintelligible mutter of subdued conversation. Lisa, Jack, and the sheriff exchanged tense glances.

Rainwater rubbed his cheek with one hand. "Miss Kemper, would you call Buddy's mother and see if he got home? She'll prob'ly faint if I call."

Lisa dialed the sheriff's phone. When a middle-aged female voice answered, Lisa said, "Mrs. Robinson, this is Lisa Kemper. May I speak to Buddy?"

"He's out in town somewhere," the tired voice replied. "I hardly know where he is these days. Do you want him to call you?"

"No, thank you." Lisa's body tensed, though she kept her voice calm. "I'll see him at school next week."

Rainwater took the phone from her and dialed. "Deputy Brown? Sorry about your lunch, but something's come up. Cruise around town and see if you can find Buddy Robinson." He listened briefly. "Naw, don't pick him up. Jus' call in an' say where he is. And look for a truck with tag number two-oh-oh, one-four-five. I want to know where it is an' who's driving it."

He re-cradled the phone and turned up the volume on his police radio. "Y'all look mighty worried, but you ain't had much experience with teenagers. When they get out of pocket you fret yourself sick over what might be happening, but ninety-nine times out of a hundred they only stopped off to visit somebody." His troubled expression belied his words.

The office grew quiet. Lisa noticed that it smelled of tobacco, leather, and gun oil. From the next room came the low mumble of Patterson's conversation. Presently, the sheriff's radio crackled. The static faded and Deputy Brown's voice came through.

"I've cruised ever' street in this town, Sheriff, and that kid ain't nowhere to be seen. Neither is the truck. Do I keep looking or finish my lunch?"

Rainwater lifted the radio's microphone and said, "Keep looking." His eyes darkened.

In the next office, Patterson's conversation ended with a decisive click. The big man re-entered, his face a picture of angry satisfaction. "The truck is a black Ford pickup," he said. "New registration. It belongs to James Fletcher."

The name drew a groan from Jack and a gasp from Lisa. Questions sprang up in her mind. Jimmy's truck? In the woods behind Vesta's house? Vesta and Jimmy Fletcher? The thought sickened her.

Jack spoke as if to himself. "I saw Jimmy's truck a few minutes ago, not three blocks from here." His face became a mask of fear and pain. "That's between here and Lisa's house. I wonder . . . I wonder if Buddy . . ."

His thought remained unfinished. Nor did anyone speak as all four persons stared at each other in alarm.

Chapter 35

Earlier that afternoon while Lisa and Jack talked on the phone, Buddy Robinson grew more excited. He was an important witness in a murder case. He'd be a hero if his information helped find the murderer. No more standing aside and watching. He'd be welcome in any group.

But if Miss Kemper took him to the sheriff, *she* would be the hero. He couldn't let that happen. He'd go by himself. What if he *did* go to jail for putting the cow in Mr. Ricketts' house? Then he'd be a martyr as well as a hero. He'd be known as the boy who told the truth even when he knew he'd be punished.

Buddy slipped out of the house and eased the door shut behind him. He ran the first block so Miss Kemper couldn't call him back. Then he walked, striding boldly like the cowboy heroes in the movies. He pictured himself marching bravely toward Main Street for a face-to-face shootout with the villain. He glanced around to see if he had an audience, but the street was deserted. Not to be discouraged, he added more swagger to his stride.

Two blocks from town, he saw a black Ford pickup parked at the curb. A big man wearing an olive-drab field jacket squatted beside it, checking the tires.

Buddy's bravado instantly dissolved into confusion. The truck had the same tag number he'd seen behind Miss Childress's house, but the man crouched beside it was Jimmy Fletcher. If Beneficent had a real hero, it had to be Mr. Fletcher. He'd led the team of 'forty-two to the state tournament, and people still talked about it. A hero like that couldn't be involved in Miss Childress's murder.

It wouldn't be right to squeal on him without letting him explain. Buddy approached the truck. "Mr. Fletcher, I'd like to ask you something."

"Yeah? What's that?" The man did not look up.

Buddy wet his lips. "How come your truck was parked behind Miss Childress's house Wednesday night?"

Fletcher met Buddy's gaze with a frown. "What makes you think it was my truck?"

"The tag number. I wasn't meaning to pry, but I ran into your truck in the dark. When I struck a match, there wuz the tag. I'm s'posed to tell the sheriff, but I know you can explain."

"I sure can."

Fletcher stood up. Buddy was surprised at how big he was. Not just tall, but so broad he looked ready to burst the buttons on his jacket. It must have been terribly hard to guard a giant like that on the basketball court. And he'd been a Marine, too.

The man's frown relaxed into a secretive smile. "I was working on an investigation that night. I'm not ready to go public, but it looks like I'll have to take you into my confidence. Can I trust you to keep a secret?"

"Of course, Mr. Fletcher." Something about this didn't feel right, but Buddy smothered his doubts. Why shouldn't he take the town hero at his word?

"It's too complicated to explain." The big man looked up and down the street, then opened the door of the truck. "If you'll get in, I can show you."

Buddy's misgivings grew, but he pushed them aside. Town heroes didn't get kids into trouble. He climbed into the truck.

Fletcher cranked the engine and drove toward the western road. With each block they traveled, Buddy's uneasiness grew.

"How far do we have to go, Mr. Fletcher?" he asked. "I have to get Mama's permission to go outside of town."

The big man's eyes looked straight through him. "You can't do that. This is a secret for just the two of us."

Buddy's heart sank. Why all this secrecy? He saw no good reason unless . . . The thought hit him like an electric shock. Fletcher's scowling face confirmed his worst fears.

Oh, Mama … How'm I ever going to get out of this mess?

***

While the sheriff's office bustled with unaccustomed activity, Jack and Lisa sat in a corner and read Jimmy Fletcher's service record. The sheriff had ordered both Jimmy and Buddy Robinson brought in for questioning. Although no one knew where they were, Rainwater said he and Ben Patterson would check out the Fletcher farm on the western road. If the boy had been abducted, that was the most likely place to look.

Jack's sorrow grew with each line he read. He'd worked with Jimmy's unpredictable temper on the ball court, so he wasn't surprised his friend had trouble with military discipline. Murder was something else. Jack's vague suspicions of Jimmy as the sniper had never thought of any motive beyond a practical joke. The idea of his teammate as a murderer was new to him, something he had to think through.

Lisa touched his arm. "I'm sorry, Jack. I know how much the team members mean to you. And we don't *know* he had anything to do with Vesta's death."

Jack sighed. "I'll believe anything after the stunt Harry Pendleton pulled. Jimmy's truck parked behind Vesta's house does look suspicious."

Rainwater and Patterson left the office. Car doors slammed outside. An engine started, then faded into the distance.

"Suspicion isn't enough," Lisa insisted. "Jimmy may have had good reason to be there."

"We can hope so," Jack said, but some inner voice told him he hoped in vain. Shame for his friend's service record now deepened into grief for what he feared his friend had become. With it came the familiar weight of responsibility Jack had never sought but never seemed to escape.

"Jimmy could never think his way out of anything," Jack mused. "When he tried, he only got in deeper. But he'd listen when we reasoned with him. In the end, he'd usually do the right thing." Jack's sense of duty moved powerfully, impelling him to a decision. He rose from his chair.

Lisa also stood. "You're afraid he's guilty. You're worried about what he'll do next."

Jack nodded. "That's why I have to go with the sheriff." He moved toward the door. When dismay showed on her face, he added, "I hope you understand."

"You don't have to go," she pleaded as she followed him to his truck. "Jimmy is old enough to handle this for himself."

Her plea wrenched Jack's heart, but his burden of responsibility outweighed it. "I have to go. He's my teammate and my friend." As he got into the truck, he saw Deputy Brown talking excitedly with Hollis Wilson and Otis Hahn in front of the bank. While Jack started the engine, Lisa opened the passenger door and jumped in.

"You can't go out there," Jack said. "It may be dangerous."

She flashed a determined look at him. "Dangerous or not, Jack Davis, you're not running away from me again." She folded her arms across her chest and stared out the front windshield.

Jack's whole being flooded with admiration for her. Without further argument, he drove toward the western road and whatever dangers it might hold.

***

A few miles ahead of them, Sheriff Rainwater sped toward Jimmy Fletcher's place as fast as the gravel road allowed.

"Ain't no way this'll be easy," he told Ben Patterson. "Jimmy's old man was a real ringtail tooter, a bootlegger an' willing to fight about it. Built his house—I guess you could call it a house, though it's not much more'n a cabin—built it on a hill as bald as Jacob Weaver's head. No trees for more'n fifty yards in any direction, and the only approach goes across an open field."

Patterson showed a humorless grin. "Didn't want anyone sneaking up on him, I guess."

"That's about it. Not that he ever gave me any occasion to." Rainwater paused to navigate a sharp curve. "He sold his likker quiet-like and never made any trouble, 'least until Jimmy went off to the war. Then rumors said he was branching out into drugs. Somebody told him I was investigating, and he hightailed it out of the county. Never heard no more about him."

"You think Jimmy takes after his father?"

"I *didn't* think so. Now I'm worried about that open field."

"Is there a back entrance?"

"A trail half a mile north of the house. I sent two deputies to stake that out just in case."

They descended the final ridgeline into Branch Bottom. The road lay flat and straight from there to the creek. After a quarter of a mile, Rainwater turned into a primitive driveway formed by two ruts worn into the rough surface of a pasture. The drive paralleled the road for perhaps a hundred feet before twisting back across the field to the Fletcher cabin atop the hill.

"I see what you mean," Patterson grumbled as he eyed the eighty yards of open terrain between them and the cabin. "They'd have a good view of the side of your car. Fletcher would see the star, or whatever, and know if it was you or the feds." His gaze lifted to the house. "I don't see a truck."

Rainwater grunted. "You won't. They allus parked in back so nobody'd know if they was there." He eased the car along the rough drive, slowing for each bump so as not to drag his muffler. "Maybe we're only borrowing trouble," he said as they approached the turn toward the cabin. "We don't know for sure that—"

Dirt flew upward from the trail ahead of them, and a loud cracking sound assailed their ears. The thump of the rifle shot reached them a second later. Patterson scrambled out of the car and took cover on the side opposite the house. Rainwater followed close behind. As the two men crouched beside the car, a Chevrolet truck turned off the road and pulled up behind them.

Rainwater recognized Jack and Lisa. "Git out o' there an' take cover," he shouted. "There's shooting."

As if to punctuate his sentence, another shot kicked up dirt ahead of the sheriff's car. Jack and Lisa scurried out on the side of the truck away from the cabin.

"Jack, you stay out o' this," Rainwater commanded. "We got enough trouble without taking care o' you two."

He watched long enough to see Jack position Lisa so she was shielded by the truck's cab, then turned his attention to the cabin. The windows on this side were open. There were no screens. Despite the bright afternoon sun, the house appeared dark inside.

Deciding to take a chance, Rainwater stood up and shouted across the top of the car, "Jimmy, I want to talk to you."

No movement showed at any window, but a returning shout answered, "Leave me alone. I'm not bootlegging."

More hopeful now, Rainwater called again. "It ain't bootlegging, but I got to take you in for questioning."

Still no movement, but the shouted answer returned, "You're not taking me nowhere. Don't try to come up here or I'll shoot."

Rainwater tried a new tack. "You got Buddy Robinson there?"

There was a moment's silence. Then a frantic, high-pitched voice yelled, "I'm here, I'm here. Don't shoot."

The boy appeared briefly at a window, then was yanked away into the darkness. A yelping sound like a kicked dog came from the cabin.

"Jimmy," the sheriff called, "your holding that boy is kidnapping. Let him go and come on out."

Only silence answered.

"You can't escape, Jimmy," Rainwater shouted. "There's deputies waiting on the trail north of your house, and we ain't going nowhere. The longer you wait, the more of us there'll be."

The cabin remained silent.

Vaguely aware of two more vehicles arriving, the sheriff looked back and saw Deputy Brown emerging from his patrol car behind Jack's truck. Hollis Wilson and Otis Hahn got out of a pickup parked behind Brown's car. At Rainwater's shout, all of the newcomers took cover behind their vehicles.

What a mess! It was bad enough for three lawmen to face an armed felon without more complications. But now he had four other people to look after, one of them a woman.

While Rainwater desperately searched for a solution, Ben Patterson's disgusted mutter came from behind him. "Enough of this foolishness."

Too quickly for the sheriff to stop him, Patterson walked several feet in front of the car and bellowed, "James Fletcher, we're arresting you for kidnapping and suspicion of murder. You're already in deep trouble, boy. Don't make it worse."

Before Rainwater's horrified eyes, an unseen force spun the big man like a top. With a sharp cry, he staggered and fell. As the sound of the rifle shot reached the sheriff's ears, Ben Patterson lay writhing on the ground, his immaculate blue-checked suit smeared with dirt and blood.

Chapter 36

Huddled with Lisa against the cab of his truck, Jack watched the standoff between Jimmy and the sheriff with growing alarm. Jimmy had always resented authority. His teammates had had their hands full keeping him out of trouble with the school principal and any number of referees. Yet Jack had never imagined his friend would defy lawmen in the performance of their duty.

His sorrow deepened as he watched, but his chief concern was keeping Lisa safe. He shouldn't have let her come. Her blue eyes searched his face as if seeking assurance, but he had none to give. As the tragic scene developed, his deeply felt conviction of responsibility weighed ever more heavily upon him.

While the exchange of shouts continued without progress, a patrol car and a pickup turned from the road into the primitive driveway. For a moment, Jack wondered what Hollis Wilson and Otis Hahn were doing here with Deputy Brown. Then he remembered he'd seen them talking to Brown. Their friendship with Jimmy ran as deep as his, so they must have come for the same reason he did.

Hearing the sheriff's warning, the newcomers hugged the side of Otis Hahn's pickup. When several minutes passed with no firing, they ran forward to take cover with Jack and Lisa.

"How bad is it?" Wilson asked.

"Couldn't be much worse." Tersely, Jack told of Jimmy's truck behind Vesta's house, his abduction of the one witness against him, and his holding the sheriff at bay with rifle fire.

Ben Patterson's bellowing challenge drew their attention. As they watched, the detective spun and fell before Jimmy's fire.

Without conscious thought, Jack ran past the sheriff to the open ground where the detective lay. Seizing Patterson's good arm and coat collar, Jack dragged him back toward safety behind the car. Patterson was conscious, but too traumatized to help. A few feet behind them, dirt exploded upward as a rifle bullet struck with a vicious slap.

Jack flinched but kept dragging his burden toward the car. He thanked his stars that Patterson was wounded in the shoulder rather than the chest as he had feared. Another bullet struck the ground, this time closer to them. It ricocheted and sang its way off into the distance. Before the sound died, Jack delivered Patterson to safety beside the patrol car and propped him in a sitting position against the door. The man appeared dazed and bordering on shock.

Sheriff Rainwater broke open the car's first aid kit while Jack stripped away Patterson's clothing. The wound proved to be on the outside of the arm, a wide gash ripped through the pad of the shoulder muscle. Jack applied direct pressure with a prepared dressing much like a military first aid packet. When the flow of blood stopped, he used a fresh dressing to bind the wound.

"Thanks," Patterson murmured. Color returned to his face as the threat of shock retreated. "I guess I asked for that."

No one commented on the big man's self-judgment.

As the silence grew, so did Jack's sense that something must be done to break the impasse. But what? Jimmy held all the advantages: the high ground, an open field of fire, a powerful weapon in expert hands, and a hostage whose presence prevented the sheriff's returning fire. Only one thing could move the deadly situation toward peaceful resolution: a change in Jimmy's heart.

But what could bring about that change? Jack had known few people as stubborn as Jimmy. Once the man had an idea in his head, no one could change it. Jack knew only one chink in Jimmy's case-hardened armor: his sense of belonging to the team of 'forty-two. That provided the only approach Jack could think of, yet using it involved risking his own life. If he guessed wrong, he would be dead within the instant.

He thought of Lisa and his hopes for their future. Even now, she watched him. Worry was written on her face, yet she somehow exuded a deep calm beyond his comprehension. The thought of bringing her sorrow wrung his heart. Then he remembered that Jimmy's rifle threatened her life, too. Indeed, it threatened the lives of all six persons crouched behind the cars as well as the life of the kidnapped youth.

At that thought, the sense of responsibility rose powerfully within him, and he could not abide further inaction. He stood up and shouted across the hood of the sheriff's car, "Jimmy, this is Jack. I have to talk to you."

The reply was immediate. "Don't come up here. I'll shoot."

Relieved that the reply was not a bullet, Jack sought to keep the words flowing. "Teammate, we've been in bad situations before, but we've always worked through them together." He stepped out from behind the sheriff's car and walked toward the bend in the trail some twenty feet away.

"Jack, stay where you are." The pitch of Jimmy's voice climbed several notches. "Stay there. I don't want to shoot."

"Then don't shoot." Jack forced out the best laugh he could muster. He kept walking, waiting in the silence for Jimmy's reply. Almost to the bend in the trail. Just a few steps more—

With a loud crack and an explosion of dust, a bullet struck the ground at Jack's feet.

***

Standing with Hollis Wilson and Otis Hahn beside Jack's truck, Lisa had held her breath as Jack dragged Ben Patterson back to safety. Her fear turned to relief when they reached cover. She savored that relief while Jack bandaged Patterson's wound.

Then, to her surprise, Jack stood erect and called out to Jimmy Fletcher. Surprise changed to alarm when Jack left the protection of the sheriff's car and walked openly onto the trail. She wanted to scream, "Come back!" But some inner impulse stopped her. Close behind that impulse came her memory of Jack's words: "Whatever situation came up, it seemed I could find a way to handle it. I guess that's the basic philosophy I live by."

He was living by it now, and her duty was to support him. But how? She wanted to run out and walk beside him, yet that might upset the precarious balance between him and Jimmy. Through swirling anxiety, she reached down and again touched the enduring calm that lay beneath. With that touch came her answer. Still watching Jack's every move, but now in trust, she began to pray.

***

As the bullet struck the ground in front of him, Jack hesitated. How foolish he'd been to bet his life on the bond of team loyalty, a bond that Jimmy might feel less strongly than he! Then logic took over. Jimmy was a trained expert with the rifle, and the range was less than one hundred yards. If he had aimed at Jack's heart, the bullet would not have struck five feet from its target. Jack took another step forward.

A shout came from behind him. "Hey, Panther. Wait up."

Jack turned and saw Hollis Wilson walking toward him. The handsome senator advanced as calmly as if he strode forward to address the Senate. He extended his right hand, and the two men exchanged their team's traditional handshake, each one's hand grasping the forearm of the other. The symbolism, Jack knew, could not be lost on Jimmy.

Wilson met Jack's eye and said, "I let you go it alone in the Army, Jack. I took the safe desk job while you stayed with the tough one. This time you'll have company."

Jack held his grip on the other's arm. "Hollis, are you crazy? Jimmy may shoot you."

"That's true." Wilson gave a cynical laugh. "But if he doesn't, this will get me reelected as long as I want to run."

"Hey, you guys." Otis Hahn approached with his lumbering gait. "I don't guess flat feet will keep me out of this one."

Jack wanted to argue that Otis had a wife and family to think of, but the steel in Otis's eye stopped him. The three exchanged the familiar handshake, then fell in abreast with Jack on the right and Otis on the left. From the center, Wilson extended his arms and his friends grasped the forearms with the interlocking grip they'd used years before when they blocked the highway to celebrate their victory. Together, they turned the bend in the trail and advanced on Jimmy's cabin.

"Jimmy," Jack called, "do you remember how we used to hold team meetings? We're coming up there to hold another one."

In answer, a bullet struck a few inches beside Jack's right foot. A second struck the same distance from Otis Hahn's left. Jack's ears rang from the noise as they had on the battlefield during the war.

"Cut it out, Jimmy," he shouted. "Don't make this mess any worse."

They closed to within sixty yards of the cabin. Then fifty. Then forty. Jack began to hope his message had gotten through. Another bullet-strike dashed his hopes. This one hit the ground between Jack and Hollis. Instinctively, they flinched away from it, but their grip held and drew them back into position.

Almost immediately, another round struck between Wilson and Hahn. They leaped apart, but quickly regrasped arms.

"Stop it, Jimmy," Jack called. "We're coming in to talk."

An ominous silence followed, broken only by the ringing in Jack's ears. The three men continued their advance.

Thirty yards, then twenty.

Now came the sound of Jimmy talking, his voice too low for Jack to make out the words. Nor could he tell if Jimmy spoke to himself or to the youth he held captive. The voice grew more impassioned, though still unintelligible.

Ten yards.

Jimmy's voice, now bordering on hysteria, came from the cabin's dark interior. "I'm warning you, Jack. Don't come any closer. I'll shoot."

Desperately, Jack searched for a reply. "It won't hurt to talk with us, Jimmy. Don't do anything foolish."

No answer came back. In silence, the trio advanced to the steps leading onto the front porch. Jack held his breath as all three, together, trod on the first step.

With a deafening sound, one shot rang out. Its brilliant muzzle flash transformed the dark rectangle of the cabin's doorway into momentary noon. The three teammates stopped, each frozen with one foot on the cabin step and the other on the dry earth of the grubby yard, their gaze locked on the open doorway.

As they stood, Buddy Robinson rocketed through the door, his youthful face a mask of horror. Emitting a gurgling sound more animal than human and looking neither left nor right, he leaped from the porch and ran frantically down the hill toward the sheriff's car.

With a sick feeling in his stomach, Jack led the others across the porch and into the cabin. Too impatient to wait for their eyes to adjust to the dim light, Jack felt for the light switch and flicked it on.

Jimmy Fletcher lay on his back, his long arms half-extended in either direction, elbows bent as if blocking out a basketball opponent from a rebound. His M-1 rifle lay where it had fallen, near his feet. The fabric of his olive-green field jacket, still bearing the boast of its unearned golden eagle, smoked and smoldered around a small entry wound in the left chest. Jimmy's eyes stared sightlessly at some other-worldly vista beyond the walls of the cabin, his lips stretched wide in something that could have been either grin or grimace.

His three comrades stood above him, silently grieving over their friend's pathetic end.

At length, Jack lifted his gaze and said, softly, "I never found the words that could reach him."

"No one did." Wilson's voice choked. "He kept the barriers up, and no one ever could."

They moved to the front porch and waved the sheriff forward, then stood in quiet sorrow awaiting his arrival.

Presently, Hollis Wilson showed a sad, sardonic smile. "Folks in Beneficent have one thing right: They'll never forget the team of 'forty-two."

Chapter 37

Saturday, February 27

As Sheriff Rainwater went about his duties, he sensed something different about Beneficent. It wasn't just the sudden break in the weather, the warm and gentle wind that whispered of coming spring. The change was in the town itself. He'd thought people would react to Jimmy Fletcher's death with the same shock they'd shown for the two murders—fear compounded with a wish to deny unwelcome truths—but today brought a subtle change in the tone, an acceptance and modesty that Rainwater hadn't seen before.

Not that he had time to think about it. He'd been too busy wrapping up the two murder cases to the satisfaction of a skeptical district attorney. He didn't blame the man for skepticism, for the wrap-up was almost too neat to be believed.

Buddy Robinson had run from the cabin straight into the arms of Lisa Kemper. Weeping in near-hysteria, he'd poured out the story of his abduction. The key element, from the sheriff's point of view, was that Jimmy had mumbled a confession to himself as his three teammates closed in on the cabin.

"I can't do it," Jimmy had cried, "I can't kill them." His breathing came quick and shallow, with an occasional gasp or sob. "I didn't mean to kill Callie, either. She hit me with her elbow, and all of a sudden there she was, dead." Then the rant became a babble of long-held grievances against the town. He'd never been accepted, Jimmy said, never been a part of anything but the basketball team. When people invited him to church, he thought they meant they were better than he was. They wanted Jimmy to be more like them so they could feel good about themselves.

Things were no different when he came back after the war. The local girls wouldn't date him and the new girl, Lisa Kemper, snubbed him in front of the drugstore checker players. That was why he'd put dead squirrels on her porch and why, when she dated Jack Davis, he'd harassed them both with rifle shots. He hadn't meant to hurt them, he said again and again, but they seemed so . . . so complacent about everything.

Thus Jimmy raved to himself while the kidnapped boy cowered in a corner, terrified that his captor would remember his presence and kill him. So it continued until Jimmy's final warning to his teammate. After that he sobbed, "I can't, I can't," and turned the weapon on himself.

Rainwater left the boy crying in Lisa's arms and took Deputy Brown up to the cabin. Hollis Wilson told him what they'd found inside. He also volunteered to drive Ben Patterson to the hospital in Shipley, an offer Rainwater gladly accepted. After asking the three teammates to make statements, he and Brown marked off the scene and gathered evidence.

Their findings included Vesta's diary recording Jimmy's drunken confession. Inexplicably, Jimmy had not destroyed it. Ballistic technicians could match the cartridge cases on the floor with those from the two sniping incidents, and Jimmy's fingerprints appeared to match the ones in Vesta's house.

That left only the problem of convincing the district attorney it was physically possible for anyone to shoot himself through the heart with an M-1 rifle. This required actual measurement of Jimmy's long arms and the coroner's statement that the weapon's muzzle had been pressed directly against the chest.

So by Saturday noon, all the loose ends were neatly tied up, and yet Rainwater felt strangely let down. He'd taken every action possible to solve Callie's murder, but none had led to the guilty party. The solution had come by chance or Providence: Buddy Robinson's stumbling onto Jimmy's truck and remembering its tag number.

That afternoon when Rainwater visited Ben Patterson in the hospital, several visitors of greater interest had arrived before him: three attractive local women, two unmarried and the third a spritely young widow. They waited outside while the sheriff briefed Patterson on the case's final details.

The big detective enjoyed his visitors too much to worry about mere business. "I should have got myself shot before," he said. "That widow donates blood every month. She says I probably have some of hers inside me already." He laughed. "I like that word *already*."

Rainwater left him with his admirers and drove back to Beneficent, musing on the strange mixture of good and evil that was Jimmy Fletcher. How could a man commit two brutal murders of women whom he knew well, and yet choose suicide rather than harm his teammates? Rainwater found no answer.

In town, shoppers told him the church's deacons had met Friday night and the town council had convened Saturday morning, but no one knew what either meeting was about. To compound the mystery, one man said Shiloh Simpson had gone directly from the council meeting and bought two cans of outdoor paint.

Rainwater wondered idly if either meeting was connected to the different tone of the community, but he found no answer. Time would tell if the change in Beneficent's atmosphere proved real, and whether it would be for better or for worse. Not given to much reflection, he shrugged and headed for home.

Chapter 38

Sunday, February 29

Lisa also sensed something different about Beneficent as the church service began. She'd been too preoccupied to notice it before. The grief and terror of the past few days had burdened her with knowledge of the world's all-corrupting evil: Callie murdered by a teammate of her dead brother, Jack betrayed by a family friend, Vesta self-betrayed for reasons Lisa could not fathom. Yet through all this, Lisa's newfound certainty stood firm, an unassailable assurance that evil was only part of the world's reality, and not the dominant part.

Friday afternoon's events had bonded her even more closely with Jack. She could hardly believe she'd ever considered choosing graduate school over their marriage. And on Saturday Jack had explained his settlement with Harry Pendleton. Reluctantly, he'd accepted a sixty percent interest in the shirt factory, with Pendleton as partner and salaried manager. Shiloh Simpson had countered Jack's objections bluntly: "The man can't feed his family without a job, and no one else will hire him." Jack finally agreed, but only after Jacob Weaver and Otis Hahn promised to examine the books every quarter.

So only now, sitting between Jack and her father, did Lisa sense a change in the townspeople. The usual ones had come: Rose and Ralph McKenzie, of course; Harry and Honey Pendleton on a pew near the front, their eyes downcast; Mrs. Telebit on one side of the sanctuary and Mrs. Harding on the other; Ronnie Parker, still isolated until Otis Hahn's family joined him; Buddy Robinson looking pale and subdued beside his mother; Sheriff Rainwater, arriving at the last possible moment and sliding into a back row seat. They were the same people, and yet somehow the attitude was different.

All entered quietly, with serious faces and none of the noisy chatter that usually continued well into the organist's prelude. Some read their Bibles, some closed their eyes and moved their lips in prayer, and some merely gazed at the organ pipes towering above the choir loft or looked with somber eyes at the cross suspended behind the pulpit.

Today they were prepared to worship, Lisa thought. She was surprised to find that she, too, felt especially prepared.

The choir filed in during the prelude, and Precious Pendleton took her usual seat in the front row nearest the organ. Lisa felt a pang of guilt, for in the press of events she'd forgotten the girl's agony of crushed pride. "I can't face anyone," Precious had said. But now she was facing everyone. Outwardly, she looked the same as ever—expensively attired, face immaculately made up and every hair combed carefully in place. Yet her countenance showed something new. A quickening of awareness in the girl's eyes replaced the former boredom, and Precious now surveyed the congregation with interest as if seeing it for the first time.

Would she sing? The printed order of worship announced "Special Music" but gave no further hint.

After the prelude, the congregation sang "O God Our Help in Ages Past." A prayer of invocation followed, and then Shiloh Simpson ascended to the pulpit.

"The deacons have acted on Harry Pendleton's resignation," he said. "We've accepted it as a resignation from the active deacon body, but not as an ordained deacon."

He paused as if expecting a response, but the congregation remained silent. Pendleton sat with head in hands, as he had after his confession. Beside him, his wife gazed steadily at the floor.

"We think Harry ought to sit things out for a while," Simpson continued, "but a time will come when we'll need him to serve again. When it does, he won't have to be re-ordained."

Simpson descended, accompanied by a general sigh and a scattering of subdued amens. Jack squeezed Lisa's hand. "They took a risk to give Harry a way to come back," he whispered. "When they told me, I agreed to do the same."

Lisa returned her attention to the service, for the air of expectancy became too powerful to disregard. It grew yet greater through another hymn and a prayer by Jacob Weaver. As the time for special music approached, Lisa's anticipation grew along with her curiosity about Precious's decision.

As the last prior event, Brother Smallwood came forward and rested his hands on the lectern. "Beneficent has been a proud town," he said quietly. "We've seen plenty of virtue and good works here, and maybe that's how we got off track. Without actually saying it, we've placed our faith in our own virtue rather than in the Source of all virtue. So we were shocked when evil struck like lightning among us in the form of theft, betrayal, and murder."

He gazed out across the congregation. "Now we see that we aren't really different from other people, that we share the common heritage of mankind: original sin. And because we're no longer 'A town as good as its name,' our city council has replaced that motto with a more modest one: 'We try to live up to our name.' It's already painted on the signs at the city limits."

He opened his Bible. "The city council did the right thing because the Lord says in Second Chronicles: 'If my people, which are called by my name, shall humble themselves and pray, and seek my face, and turn from their wicked ways; then will I hear from heaven, and will forgive their sin, and will heal their land.'"

Every word he read spoke to Lisa's heart. She was not the only one thus affected, for Precious Pendleton's face showed astonishment, as if she were hearing that text for the first time.

The girl's gaze remained fixed on the minister even as she rose to sing. It shifted to the congregation only when the organist began the soft arpeggios of the introduction. Precious then clasped her hands before her, and her newly expressive eyes seemed to convey all the turmoil and heartache she had suffered during the past week. To Lisa, they also seemed to reflect the multiple sorrows that had fallen on the community.

The song was the same one Precious had sung at Callie's funeral: Albert Hay Malotte's setting of "The Lord's Prayer." But the girl's rendering of the music could not have been more different. Even in the opening *pianissimo*, her rich voice grew resonant with a new depth of emotion:

> *Our Father, which art in heaven,*
> *Hallowéd be thy Name.*

As the tempo grew impassioned and the harmony deepened, the beautiful girl's voice rose in crescendo above it:

> *Thy kingdom come.*
> *Thy will be done in earth,*
> *As it is in heaven.*

The voice that had promised its power in the first two lines now followed the harmony into perfect repose at the mention of heaven. While the voice then rested, the accompaniment shifted to a lyrical rhythm appropriate to the petitions that followed:

> *Give us this day our daily bread . . .*

To Lisa, Precious's face as well as her voice confirmed her comprehension of those words' full meaning. This was the same girl who had cried out, "We don't know how we're going to live." But an even greater show of understanding followed:

> *And forgive us our debts, as we forgive our debtors.*

With these words, Precious looked directly at her father and then at the ostracized youth, Ronnie Parker, before returning her gaze to the congregation. Tears flowed from her eyes and black streaks of mascara ran down to mar the perfectly made-up face, but the rich voice never wavered:

> *And lead us not into temptation;*
> *But deliver us from evil:*

The young beauty's dampened eyes gazed out beyond the spellbound congregation as if seeing a divine vision. The organ's harmonies deepened, and Precious's voice now rose in fulfillment of its promised strength as the music built toward a sonorous climax:

> *For thine is the kingdom,*
> *And the power, and the glory,*
> *Forever.*

Precious's voice rang clear and powerful on the word "forever," shaping the high B-flat into a perfect blend of emotion and meaning, subsiding at last with softening tone and timbre into the sustained "Amen." During the long *diminuendo*, the girl's gaze lowered from the height of its former vision to the floor immediately before her feet in a perfect gesture of humility. She ended with her eyes fully closed as the last strain of music stole away into silence.

For a few seconds, Precious remained motionless, holding onto the silence while the awed congregation savored the moment's perfection. As if awakening, the girl took one step toward the choir, but stopped abruptly as if on command. Then, her eyes flashing determination, she walked down from the platform directly to the pew where Ronnie Parker sat. The astonished youth made room for her, and the once-proud beauty with the mascara-streaked face took her seat beside him.

The congregation remained hushed, seemingly conscious, as Lisa was, of a Presence among them, a Presence that joined them all together in one harmonious body bound by love. Lisa felt love flowing out of her toward the others and theirs flowing back toward her. It was a love somehow beyond emotion and quite different from the love she felt for Jack, which kept its own uniqueness within the context of greater love for all. She saw tears on the faces of women and wet eyes in those of the men.

She had no idea how long the moment lasted before Brother Smallwood again came forward, his eyes as misty as those of any other. He lifted his sermon notes from the top of the lectern and contemplated them a moment, then slipped them onto a lower shelf.

Taking his Bible in hand, he read from Colossians, "'For it pleased the Father . . . having made peace through the blood of his cross, to reconcile all things unto himself . . ." Then at his direction, the congregation joined hands across aisles and pews to form one continuous chain as they sang the familiar hymn:

> *Blest be the tie that binds*
> *Our hearts in Christian love:*
> *The fellowship of kindred minds*
> *Is like to that above.*

Brother Smallwood ended the service with a brief benediction, yet everyone seemed reluctant to leave. For a few moments they stood quietly in place. Then the movement began, and Lisa could hardly believe what she saw. Precious and Ronnie Parker made their exit together. Mrs. Harding and Mrs. Telebit moved from opposite sides of the church to embrace and stand conversing in the middle aisle. Ralph McKenzie and other men drifted down to gather around Harry Pendleton while a number of women surrounded Pendleton's wife. Across the church, Jed Stoddard and Buddy Robinson talked quietly with Mr. Ricketts, who listened courteously if not enthusiastically. Others crowded around Hiram and Cornelia Rakestraw, who had made their first appearance since Callie's funeral. Rose McKenzie remained seated in the usual pew, her countenance graced by a secret smile as she glanced at Lisa, who nodded back her understanding.

Rose is the one person in town who doesn't need to be reconciled with anyone.

Stephen Kemper made a brief apology that he'd forgotten to tell Oleta Brooks something and moved to an aisle where the robust chemistry teacher stood waiting. For a brief moment Lisa felt his absence, then turned to find Jack watching her. His solemn expression told her he had felt the spirit of the worship service as deeply as she.

"We'll remember this morning for the rest of our lives," he said, his face filled with wonder. Then his solemnity gave way to a grin. "In the meantime, how about some lunch?"

"Lunch?" The word sounded so ordinary, yet she knew that even Moses had to come down from the mountain. Suddenly she felt ravenously hungry, as she'd felt that first day on Jack's farm more than a month ago.

"Yes, lunch," she said, remembering the tenderness and terror of that day even as she spoke, "but this time let's not get shot at."

"I'll try to arrange it," he said, guiding her toward the door.

Sheriff Rainwater fixed his gaze upon them as they reached the back row. He appeared unchanged, though Lisa thought his deadpan stare might contain a subdued twinkle.

The church door opened into early spring, fulfilling the promise of yesterday's warm breeze. As they drove past the familiar landmarks toward Jack's farm, Lisa savored a new sense of contentment and completion, the bedrock foundation of the Lord's assurance within and the certainty of Jack's love without.

Soon the row of dogwood trees would bloom on Jack's farm in a profusion of white, divided in the center by one burst of pink. She looked forward to seeing its burgeoning beauty this spring.

This spring, she thought fondly, and many springs afterward.